SEEING IS DECEIVING

OTHER PHOEBE FAIRFAX MYSTERIES

Healthy, Wealthy & Dead

SEEING IS DECEIVING

A PHOEBE FAIRFAX MYSTERY

Suzanne North

Canadian Cataloguing in Publication Data
North, Suzanne, date
    Seeing is deceiving

"A Phoebe Fairfax mystery"
ISBN 0-7710-6805-0

I. Title.

PS8577.068S44 1996   C813'.54   C95-933059-3
PR9199.3.N67S44 1996

The publisher acknowledges the support of the Canada Council and the Ontario Arts Council for their publishing program.

Typesetting by M&S, Toronto
Printed and bound in Canada on acid-free paper

McClelland & Stewart Inc.
The Canadian Publishers
481 University Avenue
Toronto, Ontario
M5G 2E9

1 2 3 4 5   00 99 98 97 96

For
Ingrid Olson Mercer and Martha Gould

I

———

"Okay. First question. I ask her what a psychic symposium is. Next I ask why they're holding it out in a little place like Okotoks instead of in Calgary. Right. I've got those." Candi ticked the questions off Ella's list. "But I still think we should start the interview by asking her who's the most interesting person she's ever been in a previous life. After all, it says right here in their pamphlet that she studied with North America's foremost expert on past-life regression. Shouldn't I ask her something about that?"

"Everyone knows Maud's crazy. Why encourage her? Just stick to the script." Ella glanced up from her clipboard and looked out the window for the first time since we'd left the TV station's parking lot for the Okotoks First Annual Psychic Exposition and Symposium. "Where are we, Phoebe?"

"The Okotoks junction." I turned the van off the MacLeod Trail and pointed us west to the Rocky Mountains. It was early June and their upper slopes were still covered in snow. The distant white peaks shone in the morning sun, a glittering divide between the soft greens of the foothills and the sky's pellucid blue.

"How long before we get there?" Ella changed sheets on her clipboard.

"Ten, fifteen minutes," I answered. "Don't worry, we have lots of time."

"You know we only have a couple of hours for this whole assignment. I have to be back in Calgary for a production meeting at two, so I want to be set up and ready to go out here by eleven. No slip-ups. No delays." For some reason Ella was even more twitchy than usual about today's assignment. Maybe it was because she was so far along in her pregnancy that it was a race to see which she would produce first: the season's last edition of "A Day in the Lifestyle" or her baby. "Come on Candi, we have enough time to finish going through the interview. What's your next question?"

"Why do you think people's past lives were always so much more interesting than their present ones?" Candi tapped her perfect front teeth with her pencil.

"In the script," Ella persisted. "What's the next question in the script?"

"Think about it. Have you ever met anyone who was an accountant in a past life?" Candi remained lost in her own musings. "Why is it that everybody was always somebody glamorous like the Queen of Sheba or Casanova back then, but in this life they're used car salesmen or they work at Wal-Mart or something? I mean, how could so many people all have been Cleopatra? Did her soul clone itself or what?"

I thought this was a pretty interesting question. Ella didn't. "Look, we're nearly there, so could we please get back to business and get through this script."

I've been hearing this conversation, give or take a few minor variations according to subject and place, since the day that Candi and Ella and I began working together. My name is Phoebe Fairfax. I'm a television photographer. I work part time for the Calgary station that produces "A Day in the Lifestyle." Legend has it that our station manager thought up the title all by himself and, as it suggests, the program takes a weekly half-hour look at what the local movers and shakers are up to. Ella's the producer, Candi's the on-camera host and interviewer, and I take the pictures. "Lifestyle" has a surprisingly large and faithful following all over southern Alberta. I'd like to believe this is the result of my brilliant photography but it's more likely due to Candi's interviews. Like Candi herself, they are irresistible.

Candi is young, blonde, and beautiful. Actually, that last is not quite true. Candi is not simply beautiful, she's a stunner. She's the kind of beautiful that makes men have trouble remembering to breathe when she's around. You'd assume this would automatically brand her as the woman other women love to hate but, oddly enough, it just isn't so. Most women are charmed by her, as well. Even animals seem to feel an instant trust when Candi stretches out a hand. According to my friend Cyrrie, some of this comes through on television and that's why "A Day in the Lifestyle" is so popular.

"Come on, Candi. What's the next question?" Ella insisted. Ella is a highly intelligent, thirty-five-ish brunette, attractive in a starched and tailored way, and as stubborn as Candi is beautiful. For every edition of "A Day in the Lifestyle" she writes Candi a script. The interview questions in it sound just like Ella – straightforward, straight-laced, and very straight-faced. Before every interview she reviews the script with

Candi. Finally, when the camera is running, she watches in stony silence while Candi shreds her meticulous questions into a cheery verbal confetti. It's the same story every time but Ella never gives up. Today was no exception.

"Maybe we should ask Maud why most people always seem to have been human beings in their previous lives." Candi blissfully ignored Ella's growing irritation. "I mean, why couldn't they have been animals? Instead of being Alexander the Great, why not be his horse?"

"You should ask Maud if she can arrange an exclusive interview with Bucephalus for you." This suggestion won me a look from Ella that could have withered a plastic plant.

"You know, Phoebe, that's not a bad idea," Candi said. "Talking to animals from the past I mean. It would make a great way to study evolution. Think of it. You wouldn't have to bother with rocks and fossils. You could ask the animals themselves."

"Sounds to me like you've just invented a whole new branch of geology," I said. "Psychopaleontology."

Candi looked straight up and held an imaginary microphone above her head. "Could you tell us, Mr. Rex – or may I call you Tyrannosaurus? Why thank you, Ty. Well, as I was saying, could you tell us what really happened to you and all the other dinosaurs?"

"I'm sorry to interrupt, but if you two can spare the time we do have this little matter of an interview with Maud. It might be nice to have a real question or two ready for her." Unfortunately, Ella fails to see the funny side of what Candi does and even if she did she wouldn't approve. Humour is not her strong suit.

Today, Ella's sense of humour was even less in evidence than usual. The whole assignment had annoyed her from the start.

Ella takes a certain pride in what she considers the cultural tone of "A Day in the Lifestyle," and a fortune-tellers' fair, even one with its title tarted up to Psychic Symposium, just wasn't her cup of Earl Grey with a thin slice of lemon. Nevertheless, even producers have to do what they're told, especially when their station-owner's wife is a devotee of New Age mysticism and the chief organizer of the Okotoks First Annual Psychic Exposition and Symposium. They do not, however, have to do it with good grace.

"The next question asks about the papers that are being given at the symposium." Candi came back to earth. "Honestly Ella, do you really believe anybody gives a hoot about a bunch of lectures? Nobody comes to a psychic fair to get lectured at. What people really want to know is how many fortune-telling booths they're going to have? How much does it cost to have your tarot read or your aura analysed? Nobody's going to pay any attention to the symposium. It's just an excuse for all the good stuff."

"There's no point in asking a lot of what's-to-see, what's-to-do questions," Ella countered. "The whole thing will be over before the program is broadcast. Come on, Candi, it's bad enough that we have to cover this garbage so don't make it any worse. Stick to the script." She grimaced and gripped her clipboard a little tighter.

"Are you feeling okay, Ella?" Candi asked. "You look a little strained. This close to your due date we don't want to take any chances. Are you sure you're all right?"

"I'm fine. It's nothing. The baby isn't due for at least two weeks."

"Better safe than sorry," Candi intoned. "Besides, you don't know for absolute certain that it's two weeks from now. What if Dr. Kyle was right all along? That would make it more like two days than two weeks." The baby's estimated time of arrival was a source of some dispute between Ella and her obstetrician.

"Dr. Kyle is not right. I'm right, and this baby is due two weeks from Monday." She shifted awkwardly in her seat in an effort to ease her obvious discomfort.

"Candi's got a point," I said. "Having a baby isn't like timing a television program. You can't make babies start on cue at the top of the hour."

"Phoebe, pregnancy has increased my waistline – it has not decreased my IQ. I know how to count as well as Anna Kyle and I'm telling you this baby is not due until after the fifteenth. Besides, everyone knows that first babies are always late." Ella's repetition of this old wives' tale was the first time I'd ever heard her acknowledge that maybe nature didn't run on Greenwich Mean Time.

"Oh no they're not. Not always," Candi chimed in. "Look at Cyrrie's mare. She had her foal a whole week and a half earlier than anyone expected and it was her first baby. Elvira just snuck off into a corner of Phoebe's pasture and next thing you know she was walking back to the barn with a foal at her side."

"I'm afraid we didn't discuss the pasture alternative at Lamaze class."

"That foal is so beautiful. He's all legs," Candi rhapsodized, oblivious to Ella's sarcasm. "Doesn't it make you wonder how mares manage to tuck up all those legs inside?"

"Remind me to ask Elvira's advice next time I decide to have a horse. In the meantime," Ella tapped her clipboard, "could we please get on with this? We're nearly there."

We arrived in Okotoks at a quarter to eleven. Okotoks is a small town about thirty kilometres southwest of Calgary on the Sheep River, right at the edge of the Rocky Mountain foothills. It began life, sheltered in its pretty poplar-lined valley, as a service community for the surrounding ranches and farms. Now it's a bedroom town for Calgary commuters, and new subdivisions sprawl out of the valley and up the surrounding hills.

The large hall the Psychic Symposium had rented was on the outskirts of one of Okotoks' new housing developments. The symposium had opened for business at ten and already the parking lot was more than half full. I parked the van in front of the No Parking sign at the main entrance and unloaded the equipment. Candi and Ella are always very good about helping me carry the camera and tripod and lights and all the other bits of paraphernalia necessary to tape a television interview, although these days Ella is so pregnant she can't manage much more than the microphone case. She tucked this under her left arm, secured her clipboard under her right, and, leading with her very prominent prow, sailed through the hall's front door and past a table at which a wispy young man sat selling admission tickets. Candi and I, loaded down with the rest of the gear, staggered along in her wake.

The hall was one of those all-purpose structures designed to handle everything from political rallies to basketball tournaments. Today the nets and collapsible bleachers were pushed out of the way to make room for the rows of booths that now occupied most of the available space. Large signs naming the speciality of the resident psychic and the prices charged hung from the tables at the front of each booth. The occasional waft of incense added a rich and exotic new layer to the room's permanent olfactory substratum of old gym socks and hot dog mustard.

There must have been over a hundred booths in the place but Ella hustled us through the crowd so fast that I didn't have time to do much more than read the signs. One thing I did notice on our fly-past was the large number of booths devoted to various forms of healing. Granted, I am not exactly *au courant* with the latest New Age trends but, given the scene, I did find this preoccupation with mortal clay surprising. For every couple of tarot readers or astrologers there was a healer or therapist of some sort. In the row we charged down, I saw a crystal healer, a psychic healer, a music healer, a magnetic therapist, and two aromatherapists. I wasn't altogether certain of what any of them actually did but their names gave enough of a clue for me to speculate. However, the last booth in the row was a total mystery. According to its big, red-lettered banner it was "The Ozone Lair." Its sole occupant, a sleekly tailored man with a salon tan and too many teeth, was busy explaining to one unconvinced-looking customer the workings of a small stainless-steel machine prominently displayed on the table in front of him.

Beyond the Ozone Lair, food concessions and tables occupied most of an entire basketball court. However, a small area near the back had been curtained-off and furnished with a lectern and a dozen folding chairs. This was the space provided for the symposium part of the Psychic Exposition and Symposium, and, if square footage was an indicator of importance, then Candi had assessed things correctly. The lectures were simply along for the ride. Ella held a heavy black curtain to one side while we lugged in the gear.

"It's pretty dreary in here." I put the tripod and camera on the floor behind the chairs. "Maud's interview would look a lot more interesting if we taped it out in front of the booths."

"Too many people. Too much ambient noise." Ella plunked herself down in a front-row chair. She looked drawn and tired.

"We'll do the interview here in front of the lectern. Come on Candi, let's finish going over these questions."

While Ella and Candi completed their review of the script, I put two chairs in place and set up the lights. I had just finished mounting the camera on the tripod and plugging in the microphones when the young man from the front door materialized behind me.

"Mrs. Gellman said to give you this." He handed a note to Ella and vanished back through the curtain.

Ella read the note. "Maud is going to be late. She can't do the interview until noon. Shit!" This was astounding. Not Maud's lateness, but Ella's emphatic expletive. Ella never swears, not even mildly. She regards verbal vulgarity as the mark of an impoverished vocabulary. "Shit, shit, shit."

"Come on, Ella. An hour one way or the other is nothing to get upset about." Ella's language had startled Candi too. "We can go out and walk around the fair and get some cover shots before the interview."

"Phoebe's scheduled to come back and do the cover shots tomorrow morning. Besides, I haven't finished the shot list." Ella was not to be cheered so easily.

"Then I'll do some short interviews with the people running the booths," Candi persisted optimistically.

"How can you? I haven't written any questions for you."

"For heaven's sake Ella, we're talking astral projection here, not astrophysics. I don't need a script just to talk to somebody who likes to fly without an airplane."

"Then make sure you're back here no later than ten to twelve so we can be set up and ready for Maud." Ella pulled a fresh sheet of paper from the bottom of the stack on her clipboard.

"You mean you're not coming with us?" I couldn't believe that she would allow Candi to go off interviewing on her own.

"I want to have a look around by myself so I can get this shot list finished. Candi's right. You don't need me for something this simple." She rested the clipboard on her enormous front and began to write. Really, our producer was not herself today.

"Ella," I began, "are you sure you're feeling . . ."

"Phoebe, for the very last time, there is absolutely nothing wrong with me. I am fine." She glowered up at me and pointed an exasperated finger in the direction of the booths. "Now go take a picture of something."

I slung the camera off the tripod and onto my shoulder, Candi grabbed the microphone and a portable floodlight, and we set out to roam the rows of booths. Most of the occupants were very pleasant people, even if their explanations of what they thought they were doing seemed, at least to me, totally lunatic. We talked to tarot readers, clairvoyants, palm readers, aura photographers, phrenologists, astrologers, dowsers, channellers, numerologists, dream interpreters, and one lone tea-leaf reader. In most instances, I was no more certain of what they actually did after they explained it than I had been before we started the interview.

On a more worldly plane, I learned that the psychics came from all over Canada and the States and spent a good part of each year travelling from psychic fair to psychic fair. Television coverage of these events, they assured Candi, was unusual. Maybe that's why they were all so keen to get in front of the camera and talk to her.

For the most part Candi stuck to simple questions of the "exactly what is . . .?" or "how did you get started in . . .?" variety. They seemed to work, although I suspect that simply standing there holding the microphone would have done equally well as the vision of free publicity had made the psychics positively garrulous. One tarot reader even tried to bribe Candi into giving him extra airtime with the promise of a full reading on the house. Then again, maybe he was just being generous. I gave him the benefit of the doubt after a woman with a crystal ball offered to tell me about my love life free of charge. I declined. I didn't want her wasting her time gazing into empty space.

The astrologers were enthusiastic talkers too. Most of them, at least the ones with computers, wanted to do our charts. The practice of the stellar art has been revolutionized by the silicon chip, and what used to take hours of painstaking labour over volumes of *The American Ephemeris* is now available at the tap of an enter key. Even palmistry has not remained untouched by technology. In a game effort to keep her analogies up-to-date, one elderly palmist told Candi to think of her brain as a computer, her hands as its printer, and the lines on her palms as the hard-copy printout of her spiritual and physical state. Hers was my favourite in a morning of interviews that mostly reinforced my conviction that there is no theory so illogical, no practice so outlandish, no notion so daft, that someone won't believe it.

"I think we've talked to enough fortune-tellers now, don't you Phoebe?" Candi waved a cheery toodle-oo to the palm reader. "Maybe we should get a healer or two."

"Why don't we see what that guy at the Ozone Lair is up to?" I suggested. "Maybe he's some kind of healer."

"The Ozone Lair?"

"No joke. The Ozone Lair. Didn't you notice it when we came in? It's the last booth before the refreshment concessions."

We strolled towards the smell of coffee and stopped in front of the booth where tanned and toothy was showing off his peculiar little machine to another customer. A good-looking woman of about Candi's age joined him behind the front table. She wasn't part of the sales pitch and stood well to one side of the action. She frowned in concentration as she brushed a strand of shiny black hair out of her eyes and adjusted the placement of a small sign that announced in elegant calligraphy, "Tarot Readings by Tracy."

"Tracy! Tracy McMurtry!" Candi shrieked with delight. The woman looked up, startled.

"Candi!" She rushed out from behind the table and threw her arms around Candi.

After much hugging and high-pitched laughter, Candi collected herself and introduced us. "Tracy is one of the all-time best hairstylists in Alberta," she announced. "We went to high school together. She took my head to all the shows."

"Candi means that she was my model in styling competitions," Tracy explained. "They used to have a contest every semester for all the beauty culture students."

"Tracy won every show she entered, including the provincial championship."

"Only because you're so gorgeous and a lot of the judges were men. They took one look at Candi and it was contest over," Tracy smiled at me and shrugged. "I could have cut her hair with a weed whacker and they'd still have picked us. But I never did anything this good." She cast a professional eye over Candi's golden mop of cascading curls. "This cut is great. Better than great. It's mega-great. Who did it?"

"Can you guess?" Candi asked.

Tracy walked a slow circle around Candi, giving her head a long, critical appraisal. As she turned, I noticed the greenish-purple remains of a large bruise under her left eye. She had done her best to hide it with makeup. She took a lock of Candi's hair, lifted it up and let it fall back into place. She did this several times before she spoke. "I'd say it was somebody at My Mane Man. Maybe Kevin." She tested one more lock. "No, not Kevin. This is so good it could only be Ralph. It has to be Ralph."

"Right on. I've been going to Ralph for the last few years. But how could you tell? You're amazing."

"Work in the business long enough and you could do it too." Tracy shrugged off the compliment but I could see that Candi's praise had pleased her. "You get so you can recognize someone's cuts like you can recognize their handwriting." I wondered if she could identify the author of the scrawl on my head. Actually, I don't think my haircut is too bad considering how hard it is to see the back properly, even with a couple of mirrors.

"What are you doing here?" Candi asked.

"Well, working, I guess." Tracy waved a tentative hand towards her hand-lettered sign.

"You mean you're not doing hair anymore?"

"Not exactly. At least not right now. I've been doing tarot readings for a while. This is my fourth psychic fair." Tracy sounded like that was about three too many. "I'm here with Jonathan."

"Who's Jonathan?" Candi asked.

"Jonathan Webster. The guy I live with." Tracy nodded towards the man in the booth. He was still trying to sell his machine to an ever more dubious and distraught-looking customer. The sale was not going well. Actually, Jonathan and the customer seemed to be having an argument. The customer's angry voice became louder and louder. "He sells the SuperO ozone box," Tracy practically shouted this bit of information in an effort to drown out the row from the booth. She did not succeed. The customer thundered his way to a full crescendo of indignation.

"Either this is some sort of joke," he boomed, "or you should be reported to the Canadian Medical Association. This thing is disgusting and so are you." The customer spun on his heel and stalked off. I learned later that Jonathan frequently had this effect on people.

"Sweetheart, aren't you going to introduce me to your friends?" Jonathan gave the finger to the back of his departing customer and strolled out from behind the table. He draped his arm over Tracy. It was a gesture of possession, not affection. Tracy didn't actually squirm, but I could see as she introduced us that the arm made her uneasy. Up close, Jonathan didn't look all that comfortable himself. Despite the tan, his skin had an unhealthy, pasty look and his face was covered in a light sweat. He flashed a few teeth and offered me a hand. It felt damp and cold in mine.

"Why did you quit hairdressing?" Candi asked.

"Tracy thought she needed a change. She was getting stale, weren't you Trace?" Jonathan tightened his grip on her shoulders. "So I said she could use a corner of my booth for her card readings, didn't I darling?" Tracy nodded in mute discomfort. "You girls should get her to do a reading for you. She's one of the best. I'm sure we could give you a deal since you're old friends." I could see this offer did not have the effect on Candi that Jonathan intended. His snake-oil charm merely made her look like she wanted to be quietly sick.

"How did you learn to read tarot cards?" I asked Tracy.

"Her grandmother taught her. And if you think this little lady is good, you should go talk to Grandma." Jonathan widened his smile, favouring us with the full panorama of his dental perfection. "There's not a reader in this room who could hold a candle to her, is there Trace?"

"How is your grandma?" Candi said. "Is she still living here in Okotoks?"

Tracy opened her mouth to answer but again Jonathan beat her to it. "She had her seventy-eighth birthday two weeks ago, and on my way over here this morning I saw her out digging in her garden. We're living in the house next door to her right now. Tracy likes to be close so we can keep an eye on the old girl, don't you sweetheart?"

"Candi, it's almost time for Maud's interview," I interrupted. "I have to set up pretty soon so if you still want to talk to Jonathan about his machine, maybe we should get started?" If we hung around the Ozone Lair much longer, my urge to strangle Jonathan with the microphone cord might grow too strong to resist.

Not surprisingly, he was more than eager to do an interview. I checked the microphone connection and turned on the portable flood. Under the bright light he looked even more unwell. His tan had taken on a greenish tinge and his hands trembled as he wiped the sheen of sweat off his forehead with an already damp handkerchief. He stood next to Candi directly behind his machine. Tracy tucked her little sign out of sight under the table and then came to stand behind the camera. I began with a close shot of the machine taken at an angle that minimized all the lens-flaring highlights on its polished surface. It was a stainless-steel box about the size of a small suitcase with what appeared to be an oxygen tank attached to one end and a little nozzle at the other. As Candi asked her first question, I pulled back to include both her and Jonathan in the frame.

"Well, Jonathan, what does this machine of yours do?"

"Simply put, Candi, the SuperO is a device for turning the oxygen in this tank into super-oxygen. As you probably know, super-oxygen is another name for ozone. But the machine does a lot of other things too. For example, it's a good way to take medications, especially ones that taste terrible or might upset your stomach. You can simply include them in powdered form in your regular ozone treatment. I use it myself to take a herbal powder that cleanses the blood. However, I'd say that basically and most importantly, the SuperO produces ozone."

"And why do you want to produce ozone?"

"Why? Because oxygen is the element most vital to all living things and these days we're just not getting enough of it. Did you know, Candi, that according to top scientists, oxygen made up almost forty per cent of the earth's atmosphere a thousand years ago? But now, thanks to pollution and deforestation and all the other unnatural things we're doing to the earth, that figure has dropped to less than twenty per cent." I moved in for a closeup of Jonathan. Beads of sweat had reappeared on his face.

"Think of it," he said. "We're only breathing in half as much oxygen as our ancestors. This lack of oxygen is our single greatest modern health problem. It's a disaster. It weakens our entire body and leaves us vulnerable to the first disease to come along. No wonder viruses and cancers are flourishing. And other diseases are increasing too. Alzheimer's, AIDS, heart disease, diabetes, cancer, asthma – they're all on the rise. And why? A simple lack of plain old oxygen." Jonathan swallowed uneasily and tugged at his collar as if his tie were too tight.

"It's a very big problem but there is a very simple solution." He paused dramatically and patted the machine. "The answer to our health problems is ozone. With super-oxygen treatments we can overcome and prevent disease. Just by using this simple machine twice a day we can reclaim the natural, vibrant kind of good health we were all meant to have."

"Are you claiming that this machine can cure AIDS and prevent Alzheimer's?" Candi asked.

"I'm not simply claiming it, Candi, I have scientific proof that it can do that and a whole lot more. For instance, why do you think violent crime is on the rise? Because we have to fight for every breath of air we take, that's why. Lack of oxygen shifts the whole chemistry of our brains and nervous systems and that ends up in murder and rape and war. But . . ." Jonathan paused again.

"Wow! Just think of all the people who have asthma." Candi spoiled his dramatic effect. "They must be really violent because they breathe in even less oxygen than the rest of us. Jonathan, do you think Bonnie and Clyde were asthmatics?"

"I take your point, Candi," Jonathan flashed another smile, "and you're absolutely right. We shouldn't be discussing lack of oxygen in big, intellectual terms. We should be talking about the effects of low oxygen levels on the health of individual people and what they can do about it with the SuperO machine. I can tell you from my own experience that with only two treatments a day you can hardly believe how much better you feel. It's made an incredible difference to my own health." A drop of sweat rolled from Jonathan's temple, down his cheek to the tip of his chin. "The second that ozone enters my body I feel vital, I feel in tune with the earth, I feel truly alive!" The sweat drop continued its journey and plopped onto the machine's shiny surface.

"So you use the SuperO machine yourself?"

"Every day, morning and night," Jonathan assured her. "This very machine."

"How do you get the super-oxygen into your body?" Candi fiddled with the machine's nozzle. "Do you breathe it in or what?"

"Well, not exactly," Jonathan said. "The super-oxygen is actually introduced into the body by means of rectal insufflation." A long pause followed.

"You mean you shove this thing up your . . ." Candi's voice trailed off as the full implication of Jonathan's words sunk in. She snatched her hand away from the nozzle. "And then you turn on the gas and pump it in like you're some sort of human bicycle tire?"

"I know there are some people who might think that the whole process sounds . . ." Jonathan hesitated, searching for the right word. "They might think it all seems a little . . ."

"Crazy," Candi finished the sentence for him.

"A little unusual," Jonathan continued as if he had not heard her.

"And what does the Canadian Medical Association have to say?" Candi asked. "I would imagine they find your machine more than just a little unusual."

"Establishment doctors fight new ideas all the time," Jonathan replied. "But that doesn't mean they're right. I'm sure your viewers have far more open minds than the medical profession."

"What about the Department of Health? Has your machine been approved by them?"

"Candi, all radical new ideas in medicine are considered crazy at first, especially by the kind of bureaucrats who work for Health and Welfare. What do you think would happen to all those paper pushers if everyone in Canada suddenly got healthy. They'll never approve the SuperO because it would put them out of a job."

Candi signalled me to turn off the camera. "I'm sorry Jonathan but we might as well stop right now because we can't put this interview on the air. 'A Day in the Lifestyle' isn't allowed to give airtime to things that could hurt people." Candi had a point. We didn't want to encroach on the news department's territory.

"If the SuperO had been approved by Health and Welfare then it might be different," she continued. "So thanks for your time and I'm sorry it didn't work out." She held out her hand to him but he ignored it. Jonathan's affable veneer had begun to crack. "Come on Phoebe," Candi moved out from behind the table. "We don't want to be late for Maud."

"Don't go, Candi. Please." Tracy put her hand on Candi's arm. "It's not that bad. Really it isn't. Jonathan's machine never hurt anyone. He hasn't even sold one."

"Shut up, you moron," Jonathan snapped at her. The snake-oil charm had vanished. "I don't need this kind of crap from you." But the snake remained. "And I don't need any help from your goddamn girlfriends." Jonathan's skin now looked almost as green as a snake's and his hands shook uncontrollably. In hindsight I realize that the shaking was a symptom of more than emotional stress, but at the time I was only aware of his startling and disproportionate anger. In a matter of seconds, he had worked himself into a rage. He made no effort to control it and, for a moment, I actually thought he might hit Candi.

"Lady, you are some interviewer. Where do you get off deciding what's good for people? You couldn't tell that pretty little ass of yours from a hole in the ground even if it did get you a job on TV. Now get out of my face." He retreated to the depths of the Ozone Lair.

"I'll call you soon," Candi promised as we said our awkward goodbyes to Tracy. We turned and walked past the concession booths, towards the black curtains and Ella. You didn't have to be psychic to know that Jonathan gave our backs the finger, too.

2

"Get some good stuff?" Ella leaned back in her chair and stretched.

"Not bad," I replied noncommittally.

"Good. Why don't you get set up for Maud. I'm almost finished this." She went back to work. Earlier I had noticed her plodding from booth to booth, making notes and additions to her shot list while Candi and I taped interviews.

"Phoebe, I think he beats her," Candi said quietly. "Did you see that bruise on Tracy's cheek?"

"Yeah, I saw it. But just because she has a bruise doesn't mean he gave it to her." I took the used tape out of the camera and replaced it with a fresh one.

"Well she didn't get it by walking into a door. Someone punched her, and you don't have to be Sherlock Holmes to figure out who. What a creep."

Before I could agree with Candi, our station-owner's wife breezed in, all ready to be interviewed.

"Ah girls, there you are and don't you all look pretty. The three of you are a real breath of spring." Maud is a tall, elegant woman of sixty with a perfection of grooming and dress that says money is no object. She looks like the kind of woman who would be at home organizing charity balls for the symphony or masterminding fund-raising dinners for cabinet ministers. Actually, Maud does have a flair for organization but unless the minister in question had served in Sir John A. Macdonald's cabinet I doubt that she'd be interested. After dabbling in tarot, flirting with crystals, and experimenting a little with astrology, Maud finally found her psychic niche in past-life regression therapy. She firmly believes that the loves, the hates, the successes, and the failures we experienced in our past lives can affect and influence our present lives. She claims that by going back and resolving the conflicts and miseries in our previous existences we can do our present selves no end of good. The kind call Maud eccentric.

"That dress is so becoming, Phoebe. It just proves there's no reason you can't look feminine simply because you're doing a man's job." She beamed approvingly in my direction.

"And Candi, gorgeous as always. Honestly, you're enough to make a person green with envy. You know, if I did that with my hair everyone would think I was a crazy old lady who never used a comb. You do it and you look like an angel. Life's so unfair!" She kissed the air somewhere west of Candi's left ear and wafted on to Ella, who had struggled to her feet.

"My goodness, who ever would have thought it, Ella. You're simply blooming. You look like that baby of yours could be on his way any minute now." She reached out to take Ella's hands but as both were full she compromised by giving the free end of her clipboard a warm waggle.

"Isn't this exciting? Are you all ready to interview me? You know, Sam has owned that station for fifteen years but this will be the first time I've ever been on television." Maud rattled on. The woman has a genius for speech. She can squeeze more words into a minute than the ear can hear or the brain can process. However, her supersonic speech is more a physical phenomenon than a means of communication, especially as she combines it with the habit of rarely listening to a word anyone else says. Talking with Maud is like trying to have a conversation with your washing machine on spin cycle.

"Did you girls manage to have a good look around out there?" Maud fluttered a beautifully manicured hand at the activity in the hall behind her. "There's just so much to see and so much to talk about that I couldn't even begin to fill you in on everything. Did you visit the aura photography booth, Phoebe? As a photographer yourself I'll bet you were amazed, weren't you? Imagine, capturing the very essence of the life force on film."

"We're rather pressed for time," Ella said very loudly, managing, by sheer volume, to override Maud for a few seconds. "I think we'd better get this interview started."

Maud kept up a constant prattle while I set up the camera and settled her and Candi into their chairs in front of the lectern. I clipped microphones to their collars, plugged the leads into the camera, and put on my headphones.

"Time to check sound levels," I said to Ella. She pulled up a chair and put it in her customary place, behind me and a little to the left.

"Forget it. Just take a level off Maud right now and go with Candi's usual." This was most unlike Ella. She's normally ultra-meticulous about the technical aspects of our work. "Is everybody ready?" she hollered.

"My goodness Ella, there's no need to shout," Maud said. "We can hear you quite well, and of course we're ready. I can hardly wait to hear what Candi's going to ask me first. I'll bet it's going to be something about a past life and then . . ." Maud chattered away.

"You might as well roll the tape, Phoebe." Ella turned to me with a what-the-hell shrug, gave Candi a silent cue, and sat down heavily in her chair. I started the tape and put my eye to the viewfinder but I was very worried. Ella usually spends every interview on the edge of her chair, gripping her stopwatch and grinding her teeth. I can sense her behind me suppressing screams of frustration. But today felt different. Granted, Maud was impossible but, even so, this apathy was just not Ella.

"Maud! You've got to let me talk," Candi bellowed. "It's time for me to ask you a question."

"You mean we're going to start the interview?" Maud asked.

"We've already started. See," Candi pointed at the camera, "Phoebe's taping us right now."

I raised my hand above the camera and gave Maud what I thought was a friendly, reassuring little wave. I was not prepared for what came next. The impossible happened. Maud stopped talking. She simply dried up. Her flow of words ceased as abruptly as a turned-off tap. I know that many people find the video camera's staring cyclops lens intimidating, especially if it's their first time in front of one. Sometimes "Lifestyle" guests who are perfectly relaxed and talkative the minute before I turn on the camera can have trouble remembering their own names the minute after. But I never dreamed it would happen to an Olympic-calibre yack like Maud. She peered at the camera, as wide-eyed and silent as an owl on a fence post.

"We're talking today with Maud Gellman," Candi spoke directly to the camera. I wondered if she'd noticed the change in Maud. "Maud is the organizer of the Okotoks First Annual Psychic Exposition and Symposium. Its official title is 'Good Vibrations and Celestial Harmonies: A Psychic Symposium for the Nineties.' Maud, could you tell us just what a psychic symposium is?"

"Yes," said Maud. A long pause followed.

"Perhaps you'd like to elaborate a little on that for us," Candi prompted.

"On what?" Maud's lips barely moved. She continued to gaze unblinkingly at the camera.

"The Psychic Symposium," Candi repeated. "Could you tell us what a psychic symposium is?"

"Yes I could." Maud mumbled and then fell silent again.

"Then please, Maud. Tell us," Candi begged. "What's a psychic symposium?"

"It's a kind of meeting," Maud stated with an air of finality that indicated she felt they had exhausted the subject.

"But what kind of meeting?" Candi insisted.

"A psychics' meeting."

This time the pause lasted so long I wondered if I should turn off the camera. I felt very sorry for Candi. In her own way, she usually manages to coax even her most nervous interviewees into relaxing after the first couple of questions. This was different. Nothing short of a horse tranquillizer was going to relax Maud.

"What made you decide to hold the symposium out here in Okotoks rather than in Calgary?" Candi was desperate. I could tell. She was following Ella's script. Maud looked at her blankly and blinked once. "Why not have your symposium in Calgary?" Candi repeated, loudly and slowly. "Why Okotoks?"

"Cheap. Rent's cheap. Cheap."

Inspired by this gushing response, Candi launched into Ella's next question. "I know some of our viewers will be interested in the papers being presented at the symposium. What about this one?" Candi read from her notes. "'Personal and Planetary Healing: An Inner Journey to Serenity and Cosmic Awareness.' What will that be about?"

Maud shrugged, shook her head, and relapsed into total silence.

"Well, Maud." Candi drew herself up in her chair and squared her shoulders. When I see that look through my viewfinder I know it's time to hold tight to the tripod and get ready for a ride on Candi's conversational roller coaster. Usually, this is when I can sense Ella's silent screams at their loudest but today I couldn't feel a thing from her direction. "Well, Maud," Candi repeated firmly, "I understand you're an expert on past-life regression so I think it's time for us to talk about some of those previous lives you've led. Who's the most interesting person you've ever been?"

At last, Maud came alive. It was like watching someone wake from a trance. A flicker of animation crossed her face. Life and warmth returned to her eyes. She smiled at Candi. She took a breath. She opened her mouth to speak. But, before she could say Cleopatra, Ella interrupted. For the first time in the four years we'd worked together, Ella actually stopped an interview.

"Phoebe," she tugged at my sleeve. "Phoebe, I guess maybe Dr. Kyle was right. I think I should probably get to the hospital." She grasped my arm. "Soon."

"What's the matter?" Candi asked.

"Ella needs to get to a hospital," I said. "I think the baby's on its way."

"I'll call an ambulance." Maud leapt from her chair and

promptly tangled her feet in her microphone cord. By the time she'd snarled it twice around her left leg and jerked the clip off her collar, Ella had managed to recover from her latest spasm.

"Please Maud. No ambulance. I'm perfectly capable of walking to the van."

"Are you sure, dear?" Maud gave the cord an almighty yank and pulled the microphone plug out of its socket in the camera. I swear I heard the camera scream. She absentmindedly looped the dangling cord around her neck, then linked her arm through Ella's. "Now hold on tight and let's go," she ordered. "Candi, you take her other arm and we'll just go nice and slowly out to the front door. Phoebe, you get Ella's things. There's a hospital at Black Diamond, Ella dear. Don't you worry. We'll have you there in no time. I really do think you should let us call an ambulance. Slowly now," she added somewhat superfluously as she attempted to drag the resisting Ella after her.

"Please Maud, I'm not an invalid." Ella dug in the heels of her sensible shoes. "I can walk to the van on my own." Maud looked hurt. "Besides," Ella added, a trifle more gently, "I really don't think you should come with us. You can't leave your post. You're the fair's organizer, and I'd feel terrible if you left on my account when people here are depending on you. Phoebe and Candi are perfectly capable of getting me to the hospital." Ella detached herself from Maud's arm. She seemed to have regained a little of her composure. "Shall we?" She looked at Candi and me.

"Right," I said, relieving Maud of her microphone. "Just let me square away the gear and we'll be on our way."

"For God's sake, Phoebe, couldn't you leave the damn equipment where it is for once?" So much for Ella's composure.

"We need an ambulance," Maud worried aloud. "I know we need an ambulance."

Finally, Candi organized us. "Come on, Ella," she said gently. "Let's go. Phoebe will catch up to us at the door. Maud you go ahead and make sure the way is clear. Phoebe, don't take forever. Just bring the camera and leave the other stuff. Maud's staying here so she'll make sure nothing happens to it, won't you Maud?"

I followed Candi's orders but it still took a couple of minutes to unplug the lights, tuck them out of harm's way behind the lectern, and drop the microphones in their small case into my workbag. I was taking the camera off its tripod when I heard sirens approaching. I wondered how Maud had managed to call an ambulance so soon. Maybe there was more to psychic communication than I thought. I collected my workbag and the camera and stepped through the black curtain just as I heard the sirens cut out. A crowd had gathered in front of the Ozone Lair. They moved back to make way for a uniformed paramedic who ran past the row of booths carrying a medical bag. Another paramedic, this one pushing a stretcher, followed close behind. I hoisted the camera onto my shoulder and started taping.

Jonathan Webster lay on the floor in front of his booth. His eyes were closed, his breathing shallow and erratic. Tracy stood looking down at him while one of the paramedics did things with a stethoscope and the other hooked Jonathan up to an oxygen tank. Then the two of them lifted Jonathan onto the stretcher. The crowd stood silently as they wheeled him feet first towards the entrance. I went too, walking backwards slightly ahead and to one side of the stretcher while I kept on taping. I got a great shot. Jonathan's oxygen-masked face poked out from under a blanket. The paramedics, one on either side of the stretcher, leaned forward in their effort to hurry their patient to the waiting ambulance. A distraught Tracy followed directly behind. I had to step aside to let them through the front door but I kept right on taping. I didn't stop the camera until the paramedics had bundled Jonathan and Tracy into the ambulance and driven off, siren blaring.

"Phoebe, don't you have any feelings at all?" Maud was incensed. She stood beside the open door of the van with her arm looped through Ella's. Candi was already behind the wheel.

"How callous can you photographers get?" Maud continued in full indignation. "How could you stand there taking pictures while they wheeled poor Jonathan Webster away?"

"It's Phoebe's job, Maud." Ella came to my defence as I detached her from Maud and boosted her into the front seat. "That's what she gets paid to do."

"You mean that Phoebe gets paid to behave in a totally vulgar and insensitive manner in public places?" All in all, it seemed to me that Maud had come up with a pretty good description of news photography. "I thought she was being paid to come out here and photograph our psychic fair, not to take up ambulance-chasing. You may be doing a man's job, Phoebe, and although I certainly can't call you a lady after what I've just seen, you might at least try to remember that you are a woman. I don't understand how a woman could do what you just did. How could you? How could you be so crass?"

I was spared having to justify my lack of the finer feminine feelings by Ella. "Hurry up Phoebe, let's go." The "o" in Ella's "go" turned into a loud groan as a new contraction hit.

I hopped into the back of the van and slammed the door. Candi waved to Maud as she spun gravel and we roared out of the parking lot and down the hill to the town centre at a good thirty kilometres over the posted speed limit. Even on ordinary days Candi drives likes she's in training for the Indy 500 and this afternoon was anything but ordinary. We slewed to a halt at a four-way stop sign.

"Where is this hospital Maud was talking about?" she asked.

"It's in Black Diamond," I said. "Turn left and then follow the highway signs."

"Do you think that's where they'll take Jonathan?"

"It's closest but who knows."

"I'm supposed to go to Calgary," Ella announced, "to the Grace Hospital."

"Sorry, Ella, we're off to Black Diamond." Candi hit the gas.

"But my obstetrician works at the Grace Hospital," Ella protested.

"Ella, you're in labour and the Grace is over an hour away," I tried reasoning with her.

"We've got lots of time," she stated confidently. "First babies always take a long time coming."

"Where did you hear that one?" Candi asked. "Same source that told you first babies are always late?"

"Look, it would be silly to take any risks when there's a perfectly good hospital a few minutes from here," I said.

"But we had our pre-natal classes at the Grace," Ella persisted. "They even gave us a tour. I know the Grace Hospital." She gave a sudden gasp and clutched her clipboard so tightly that her knuckles turned white.

"Ella, stop being such a jerk," Candi ordered brusquely. "Unless you want to have your baby right here in the van with the assistance of Dr. Phoebe, we're going to Black Diamond and that's that."

That was indeed that. Ten minutes and three contractions later, we pulled up to the door of the emergency ward of the Oilfields Hospital in the town of Black Diamond. The big doors to the ambulance bay stood open revealing an ambulance parked inside.

"That's gotta be Jonathan's," Candi said.

"I'll go find a wheelchair," I volunteered.

"I do not need a wheelchair," Ella objected vehemently. I was encouraged to see a little of her fighting spirit back. She climbed out of the van and strode towards the doors which swept open automatically at her approach. Candi and I hurried after her.

Inside, the two paramedics from Jonathan's ambulance stood near a desk filling out some forms. Tracy sat weeping quietly to herself, huddled into a chair in one corner of the otherwise empty emergency waiting room. Candi immediately went to sit beside her and put a comforting arm around her shoulders. Ella and I continued down the hall to the general admitting desk. The nurse on duty looked up from her work as we approached.

"May I help you?" she asked pleasantly. Her name tag said Hilda Adams, R.N.

"My friend is having a baby," I said.

"So I can see," she smiled.

"No, I mean she's having a baby right now," I said.

Ella picked that moment to groan loudly. Her knees began to buckle and she grabbed at the desk.

"You girls don't waste any time, do you?" Mrs. Adams whisked a wheelchair out from behind the desk and helped Ella to sit. "I think we'll find you a doctor now and ask questions later." She patted Ella's shoulder reassuringly. "Do you have a partner we should contact?"

"Marty. My husband." Ella spoke through pain-clenched teeth.

"How soon can he get here?" Mrs. Adams asked.

"Fifteen, twenty minutes," I said.

"Better tell him to hurry," Mrs. Adams began to wheel Ella down the hall.

"Phoebe," Ella called back over her shoulder, "would you phone the station and tell them I might not make that two o'clock production meeting. And here," she held up her clipboard, "here's your shot list for tomorrow."

Marty's the lifeguard at a health resort near Millarville. He must have been standing right by the telephone because he answered almost as soon as The Ranch's operator put my call through to the swimming pool. He did not take my news calmly.

"Oh no, Phoebe, this is way too soon. Are you sure she's okay? How far apart are her contractions? How many . . ."

"Look Marty, your kid is being born. Stop playing twenty questions and get over here."

"Yeah, you're right. I'm on my way. But why didn't she say anything this morning? Do they have a good obstetrician at Black Diamond? How long . . ."

"Goodbye Marty." I hung up.

My phone call to the station created almost as much excitement as my call to Marty but the furore there was not fuelled by sentiment. The arrival date of Ella's offspring was the subject of one of the richest office pools on record. Over two hundred and fifty bucks were riding on this kid, not to mention the added fifty in side bets on its sex. Phone calls completed, I went to sit with Candi and Tracy.

"How's Jonathan?" I asked.

"I don't know." Tracy had stopped crying. She and Candi

sat drinking the coffee that Candi had bought in the small cafeteria off the main lobby. "We got here and they wheeled him away. Then they asked me some questions and said I should wait. Nobody told me anything."

"The ambulance men think it might be a heart attack," Candi said. "They told Tracy he had all the symptoms."

"It can't be his heart. How could it? Jonathan's a health freak. He exercises all the time and he never eats anything but health food. You know, all organic stuff."

"He is a little young for a heart attack," I agreed. "What happened?"

"He said he didn't feel well and that he was going to the refreshment area to get himself a cup of herbal tea. Then he walked out of the Ozone Lair and just keeled over. He's going to be all right, isn't he Candi?"

"How long have you lived with him?" Candi tried to distract her.

"A couple of years, I guess. I met him while I was at La Maison."

"You mean Jonathan's a hairdresser too?"

"He even had his own salon for a while. He got real sick of working at La Maison. He figured he could make a lot more money on his own so he and his friend Edward Sedge started up a new salon, Foxy Locks. That was just before Jonathan and I started living together. He and Eddy asked me to come work for them and I did. It was great. Pretty soon there was so much business we had to hire more stylists. Eddy and Jonathan were terrific to work for. They even gave me a few shares in the business. Jonathan said I deserved it because I was in on the ground floor and helped build it up."

"What happened?" Candi asked. "Why aren't you still there?"

"The place went belly up," Tracy stated flatly.

"But how could you go bankrupt when you were doing so well?"

Tracy shrugged. "Cash flow or something, Jonathan said. I never really understood. I only know that he and Eddy had a big fight and they haven't spoken to each other since. Jonathan says Eddy tried to rip him off when they had to declare bankruptcy. It was all pretty ugly."

An elderly doctor in an immaculate white lab coat entered the waiting room. A fringe of equally white hair ringed his bald head. "Which of you is the woman who came in with Mr. Webster?" Tracy raised her hand. "I'm Dr. Addison. Are you his wife?"

"Well, sort of I guess. Although I'm not exactly . . ."

"Yes, she's his wife," Candi answered decisively.

"How is he? Has he had a heart attack? Is he going to be okay?" I noticed that Tracy did not ask to see Jonathan.

"Mrs. Webster, I'm not going to beat around the bush here. You should know that your husband is a very sick man. We're pretty sure it isn't his heart but we don't know exactly what is wrong yet. Right now we need some more information from you. When did you first notice that your husband wasn't feeling well?"

For the next few minutes, Candi and I sat silently while Dr. Addison asked Tracy a lot of questions regarding Jonathan's symptoms.

"And you're absolutely certain he didn't eat or drink anything unusual in the last twenty-four hours?"

"Most of what Jonathan eats is unusual," Tracy said. "He's a health-food nut. He's eaten the same weird stuff ever since I've known him. He didn't eat anything different today."

"What about the SuperO machine?" I suggested.

"What's a SuperO?" Dr. Addison asked.

I told him.

"Lord help us," he shook his head. "Four months from retirement and I thought I'd seen it all."

"But Jonathan has used that machine for months. Twice a day," Tracy said. "Why would it hurt him now?"

"And you're sure Mr. Webster said that you can introduce other substances into the system besides oxygen?" Dr. Addison looked like he still didn't quite believe what I had told him.

"I did an interview with him today for the television program I work for. Jonathan told me that he sometimes uses the SuperO to take some herbal powder that's supposed to cleanse the blood. It's all on tape if you want to see." Candi corroborated my story.

"Every Friday morning," Tracy agreed. "He cleanses his blood every Friday morning."

"Where is this SuperO thing?" Dr. Addison asked.

"Back in our booth at the psychic fair," Tracy said.

"And Mr. Webster used it this morning?"

"Yes."

"And the blood cleansing powder. He used that too?"

"I guess so."

"What's in it?" he asked. Tracy looked blank. "The powder. What's it made of?"

"I don't know. It's some sort of white stuff."

"Did you actually see him use it?"

"No. But it's Friday so I'm pretty sure he did. Jonathan is very fussy about stuff like that."

"Mrs. Webster, as soon as your husband is stable we're going to have to move him to a hospital in Calgary. I think he should be seen by a toxicologist."

"A toxicologist?" Tracy said.

"A poison specialist," Dr. Addison explained.

"You think Jonathan was poisoned?"

"Right now we're still exploring possibilities. When we find out anything positive, I'll let you know." He turned abruptly and walked back to the ward.

"He thinks Jonathan was poisoned." Tracy's voice cracked a little as if she were nearing the end of her emotional rope. "But he uses that machine everyday. Jonathan couldn't have made that kind of mistake, could he?"

Candi and I were spared having to provide the obvious and unpleasant answer to her question by Marty. He ran through the sliding doors and, with a screech of his big white running shoes on the linoleum, all six-foot-four of him lurched to a stop directly in front of us.

"Where is she, Phoebe? I'm her coach. Candi, where is she? She needs me."

Marty and Ella are one of the oddest love stories I've ever come across. Talk about opposites attracting. He's an impossibly good-looking jock, almost ten years Ella's junior and as dashing and devil-may-care as she is prim. Nevertheless, it was love at first sight, marriage a few weeks later, and, at least so far, passionately happy ever after.

"Marty. Marty. Calm down. Let's go ask the nurse." I walked him down to the main admitting desk.

"Your wife is in the delivery room," Mrs. Adams said. Marty started down the corridor. "But you can't go down there." She ran out from behind the desk and dashed after him. Mrs. Adams was one very nimble nurse. She caught up with him halfway down the corridor and hauled him back to the desk. "You've got to wait out here for the doctor's permission."

"But she needs me. I'm her coach. She can't breathe without me!"

"I wouldn't worry too much, Mr. Bradshaw. Your wife seemed to be breathing very nicely last time I looked. Now wait here and I'll find out when you can see her." Mrs. Adams disappeared down the corridor. Marty writhed in an agony of worry until she returned a couple of minutes later.

"The doctor says to come join the party, Mr. Bradshaw, your baby will be here any time now." Marty took off down the hall like a sprinter from the blocks. "There's a nurse waiting for you with a mask and gown," Mrs. Adams called to his disappearing back. "Well," she grinned at me, "maybe his wife can calm him down."

I rejoined Candi and Tracy in the waiting room. We sat for another half-hour, mostly in silence. Tracy picked at the rim of her empty styrofoam cup. I read an antique *Reader's Digest*. Candi made a second trip to the cafeteria and brought us all back another cup of coffee. I had just finished the last of mine when I saw Dr. Addison coming down the corridor. I don't know why, maybe it was the grim look on his face, but something made us all stand when he came into the room.

"I'm very sorry Mrs. Webster. We did everything we could but your husband didn't make it. He died a few minutes ago." He paused, almost as if he were waiting for Tracy to break down. She didn't. She was shaky but she managed to maintain control.

"Jonathan's dead," Tracy said. I couldn't tell whether it was a question or a statement.

"He died without regaining consciousness," Dr. Addison said.

"Jonathan's dead," Tracy repeated.

"I'm sorry Mrs. Webster."

"So you don't know what happened to him," Candi said.

"Not right now," Dr. Addison acknowledged. "But we will. Right after the autopsy.

"The autopsy?" This time Tracy did react. She collapsed onto her chair like the wind had been knocked out of her. But still, she was dry-eyed.

"We have to determine the cause of death before I can issue a death certificate," Dr. Addison continued. "Also, in cases like this, I'm required to notify the police. Nurse Adams will give you all the details on that and on when you can claim the body for burial."

"Phoebe! Candi!" A masked Marty ran down the hall towards us, his green surgical gown streaming out behind him. "I'm a father!" he shouted. "I have a daughter and I'm her dad!" He pulled off his mask, flung his arms around me, and burst into tears.

3

After we mopped up Marty and sent him back to Ella and their new daughter there was nothing more we could do at the hospital. We waited while Mrs. Adams talked to Tracy and got her to sign a couple of forms. Then we drove her back to Okotoks with us.

"Would you like us to drop you off at home?" Candi asked.

"No, I don't think so. I guess I should pick up the car before I go home." Tracy sat slumped in a corner of the backseat. "It's in the parking lot at the psychic fair. And the SuperO. I'd better get that too. They'll probably want the booth for someone else."

But Tracy was too late to collect the SuperO. The police beat her to it. We met Constable Jennifer Lindt coming out of the door to the psychic fair. Jenny works with the local RCMP detachment. She once saved my life so I'm kindly disposed to her even though she can be a pompous pain when she's busy playing supercop. She carried Jonathan's machine wrapped in a clear plastic bag sealed with a police tag.

"Hi Phoebe. What are you doing here?"

"You can't take that." Tracy grabbed a handful of the heavy plastic and tried to yank the SuperO out of the constable's arms. "It belongs to Jonathan. Give it to me."

"Tracy, take it easy," Candi said sharply. "It's okay. I know Constable Lindt. She's a good friend of Phoebe's." This last was an exaggeration but it did seem to have a calming effect. Tracy stopped struggling.

"I'm sorry, Constable." She let go of the bag.

"What's your name?" Constable Lindt used her best third-degree voice.

"Tracy. Tracy McMurtry."

"Ms. McMurtry, you have just assaulted a police officer. This is a very serious offence and . . ."

"Oh for God's sake Jenny, all she did was grab your plastic bag. Come on, give her a break. The guy she lives with has just died. That's his machine your carrying."

"Do you have some identification, Ms. McMurtry?"

"Why on earth do you need to see her ID?" Sometimes Jenny is the absolute limit. Maybe it's because she's so young and pretty that she's afraid no one will take her seriously unless she sounds tough. "Candi and I can both vouch for who she is. Tracy and Candi have been friends for . . ." Candi jammed a none-too-subtle elbow into my ribs and shut me up. I guess she was right. The constable needed a face-saver in order to back off from her tough-cop routine and the ID gambit was as good as any. Tracy showed her a driver's licence.

"Ms. McMurtry, you lose control like that again and you're going to be in big trouble. I'd advise you to get a grip on yourself."

"I really am sorry, Constable Lindt. I guess I kind of lost it when I saw Jonathan's SuperO. Where are you taking it?"

"It's going to the RCMP lab. I've left a receipt for it with Maud Gellman. It's made out to the Ozone Lair."

"When can I get it back?"

"I don't know. That all depends on what they find at the lab." The constable turned to leave but changed her mind and looked at Tracy. "Ms. McMurtry, how did you get that bruise on your face?" Tracy's careful makeup job had long since disintegrated, leaving the large greenish-purple blotch without camouflage. It looked painful.

"I don't think that's really any of your business. But if you want to know, I stumbled getting out of the bathtub and hit my head on the sink." The lie flowed so smoothly that I knew Tracy had used it before. So did Constable Lindt.

"The bathroom sink. Are you sure about that? It looks more like someone hit you."

"It's my face so I guess I should know what happened to it. I hit it on the sink."

"Then I guess there's nothing more to say, is there?" The constable walked over to her police cruiser and opened the trunk.

"You two go ahead," I said to Candi. "I want to talk to Jenny." I followed her over to the car. "Come on, Jenny. What's up?"

"You know I couldn't tell you that even if I knew. And this time I don't. It's exactly like I said. They told me to come get this thing and take it to the lab." She settled the SuperO carefully into the trunk. "Who was this Webster anyway? And what about this machine? What does it do?"

Instead of getting any information from Jenny, I ended up telling her what I knew about Jonathan and the SuperO.

"No wonder they want it at the lab." She closed the trunk.

"Phoebe, have you ever noticed bruises on your friend before?"

"I met Tracy for the first time today. She's really Candi's friend, but I don't think Candi could give you an answer either. She hadn't seen her for quite a while."

"How long?"

"I don't know. A few years maybe. Before Tracy started living with Jonathan Webster anyway. Why?"

"Because I think someone beat her. And I don't think it was the first time."

"Come on, Jenny. How can you tell all that from one bruised cheek?"

"Because she lied about how she got it and she lied too well. Like she's had a lot of practice lying about her bruises. I've seen it too often."

"In your many years as a cop?" I said and immediately wished I hadn't. Jenny is very sensitive about her youth and lack of experience.

"I may only have been a police officer for a couple of years but I have seen a thing or two and one of them is domestic violence. You do this job for two weeks let alone two years and you see enough battered women to recognize one when she stares you in the face."

"Sorry, Jenny. I didn't mean . . ."

"That bathroom sink is going to knock her around some more. Guaranteed."

"I don't think so. If you're right then I think the sink just had his plug pulled at the Oilfields Hospital. Permanently."

"If Webster did die of poison then Candi's friend is in for a very unpleasant time no matter what the lab finds in this machine. She's going to have to answer so many questions that her head will spin. If he beat her up then that's going to make things even worse. Tell her to make sure she has a lawyer."

The psychic fair was packed with people. I struggled through the crowd in the direction of the Ozone Lair. The booth stood empty, its big, red-lettered sign down, all traces of Jonathan removed. I found Candi and Tracy in the lecture area. Tracy sat quietly, the neatly folded Ozone Lair sign on her lap, watching Candi rewind the last of the light cables. The rest of the equipment was stacked by the lectern.

"Thanks," I said. "When do you want to finish the interview with Maud, or are you going to bother?"

"I've already talked to Maud. I made arrangements to finish up tomorrow morning at eleven. She was so overwhelmed when I told her about Ella's baby and Jonathan that she actually shut up for a minute and let me talk." Candi put the cable in the light case and snapped the lid closed. "I figured that tomorrow would be okay since you have to come out and do the shots on Ella's list anyway."

"Tomorrow morning is fine," I agreed. "But do you think you can get her to say anything? Today's session was pretty grim."

Candi shrugged. "I'll just have to try, I guess. She seemed to be coming around a bit when Ella stopped the interview."

"I think I should go home now." Tracy sounded more like she was trying to convince herself than inform us. "I have to tell my grandma about Jonathan. I don't want her finding out from anyone else." She tucked the folded sign under her arm.

"I don't think you should be driving. Phoebe and I will come with you. One of us will drive you home."

"No, that's okay. I can drive. It's only a few minutes from here." She dug around in her purse and pulled out her car keys.

"And thanks. I don't know what I'd have done if you guys hadn't been there." A single large tear rolled down her cheek, tracing a glistening path across the bruise.

"Look, I really think you should let one of us drive," Candi said.

"Really, I'm okay," Tracy insisted a little impatiently.

"You've had a shock. Maybe you aren't as okay as you think you are."

"Candi, I'm fine." This time there was a snappish edge to Tracy's voice. "I just need to be alone for a little while."

"Tracy, do you have a lawyer?" I figured I'd better make some effort to pass on Constable Lindt's message minus its more ominous overtones.

"No. Why? Do you think I need one?"

"Well, maybe it might be easier if you had some help dealing with all this stuff. You know, autopsies and all that."

"I guess you're right. I'll ask my grandma. I think she knows somebody here in Okotoks."

"I'd like to come see you sometime this weekend if that's okay," Candi said.

"I'd really like that," Tracy said.

"I have to work tomorrow so it probably wouldn't be until Sunday. Would Sunday afternoon be all right?"

"That would be fine," Tracy said. "Will you come too Phoebe? I'd like you to meet my grandma."

"Sure," I said, surprised by the invitation. I've never exactly regarded myself as the comfort-in-time-of-sorrow type. "See you on Sunday."

Candi and I hauled the gear out to the van. Tracy waved to us from her dilapidated green Honda on her way out of the parking lot.

"Why don't I drop you off at your place?" Candi offered. I

live on an acreage in the foothills about an hour's drive south-west of the city, so Okotoks is in my neighbourhood. "There's no sense in your coming all the way back to Calgary. I can take the equipment back to the station. I left my car there so I've got to go back anyway."

"Thanks. I'd just as soon not waste the rest of my afternoon driving back and forth to town. But that will mean you have to collect all this stuff again in the morning and bring it back out here."

"No problem. It'll only take ten minutes to stop off at the station." Candi started the van and we pulled out of the parking lot, this time at a speed that was at least in the same general range as the legal limit.

"While you're at the station would you mind giving News that footage I shot of Jonathan being wheeled away to the ambulance?"

"You think Jonathan's going to make the news?"

"Health weirdo croaks at local psychic fair – if it's a slow day, why not? Besides, I really did get some great shots. Remember to tell them we have some shots of him just before he collapsed too. He sure looked green in that interview but I'm not certain that will show up on the tape."

"You know, I'm beginning to think Maud's right about you, Phoebe," Candi laughed. "For a nice nature photographer you do have some very crass tendencies."

I refrained from reminding Candi that my deplorable ten-dencies were what paid for the nature footage. That's why I work for television. My two or three days a week with "A Day in the Lifestyle" pay the bills and leave me with time for my own work, which, as Candi said, is the making of natural history documentaries. Although I have sold most of them for broadcast on educational television, my nature films are hardly able to support themselves, let alone me. I consider myself lucky if I break even on film stock and processing. I've given up even hoping to be paid for my time. Candi claims that this is a defeatist attitude and that my major problem is that I'm a terrible business woman. Maybe she's right. I know the business end of filmmaking doesn't interest me much. And, to be fair, Candi does have a right to an opinion since on weekends she often helps me with the films – she's got pretty good at doing sound. Right now we're working on one called *Right in Your Own Backyard*. It's about the ecology of an urban garden and is aimed at an elementary school audience. I thought it would be really dull to work on but it's turned out to be a lot of fun. Part of what makes it so enjoyable is that I'm being paid real money up front to produce it. Candi managed to swing me a contract with a company that produces educational software and audio-visual material so, for the first time in my career as a natural history filmmaker, the bucks are big, or at least they seem big to me.

"Maybe we should drive by Tracy's grandma's place and see that she made it there all right," Candi said. We were at the four-way stop again.

"Tracy is an adult. She doesn't need a couple of keepers."

"Not everybody's like you, Phoebe. Sometimes people need a little extra looking after. Especially if they've had a shock like Tracy's had this afternoon. We won't go in. We'll just make sure her car is there."

"You know where her grandma lives?"

"Tracy lived with her when she went to high school. I came out to visit them a few times. I think I remember where the house is."

We drove through the centre of the town and on to the old

residential area that dates back to Okotoks' farming and ranching days. "That's it." Candi pointed to a tidy brick bungalow on the southeast corner of the street. There was no sign of Tracy's car.

"Maybe she parked at the back," Candi said.

"That must be Tracy and Jonathan's place." A tiny two-storey frame house occupied the next lot. "Remember, he said they lived next door."

"You know I think that house belongs to Tracy's grandma too. I remember that she used to look after the garden even though the place was rented. Tracy was always having to help her mow the lawn and stuff."

"Looks like she still does." The lawns in front of both houses were immaculately groomed, patches of perfect green broken only by a pair of small circular rose beds, one for each house. Both beds had recently been dug over and a couple of the neatly pruned bushes already sported an early bloom or two. I was impressed. The wild rose may be Alberta's floral emblem but the tea rose, its effete overcivilized cousin, is very difficult to grow in the harsh and erratic foothills climate.

"I think her grandma is some sort of gardening expert," Candi said.

"She must be if she can grow roses like that in Okotoks."

We drove down the alley at the back of the houses. Still no sign of Tracy's car. Both yards were surrounded by a six-foot white fence interrupted only by a small single-car garage on the brick house's side. The old building had a hayloft door under the peak of its eaves and had obviously begun life as a stable. Candi hopped out of the van and peered through the dusty glass in a back window. "Nothing in here but a little red car and a lot of gardening equipment. What now?"

"Home," I said, as Candi climbed into the driver's seat.

"Maybe Tracy got here and found her grandma was out and went looking for her. What do you think?"

"I think we should go home."

"I wonder where her grandma could have gone. Maybe she went shopping." We zoomed out of the alley and turned towards the town centre again. "Let's drive around town for awhile and see if we can spot her."

"Candi, this is really dumb. Tracy's grandma could be any-where. Let's go home."

"Look, there's Tracy's car. I wonder what she's doing here?" The green Honda was parked in front of a small bookstore on the main street. Candi whipped the van expertly into a parking spot on the opposite side of the street. "We'll just wait until she comes back to her car and make sure she gets home okay. She won't even know we're here."

"How could she not know when we're driving this thing?" The van has the station's call letters plastered all over it in foot-high letters. "Look, whatever Tracy's doing it's none of our business. If she'd wanted us to come with her she would have said so. But she wanted some time alone. Remember?"

"She doesn't look too alone to me. Look over there." Candi pointed to where Tracy now stood waiting outside the bookstore while a slight, sandy-haired man in a pale lemon polo shirt and grey trousers turned the sign in the window to Closed and locked the front door. They both got into Tracy's car and headed in the direction of her grandma's house. Candi made a fast and totally illegal U-turn and we shot after them.

"How come there's never a traffic cop around when you pull that kind of stuff?"

"Phoebe, you're getting very prissy. Sometimes I think

you've been working with Ella too long." She slowed down a little but only because we were about to overtake the Honda.

"Why are we doing this? They're going to see us for sure. Tracy's fine. Someone's with her. Let's leave her to the bookstore guy and go home."

"We'll just see where they're going. Then we'll leave. I promise." We turned left behind the Honda onto Tracy's street.

"This is none of our business." I tried again but I knew I was wasting my breath. Candi is one of those rare souls who is genuinely interested in other people. She has a wide streak of natural curiosity but it isn't simply busybody inquisitiveness. She truly cares about people – she even remembers their children's names. When Candi asks how are you, she really wants to know. For someone like me who thinks that unless you're actually dead the only proper answer to that question is fine thank you, Candi's attitude is impossible to understand. It's dragged me into some odd places with her and clearly today was not going to be an exception.

The Honda stopped in front of the brick house. Candi parked the van across the street and a few houses up the block. Tracy and the bookstore man sat in the car talking.

"I wonder who he is?" Candi turned off the engine.

"They're going to see us."

"Maybe he's the lawyer."

"My lawyer never treats me like that." The bookstore man and Tracy were now locked in a passionate embrace. "Let's go. All we're doing here is snooping."

"Do you think Jonathan knew she was having an affair with this guy?"

"Candi, that's outrageous! How can you say she's having an affair with the man? All she's done is kiss him."

"She still is."

"Then let's leave before they come up for air and see us."

"Too late. They're getting out of the car." Tracy and the bookstore man went up the walk and disappeared into her grandma's house. If they saw us they did not let on.

"You want to go stick your ear to the keyhole?"

"No, that's okay." Candi is impervious to sarcasm. "You're right. It's time to go home."

Another of her criminal U-turns headed us back through the town and then on to the gravel of the secondary road that runs west from Okotoks to my place in the hills. The afternoon sun shone high in the sky and the fresh smells of damp earth and new growth blew in the van's open windows. Late spring is one of the most beautiful times in the foothills although I say the same thing about every change of season here. Even so, this spring was unusually lush thanks to heavier than average late snow followed by equally exceptional amounts of rain. We came to the crest of a hill. Before us in the valley, the juicy green of the new poplar leaves stood in bright contrast to the dark shades of the occasional spruce and pine scattered through them. Farther west, as the hills get higher and drier, the poplars become smaller and sparser until, eventually, the pines take over completely. But always, the jagged line of the Rocky Mountains dominates the horizon.

We swooped through the valley and up over the top of the next hill. My stomach rejoined me some moments after we began our descent.

"What did Constable Lindt have to say?" Candi asked.

"Not much. I don't think she knew as much as we did."

"She knew that he was beating Tracy. You know, if Jonathan did die of poison then they're going to think Tracy murdered him." Candi doesn't simply leap to conclusions, she soars.

"Candi, you see one kiss and immediately Tracy's having an affair with the bookstore man. Some doctor does his best to cover all the bases because he's trying to find an explanation for an unusual death and you decide it's murder before the corpse is cold."

"I didn't say I thought Jonathan had been murdered. I said I thought the police were going to think Tracy murdered him. There's a big difference. Besides," she added, affirming the maxim that a good offence is the best defence, "why do you care so much about getting that ambulance footage to News if you don't think there's something funny going on?"

"I'm just covering all the bases too." It sounded pretty lame, even to me. "Actually," I admitted, a little more honestly, "I wouldn't be surprised if it does turn out to be poison. But it's a long way from that to murder."

"Why? When you think of it, it's really not all that easy for an adult to get poisoned by accident, is it? It's not like Jonathan was some curious little kid who decided to see what antifreeze tastes like. Adults don't do stuff like that. I mean he wasn't a farmer or anything."

"A farmer?" Sometimes Candi's leaps of logic puzzle even me and I'm used to them.

"Yeah, a farmer. Farmers work with poisons all the time. They're always mixing up pesticides and herbicides and fertilizers and stuff. Remember that report the agriculture show did on farm safety? It said that farmers are one of the highest risk groups for accidental poisonings. Jonathan wasn't in a high-risk group like that."

"I think the SuperO put him in a high-risk group all his own," I said. "What if he got mixed up while he was taking a dose of that blood cleanser and blew something else into himself instead."

"And what if somebody hated him enough to make sure that something else was poison? For sure the police are going to check that out and you know as well as I do that the first somebody they're going to check is Tracy."

"That's pretty much what Constable Lindt said too," I conceded. "About the police I mean, not the poison. That's why she told me to make sure that Tracy had a lawyer."

"Let's hope this lawyer her grandma knows is good for more than wills and real-estate deals," Candi said.

"Why did Tracy live with her grandma?" I asked. "Where were her parents?"

"Tracy's dad died when she was really little and she and her mother went to live with her grandma. A few years later her mother got married again. Her new husband was an engineer or something and he got a job in South America. Brazil, I think. Anyway, Tracy stayed in Canada with her grandma. She used to go visit her mom for the summer holidays sometimes but it was really her grandma who brought her up."

"What about the card reading? Did her grandma teach her?"

"I guess she must have," Candi said. "But I don't think Tracy ever got into it seriously. I mean she used to do readings at pyjama parties when we were kids, but she was never all that good at it."

We turned off through the pine-pole gate at the entrance to my place and stopped at the end of the drive in the small poplar grove behind the house. I'm very lucky to live where I do. Being only an hour's drive from Calgary puts me right in the heart of foothills acreage country. Land is very pricey here and parcels like mine with a stream and a view of the Rockies are especially expensive. I couldn't afford to buy even one acre here let alone the forty I inherited from my Uncle Andrew.

"How's Elvira's foal?" Candi asked.

"Growing like mad. Come see for yourself."

We had just stepped out of the van when the dog came bounding out to greet us from wherever he had been sleeping. With much undignified wriggling and yelping, he flung himself at Candi's feet. Bertie is one of Candi's most devoted fans. He's also supposed to be a watchdog, which is a laugh. According to my ex-husband, generations of careful genetic selection had bred a fierce guarding instinct into Bertie's German shepherd bones. But, much to Gavin's disgust, his warrior pup grew up to be a pooch pacifist, a shameless advocate of non-violence who never growls and rarely barks. Although he's so enormous that he looks ferocious, to my knowledge Bertie has only once raised a protective tooth in anger and all that episode got him was a knock on the head for his troubles. I think he must have been almost as big a disappointment to Gavin as I was. In any case, when Gavin left he not only shook off the dust of our crumbled relationship but the dog hair as well, and Bertie stayed with me.

He danced along beside us as Candi and I walked to the house where I collected half a dozen carrots for the horses and found us each a pair of gum boots. The big black rubbers with their red toes looked a little odd sticking out from under our summery skirts but the recent heavy rains had left the path to the pasture far too muddy for sandals.

The three horses came running to meet us and the carrots at the fence. The foal imitated his elders and sniffed at our hands. The little fellow didn't quite know what to do with the carrot stump Candi held out to him. He mumbled at her fingers with his soft muzzle and then went to lean against Pete, the pinto gelding, who was his mother's lead pony at the racetrack and is now her faithful companion in retirement. Elvira kept a loving eye on her baby while she applied herself to the carrots. The loving-eye stuff is a new development for Elvira. Really, she's one of the bitchiest mares I've ever met. Or at least she used to be, especially during her racing days. At the track, she was more temperamental than an opera full of sopranos. However, motherhood seems to have mellowed her and her new-sprung well of maternal feeling has overflowed to include the rest of her world. The tempestuous champion Thoroughbred has turned into an absolute sap. I'm quite enjoying the change although I still count my fingers after every carrot.

"Elvira's a different horse, isn't she?" Candi offered the mare another carrot. "Motherhood must really agree with her. I've never seen her this friendly and gentle."

"Do you think motherhood will do the same thing for Ella?"

"I wouldn't bet big bucks on it," Candi laughed. "Say, has Cyrrie come up with a name for this little guy yet?" She stroked the furry baby hair along the foal's neck.

"He's come up with about ten and all of them are characters from Noel Coward plays. I think Mr. Condomine is still at the top of the list. It's the *Blithe Spirit* connection I guess."

Although the horses live on my land, they are not mine. They belong to my friend Cyril Vaughn. Actually Cyrrie is more than a friend. He's more like an uncle.

"I wonder how Ella and her baby are doing?" The foal had begun to nibble on Candi's fingers. "With all the confusion over Tracy and Jonathan I forgot about her. We should stop by the hospital tomorrow and see how she's doing."

"If she's still there," I said. "They send you home so fast these days she might not be there tomorrow."

"I'll phone and check. Want to go half on some flowers? I could pick them up on my way out of town."

"Okay," I agreed. "But only if we go to see her after I've done all the stuff on that shot list. I refuse to be nagged by somebody in a hospital gown." We started back to the house.

"What time should I pick you up?" Candi put on her sandals and gave me back the gum boots.

"Don't bother. I'll catch a ride with Jack and Barbara. They're off to an auction in High River tomorrow morning and I'm sure they won't mind dropping me off." Jack and Barbara are my next-door neighbours.

"See you tomorrow then." Candi climbed into the van. I had to hold Bertie's collar to stop him from following her.

"Hey," I called as she backed down the drive. "Who do you think won Ella's baby pool?" It sure wasn't me. I had taken Ella's estimated date and then added an extra week because of the old wives' tale about late first babies. All of this put me three weeks out of the money. "Can you remember who bought today?"

"I did," Candi said. "Everybody else believed Ella but I took Dr. Kyle's date. I bought it and the two days before it. I figured Dr. K's had a lot more babies than Ella ever will, so I went with experience."

"Don't tell me you got the sex right too?"

"How many choices are there?"

"Maybe you should set up a booth at the psychic fair."

"What can I say? It's a gift. And lunch is on me tomorrow." She gunned the engine and the van shot out onto the road.

4

Barbara and Jack dropped me off at the psychic fair at a quarter to ten, fifteen minutes before the doors opened for the day. I sat outside basking in the morning sun, reading the *Herald* and drinking a cup of coffee from the convenience store at the gas bar where we'd stopped to fill the car. There wasn't any mention of Jonathan's death in the Calgary newspaper. By the time I finished the funnies and decided to have a glance at the stuff on Ella's shot list it was ten-fifteen and the parking lot was filling fast. Inside the fair, people milled along the rows of booths talking to the occupants, reading the free pamphlets, deciding which of the psychic arts they would entrust with their futures.

"Phoebe. Phoebe Fairfax." A resonant, well-projected baritone called my name. "Over here, Phoebe. I'm over here." The voice belonged to my actor friend, Nicholas Quentin. The rest of his large, handsome self waved to me from the business side of what had been the Ozone Lair. I wondered what Nick was doing at a psychic fair. In the ten years I'd known him he'd never shown the slightest interest in that kind of stuff. But here he was, not only at the fair but, it seemed, actually participating in it.

"How's the world's sexiest nature photographer?" He leaned across the table at the front of the booth and planted a beardy kiss on my cheek. "Things going well at Fuzzy Bunny Films?"

"If you mean how am I progressing in my noble efforts to capture the beauty and truth of Alberta's wildlife on film, then they're okay for a change. I actually have a job – a real, for-money job." I told him about *Right in Your Own Backyard*, including the production fee Candi had negotiated.

"Good God! You mean they're paying you that much to take pictures of Cyrrie's backyard? I'm in the wrong business."

"Just what business are you in, Nick? What on earth are you doing here?"

"Exactly what it says on my sign." He pointed to the large sign complete with handwritten price list that hung down in front of his table. "I'm a pet channeller."

"You're a what?"

"A pet channeller," he repeated. "I'm a sensitive who works with companion animals. You know, a sort of medium who channels pets."

"Come off it. What are you really doing here?"

"I'm doing exactly what I told you." His voice began to ring with sincerity. "I'm communicating with non-human consciousnesses." When Nick starts to sound this resonantly candid, you know he's lying. He's like a politician that way. "You see Phoebe, animals convey their thoughts and feelings through me to their human friends. I guess you could say I'm a sort of conduit for dumb creatures."

"At forty bucks a go, I'd say you're more of a hose for dumb people."

"I suppose it might sound a little odd at first," he conceded huffily, "especially to someone so obviously out of touch with the spiritual plane as you. But I assure you, animal channelling is one of the newest areas of the psychic service industry. It's cutting-edge stuff and I'm right in the vanguard." A certain theatrical flourish had begun to creep into his gestures. I could see the improvisational actor taking over and stood back to enjoy the performance.

"Let's say you've always wanted to know what your dog really thinks of you. Or maybe you've always wondered who your cat was in one of its previous incarnations. All you have to do is bring Fido or Fluffy to see me. If you can't bring the animal, a collar or a favourite blanket or toy will do almost as well." He somehow managed to put this last in vocal parentheses. "Then I either listen directly to what your pet has to say, or feel what they're trying to communicate via the collar or toy, and presto, I pass the message on to you. Simple, eh?"

"Nick, that is the biggest crock I have ever heard in my entire life. It's a real prizewinner. Even for you, it's spectacular."

"I know you don't have an ounce of sensitivity yourself Phoebe, but that's no excuse for being rude to those of us who do." He passed me a silver-papered business card embossed with a tangle of curlicued script. "I do livestock too."

"I thought you were supposed to be doing a Neil Simon out in Victoria."

"I did," he said. "But that was back in February. Now it's June and I'm doing this. Here." He handed me another of the cards. "Give this one to Cyrrie. Tell him I have a very special rapport with racehorses."

"If you don't watch it, you're going to have an even more special rapport with the fraud squad."

"Come off it, Phoebe," he said in his real Nick voice. "Take a look around you. This place is the Tiffany's of flimflam. You think the fraud squad is going to come after one little rhine-stone cufflink like me when there are diamond tiaras every-where they look?"

Nick had a point. The Okotoks First Annual Psychic Exposition and Symposium was not the sort of gathering in which one out-of-work actor turned pet channeller would stand out.

"If you think what I'm doing is bats, you should hear what happened to the weirdo who had this booth before me. He was peddling a machine that blows ozone into your body. It's supposed to be some kind of health treatment. Anyway, he used the thing on himself and they think it killed him. Instead of ozone, they figure he whooshed some sort of poison up his ass and croaked. Met a sad end, so to speak."

"Who told you that?"

"A couple of astrologers I had coffee with before the place opened this morning. But everyone here knows. It's all they're talking about. And nobody seems very sorry, either. This Webster must have been a real scumbag."

"How do they know what he was like? The fair only opened yesterday. I bet you most of them never even met him. And don't give me the line about how psychics just know those kinds of things."

"It's nothing like that. Apparently Webster and his girlfriend had a booth at a few other fairs before this one. A lot of these people travel the circuit so they had run into them before. There's nothing psychic about it – it's just a small world," Nick paused. "Smaller than you think sometimes. I didn't know Webster but I've met his ex-business partner. He's a hair-dresser in Calgary. He did the wigs for that Molière I was in last year. Big, tall guy. Edward something-or-other."

"Sedge," I said. "Edward Sedge."

"Yeah, that's right. How do you know?"

I told him.

"You mean you were actually there when old Jonathan bought the farm? Everybody here thinks someone bumped him off, and if he was as much of a slime as they say then they're probably right. Edward Sedge sure hated him enough. From what I heard, Webster screwed him but good."

"What did he do?"

"I can't remember all the details, but it was pretty hot green-room gossip that Eddy Sedge was having big financial problems because of his partner. There was even a panic that the bailiff was going to seize all our wigs on opening night. Eddy had rented the wigs through his hair salon and then leased them to the theatre company. But, in the meantime, Webster bankrupted the business so our wigs were in lockout or lockup or whatever the hell it is you call bankrupt limbo. In the end, they let us keep the wigs for the run of the play, but Eddy's credit rating went right into the toilet. After Webster was through with him, the poor bugger couldn't have raised enough money to open a lemonade stand. Last I heard he got a job in somebody else's salon. Must feel like kind of a comedown after you've had your own place."

"Not as much of a comedown as selling ozone machines in Okotoks."

"Yeah," Nick agreed. "That could make you feel sorry for Webster even if he was a bastard."

"You should talk – pet channelling. Really Nick, what are you doing here? I know you don't actually believe any of this stuff."

"You can scoff all you like Phoebe, but pet channelling has never killed anyone. Besides, I am not a fraud. Just ask Teddy here. He'll vouch for me, won't you Ted?" Nick poked a finger into the mound of rumpled grey fur that occupied a basket on one side of the table. The mound opened a golden eye and began to purr.

"What's Teddy doing here? He supposed to be your familiar or something?"

"Don't be insulting. Ted's my business partner. Yeah Ted, I know we haven't seen her for months." He spoke to the mound which by now had reclosed the eye and shut down the purr. "I don't know where she's been." Nick returned his attention to me. "Ted says hello to the beautiful-lady-who-carries-the-box-with-the-big-eye. He wants to know what you're doing here. He doesn't think a psychic fair is quite your scene."

"Tell Teddy he's right. It isn't. Tell him I'm here finishing up the work I started yesterday."

"You know Phoebe, you can talk to Ted directly. I don't have to channel what you say to him, only what he wants to say to you. You can talk right to him." He poked the mound again, the eye reopened and the purr hiccupped back to life.

"Well Teddy, I just want to say that I think you should hire yourself a lawyer." I stroked the soft woolly fur and the purr grew louder. "We both know your partner's a flake. So take my advice, pussycat. Get yourself out of this mess while you've still got the fur on your back and a can of tuna in the cupboard."

"Ha ha ha. Just ignore her, Ted. That's Phoebe's idea of funny. She doesn't realize that cats have no appreciation of irony."

"Who's being ironic?"

Nick ignored this last remark. "Ted wants to know if you're here on a job then where's your camera?"

"My box-with-the-big-eye?"

"Don't be snotty, Phoebe. I don't always do literal translations."

"The woman I work with is bringing the equipment out from Calgary. We're doing an interview at eleven."

"You mean Candi Sinclair is coming here this morning?" He unconsciously straightened his tie and ran a hand over his wiry brown hair.

"Why Nick, I do believe you're a fan. I think you've fallen for a face on the box-of-small-pictures-that-move."

"God, you can be a pain in the ass when you try, Phoebe. It's Sinclair's interviews," he protested. "They crack me up."

"And I'll bet you buy *Playboy* for the articles."

"Since when did 'A Day in the Lifestyle' go New Age?" Nick ostentatiously changed the topic.

"Since our station-owner's wife decided to organize this hoopla."

"You mean our Maud Gellman is your boss's wife?"

"Ah there you are, Phoebe. I've found you at last." As if on cue Maud sailed up to Nick's booth. She seemed to have forgiven me for behaving like a news photographer the day before. "And hello to you too Nicholas. All settled in I see. But Phoebe, where's your camera? And where's Candi? Oh dear, nothing seems to be going right this morning."

"Don't worry Maud. Candi will be along soon. We'll be all set to interview you by eleven like we promised."

"Well thank God we don't have to tape it in that dreary little curtained-off hole. There are lectures in there this morning so we'll have to find somewhere else to talk. Being in this booth doesn't bother you, does it Nicholas?" Maud did one of her one-hundred-and-eighty-degree shifts of topic. "I was so hoping the bad vibrations from yesterday wouldn't linger but

I feel they've focused themselves right here on this spot. I guess you can never tell how long these things will hover around, can you? Especially with murder. Really, it's a miracle that any of you can work in this place today. Poor Jonquilla's crystal ball was so clouded this morning that she's had to send home for a spare."

"Whoa, Maud! What's all this about murder?"

"Oh Phoebe, everyone knows that Jonathan Webster was murdered. Why, simply oodles of people here have told me that they felt something dreadful was about to happen yesterday and, sure enough, it did, didn't it? One of the clairvoyants even had a vision of a woman putting the poison in that nasty little machine of his. I should never have let him bring that thing in the building but it was Tracy's booth and he just sort of appeared in it selling that awful machine. I wouldn't call that real healing would you? Selling some machine? But what could I do? I couldn't humiliate poor Tracy in front of everyone by refusing to allow Jonathan's machine in the building, could I? But now that he's been murdered and these horrible, violent vibrations are polluting the building I wish I had."

"But Maud, Jonathan didn't actually die here," I offered by way of comfort. "Wouldn't most of the bad vibes be in Black Diamond at the hospital?"

Maud didn't even attempt to answer my question. Instead, she sighed and gave me a look that said she'd sooner try explaining the theory of relativity to a roomful of golden retrievers. "I simply can't bear to think what all this is doing to Sadie Nightingale. A woman of her sensitivity could be badly damaged."

"I think I just got left behind," Nick chimed in. "Who's Sadie Nightingale?"

"Tracy McMurtry's grandmother and the finest cartomancer in Alberta," Maud stated.

"You mean Sadie Nightingale is Tracy's grandma?" I said. "The Sadie Nightingale who's the gardening expert?"

"Like most sensitives, Sadie is in harmony with all living things," Maud said. "She's very gifted with greenery."

"Am I the only person in the province who doesn't know this Sadie person?" Nick asked.

"I've never met her," I said. "But Cyrrie knows her. Cyrrie loves gardening. He even belongs to a gardening club and I think that's how he met her. Somebody at his club told him that Mrs. Nightingale is an expert on foothills growing conditions so he went to her to find out how to grow roses here." Cyrrie is English so he grew up thinking that roses just happen. A few year's gardening in Alberta straightened him out. That, and what he now refers to as the Nightingale Method.

"I'm afraid more people know Sadie through her gardening than through the cards," Maud said. "I can't think how many times I've tried to get her to participate in some of the New Age activities I organize. Like this psychic fair, for instance. But nothing doing. Sadie has always refused to do public readings. She says the gift is not for sale. And, my lord, is she gifted. Although I do think she could be a little more help with this dreadful lawsuit of mine. She's been so discouraging about it. But maybe she was right, you know. The whole thing seems to be dragging on and on. You know I had simply no idea that suing someone could be so spiritually exhausting."

"You're suing someone?"

"Oh yes Phoebe," Maud said. "I'm suing the Queen."

"You mean *the* Queen, as in Queen Elizabeth the Second of England?"

"That's exactly who I mean. Not that I have anything

against Her Majesty personally you understand. I have nothing but the greatest respect and admiration for her and for the work she does. And how she manages to cope with that awful family of hers I'll never know. When you think of some of the things those children . . ."

"Why are you suing the Queen?" Nick interrupted the flow.

"Well," Maud paused and took on some extra breath, indicating that a long explanation was about to follow. "You see, when I lived in England I was a witch. Or at least a lot of people said I was and that's what caused all the trouble."

"I didn't know you'd ever lived in England," I said.

"I lived there all my life," Maud stated. "Not that it was a very long life. I was executed for witchcraft the day before my twenty-eighth birthday in 1685. And what a terrible experience that was. Thank God nothing like it has ever happened to me again, before or since. It was such an injustice. I was no more a witch than you are but they were jealous of me. You see, I was a rich widow and I owned a lot of very valuable land in what's now the Hampstead district of London."

"What's all this got to do with the Queen?" Even the pet-channelling Nick was having a little difficulty following this one.

"Well, after they executed me, the Crown confiscated all my property. So that's why I'm suing Her Majesty. I want my land back or at least some proper compensation."

"Let me see if I've got this straight, Maud," I said. "You're suing the Queen because in one of your previous lives the Crown wrongfully executed you for witchcraft and then confiscated all your property."

"Exactly," Maud nodded emphatically. "And if I win this one I may consider launching a class action on behalf of all wrongfully executed witches."

"I didn't think it was possible to sue the Queen." Nick pondered this legal nicety for a moment. "Suing the Queen isn't the same thing as suing the Crown, is it?"

"Nick, I'm not sure that's Maud's biggest problem at the moment." I turned to Maud. "And Sadie Nightingale is trying to discourage you from continuing with the suit?" For a card reader, Sadie sounded like a pretty sensible sort to me.

"It's really too bad," Maud said. "I only want to consult her and her cards in order to help plan my strategy. You see, I don't feel I can rely on lawyers to do it all. Besides, you've no idea how obtuse those English lawyers can be. You'd think my lawsuit was some sort of a joke."

"But Mrs. Nightingale won't help you."

"She absolutely refuses to so much as discuss it with me, even without the cards. And it's such a loss. Really it is. Sadie truly is a brilliant reader. She'd be the star of this fair if only she would come. I had so hoped that just this once she'd break her rule and be a part of things. You know, I even saved this booth for her right up until the last minute in case she changed her mind."

"But you couldn't persuade her?"

"No. Sadie won't even leave home to do readings let alone charge for them. If you want her to read your cards you have to go to her house," Maud said. "So Tracy came to the fair instead. She's a nice enough little thing but she can't hold a candle to her grandmother when it comes to cards. And she would insist on bringing Jonathan Webster with her. Now he's gone and got himself murdered. Right here in Okotoks." Maud shook her head in dismay. "You know Phoebe, I just don't understand what's happening to the world. It's all getting to be too much. But I guess what's done is done and we'll just have to make the best of it and hope nothing else happens to disrupt things."

Maud's hopes were promptly dashed when the wispy kid from the front door appeared at her elbow.

"Mrs. Gellman, there's a policeman here to speak to you. I told him you'd meet him at the main door."

This announcement really upset Maud. I could tell because she turned and walked up the row of booths without another word.

"And good luck to that poor cop," Nick laughed. "Can you imagine what it would be like to question Maud?"

I was spared this daunting speculation by Candi, who came through the fair's front door carrying the camera. She stopped and spoke to Maud, who pointed back down our aisle and then bustled off to meet her policeman.

"Do you think we're ever going to get through this interview?" Candi handed me the camera. "Now we have to wait until Maud's finished talking to the RCMP. I may be stuck in this dress for the rest of my life." In the interest of continuity, she was wearing the same dress she'd had on yesterday, a teal cotton print that set off the blue of her eyes to perfection.

"I'll work on Ella's cover shots until you're ready to do the interview. Give me a shout when Maud appears." I used to feel a little discouraged working with a woman as gorgeous as Candi. I suppose this is a natural enough feminine reaction. Not that I think I'm ugly or anything. I'm okay looking. But, around Candi, okay sort of disappears. However, I realized very early in our friendship that envying her kind of beauty was pointless in the same way that envying a sunset or a mountain morning or any other lovely phenomenon of nature is pointless.

I was about to go off and start work when a theatrical throat clearing erupted behind me.

"Oh sorry, Nick. Nicholas Quentin, I'd like you to meet Candi Sinclair." I did the introductory honours. "Nicholas is an actor and he . . ."

"I know he's an actor," Candi shook Nick's hand. "I've seen you in three plays now and I really admire your work, Nicholas. Your Jaques was far and away the best thing I saw all last year. It was really remarkable. I've been after our producer to get you on 'A Day in the Lifestyle' ever since. Would you consider doing an interview for us some time?"

"I'd be delighted to do an interview with you," Nick kept Candi's hand in his. From the look on his face I could tell that an interview was not all he'd have been delighted to do with her. Usually Candi doesn't take much notice of the stacks of smitten men strewn at her feet. I suppose by now she's used to stepping over them. But, this time was different. She made no move to withdraw her hand.

"Maybe we should get together to discuss it," Nick continued. As lines went, it was certainly an oldie. I'd have thought an actor as good as he is could have come up with something a little more original.

"That's an excellent idea," Candi agreed. "When are you free?" Then again, why mess with success?

"The fair closes at nine tonight. What would you say to a late dinner in town?"

"Where will I meet you?"

"Do you like Japanese food? How about Sugamoto's at ten?"

"I'll be there."

I left them standing in front of Nick's booth, still holding hands. They didn't notice me leave.

Ella's shot list was a little on the short side but she really hadn't had her full powers of concentration up and running yesterday when she prepared it. Still, even though she may not have approved of this assignment, she had put together a totally professional package. It would be a simple enough job to add the few shots necessary to cover the brief interviews Candi and I had done yesterday.

It was after twelve by the time I'd worked my way to the end of the list. As I packed away the portable flood, I noticed Candi and Nick having coffee together at one of the refreshment tables. If this was Nick's idea of a hard morning's pet channelling, then Teddy's tuna fund was in big trouble. Candi stood and waved to me. Nick never took his eyes off her as she walked to where I stood in front of the lecture area. A very subdued Maud joined us a few moments later.

We decided to do the interview outside in natural light. I set up the camera in a convenient grove of poplars in back of the building. A breeze stirred the leaves and the scent of sun-warmed sap filled the air. I heard a robin singing. The quiet freshness was a relief after the noisy crowds and incense-laden air of the fair. Even Maud seemed more relaxed out here, although she was still unnaturally quiet while I set up the camera and clipped on her microphone. Nevertheless, she managed to remain sufficiently calm during the interview that she actually listened to Candi's questions. She even came up with some pretty sensible answers although, surprisingly, she resisted talking about her own special interest in past lives. Maybe Maud was finding today's present so vexing that she was reluctant to summon extra trouble from the past. All in all, compared to yesterday's zombie monosyllables, today's interview was a triumph.

"How did it go with the Mounties, Maud?" Candi asked the second I turned off the camera. I knew she had been dying to question Maud about her police interview but she had been restrained enough to wait until we had our own interview safely on tape.

Maud shook her head and started to cry.

"Were they really awful to you?" Candi fished a Kleenex from her pocket and gave it to Maud.

"They weren't awful at all." Maud blew her nose loudly. "They were very nice."

"Then why are you so upset? What did they ask you?"

"All about Jonathan Webster. He was poisoned. It's official. He really was poisoned." The tears welled in Maud's eyes once more. "The police aren't coming right out and saying that it was murder but they're out here investigating it as a suspicious death. It's simply a nightmare."

"But Maud, you told me yourself this morning that you thought Webster was murdered," I said. "So why are you so upset now?"

"Because the fair is ruined. I wanted this to be the best psychic fair ever held in Alberta but how can it be when it's going to be swarming with police? They're calling in a team from Calgary this afternoon to question everyone who was working here yesterday. How can anyone be expected to function with an army of Mounties crashing around the place?" Maud made it sound like the entire musical ride was about to charge through the building.

"Come on, Maud. They're not going to come out here wearing their scarlet tunics," I said. "Most of your customers won't even know they're around."

"I'm not thinking of the seekers," Maud said. "It's the sensitives I'm concerned about. It's bad enough this evil happened in their presence but that they should be subjected to police grilling is beyond endurance. Think of the grotesque emanations. Think of the harm they could do." She turned sadly and walked back to the fair and the helm of her sinking ship. Yesterday's bounce had vanished from her step. She looked every one of her sixty years.

Maud may have been overreacting but she was right about one thing. If the police were going to all the trouble of sending for help to question the psychics then Jonathan's was more than a suspicious death. The police were investigating a murder.

5

"See, it's official," Candi said. "He was murdered. Now Tracy's going to be up to her neck in it for sure. We've got to go over there and help her."

"Candi, we can't go barging in uninvited. We should wait and go tomorrow like we said we would." I put the camera case on the floor of the van and made certain it was braced against the back of a seat. "Besides, Sports needs the camera this afternoon so I have to have the equipment back in town by three."

"It's only one. We've got lots of time."

"What about Ella? I thought we were supposed to be taking her some flowers on our way back to town."

"They're in the van and we have time to do both. Come on, Phoebe. Tracy needs us."

"She doesn't need me. She doesn't even know me."

"We won't stay very long. Twenty minutes, tops."

"I'm not staying at all. You're on your own with this one. I'm not going in. I'll wait for you in the van."

As it turned out, neither of us went in. When we got to Tracy's we found an RCMP cruiser and a police van parked in front of her door. The cruiser contained Constable Lindt, the van was empty. The constable spoke into her radio and then came over to talk with us.

"Are you part of this murder investigation, Jenny?" Candi asked.

"It's still a suspicious death and yes I'm part of the team."

"We heard from Maud Gellman that Webster was poisoned. That it's official. She says you're bringing in a team from Calgary."

Jenny nodded a cautious agreement. "Inspector Debarets is heading up the case. He's inside with Miss McMurtry now." I had met Inspector Debarets while he was working on another case in our district. I liked him. He was an intelligent cop, and a fair one. He was also a very attractive man.

"Did you bring out the paddy wagon just in case?" I pointed to the van.

"That's not a paddy wagon. It's from the lab. Forensics."

"Forensics?" Candi seemed genuinely shocked. "At Tracy's place?"

"Webster was poisoned. We have to find out where the poison came from. The victim's home is the first place to look."

"What kind of poison was it?" Candi asked casually.

"An agricultural pesticide." The words popped out of Jenny's mouth and then she realized she'd said too much, especially to people who worked in television. "But that's confidential and off-the-record," she blustered.

"Don't worry Jenny. We won't tell the News guys until it's official," Candi assured her. "Can we talk with Tracy now?"

The constable shook her head. "I'm afraid not. But why don't you come back later? Inspector Debarets will probably be finished here around three."

Candi was unusually quiet as we headed out of Okotoks on our way to see Ella at the Oilfields Hospital. Our luck was much better there. Mrs. Adams directed us and the big bouquet of pink roses that Candi had brought from town to the ward where Ella and her baby had moved. The starched dragon on duty there marched us down the hall and left us at Ella's door with firm instructions that we were not to stay more than ten minutes. She would return.

Ella sat in an easy chair in the corner of the room, gazing into the bassinet that rested on a low table next to her. With a little difficulty, she got out of the chair and gave Candi a kiss and an enormous hug. She repeated the procedure with me. I was stunned. Ella is not a demonstrative person. Once, when we first met, she shook my hand. Until today, that was the biggest spontaneous outburst of affection she ever directed my way.

She led us over to the bassinet. A tiny red face topped by a mass of black hair poked out from the blanketed interior. It opened its eyes and squinted up at us. It obviously didn't approve of what it saw and began to cry. The noise stopped as soon as Ella picked it up.

"Oh Ella, she's beautiful," Candi said. "Look, she has your nose." It always amazes me how people can see these family resemblances in babies. Newborn infants all look pretty much the same to me, wrinkly red and kind of irritable.

"She has Marty's hands," Ella cooed. "Look at the length of her fingers. Would you like to hold her? Come on, time to go to your Auntie Candi." Auntie Candi? Maybe they'd given Ella some sort of anaesthetic or painkiller and she was suffering from lingering after-effects.

"Where's Marty?" I asked, hoping to inject a little sense into the proceedings.

"I sent him home to get some sleep. The birth was really hard on him. The poor man was exhausted."

"Would you like to cuddle with your Auntie Phoebe?" Candi said wickedly and passed the pink-blanketed bundle to me. I held the new person close as she nestled into my arms, her body so amazingly small and warm next to mine. I watched the regular beating of the pulse under the downy skin that covered the soft spot at the top of her head. She smelled of clean blankets and sleepy baby with maybe just the slightest whiff of hospital. She looked up at me and yawned mightily.

"What's her name?" Candi asked.

"It was supposed to be a surprise. I promised Marty I'd wait until he was here but he'll just have to understand. I can't wait to tell you." Ella primed herself for the momentous announcement. "Ladies, I'd like you to meet Margaret Phoebe Candida Bradshaw."

The shock was so great I damn near dropped Margaret Phoebe Candida right on her nose that looked like Ella's. Even Candi seemed at a loss for words.

"Ella, you can't stick some poor innocent little kid with a name like Phoebe," I said.

"Your parents did."

"Only because of my Great Aunt Phoebe but, believe me, it's not a name to grow up with."

"You think Candida is a treat?" Candi piped up. "Everyone thinks your parents named you after a vaginal infection."

"But I thought you'd both be pleased." Ella sounded hurt

and dismayed in equal measure. I thought I saw her eyes begin to fill with tears but she managed to regain her composure before I could be certain. "Besides," she continued briskly, "Margaret is the name she'll go by." Then Ella gave her daughter a look that for sheer sappiness had Elvira beat all to hell. "My little Maggie."

"Ella, I am pleased," I said. "It's just that you took me by surprise. But really, I'm very pleased." And the funny thing was that even as I said it I realized it was true. I was pleased, and more than a little touched. Wee Phoebe opened her eyes, looked up at me for a moment, and then settled back to sleep in the crook of my elbow.

"And very honoured," Candi said. "Margaret Phoebe Candida. It's going to take some getting used to but it's wonderful, Ella. It really is."

"I knew you'd love it." Ella reclaimed her daughter and settled back down in the chair with her just as the nurse came to toss us out.

"Say Ella," I hesitated for a moment at the door, not quite certain how to frame the question. "Did they give you anything for pain, an anaesthetic or something?"

"Really Phoebe," Ella looked horrified, "Marty and I trained in the Lamaze method. We had a completely drug-free pregnancy and delivery. Margaret is a natural baby, aren't you Maggie?"

"We'll drop in again tomorrow," Candi said.

"But not here. We're leaving the hospital this afternoon. You'll have to come see us at home, won't they Maggie? Now say goodbye to Auntie Phoebe and Auntie Candi."

"They must have given her something," I said to Candi as we walked down the hospital corridor. "She didn't even ask about the shot list or if you'd managed to finish Maud's interview."

"I don't think she cares right now," Candi said.

"That's exactly what I mean. It's not like her."

"Phoebe, if you had just produced something as wonderful as that baby, would you care about producing one week's worth of 'A Day in the Lifestyle'?"

"No, but I'm not Ella. I'm normal."

I thought Candi's laughter was inappropriately loud for a hospital. However, she had herself under control by the time we reached the parking lot where we met Dr. Addison on his way to work.

"You're Miss McMurtry's friends from yesterday, aren't you?" He collected a slim leather briefcase from the backseat of his grey Mercedes. "How is she? I was a little concerned about her yesterday. You should make certain she sees her doctor." The car door closed with an expensive thunk. "If you've come to pick up Mr. Webster's personal effects for her then I'm afraid you're too late. The police took everything away yesterday."

"The police told us that Jonathan was killed by an agricultural pesticide," Candi said, with a puzzled little shake of her curls. "But I don't understand." She opened her big blue eyes a little wider. "I mean, he wasn't a farmer, so how could that be?" She turned the full dazzle of her best dumb-blonde smile on the poor old doctor. He didn't have a chance.

"My dear young lady, you don't have to be a farmer to come into contact with pesticides. Most people with a garden keep some kind of bug killer around the place." Dr. Addison's ponderous gallantry was a sure sign that Candi had him firmly hooked. She proceeded to reel him in.

"The stuff that killed your friend Webster is quite common. You can buy it in small quantities at any garden store. Farmers use it mainly for grasshoppers but I believe it's quite an effective general pesticide as well. The garden-store kind is called HopAway and it's much less concentrated than the kind sold for agricultural use." Most men love explaining things to Candi, but I'd seldom seen one enjoy his own voice more than Dr. Addison. Maybe it was because he was a doctor and had had so much practice in being pompous and condescending that it now came naturally.

"Could the garden-store kind actually kill you?" Candi asked earnestly. "I mean, if it's not as concentrated as the agricultural stuff."

"HopAway is a dangerous substance, no matter what form it's in. You want to be very careful how you handle it. It comes as a powdered concentrate and then gets mixed with water and applied to the crop as a liquid spray. It's the mixing part that's the most hazardous because that's when you have to handle the powder. I'm afraid the damn stuff gets at least a couple of farmers every year. The symptoms look a lot like a heart attack."

Before Cyrrie gave up on chemical poisons and started gardening organically, he had occasionally used HopAway. I remembered the name because I'd watched him mix up a batch one day, and the elaborate care and precautions he'd taken when handling the stuff had stuck in my mind. He'd worn rubber gloves and a mask. The powder Cyrrie used had not come from a garden store but from a farmer he knew who had bought the agricultural concentrate in bulk and given him a little of it to use on his garden.

"Do you think the poison was actually in his SuperO machine?" Candi asked, batting her eyelashes so briskly I swear I felt a breeze. It was one question too many. At last, it dawned on the doctor that the charming young woman he'd been so gallantly instructing on the finer points of pesticide poisoning was not quite as dumb as he first thought. Too late he realized she was pumping him for information and had been far too successful for comfort. I had to hand it to Candi. She had taken Constable Lindt's vague indiscretion about pesticide and adroitly parleyed it into Dr. Addison's particulars of kind and effect. He'd been sandbagged by a butterfly.

"You'll have to ask the police about that," he answered curtly. "And if you young ladies will excuse me, I'm late for a patient."

"Now we know exactly what poison the killer used." Candi started the van. "At least we've made some progress."

"You bamboozle what you know is confidential information out of that poor old guy and you call it progress? Progress with what, I'd like to know?"

"Progress with our murder investigation."

"Candi, have you lost your mind?"

"Somebody has to help Tracy. Somebody has to find the real killer. And we've made a start."

"If you think I'm going to go charging around the country like some superannuated Nancy Drew, you can think again. If it is murder, and that's still a big if, then the police are perfectly capable of solving it all on their own. Besides, how do you know they're going to go after Tracy? This is not the TV mystery-of-the-week, for God's sake. It's real life."

"Well it's weirder than any mystery I've ever seen on TV."

"And Inspector Debarets can work on it very well without our help. The last thing he needs is a couple of amateurs messing around."

Candi didn't argue the point but I knew she wasn't convinced. We drove in silence for a few minutes.

"Would you mind stopping at my place? I want to take the dog into town with me," I said. "I'm going over to Cyrrie's after I drop off the equipment. I'm invited for dinner and Bertie always comes along. And speaking of meals, what happened to my lunch that you're supposed to be paying for?"

"We have time to stop for a Big Mac on the way in to town."

"In your dreams. I'll take a rain check. For La Chaumière, I think."

"Would you settle for Howie's Cafe? I could actually afford to eat with you if we went there."

"I'll think it over."

It was a few minutes past three by the time we'd collected the dog and driven back to town. Fortunately the Sports cameraman was a little late too so we had the camera back at the station in plenty of time. Bertie followed quietly as I hung the keys to the van in the equipment room and locked the door behind me.

"I'm starving. I need to eat something. I'll never last until I meet Nick tonight," Candi announced as we walked back to our respective cars. I'd left mine parked at the station the morning before. "Phoebe, about Nick. You're not interested in him, are you?"

"Of course I'm interested in him. He's my friend."

"You know that's not what I mean. What I mean is," she hesitated, "you're not . . . he isn't . . . I mean you aren't . . ."

It was my turn to laugh. "If you're trying to ask me if I'm lusting after Nick's beautiful body or, God forbid, in love with the man then the answer is no on both counts. He's a friend and that's all."

"You're sure?"

"Positive. We once tried to make it something more but that was a long time ago when we were both in university and it was a disaster. We fought all the time. Either that or we laughed in the wrong places. So we gave up and became friends instead."

"I can see why you tried. He's a very attractive man."

"Yes," I agreed. "He is."

"And it's okay with you? Nick and me, I mean. You're sure?"

"Candi, don't be a jerk. You don't need my permission to find Nick attractive. Go for it."

"Got time for coffee?"

"Cyrrie's expecting me. I told him I'd come over as soon as I got off work. His sister arrived yesterday on a visit from England."

"The famous Edith?"

"The very one. Why don't you come with me? I'm sure Cyrrie could find you a sandwich and a cup of coffee."

"You're sure he wouldn't mind?"

"I know he wants you to meet Edith, so why not now? But no mention of anything about Webster, okay? Cyrrie and Edith might as well enjoy their first day together without hearing about that mess."

I bundled Bertie into the back of my car and did my best to keep up with Candi as she drove to Cyrrie's house. No one answered our ring at the front door so we strolled around to the backyard where the sound of English voices and the clink of china told me Edith and Cyrrie were having tea in the garden and catching up on the gossip from Edith's village in Essex.

"Bodger still fighting the Battle of Britain?" Cyrrie's accent always sounds more English when he's around Edith.

"And soaking up my gin. The man must have a liver like a

block of wood." Edith answered with that slightly imperious quaver in her voice that always reminds me of Dame Edith Evans playing Lady Bracknell. Actually, Edith even looks a little like the older Edith Evans – tall, spare, ramrod straight, and totally indomitable – with maybe a touch of that other eccentric English Edith, Dame Edith Sitwell, tossed in for good measure. Perhaps there's something about the name Edith that has an odd effect on English women of a certain age.

"What about his wife?" Cyrrie asked. "Such a nice woman. I do like Diana."

"Gallstones," Edith replied sepulchrally. "The poor thing is an absolute gravel pit these days."

I opened the gate and the dog bounded into the yard ahead of us. Cyrrie is a great favourite of Bertie's. He's right up there with Candi. To have them both in the same place at the same time can be something of an emotional overload for the poor beast. With much wriggling and squeaking he threw himself in front of the garden swing where Cyrrie and Edith sat drinking their tea. He rolled over on his back, his huge paws flailing the air perilously close to the tea trolley.

"Sit!" Edith commanded with such an emphasis on the T that I feared for her upper plate. The dog obeyed instantly and, if it's possible for a dog to sit at attention, then Bertie did. He practically saluted.

"My darling Phoebe, how wonderful to see you again." Edith leapt to her feet with an agility many women much younger than her seventy-eight years might envy. After the greetings and introductions were out of the way and we'd told Cyrrie all about Ella and Margaret Phoebe Candida, he and Candi went off to make extra sandwiches and a fresh pot of tea. The dog trotted after them, lured by love and lobster paté. Edith and I sat together on the swing.

I have known Edith since I was a child. She is older than Cyrrie. Their mother died of tuberculosis when he was six, and the two of them have that special closeness that sometimes develops between motherless children. It is a bond cemented by a lifetime of friendship and a little motherly bossiness on Edith's part, which Cyrrie takes with his usual good grace.

"Cyril is so lucky to have you nearby, my dear." She took my hand in hers. "I hope you know that you are a very great comfort to him. Andrew's death was such a blow. So unexpected."

Cyrrie and my Uncle Andrew had met during the Second World War when Andrew was a pilot in the Royal Canadian Air Force stationed in England. They fell in love and after the war when Andrew came home to Canada, so did Cyrrie. He never left. He and Andrew lived together for over forty years. I have been told that Andrew fought some terrible battles with my grandparents over his relationship with Cyrrie. After he and Cyrrie moved into the house they bought together, my grandfather never spoke to Andrew again. But all of that happened long before I was born. By the time I came along it was ancient history and Cyrrie was as much a part of our family as any of our more orthodox relatives. One of my uncles still upheld grandfather's condemnation but he had long been a voice of one.

"Cyril does seem much better now, more cheerful, don't you think?" Edith continued. "But then I suppose he should. Time helps, it truly does. I learned that after Tom died."

"It will be four years this November," I said.

"Four years! It hardly seems that long since I was in Canada." Edith's last trip to Calgary had been to attend Andrew's funeral. "But I suppose since Cyril comes to see me every year in England that it's easy for me to lose track of visits. And when are you coming to England again, Phoebe? They ask about you every Sunday at the Fox." The Fox and Hounds is the pub in Edith's village. Every week, on her way home from church, she pops in for two small Dubonnets with lemon and the latest village gossip.

"Not this year, I'm afraid. Too much work to do here." And too little money, I didn't add. "How long are you staying?"

"Four weeks," Edith said. "I'm afraid I'm going to miss your parents this time but they have a stopover in London on their way home from Istanbul so I'll see them later in the summer." My parents are retired and now spend at least half of each year travelling. They had left in early May for three months in Turkey.

"You could stay until they come home," I cajoled. "It would only mean a few extra weeks."

"You're as bad as Cyril," Edith laughed. "He wants me to stay through July but I simply can't. As it is, my garden will be in tatters by the time I get home."

"Cyrrie probably wants you to stay so you can see his horse run," I said. "I think he and his trainer are hoping Prairie Fire will be ready for some big races in July."

"And I would love to go with him and watch, truly I would. Really, buying himself a new racehorse and having Elvira bred are the most hopeful things he's done since Andrew died. I never thought he'd go back to racing on his own."

For the last few years before Andrew's death, he and Cyrrie had shared an interest in Thoroughbred racing. They started their Blithe Spirits Stable modestly with a couple of honest geldings who earned their oats every season in the mid-claiming ranks. But it was Elvira who, a couple of years later, catapulted them to the top of the western Canadian racing scene. She piled up the stakes wins and capped her three-year-old season by beating the colts in the Alberta Derby. That victory marked the end of the Blithe Spirits Stable. Two months later Andrew was dead and Cyrrie sold all the horses except Elvira. He never raced her again. It was as if his interest in racing had died with Uncle Andrew. However, last year, almost on a whim, he purchased a promising two-year-old and followed up that surprise by breeding Elvira to a top local stallion. The Blithe Spirits Stable was back in business.

"Then stay. Just until July. I know it would mean a lot to him if you saw his horse run."

"For that matter, I'll be delighted if anyone sees Prairie Fire run." Cyrrie and Candi returned with the replenished tea tray and the dog. "There's something wrong with him. He's just not training like he should."

"What does Sandra say?" I asked. Sandra is Blithe Spirits' trainer.

"She doesn't know what's wrong. Neither does the vet. We've had him in twice but he can't find a thing. Prairie doesn't seem sick, but he isn't right either."

"What about Nick?" Candi asked. "Maybe he can figure out what's wrong. Why not give him a try?"

"You mean Nicholas Quentin?" Cyrrie said. "Your actor friend, Phoebe? I didn't know he was a horseman."

"He's not," I said. On a good day Nick might be able to figure out which end bites and which end kicks but that would tax his equestrian expertise to the limit. "He's taken up something he calls pet channelling." I filled Cyrrie and Edith in on the details of Nick's adventure in animal communication at the psychic fair. "He said to give you this." I fished the silver card out of my purse.

"Perhaps you should call this Mr. Quentin, Cyril," Edith said.

"Edith, really," I protested. "You can't be serious."

"Why not? Cyril says nothing else is working."

"But Nick's a total fraud, and even if he weren't, you don't really believe in that sort of nonsense, do you?" The basilisk gaze Edith fixed on me said that she was, indeed, a believer in just that sort of nonsense and probably in a few other related nonsenses as well. No matter how long you know people, they can still surprise you. "Not that I'm saying certain unexplained phenomena don't exist. It's how people go about explaining them that's crazy. You should hear some of those lunatics at the psychic fair." I fumbled on trying to undo the damage of my tactlessness.

"There are more things in heaven and earth, Phoebe, than are dreamt of in your philosophy," Edith said in that infuriating half-patronizing, half-loving way that even the nicest old people indulge in occasionally when addressing the young. She smiled serenely. "Perhaps when you have been in this world a few more years, you will begin to realize what a very curious place it can be."

"Edith's right, my dear. Sometimes you are far too rational for your own good," Cyrrie said. "Everyone needs a little magic from time to time, a little holiday from drab reason."

"You can't mean that Cyrrie," I said.

"Why can't I?"

"Because if people aren't rational and reasonable then what are they?"

"Religious, I suppose," he said. "Really Phoebe, you mustn't be so hard on the poor psychics out at Okotoks. When you come right down to it, all religious belief is basically irrational. It defies logic and flies in the face of reason. That's why it's called faith. It doesn't matter whether it's traditional religious doctrine or the kind you ran into out at your psychic fair; at some point it all demands that reason be suspended. Orthodox or esoteric, it's the same blind leap of faith."

"You mean you don't think there's any difference between the Pope and Shirley MacLaine?" Candi asked.

"Of course there's a difference," Cyrrie said. "Shirley MacLaine is much prettier than the Pope, and a much better dancer too."

"Really Cyril, you mustn't tease about these things," Edith said. "People can't tell when you're joking and when you're serious. They're never sure whether or not you believe all the outrageous things you say."

"But Edith, you know I'm always serious," Cyrrie protested. "And believe me," he smiled into his tea cup, "I truly am a great fan of Miss MacLaine's. Another sandwich anyone?"

"Then you really are going to call Nick?" I asked.

"As soon as I've finished my tea."

"You won't get him at the number on his card because he'll be working at the psychic fair until nine," Candi said. "But I'm having dinner with him tonight so I could deliver a message if you like."

"Maybe you should go out to Okotoks and see him yourself," I said. "The psychic fair is on until six tomorrow. You could have your cards read at the same time, do a little crystal gazing, maybe indulge in a bit of aura analysis."

"What a splendid idea, Phoebe." Sarcasm has about as much effect on Cyrrie as it does on Candi. "Edith and I may just do that. We're off to Okotoks tomorrow anyway so we might leave a little early and drop in at the psychic fair. Good of you to suggest it."

"What are you up to in Okotoks?"

"We're off to visit Sadie Nightingale. You've heard me speak of Sadie. She's the one who taught me to grow roses here. I ran into her buying a new hose out at the Green Thumb last week and she invited me to bring Edith to see her garden. So we're off tomorrow afternoon to drink tea and talk horticulture."

"Cyrrie, I don't think that's such a good idea," I said. "Maybe you'd better phone Mrs. Nightingale before you and Edith go out there." There was no way out of it so I told them the whole story of Jonathan Webster's death.

"And this Webster person was Mrs. Nightingale's granddaughter's boyfriend? Have I got that right?" Edith asked.

"Tracy and Jonathan had lived together for two years." Candi put the relationship in perspective. "They were living in the house next to Mrs. Nightingale's."

"Poor Sadie, this is a terrible business," Cyrrie said. "And you're quite right Phoebe. I must call her. I wonder if there's anything I can do to help." He hurried inside to make his call.

Candi and I cleared away the tea things while Edith strolled down the flagstone path that curved the length of Cyrrie's garden, closely inspecting the plants on either side.

"No luck." Cyrrie emerged from the house. "The line is busy. I'll have to try again later."

"Cyril," Edith called from the bottom of the garden. "This honeysuckle is looking thrippy. Where's your spray?"

"Nonsense, Edith. I checked that bush yesterday and it was perfectly healthy. Besides, you know I've stopped using chemical poisons."

"Still going in for that organic stuff, are you?" Edith sniffed. "If you ask me, all that kind of thing gets you is very small, unhappy plants and very large, jolly thrips."

"Ah Edith, still the Lucretia Borgia of the garden club, I see."

"Laugh all you like Cyril but, used judiciously, a little poison can work wonders."

6

The alarm clock hauled me out of bed at twenty to five on Sunday morning. At first I couldn't remember where I'd put the damn thing. I knew I'd been careful to place it well away from the bed so I couldn't simply stick an arm out from under the duvet, turn it off, and forget that in a moment of weakness I'd agreed to meet Cyrrie and his trainer at the racetrack at six. I stumbled around the room searching for the source of the plaintive little beeps. Because my house is mostly one big room where I sleep and work and eat, there were lots of places to look. I finally found the clock on the film-editing bench, silenced the beeps, and leaned against the bench doing my best to remember why I was needed at the track. I was supposed to tape Prairie Fire's workout. That was it. I was awake.

By five I was showered, dressed in jeans and a T-shirt, and out the door with my little home video camera and a couple of fresh tapes stuffed in my workbag. I'd even managed a cup of coffee. Instant, of course. I like instant but that's probably more a reaction to my ex-husband than a matter of taste. Gavin regarded instant coffee as a form of sewage. I swear that every morning we were together, he lectured me on the merits of fresh beans freshly ground while he fussed with his cappuccino machine. You'd have thought he was preparing the sacrament, not a morning cup of heart-starter. I suppose it was one of those little annoyances that people who love each other eventually learn to overlook. It drove me crazy. Oddly enough, when we split up, he left the cappuccino machine with me. Maybe he thought I might reform. More likely he wanted a good excuse to buy himself a fancier model. The old one is somewhere at the back of a cupboard.

The sun was warm on my face but I was still glad of the thick sweatshirt I'd pulled on over my T-shirt. Mornings in the foothills are chilly, even sunny ones that hold the promise of a glorious June day. The ground was wet with dew and a few steps through the grass on the path to the garage had my runners soaked. I stopped to watch a honeybee who had worked too late the night before and been caught away from its hive at dark. It inched along a fence rail, struggling to move its chilled wings. Another hour in the sun would warm its muscles and have it back hard at work in the Icelandic poppies that line my driveway.

The dog rode with me as far as the gate, a journey of twenty-five yards. For some reason best known to himself, this is part of his morning ritual of seeing me safely off to work. My usual mornings aren't quite this early and I think he was still asleep when I let him out at the mailbox. Bertie is a firm believer in a solid twelve hours a night supplemented by daytime naps as needed. This morning, I had every sympathy with his point of view. It was five after five when I pulled out of the driveway and headed for Calgary.

The racetrack is right in the middle of the city. A few blocks to the west, glass office towers shone gold in the cloudless sky.

Behind them, the Rockies looked larger and closer than usual. Sometimes, on clear Calgary mornings, tricks of light defeat distance and create the illusion that the white peaks are no more than a short stroll from the edge of town. To the east, the shades were still drawn in the upscale condos perched precariously on the Elbow River's steep-cliffed bank.

I checked at the race office where Cyrrie was already waiting to sign me in. He looked his usual spruce self in cavalry twill trousers, a plaid shirt, and a Tilley hat, but he was very quiet. I think he was more worried about his horse than he wanted to admit. I collected my guest pass and showed it to the security officer at the gate who waved us through into the world on the other side of the fence.

The backstretch of a racetrack has a smell all its own – a rich blend of horse, hay, manure, and leather with the occasional sharp dash of liniment for accent. Every morning of the racing season, while most of us are still in bed, it's alive and at work, bustling with horses and people, all of them absorbed in the task at hand. It is a community of common purpose, a mini-society closed to outsiders.

The backstretch was at the peak of its morning business. Horses headed out to the track for their workouts, their helmeted riders high in the stirrups. Horses trotted back from the track still charged up from their run, nostrils flared, necks arched, legs like loaded springs. Horses stood under splashing hose pipes, steam rising from their backs as their grooms bathed them. Inside the barns horses dozed in their stalls or ate their breakfast oats or hung their heads over their doors and watched the business all around them. I hurried along behind Cyrrie, doing my best to avoid being stepped on or stepping in.

As a visitor, the insularity of the backstretch has always

made me a little uncomfortable. Not that racetrack people are hostile to outsiders. Far from it. They're more than hospitable. It's just that they can't understand anyone who does not eat, breathe, sleep, and dream horses the way they do. For them, real life is the track and everything else is somewhere on the edges. Gavin claimed that I'm the same way when I work on one of my films, but I don't think so. I've never been quite that obsessive.

"He's working from the gate today," Cyrrie said over his shoulder as he hustled us into the barn. "Sandra will tell you what part of the workout she wants you to film. She's waiting for us at Prairie's stall."

A half-dozen long noses followed our progress down the row of stalls to where Sandra Doyle stood on tiptoe brushing Prairie Fire's back. Her bright-copper Orphan Annie curls bobbed just above the dark line of his withers. "Hi Phoebe. Thanks for coming. We really need some help with this guy." All five-feet-nothing of her walked under Prairie's head and continued to brush his other side.

"He doesn't look so bad," I said. The horse stood docilely while I patted his neck.

"But he doesn't look so good, either. Does he?"

I had to agree with Sandra. While he wasn't actually sick or lame, Prairie's dark bay coat did not have its usual dapple and he was standing far more quietly than was normal before his morning run.

"He's lacklustre," Cyrrie said. "That's the only word for it. Lacklustre."

"Whatever it is, it doesn't win races." Sandra shoulder-heaved Prairie to one side, picked up a back hoof, cleaned it, and moved on to the next one. It always amazes me to watch one hundred pounds of Sandra manhandle twelve hundred pounds of horse. I suppose it's all in knowing what you're doing and that she certainly does when it comes to horses.

"We're going to work him four furlongs from the gate. Full out. I'd like you to take as much of a closeup as you can for the last couple of furlongs, Phoebe. That's where the trouble is. He's okay at the start but he runs out of gas."

Cyrrie and I left Sandra to saddle Prairie while we went to put the camera in place. We walked the quarter-mile to the grandstand along the same path that the horses use coming to and from the paddock on race days. It passes close to the river. I took a quick detour to the water's edge to check for fish. As it flows past the racetrack, the Elbow is so clear that you can stand on the bank and watch trout basking near its rocky bottom. There's usually a string of little boys fishing off the footbridge but I've never seen them catch anything. I think the trout have the game figured. They're city fish, street-smart with fins.

"Do hurry along, Phoebe. You can look at the fish on the way back." Sometimes Cyrrie can make me feel ten years old again.

We walked past the paddock and climbed up into the empty grandstand where I could get a clear shot of the four workout furlongs. Four furlongs is half a mile and for a three-year-old Thoroughbred like Prairie, it's no distance at all. I set the camera on its monopod right in line with the track's official finish wire. "Ready to go."

Cyrrie raised his binoculars and scanned the track. "There he is. Out on the track warming up. The exercise rider has a red shirt and a blue helmet."

I picked up the shirt and helmet in the viewfinder and put the zoom lens to maximum. Prairie cantered through my field of view. "He looks fine."

Cyrrie shrugged. "I only wish he were. It's so worrisome not to know what's wrong. I've almost decided to take him out of training for the rest of this season. Give him a rest and bring him back next year." The policy of the Blithe Spirits Stable had always been to put the welfare of its horses first and the winning of races second. Still, in Prairie Fire's case, Cyrrie's decision did seem a little premature.

"That's a bit drastic, isn't it?"

"I don't want him hurt," he snapped. "I won't risk it. Racehorses are flesh and blood, not machines. Maybe they wouldn't break down so often if more people would remember that."

"Cyrrie, take it easy. You're talking to one of the good guys, remember?"

"Oh, my dear girl, I do apologize. I don't know why this business has got me down so."

"It must be hard without Uncle Andrew. Going back to racing, I mean."

"Everything's hard without Andy but that's no excuse for taking your head off like that. I'm sorry." This was the first time since Andrew died that Cyrrie had ever admitted to me that life was difficult without him. I didn't know what to say.

"Maybe this tape we're shooting will help. It'll give you and Sandra and the vet a chance to study his action in slow motion."

"At least it feels like we're doing something." Cyrrie trained his binoculars on the starting gate.

"You're not really going to call Nick, are you? That was just a joke, wasn't it?"

"Phoebe, get ready. They're starting to load. There are four of them. He's the last one in." I centred the starting gate in the frame and started the tape rolling. "They're off." I heard the click of Cyrrie's stopwatch.

Prairie may have been the last horse into the gate but he was the first one out. He burst onto the track, took the rail, and led by daylight for the first two furlongs. Then he seemed to give up. There was nothing different in his action that I could see in the viewfinder. He just quit running. He dragged under the wire a good fifteen lengths behind the others. I heard Cyrrie's stopwatch click again, but I kept on taping until Prairie had slowed to a trot.

"He looked great for the first couple of furlongs," I said. Cyrrie said nothing. He didn't bother to tell me Prairie's final time. We walked back to the stable in silence. Sandra looked almost as gloomy as Cyrrie while we waited for the exercise rider to bring Prairie in off the track.

"Well, Sandy, he ain't no morning glory, that's for sure." The rider hopped down and handed her the reins. Morning glory is racetrack slang for a horse who runs brilliantly during its morning workouts but fizzles out in an actual race. "I couldn't feel anything wrong with him. He run a hell of a first quarter but then he just quit. Too bad he ain't a quarter horse."

"Ladies, ladies. Don't look so glum. It's only a workout, not the Derby," Cyrrie said. "Come on. What the three of us need is a slap-up Sunday breakfast, my treat. Phoebe, you go ahead to Howie's and find us a table while Sandra and I get this horse cooled down and in his stall."

Howie's Cafe, The Palace of Eats as the subtitle on the faded sign above its door proclaims, is the best greasy spoon in Calgary. It's probably the best in Canada. Howie's is only a few minutes from the racetrack in a corner of east Calgary that somehow escaped the city's last wave of urban redevelopment. Tucked into the ground floor of a two-storey red-brick building built before the First World War, Howie's and the two frame houses on either side of it are a reminder of old Calgary and a time when the city's economy was based on agriculture, not oil.

Early as it was, three of the cafe's six tables were already occupied as were most of the ten revolving stools at the lunch counter. My favourite table near the window was taken so I sat at one close to the kitchen instead.

"Hey Phoebe, where ya bin?" Howie himself plunked a coffee cup in front of me and filled it from the steaming pot in his hand. Howie is small and wiry and somewhere on the grizzled side of sixty. He and his wife, Chantelle, take turns cooking and waiting on tables. Chantelle was working the grill this morning. "You all alone, sweetheart?"

"Cyrrie and Sandra Doyle will be along in a few minutes. They're still at the track getting Cyrrie's horse cooled down and in his stall."

"Here." Howie tossed me a newspaper with his free hand. "You can read the *Herald* while you wait." He whipped off to patrol the room for half-full coffee cups. It's a point of pride with Howie that Palace of Eats customers never see the bottoms of their cups.

I've been coming to Howie's since I was ten years old, when Andrew and Cyrrie began taking me with them to the races on an occasional Saturday afternoon. The outing always began with brunch at Howie's and nothing much has changed in the restaurant since then. The red and white pattern on the tables' Formica surfaces may be a little more scratched, but it still manages the same gallant imitation of a checkered tablecloth that I remember from my childhood.

As a special indulgence, I stirred a dollop of cream into my coffee. Cream at Howie's is real and comes in pitchers, not those nasty little individual plastic containers. The spoon clinked solidly against the thick crockery cup. It didn't match either the fork or the knife that were already on the table in front of me, resting neatly on a white paper napkin. I pushed the cutlery to one side and spread the newspaper open.

The news part of the Sunday paper is a fast read. I had hardly started to drink my coffee when I came across the article on Jonathan Webster's death, buried in the back pages of the first section. "PSYCHIC FAIR DEATH" was a short item, about four inches of a single column, but there was a head-and-shoulders photo of Jonathan along with it. The article referred to him as a "prominent local hairstylist," briefly outlined what happened in Okotoks, and concluded with the tantalizing statement that the police were investigating. I had the feeling that by tomorrow, if the police released any more information or if the *Herald*'s reporter did some digging, Jonathan would make a fast trip to a page with a smaller number.

"Your pals are here." Howie topped up my coffee with a slosh of fresh and poured a cup each for Cyrrie and Sandra who had just walked in the door. "You guys ready to order?" he asked as they sat down.

At Howie's no one bothers with breakfast menus. You simply match whatever combination of cholesterol you fancy with pancakes or toast, white or brown. I ordered scrambled eggs with sausages and brown toast, Cyrrie went for poached with ham and brown, and, after some preliminary hemming and hawing about her diet, Sandra settled on sunny-side up with bacon (extra crisp) and white.

"Here's your tape." I put the videocassette on the table in front of Cyrrie. "I hope it helps."

"Thank you for cracking yourself out of bed so early, my

dear. It's appreciated," Cyrrie said. "And that's enough about Prairie Fire and his troubles for one morning. Tell us what's new in the *Herald*."

I turned the paper around and showed them the article about Jonathan Webster.

"Hey, I know him," Sandra pointed to Jonathan's photo. "That's the Big Spender."

"Who?" Cyrrie asked as he skimmed the article.

"The Big Spender. B.S. for short. He practically lived in the clubhouse last summer. Talk about your high rollers. This guy must've shoved thousands through the wickets. That's how come everybody called him Big Spender. What's his real name?"

"Webster," I said. "Jonathan Webster."

"What happened to him?"

I told her.

"So the poor old Big Spender's dead. I'll have to tell them at the track."

"And was the Big Spender a big winner?" Cyrrie asked.

Sandra shook her head. "A big loser. At least most of the time. But he always had an excuse. That's how come Big Spender got shortened to B.S. Before a race, he'd go around telling everyone why some long-odds horse that couldn't keep up with a herd of cows was going to be a surefire winner this time. After the thing lost, he'd spend the next half-hour making excuses for it – it had a terrible trip, the jock stiffed it – you know, the usual kind of loser's bullshit."

"Did he always go for the long-odds horses?"

"Pretty much. Long odds, combinations bets – the big win. I heard he was into Pick Six combinations like you wouldn't believe."

In order to win a Pick Six a bettor has to select the winning horse in six consecutive races. It's next to impossible to win a Pick Six with a straight selection of one horse per race, and the cost of playing combinations of horses can blast the price of a pari-mutuel ticket into the stratosphere. At big tracks, ones where the Pick Six pool can be hundreds of thousands of dollars, horse players form syndicates so they can afford to bet combinations.

"One sunny-side up." Howie placed the first of the three oval platters he carried in front of Sandra. I folded the newspaper out of his way and the other two breakfasts followed. "One scrambled, one poached." A paper-thin slice of fresh orange garnished the hash browns on each of our platters, evidence of Chantelle's touch. This little salute to fruit never appeared when it was Howie's turn to cook.

"So Jonathan Webster was into big money?" I tasted a forkful of the scrambled eggs. Perfection.

"Like a thousand a pop sometimes when he figured he was on to a really sure thing, and the Big Spender was always sure. If there were ten races on a card, he had at least nine sure things." Sandra mopped up egg yolk with a piece of buttery toast. "Geez, you should probably just inject this stuff right into your arteries and save your digestive system the bother. But what the hell." She popped the toast in her mouth. "It's great food."

"How do you know all this stuff about Webster?" I asked.

"The wife of a jockey I use a lot works a pari-mutuel wicket in the clubhouse. She pointed him out to me one afternoon and told me about him. But all the clubhouse regulars knew who he was. The Big Spender was famous."

"Was?" I said.

"Nobody's seen him since last year. Somebody said that he

lost a real bundle on Alberta Derby day and gave up the ponies for blackjack. Last I heard he was part of the scenery at the Elbow Lodge Casino. It's too bad, really, the guy was a one-man bonanza for racing."

I've never been able to eat a whole Howie's breakfast but that morning I came pretty close. I drank the last of my third cup of coffee just as Cyrrie got up from his chair.

"You ladies may stay, but I think I should get home to Edith. She's still suffering from jet lag but it's nearly nine so I expect she's up by now."

"Yeah, I gotta get going too," Sandra said. "I've got a ton of stuff to do at the track. We've got three horses running this afternoon."

"And I hope they do you proud." Cyrrie paid the bill, left a generous tip, and we strolled out to the street. The day was becoming beautifully warm. We waved to Sandra as she roared off in her old pickup truck, three bales of hay bouncing in its back.

"Home to Edith or your Sunday cigar?" I teased. Cyrrie used to smoke but my brothers and I nagged him about it so much when we were kids that he finally gave in and quit. However, he still allows himself one cigar a week – a very big, very expensive Havana that he lights with ceremonial pleasure every Sunday morning after breakfast.

"I may retire to the garden for a few puffs," he conceded.

"Are you and Edith still going to see Sadie Nightingale this afternoon?"

"Yes. Around three. I phoned her last night and she seemed very anxious that we not change our plans."

"Then I might see you there. I'll be next door." I told him about agreeing to go along with Candi to visit Tracy.

"I think you'll enjoy meeting Sadie."

"Maud Gellman told me she reads cards and that she's really good at it."

"I believe that's true although I've never asked Sadie about it. We stick mainly to gardening."

"Cyrrie, do you believe there's anything to that kind of crap – card-reading, crystal-gazing, astrology, all that sort of stuff?"

"I'd say it's pretty obvious that you don't." He folded his arms and leaned back against my car. "Isn't crap a rather harsh word for something that probably does more good than harm?"

"But it's all such a fraud."

"Some of it is," he agreed. "But I don't think people like Sadie Nightingale are frauds. I'd say she's a totally honest woman in every respect."

"But how can you say she's honest when what she does is basically phony?"

"Is it?"

"Of course it is. How can a stack of painted cardboard predict the future? It's ridiculous."

"You may be taking too narrow a view."

"Meaning?"

"Meaning that everyone needs a sympathetic ear. Someone they can confide in and look to for sympathy and help and guidance, especially if they're feeling troubled about something. That's where I think someone like Sadie could be a real help. She's a very warm and sympathetic woman and she certainly understands the ways of the world. You could do far worse than go to someone like her for advice."

"But Cyrrie," I protested, "you should have heard some of those psychics Candi talked with. They were crazy. Really."

"Well, maybe they were," he agreed. "But, as a group, I

doubt that they're any crazier than a great many psychiatrists or social workers or any other socially acceptable therapists. To be quite honest, if I had to choose between Sadie and the average psychotherapist, I'd take Sadie and her cards every time."

"You may have a point there," I said, remembering the marriage counsellor Gavin and I had gone to before we split up.

"Phoebe, for many people the world is a very difficult place and help is hard to find. They feel lost and isolated and with good reason. Many of them live thousands of miles from their families. Marriages are crumbling at an alarming rate. Traditional religions are in decline. Where are they to go for comfort? We all need something or someone we can trust, even if all that boils down to is having a friend to talk with. Everyone should have somebody who's willing to listen to their troubles and maybe give a little friendly advice."

"But what about all the hocus-pocus that goes along with it, like crystals and cards? You simply can't defend that."

"I'm not defending anything," he said. "I'm simply telling you why I'm not quite so down on this sort of thing as you are. And, as for the cards, what does it matter what tools people use as long as they get the job done? Ink blots, personality tests, tarot cards – they're only tools."

"But the people who go to have their cards read don't think of the tarot as a tool. They think it's magic."

"And if it works, if it helps them or comforts them, then maybe they're right. It is a kind of magic."

"Isn't that pretty patronizing? It's kind of like saying to people that what they believe in is basically bullshit but since they're dumb enough to believe it, you hope it helps them."

Cyrrie shrugged and smiled. "Phoebe, I think we're going

to have to agree to disagree on this one." He opened my car door for me. "Thank you again for the tape."

"No problem," I slid behind the wheel. "I'm glad I could do something. I only hope it's a help."

"I'll let you know what Sandra and the vet have to say." He stood back while I closed the door and started the engine. "And I'll look for you and Candida this afternoon at Sadie's."

7

The sun was high in the sky by the time I reached home. Its drowsy warmth on top of an early morning and too much food made the temptation to slip back into my unmade bed almost irresistible. I was saved from sloth by the telephone. Candi called to tell me she'd pick me up at three for our visit with Tracy. After I hung up, I removed temptation by folding the bed back into its daytime sofa self and bundling the duvet into the closet.

My one big room was once a three-bedroom bungalow that Uncle Andrew used as a country retreat on weekends and in the summer. When I inherited the property and Gavin and I decided to make it our home, we renovated. Now all that remains of the old interior is a small guest bedroom tucked in next to the bathroom. The rest is open space. One area is taken up by my desk and film-editing equipment, another by the sofa and a couple of easy chairs. A third corner is devoted to a compact but very fancy kitchen that Gavin designed. Gavin is an ardent cook and, although the kitchen is small, Julia Child would feel right at home. A stainless-steel vented grill, a convection oven, real butcher's block counters – you name it, my kitchen's got it.

A nine-foot grand piano dominates the remaining space. Its polished ebony length runs parallel to the bank of windows that are the room's west wall. I sat at the keyboard and gazed over the deck, across the sweep of the pasture and on to the mountains. A slight breeze blew through the open patio doors and ruffled the well-marked pages of my copy of the *Goldberg Variations* that stood open on the music rest. I've been bashing away at the Goldbergs on and off for a couple of years now. I'm up to "Number 29," the next to last, the one with all those wonderful tumbling triplets. At least they tumble when Glenn Gould plays them. I'll consider myself lucky if I achieve a sedate plod.

The piano was Andrew's too and, because I was the only one of my generation to play at all, he left it to me. My uncle was a fine pianist and his Steinway is far too good an instrument for a Sunday duffer like me. It should really belong to a professional musician but I have no intention of giving it up. Even if I don't play well enough to do it justice, I do play regularly. It would be a sin to own such an instrument and let it sit unused. At least that's what Cyrrie says and that's why the piano is here, instead of at his house in Calgary. I must admit I felt a little like a furniture thief on the day I watched the movers wheel it out of his living room. Uncle Andrew's piano had stood in front of the big west window since before I was born. But Cyrrie insisted and I know he was right. A musical instrument is not a piece of furniture. I played for a couple of hours before I took a break and went for a walk with the dog. I fully intended to do some work at the editing bench when I got back to the house but instead I found myself at the piano again playing some Kurt Weill theatre songs I'm learning. They're difficult, but worth it. I finished off with "September Song."

"Bravo! Bravo! We want more!" Candi strolled in from the deck, applauding and carrying on. The dog danced along beside her. "That last one was really beautiful."

"How long have you been out there?"

"About half an hour. I was early but I didn't want to disturb you so Bertie and I sat out on the deck and listened." She dropped into one of the easy chairs. The dog flopped down on the floor beside her and rested his chin on her foot. "You know Phoebe, I don't understand why you'll never play for anybody. You're not anywhere near as bad as you say you are."

Candi wore a calf-length khaki skirt and a short-sleeved white shirt, all very cool and casual and a considerable cut above my T-shirt and jeans with their faint pong of horse barn. After a quick shower, I changed into a sky-blue dress made of soft, fine-woven cotton, a recent purchase in celebration of spring.

"That new?" Candi asked.

I nodded, stumping around the room in one sandal while I searched for the other.

"It looks great. That's definitely one of your colours."

"How was your dinner with Nick?" I knelt and peered under the sofa. Still no sandal.

"Good. He had sushi and I had teriyaki shrimp."

"I didn't mean the food."

"Well, we're going out again tonight after the psychic fair closes so last night must have gone okay." She raised her eyebrows and wiggled them in the best Groucho fashion.

"You mean Nick actually stuck it out at the fair? I figured he'd give up after the first hour with no customers."

"What do you mean no customers?" Candi was indignant.

"The poor man was rushed off his feet yesterday. He was so busy that he's had to schedule house calls for next week."

"Well, at least he's got Teddy to keep his appointment book straight."

"Phoebe, I think you're being a bit unfair about Nick's pet channelling. I know you think he's a fake, but what harm can it do?"

"I found out some interesting stuff about Jonathan Webster today." I wasn't up for another discussion of the ethics of hocus-pocus so instead I paused in my shoe search and passed on the news Sandra had told me at breakfast. Candi listened without comment until I had finished my story. "If even half of what she heard about him is true, then Webster must have had a real gambling problem."

"That's what Tracy says, only from what she told me it was more than a problem. The guy was an addict, a total compulsive. Tracy called him a gamblaholic."

"You already knew about the gambling?" And I'd been so proud of my little nugget of information.

"I talked to Tracy and her grandmother yesterday afternoon. After I left Cyrrie's, I had a few hours before I was supposed to meet Nick so I drove back out to Okotoks. I was worried about her."

"How was she?" I resumed the shoe search.

"Okay, I guess. A little tired maybe but then who wouldn't be if they'd spent most of a day being grilled by the police. She'd had a lot of company after the police left too. A couple of neighbours came over with casseroles while I was there."

"That's a weird custom, isn't it?" I said.

"Bringing food to the bereaved?"

"Yeah. Her lover croaks so all of a sudden people figure Tracy's appetite should perk up. Does this make sense?"

"Considering what a creep Jonathan was, it probably does," Candi laughed. "Remember the guy we saw her with on Friday, the mystery man in the car? He was at Tracy's too. His name is David Cavendish and he owns the bookstore where she went to meet him."

"He didn't waste any time."

"He's in love with her and it's mutual. And that's not just one of my guesses." Candi cut off my protest. "I know for a fact that Tracy and David are in love because she told me."

"Did they tell Jonathan Webster too?"

"Tracy says she couldn't tell him, not while he was so down. She didn't love Jonathan anymore but she still felt sorry for him. I mean the guy had lost his house and his business. She was going to tell him as soon as things turned around for him. Besides, she says it was really all over between her and Jonathan and they both knew it. The only thing he cared about was gambling."

"It didn't look to me like he thought it was all over," I said, remembering the possessive arm draped around Tracy's shoulders. "What did the police ask her?"

"They wanted to know all about Jonathan and his ozone machine. Where he kept it, how long he'd had it, how often he used it – all that sort of stuff. Then they wanted to know everything he did during the twenty-four hours before he died. And what Tracy did too. She said it took forever to tell them because they wouldn't let her leave out anything. I mean, you go for a pee and they want to know all about it."

"That sounds like Inspector Debarets," I said. I was all too familiar with the inspector's method of questioning, having been subjected to it myself after I discovered a woman's body floating in our local health resort's swimming pool. It's amazing how much detail you can actually remember when a deft questioner like Debarets takes you back and forth, time after time, along the trail of your day.

"They questioned her grandma and David Cavendish too. Tracy says they even went from house to house and talked to all her neighbours."

"What about the lab types?" I asked. "Did they find anything?"

"If they did, they didn't tell Tracy. She said that they searched all through the house and then went over to her grandma's place and did the same thing there. They even searched her garage and all her gardening equipment. Tracy said she couldn't figure out why they were so interested in the garden stuff, so I told her what we'd found out about the pesticide that killed him."

"What did she say?"

"Nothing much really. I'm not sure if she even believed me. She didn't seem all that upset or even very surprised. But I guess so much has happened to her in the last couple of days that's she's feeling a little numb."

"Did she call a lawyer? Jenny Lindt seemed to think it was pretty important that she get some legal help."

"Her grandma's lawyer was at the house yesterday when the police were there. Tracy says the old guy hasn't done anything but real estate for the last thirty years but I suppose he's better than nothing." Candi looked at her watch. "Hurry up, Phoebe. We don't want to be late. Did you look in Bertie's basket?"

I rummaged around in the dog's bed and fished my left sandal out from under the cushion. Bertie doesn't chew shoes, he cuddles them. He takes them to his basket for company on those rare occasions when he's feeling mopish. Generally he's not a sulker but maybe he found getting up before five depressing because this was definitely one of his broody days. When he discovered we weren't taking him along with us, he sat in the middle of the driveway, a droopy mound of dejection, and glowered resentfully at the departing car.

Tracy was alone watching television in her kitchen when we arrived. It was by far the larger and more comfortable of the two rooms on the main floor of the old house. As well as the usual stove, fridge, and table, it had plenty of space for the television set and a couple of easy chairs. A big south window filled the room with light. By contrast, the north-facing living room looked dark and stuffed to overflowing by one shabby old sofa and a bean-bag chair. A disproportionately large staircase leading to the bedrooms and bathroom ran up the wall near the front entrance. Its looming bulk made the living room seem even smaller.

Today's Tracy looked very different from the bedraggled specimen I'd said goodbye to on Friday afternoon. Her long black hair was freshly washed and swept back from a face that bore no signs of grief. Even the bruise on her cheek had faded to the point where a touch of makeup hid it nicely. She wore jeans, a hot-pink T-shirt, and no bra. Tracy was not the picture of a mate in mourning.

"It's quiet here today," Candi said. "That was a real crowd scene you had yesterday."

"Yeah," Tracy agreed. "After the police left, half of Okotoks must've rung my doorbell to offer their condolences. I guess they meant well but I sure could have done without most of them."

Privately I wondered if the visits were meant quite as kindly as Tracy thought. I suspected that at least some of the condolences had been paid as the price of admission to the hottest gossip in Okotoks. Jonathan Webster's death would be the town's number-one topic and a personal chat with his live-in lover would get the goods straight from the horse's mouth.

"My grandma's asked us to go to her place later," she added. "She's having some people from Calgary over to talk about gardening and she says they're good friends of yours so we should all have tea together."

"Is that okay with you?" I asked.

"Sure," Tracy said. "At least that way I won't be home if more people come to pay sympathy calls. I don't think I can take much more of that." But Tracy spoke too soon. The buzz of the doorbell drowned her last words. She glanced out the window. "Oh no. It's the Three Graces." Her face fell. "They're from my grandma's church. They go everywhere together."

Three women in sensible shoes and the late stages of middle age stood on the doorstep bearing large dishes in their arms. Tracy opened the door and a tuna casserole marched in, followed by a lasagna and a chocolate cake.

"Now don't you bother Tracy dear, we'll introduce ourselves to your friends," said the tuna casserole. "I'm Grace Marten." She was a tiny woman and peered up at us from under straight black bangs that cut across her brow pudding-bowl fashion.

"I'm Grace Gordon." The lasagna was a touch taller than her friend or maybe it was the brush of permed hair frizzing out from her head that gave the impression of extra height.

"And I'm Alice Grace." The chocolate cake was tall with a breadth to match her height. She towered over her two friends without any help from her grey hair, which was pulled back into such a tight bun that from the front she looked almost bald.

I think I must have stood and gaped. I know Candi did. It was impossible not to stare. The Three Graces looked for all the world like the Three Stooges in drag. The resemblance was so extraordinary, it was uncanny.

"We were all so upset when we heard about your friend," said Curly Joe. "Where would you like us to put these?"

Candi and Tracy helped Curly store the food in the kitchen while Moe and Larry and I held the conversational fort in the living room. They were regular "A Day in the Lifestyle" watchers and obviously thrilled to meet Candi.

"I work with Candi." I explained my much less interesting presence there. "She and Tracy are good friends. They went to high school together."

"We've known Tracy since she was a little girl and came here to live with her grandmother. My husband and I live across the street." Moe pointed out the window to the house opposite. "Over there in the white stucco."

"I live three houses down across the alley," Larry said. "You can see my place if you look out Tracy's kitchen window. Alice lives up on the hill."

"What an interesting coincidence," I said. "Your names I mean."

"Mr. Churchill . . ." said Moe.

"He's our minister," Larry filled in.

"He calls us his Three Graces," Moe finished and they both laughed with real enjoyment at what was evidently a much-loved and well-worn witticism. Clearly, neither of them suspected Mr. Churchill of any ironic intent.

"What's all that laughing in there, you two?" Curly called from the kitchen. She bustled into the living room, herding Candi and Tracy in front of her.

"We were just telling Phoebe about how we got to be called the Three Graces," Moe explained, which got them all giggling again. Finally she and Larry pulled themselves together and sat down at either end of Tracy's ancient sofa. It was not a wise move. The tired velour upholstery camouflaged an instrument of torture, one of those sofas-from-hell whose broken springs drop unsuspecting bums to the floor while their sharp front panels cut off circulation at the knees. It dragged the two women down into its saggy depths.

"Won't you sit down too, Mrs. Grace?" Tracy inquired of the still-standing Curly who, having watched her friends struggle with the sofa, now cast a suspicious eye on the bean-bag chair. "I'll get some extra chairs from the kitchen. Would you like some coffee? Or maybe you'd sooner have tea?"

"Oh, no thank you dear, we won't have either." Moe sank still deeper into the sofa. She peered out from the tiny space between her bangs and the peak of her knees.

"You mustn't go to any trouble for us." In an effort to keep her bottom at least a couple of inches above the floor, Larry clutched the sofa's padded arm with the desperation of the drowning. Unfortunately, the wily old piece of furniture knew this ploy and managed a quick counterstrike by slump-ing its arm a few inches inward. She hit the floor with a soft thump.

"We can't stay more than a minute." Curly arranged her considerable bulk on the sturdy wooden chair Tracy brought from the kitchen, obviously relieved at having been spared trial by bean-bag. Tracy and I fetched two more kitchen chairs while Candi lowered herself gracefully onto the beans.

"We just wanted to come over and let you know that we're thinking of you," Moe said when we were all settled.

"And to tell you that if there's anything we can do for you, all you have to do is ask," Curly added.

"If you need help, any help at all, you just give us a holler and we'll be right over," Larry finished the thought.

"Thank you," said Tracy. "That's very good of you."

And it was. The Graces' offer of help was truly kind and sincerely meant. However, the three women's curiosity was every bit as genuine as their generosity and almost as obvious. I could see they were simply aching to have a good chin-wag about Webster's death. I watched with admiration as they skilfully manoeuvred the conversation towards the Big Topic.

"We would have come yesterday but there were so many people buzzing around here that we thought we'd wait until things calmed down a little. You must be worn out, you poor kid," Larry said to a very fresh-looking Tracy.

"Yes," Curly agreed sympathetically, "you must be exhausted. The police were at your place for such a long time yesterday. I don't know how you stood it."

"They questioned all us neighbours too," Larry said.

"They wanted to know if we saw anybody coming or going from your house the night before Jonathan passed away," Moe explained. "I'm afraid I had to tell them the truth. I only hope I don't get anyone into trouble. You had such a lot of visitors that evening."

"Jonathan and I were both out that night so we couldn't have had too many visitors." A hint of impatience had found its way into Tracy's otherwise perfectly polite manner.

"Oh, but you did, dear," Moe demurred from under her bangs. "I know because I saw them."

"And so did I. But I didn't see as many as Grace because I can only see the back of your house from my place. She can see the front." Plainly, Larry felt this accident of geography had given her friend an unfair advantage.

"I live on the hill so I didn't see anything," Curly admitted sadly. "I was at home watching 'Street Legal.' They have reruns on now."

"Exactly how many people did you see?" Candi asked.

"Six," Moe said.

"I thought you told us you saw five," Curly said.

"It was six if you count Sadie."

"My grandma was over here?" This was news to Tracy.

"She brought over a plate of muffins for you. She knocked on your door and when no one answered she let herself in with a key."

"You must have excellent eyesight," Candi said. "To be able to see muffins all the way from your house."

"I happened to be watching the robins. They have a nest in the spruce tree in our front yard." Moe seemed a little miffed by the implications of Candi's remark. "I'm very interested in birds so I keep a pair of binoculars on a table beside my front window. The father robin was sitting on the fence in front of Tracy's house so I couldn't help but see Sadie when she walked right in front of him."

"I'm a bird-watcher too," Larry chimed in. "Only I keep my binoculars in the kitchen. You see, we have purple martins in the backyard and it stays light so late these evenings that I can sit and watch them for hours after dinner. Stan says I'm nuts when it comes to those martins, but I think they're such interesting birds. Did you know they eat their weight in mosquitoes every day?"

"Bats too," Curly said.

"Bats what?" Larry asked.

"Eat mosquitoes," Curly answered. "Bats eat mosquitoes too."

"Bats aren't birds," Moe stated firmly.

"Well, I never said they were," Curly protested. "I only said they eat mosquitoes."

"Bats are rodents, aren't they?" For some reason Larry looked to me for affirmation. "Like rats, only with wings."

"Actually, they're not," I said. "Bats have an order all to themselves. They're Chiroptera. Did you know that there's a really interesting little bat colony near Okotoks? They live down by the river in . . ." I could feel myself beginning to babble. The conversation had entered the twilight zone.

"Did you recognize any of the people you saw at Tracy's place?" Candi yanked us back to earth.

"Well, everybody in town knows David Cavendish," Moe said. "He owns the bookstore. He was the first. He came a few minutes after Jonathan left the house and drove away. That was about seven I guess. Then ten minutes after you and David left, Sadie came over with the muffins. You left at about seven-twenty, didn't you dear?" she asked Tracy.

"About then," Tracy agreed. "We went to a movie," she added with unnecessary firmness.

"So that would mean Sadie came to your house about seven-thirty," Moe said.

"I thought you said the older woman came next," Curly said. "The one in the expensive clothes."

"No, no. She went to Sadie's house first but after she rang the bell and no one answered then she went over to Tracy's. She knocked on your door, dear, and your grandma let her in."

"And you don't know who this woman was?" Candi said.

"No, but she was about sixty and had grey hair and she was wearing a beautiful green suit," Moe said admiringly. "She was so elegant and well-groomed. You know, one of those women who always look perfect no matter what." The bird binoculars had put in a busy evening.

123

"Could have been someone for a reading," Tracy said. "Grandma sometimes does them at home in the evenings."

"Tracy's grandma reads cards, you know. She's very good at it," Curly informed us. "Tracy's inherited some of Sadie's talent too. Have either of you girls ever had your cards read?"

"First David Cavendish, then Tracy's grandma, and then the woman in the green suit. That's three." Candi was not about to let the conversation wander. "When did you see the others?"

"Well, after about ten minutes Sadie and the woman left and went back to Sadie's place. It was just after that when the tall man came." Moe paused. "My, but he was big. More than big enough to be a basketball player. My nephew plays basketball for the Dinosaurs but this man was far taller than Jim. I wonder. Maybe it's funny hormones or something."

"What did the man do?" Candi steered her back on track.

"Well, he'd been sitting a few houses down the street in his car, but after Sadie and the woman left he walked right over and rang the doorbell. When no one answered, he knocked. Maybe knocked isn't the right word. Really, he pounded that poor door so hard that for a minute I thought he might wreck it, but he finally stopped and went around to the backyard."

"That's when I saw him knock on the back door." At last, some action for Larry and the purple martins. "But when no one answered he looked in your kitchen window. Then he went and got himself a lawn chair. He put it down right in the centre of the patio. I could just see him through a clump of Saskatoon bushes. It's a good thing he was so tall or I wouldn't have been able to see him at all. He must have stayed there for an hour or more. I didn't actually see him leave – he must have gone around the time my daughter phoned – but I know he was there when those two thuggy-looking ones came. He sure skedaddled out of that chair then. Ran and hid in the bushes."

"What thuggy-looking ones?" This time it was Tracy who asked the question.

"Now they were an odd pair," Moe said. "They parked right in front of your house but instead of both of them coming to the front door, one ran around the back while the other one rang your front bell. Then when no one answered, the one at the front looked in all the windows. And I don't mean glanced, I mean he looked and looked hard."

"So did the one I saw at the back door," Larry said. "He looked in every window he could reach almost like he was casing out your place. I can tell you I came this close to calling the police. That's exactly the kind of behaviour that Neighbourhood Watch tells you to keep an eye out for. And he was a very rough-looking man, wasn't he?" She appealed to her friend.

"They both were," Moe agreed. "One of them was very fat. He had a big tattoo of a naked lady on his arm. And the skinny one, the one with the pimples, he had on the dirtiest pair of jeans I've ever seen. His hair was dirty too. A nasty, dirty ponytail. I was sure they couldn't be friends of yours."

"I don't know anyone with a tattoo like that," Tracy said.

"Did they go into the house?" Candi asked.

"I can't say for certain," Larry replied carefully. "Like I said, my daughter phoned around then so I suppose they could have gone in while I was talking to her."

"What about the tall man who hid in the bushes?" Candi continued. "What did he do?"

"Stayed in the bushes, I guess. But I'm not really sure," Larry shook her frizzy curls. "I didn't see."

"Well I did," Moe said. "He left right after the other two did. He seemed to be in an awful hurry."

The phone rang.

"I'll take it upstairs." Tracy was already halfway up the stairs when she spoke. I heard her answer the phone, then a door shut.

"It's probably David Cavendish," Curly said. "Such a nice man. Do you know him?"

"I met him for the first time yesterday," Candi said. "Tracy and I are old friends but we've been out of touch for a while."

"I'm glad you're here now," Curly said. "When she needs old friends around her."

"Were you girls friends of Jonathan Webster's too?" Larry asked.

"No, we didn't know him at all," Candi said. "Tracy introduced him to Phoebe and me on Friday morning but that was it."

"What do they think really happened to him?" Moe asked. "You know, there are all sorts of terrible rumours floating around town. Everyone's saying that he was murdered."

"They're saying that someone put poison in that weird little machine of his. You know, that oxygen thing he was the sales rep for." Curly added the details. "Do you think it can be true?"

"You're probably in a better position to know than I am," Candi said. "Why would anyone want to murder Jonathan?"

This was the question the Graces had been waiting for. They stumbled over each other in their eagerness to talk. But they were not simply indulging a natural passion for gossip. There was real anger and more than a little anguish in their voices as they told us what they knew about Jonathan Webster.

"Who wouldn't want to murder him would be more like it," Moe said.

"You're lucky you didn't know him." Curly looked grim. "I suppose he was nice looking enough and I know he could be oh-so-very-very-charming if he felt like it," she conceded. "But that was all a big phony act. The man was a monster. Why Tracy stayed with him I will never understand."

"You see, he beat her," Larry stated flatly. "And I don't mean a little smacking around. He knocked the living daylights out of her."

"Once, he hurt her so badly she had to spend two days in hospital." Moe shook her head sadly. "Broken ribs and bruises and her eyes all black and swollen. It was so bad she looked like she'd been in a car accident. And that's what she told everyone but we knew it wasn't true. That poor little girl."

"It nearly broke Sadie's heart," Larry's eyes filled with tears. "But what could she do? Tracy wouldn't leave him."

"Why do women stay with men like that?" Moe asked a question that has always troubled me. "They didn't have any children. She could earn her own living. Why did she stay?"

"Believe me," Curly said with feeling, "the world is a better place without Mister Jonathan Webster. Grace is right. Who wouldn't want to murder that evil bastard? And there's no need for you to look shocked," she said to her friends. "Because that's exactly what he was and both of you know it as well as I do. He was an evil bastard and whoever murdered him should be given a medal."

"Well, maybe not quite a medal, but I sure hope they don't catch him." Larry spoke a little more gently than her friend, but the sentiment was the same.

"Now Tracy can get on with her life," Moe said. "And I hope

that means with David Cavendish. At least the poor man won't have to wait down the street anymore when he comes to see her. He used to sit in his car just around the corner and wait until Webster left the house. Now he can march right up to the door like any honest man in love with . . ." She stopped abruptly when we heard a door open and Tracy came down the stairs.

"That was my grandma," Tracy lied. A few minutes before I had glanced out the front window and watched a grey-haired woman come down the path next door and greet Cyrrie and Edith as they pulled up in front of the house. Right now the three of them were standing talking in front of one of the rose beds. Whoever had phoned, it was not Tracy's grandmother. "I'm afraid we have to leave you and go over to her house now," she continued smoothly. No one else in the room had my view out the window. I was the only one who saw Cyrrie and the two women continue up the path and in the front door. Tracy was a very good liar.

"Don't worry about it, dear, we were just on our way, weren't we girls?" Curly rose majestically from her kitchen chair. However, things weren't quite so simple for the other two. They were still lodged deep in the sofa, which looked like it might be busy digesting them. Their friend came to the rescue. Curly extended a hand to Moe and, with a one-two-three-heave, the little woman shot from the sofa like a jack-in-the-box. A mournful twang from one of the more musically inclined broken springs accompanied the action. Back on her feet at last, she teetered over to the door. Meanwhile, through a series of involved rolls and heaves, the more athletic Larry had managed to extract herself from the sofa's velvety gullet. Unfortunately, her left leg appeared to have developed a violent case of pins and needles. She hobbled after her friends.

"And you remember what we told you," Curly said. "If you need anything you give us a call and we'll be right here." Her two friends nodded in agreement as they reached the bottom of the front steps.

"Good luck with the robins," Candi called after them. "Have any babies hatched yet?"

"I don't really know." Moe still seemed more than a little dazed. "I can't say as I've noticed."

8

"Robins my ass," Tracy snorted. "Those old bags were spying on my house." She flopped down on the bean-bag.

"Don't we have to get going?" Candi asked.

"Where?" Tracy said.

"To your grandmother's."

"Don't worry, we have lots of time. We don't have to be at Grandma's until four. I just said that to get rid of the Three Graces," Tracy said. Candi looked a little taken aback.

"You gotta hand it to them," I said. "They sure don't miss much."

"Then neither did the police. I'll bet they had a wonderful time telling the Mounties everything. They must've really enjoyed it."

"Tracy, don't you think you're being a little hard on the Graces?" Candi said. "After all, they didn't have much choice, did they? When the police investigate murders people are supposed to tell what they know."

"Jonathan wasn't murdered." Tracy spoke with more hope

than conviction. "It was an accident. A terrible accident."

"Trace, you know that isn't true," Candi said gently.

"But the police haven't said he was murdered. They told me they won't know what happened for sure until they get the results of all their tests, and that won't be until Wednesday or Thursday."

"Don't kid yourself. The police don't send in a whole homicide team for deaths they think are accidents," Candi said. "Right now, they're treating Jonathan's poisoning like a murder. Maybe all their interviews and lab tests will prove that they made a wrong assumption but I don't think so and obviously neither do they. That's why they went to all your neighbours. It's pretty clear that they think whoever killed him put poison in the oxygen machine on Thursday night so anyone who came to your house then is a suspect."

"And we all know whose name is gonna be at the top of the list," Tracy wailed. "Mine. Mine and David's. Oh, God." She put her head in her hands and rocked back and forth. "What am I gonna do? Candi, you've gotta help me."

There it was, the invitation that transformed Candi's passion for snooping into a legitimate act of friendship.

"First, we'd better figure out who else is on that list. Did you recognize any of the people the Graces described?" Our girl gumshoe plunged right in.

Tracy stopped rocking and looked up. "The well-groomed older woman in the green suit. I figure that must have been Maud Gellman. Grandma said she was coming over for a reading soon and she was in town that night anyway getting ready for the psychic fair."

"What about the tall man?"

"That could only be Eddy Sedge, except he and Jonathan

hadn't spoken to each other for months so I don't know what he was doing out here. But Eddy's the only guy I know who's that tall so it must have been him."

"And the other two, the tattoo and the dirty ponytail?"

"Beats me," Tracy said. "I haven't a clue who they were. I don't know anyone like that."

"Could they have been friends of Jonathan's?"

"It's not very likely but I suppose it's possible."

"Maybe they were gambling friends," I suggested.

"Maybe they were not such friendly gambling friends." Candi pushed my suggestion one step further. "Did Jonathan owe money to anyone?"

Tracy hesitated. "I don't know. There were parts of Jonathan's life I didn't know much about. If he did owe money he didn't tell me."

"But it is a possibility," Candi persisted.

"Of course it's a possibility. I guess anything's a possibility."

"So Jonathan may have been in debt?"

Tracy shrugged.

"He could have owed money that you didn't know anything about?"

"Candi, lay off, will you?" Tracy snapped. "You're worse than that Mountie yesterday."

"I'm sorry, Trace. I guess all this stuff really isn't any of my business." For the first time since Jonathan died I found myself in complete agreement with Candi. "I shouldn't have pushed you like that. Those are questions for the police to ask. I should just butt out." Not that I believed a word of what she was saying. I knew there wasn't a chance that Candi would give up sleuthing her way through Tracy's troubles. Tracy, on the other hand, believed every word.

"Candi, please don't. I don't want you to butt out. I don't

know what I want but I do know that." Tracy started to cry. "I don't know what I'd do if you weren't around. And you too Phoebe."

"Tracy, crying is not going to do anybody any good at all, least of all you." Candi's brusqueness surprised me. Usually she's very tenderhearted. "The police are not going to stop asking questions just because it upsets you, and the more upset you get the more confused your answers are going to be. Come on, pull yourself together." She opened her purse and fished out a Kleenex. "Here. Now let's start again."

Tracy blew her nose, sat up straight, squared her shoulders and smiled. The wan smile had overtones of plucky aristo in the tumbrel but at least she was trying.

"So Jonathan didn't owe any money," Candi resumed her questions. "At least not that you know of. Is that right?"

Again, there was an uncomfortable little pause but this time Tracy was saved by the bell. She leapt up, ran to the kitchen, and answered the phone before it had a chance to ring a second time. "That really was Grandma. She says to come over when we're ready. I guess we'll have to finish this talk some other time." She looked relieved. "Maybe we should take this stuff the Graces brought and put it in Grandma's freezer. I can't eat it all myself."

Each carrying a dish, we went out Tracy's back door, through the garden to her grandmother's. The garden itself was a surprise. I had expected the trim lawn and well-manicured rose garden at the front of the house to be continued at the back, at least in style if not content. I was wrong. There was nothing in the least formal about Sadie Nightingale's garden. The place was filled with masses of native shrubs and wild flowers mixed in with the very hardiest of traditional perennials. They surrounded a fieldstone patio where Edith, Cyrrie, and Sadie

Nightingale sat on well-cushioned willow chairs set around a white enamel table. Their three grey heads almost touched as they poured over the pages of a gardening book spread out in front of them. A large adjustable umbrella in the centre of the round table shaded them from the glare of the afternoon sun. The whole garden hummed with bees and, in the warm, still air, the civilized perfume of early French lilac fought a losing battle against the wild pungency of wolf willow in bloom.

Sadie Nightingale was taller than her granddaughter, close to my five-eight. Her quick, graceful movements as she stood to greet us betrayed no sign of age. She wore a blue and white checked blouse over a denim skirt and white runners. Her clear brown eyes looked out from behind a large pair of aviator glasses. Candi and I stood clutching our dishes while Tracy introduced me.

"Good grief, what are we going to do with all this food? Here, let me help you." Mrs. Nightingale reached out to take the lasagna.

"It's okay, Mrs. Nightingale. I can manage," I said.

"Then at least let me hold the door for you." She led us into her bright, airy kitchen. "And, please, won't you call me Sadie?"

While we stowed the food in the freezer, Sadie filled a large kettle and put it to boil on the old-fashioned gas range. Two trays, one with cups and saucers, the other with a lemon cake, stood on the counter. She took a big brown teapot from the top shelf of the cupboard and put it next to the tray with the cups.

"Grandma, let us make the tea," Tracy gave her grand-mother a hug. "You go talk to Cyrrie and Edith and we'll bring everything out when the tea's ready."

"You are a dear," Sadie said and clearly meant it. The affection between grandmother and granddaughter was real and obvious. Tracy may have had bad luck with men but she was batting a thousand in the grandma league.

"Phoebe, why don't you come with me," Sadie continued. "It doesn't take three people to make tea and I want to ask about those nature films you make."

She took my arm in hers and led me back out to the garden. Somehow, Sadie's touch managed to convey that we were now friends and good friends at that. This surprised me because I'm basically a solitary soul and it usually takes me a long time to feel even a glimmer of this kind of rapport with someone. I wondered if she had the same remarkable effect on everyone she met for the first time, this feeling of instant intimacy, unforced and totally genuine.

"I had no idea Cyrrie knew you or I'd have been certain to wangle an introduction before now. I'm a great admirer of your work, Phoebe."

"You've actually seen some of my films?" I don't know why this always surprises me but it does. I found myself a chair and sat at the table with Cyrrie and Edith. Sadie stood beside Edith's chair looking down at us. I was struck by the resemblance between the two women. It wasn't simply that they were both tall and slim and very straight and had nearly identical shades of grey hair and brown eyes. There was something in their gestures and the way they held themselves that struck a chord of similarity as well. Such likeness of demeanour and bearing often occurs among members of the same family but seeing it in strangers like Edith and Sadie was a little uncanny.

"Of course I've seen them," Sadie said. "The educational network plays them on their 'Naturally Alberta' program.

They did two last winter. That one on meadow voles and a new one I hadn't seen before about beavers. What are you working on now?"

I told her a little about *Right in Your Own Backyard*. As I did, I thought what a wonderful setting her garden would make for the film. This was followed by an immediate pang of guilt at my disloyalty to Cyrrie.

"And you're filming it all in Cyrrie's garden?"

"Not quite all. There are a few outside sequences. I want to show how a small city garden fits into a whole ecological system. For instance, I'm doing one of those water-cycle sequences. You know the kind of thing – how a drop of water gets from the sea to your garden and back again to the sea. I'll be filming some of that not far from here. The part where the drop of water melts out of its snow bank and joins a trickle that eventually runs into a raging mountain torrent. I've got everything but the last part. The Sheep River is going to star as my raging torrent only there was so much late snow and rain this year that I haven't been able to drive up there to film it. I'm going to try to make it out on Tuesday if the weather holds."

"Do you allow spectators?" Sadie asked. "Or am I presuming? I'd love to come with you and watch you work if I wouldn't be in your way. I've never seen anyone make a film before."

"There's not much to watch but I'd be delighted to have the company," I said. "I was hoping I'd be able to persuade Edith to come with me too. What about it Edith – you game for a day in the foothills?"

"Unless Cyril has something else planned?" She looked at Cyrrie questioningly. He shook his head.

"What about you Cyrrie?" I asked.

"Thank you, but I think I'd better stay home with my grant applications. I have two enormous cartons full of them to read and the meeting is a week tomorrow." Cyrrie is on the board of directors of a foundation that gives money to artists.

"I'm going to bake bread for Cyril tomorrow so I'll do an extra loaf and pack us some sandwiches for a picnic," Edith volunteered. Cyrrie's face fell. He claims that the British navy uses loaves of Edith's bread as ballast in their battleships.

"I haven't been up to the Sheep River for years," Sadie said. "It will be good to get away from all of this turmoil even if it is only for a day." It was the first reference she had made to Jonathan's death.

"When is the funeral?" Cyrrie asked.

"I don't know. The police haven't released Jonathan's body. They think he was murdered, you know." Sadie was very matter of fact.

"So I had heard," Cyrrie replied. "Are they right, Sadie?"

"They may well be," she said. "Jonathan had made himself enough enemies in the past few years."

"But could they hate him enough to murder the poor man?" Edith asked. She was having trouble believing that people one knew, or at least knew of, could actually be murdered. Murder was something that only happened to strangers.

"I'm afraid a lot of people had good reason to want Jonathan dead," Sadie said, but before she could elaborate Tracy and Candi appeared with the tea.

There was no more talk of murder. Instead, given the circumstances, our conversation was unnaturally cheerful. I got the feeling that we were all carefully avoiding any mention of Jonathan's death, especially Sadie. Maybe she was protecting Tracy. We talked about gardening, the weather, travel – the sort of topics that people who do not know each other well find to occupy a pleasant afternoon hour in one another's company. Except this was not a normal afternoon and all of us knew it. Jonathan's murder was with us like a conversational undercurrent waiting to drag us down. But still, we did our best.

Cyrrie told some funny stories about the racetrack, which led to Candi's account of Nick and his pet channelling adventures. This, in turn, brought us around to the topic of Maud's psychic fair, which pushed us perilously close to the subject of Jonathan and murder but, after a false start or two, we managed to tiptoe back to a safer topic. I noticed that Edith and Sadie seemed to have hit it off very well. Only Tracy didn't contribute to the conversation. She sat and sipped her tea in preoccupied silence.

"This has been lovely, Sadie, but we mustn't take any more of your afternoon." Cyrrie stood up to leave.

"I'm afraid I have to go too," Candi said. "I just have time to run Phoebe home before I pick up Nick at the fair."

"Please Phoebe, do stay a little longer," Sadie said. "You don't have to leave so soon, do you? I'll be glad to drive you home later myself."

"I'd love to stay," I said, wondering what Sadie wanted.

After the others had left, Tracy and I helped her carry the dishes back to the kitchen. Sadie did not have a dishwasher. Tracy ran a sink full of soapy water and put the cups and saucers in to soak.

"Grandma, would you mind if I left you and Phoebe to cope with these dishes? I hardly slept last night and it's starting to catch up with me. I'd really like to go home and get some sleep."

"You do what you need to do, my dearest." Sadie kissed her

granddaughter goodbye. She stood at the window and watched Tracy walk through the garden.

I started to wash the cups.

Sadie picked up a towel and we worked together in silence for a while. It was a comfortable silence, like the silence of old friends. She finished drying and stacking the saucers before she spoke. "Tracy's not really going home because she's tired. She's going to meet David. David Cavendish. Do you know him, Phoebe?"

"No. We've never met but I have seen him." I found myself telling her about the afternoon of Jonathan's death when Candi and I followed Tracy around Okotoks.

"I'm surprised they kissed so openly," Sadie said. "Usually Tracy and David try to be discreet but she was very distressed that afternoon. Besides, in a place as small as this I guess it's almost impossible to keep that kind of secret. Everyone in town must have known what was going on."

"Candi says that Tracy is in love with him."

"David is a very good man. He owns the bookstore here. He was a high school biology teacher in Calgary before he moved to Okotoks. He'd be very good for Tracy." She opened the cupboard next to the sink and put the stack of clean saucers on the top shelf. "Poor Tracy, lying about what she's doing when she goes to meet David has become such a habit that she can't stop even now that Jonathan's dead. She even lies to me. It hurts a little, that." Sadie closed the cupboard door. "But I suppose it's Jonathan's doing too. She never lied before she met him."

"Maybe she never had to," I said.

"She was a wonderful child, a real joy to me and such a funny little thing. They don't come any dearer." Sadie shook her head, picked up the towel again, and started on the cups. "Well, maybe it is better for her and David to try to be discreet," she said briskly. "At least until the police are finished this investigation."

"Do you think it really matters all that much?" I said, thinking about what the Three Graces had told us earlier in the afternoon. "If the whole town knows about Tracy and David then the police will know too."

"You're right, of course. But it worries me all the same – Jonathan murdered and Tracy and David so obviously in love with one another. It does look bad."

"Why did Tracy stay with Jonathan?" I asked. "It's pretty evident that their relationship was over. And you're right about things getting around a small town – the Graces told us that he beat her. Why did she stay and let herself be abused?"

"So you know about the beatings." Sadie hung a cup from its hook in the cupboard, put down her towel, and leaned against the counter. "She stayed because she was afraid and she had good reason to be. Jonathan in one of his rages was terrifying – he'd get so out of control it was almost as if he'd lost his mind. As things in his life got worse and worse, the rages and the beatings got worse right along with them. Jonathan was destroying himself and he was destroying my beautiful girl right along with him. I begged her to leave him but she was too afraid of what he'd do."

"Couldn't she have gone to the police and had a restraining order put on him?"

"How could a piece of paper protect her from a man like Jonathan? I heard him tell her myself that he'd lost his house and his business and he damn well wasn't going to lose her too."

"A restraining order is more than a piece of paper, Sadie.

The police take them very seriously. They would have helped Tracy."

"You have a lot of faith in the police, don't you Phoebe?" Sadie picked up her towel and started back on the cups. "Cyrrie says that you know the policeman in charge of Jonathan's case."

"I know Inspector Debarets but he's not really a personal friend or anything. I only know him professionally. Remember when those two people were murdered at the health resort near Millarville? He was in charge of that case too. That's when I met him. I was out doing some filming at The Ranch when the murders happened so I had to answer a lot of questions, but I really didn't have all that much to do with the case itself."

"That's not what Cyrrie told me. He said you practically got yourself killed and that if it hadn't been for you the police would never have solved those murders."

"Cyrrie's exaggerating," I said. "Even my being there was a coincidence. Take my word for it, the police would have done just fine without me. Inspector Debarets is too good at his job to need me to do it for him."

"So the inspector is a good policeman."

"In my books he's the best. He's smart, he's thorough, and he listens to what people tell him. If there's a fact to be found, he'll find it." I put the last of the cups on the draining board and looked at her. "Sadie, if you're worried about the police arresting Tracy or David you shouldn't be. Inspector Debarets is not the kind of policeman who goes around arresting innocent people just because it might look like they have a motive. I guarantee that he won't make any arrests until he's found the real murderer. And he will find Jonathan's murderer. You can count on it."

"And until he does I guess we'll just have to put up with the fact that Tracy and David are both on his list of suspects."

"Anyone who was near Tracy's house on Thursday night and had access to Jonathan's ozone machine will be on the inspector's list," I said.

"I knew he'd get himself into trouble with that stupid machine some day. It was a matter of time," she said. "If only Tracy weren't involved."

"But Sadie, Tracy and David aren't the only ones on the list," I said. "I know for a fact that there are at least five other people who were at Jonathan's that night. Any one of those five could have put poison in the SuperO."

"How do you know about the other people?" Sadie asked. "Who are they?"

I told her about the Three Graces and what they had seen.

"The Graces," Sadie shook her head and laughed. "I might have guessed. Those are the most watched birds in Alberta. And you're quite right, the woman in green was Maud Gellman. The tall man sounds like Jonathan's business partner, Eddy Sedge, but I don't know who the other two are. I can't remember seeing anyone like that around here."

"You see," I said. "You don't have to worry so much about Tracy and David. For all we know, every single person the Graces saw that night could have had a reason for wanting Jonathan dead."

"Including me."

"Including you," I agreed. "It's pretty obvious you love your granddaughter very much. You must have had some strong feelings about Jonathan."

"You're right, of course. We all had reasons for wanting Jonathan dead. At least Tracy and David and Eddy and I did.

But what about Maud? Why would she kill Jonathan? They were friends."

"Maud and Jonathan?" I was surprised. "Maud gave me the impression that she didn't know him all that well. She certainly didn't approve of his selling his ozone machines at her psychic fair. She told me that the booth was really Tracy's, and Jonathan was just there on sufferance."

"Of course Maud knew Jonathan. He'd done her hair for years, first at La Maison and then later at his own salon. He's the one who got her started on that lawsuit of hers. Did you know that Maud is suing the Queen?"

"She told me about it. It's totally crazy. I mean, even for Maud it's a bit much. But how did Jonathan factor in?"

"Jonathan knew all about Maud's psychic dabbling. He's the one who sent her to me to have her cards read. That's when I met her. I know that Maud and Jonathan talked about her latest psychic fads every time she went to get her hair done. It wasn't long before Foxy Locks went broke that Maud took up past-life regression therapy. One day she told him about having been executed for witchcraft in a previous life and that's when he came up with this crazy idea that she should sue the Queen."

"So you think Maud's lawsuit is crazy?

"Well of course I do." Sadie sounded a little insulted, as if she couldn't quite believe that I even had to ask. "The whole thing is preposterous. Jonathan must have said it as a joke but Maud being Maud took him seriously."

"So Jonathan didn't believe in it?"

"Jonathan believed in Maud's money. Maud's a very rich woman – or at least she's married to a wealthy and generous man. In any case, Jonathan told Maud that he had a cousin in

England who was a solicitor. Jonathan said this cousin of his would look after the British legal aspects of the case for her. She gave Jonathan five thousand dollars to send on to the cousin as a retainer."

"Was it true? About the lawyer cousin?"

"Jonathan hardly ever spoke about his family. He said he was an only child and that both his parents were dead, but that's all. The English cousin is news to me."

"Then you think Jonathan was taking Maud for a ride?"

"You mean swindling her? Yes, of course. I know he was. Jonathan was a compulsive gambler. He probably lost the money the day she gave it to him. But I had no real proof that the cousin didn't exist and even if I had Maud wouldn't have listened." Sadie had a point. Anyone crazy enough to sue the Queen on behalf of a former self wouldn't hesitate to send money to an unknown lawyer. Neither proof nor sweet reason could dint that kind of faith.

"But Maud spoke as if she'd heard from her English lawyer," I said. "She told me that she didn't think he was taking her case seriously enough. If the cousin wrote to her then he must exist."

"You can bet that Jonathan took care of all the correspondence," Sadie said. "He only told Maud about what the lawyer said in his letters. Ask her. I think you'll find she can't show you a single letter from her English solicitor."

"Have you told the police about this?"

"No. What would I say? If people want to do crazy things with their own money, then that's their business."

"But Sadie, you have to tell them," I said. "Don't you see, this gives Maud a motive to murder Jonathan?"

"Why on earth would she want to murder him? As far as Maud is concerned, Jonathan was helping her."

"But what if Maud had found out that there was no English cousin? That Jonathan was swindling her."

"I honestly can't see Maud Gellman murdering anyone over money, can you?" Sadie said. "Especially not for a measly five thousand dollars."

"Maybe it wasn't only five thousand. She could have given Jonathan money that you don't know about. And maybe it isn't the money at all. You say that Maud isn't rich in her own right, that the money is her husband's. Well, it could be that she was afraid of what her husband would do if he found out she'd spent his money on something that crazy."

"But Maud doesn't think what she's doing is crazy." Sadie explained patiently. "You may find it difficult to believe Phoebe, but she is very sincere about this lawsuit. She believes absolutely in the rightness of her cause. To her, it's a kind of social crusade. Besides, Maud would never be afraid of Sam no matter what she'd done. They've been married for forty years and he's still dotty about her."

"I think you should tell the police what you know."

"If your inspector is as good a policeman as you think, then he knows already."

"Sadie, that's not fair. Inspector Debarets is a cop, not some loopy psychic." The words were still coming out of my mouth when I remembered that Sadie was a card reader and, according to all reports, a very dedicated one.

"I gather that you're not a believer in the psychic arts," she laughed, not in the least offended, either by my remark or by my lack of belief. "What on earth did you make of Maud's fair?"

I felt this wasn't quite the time to compound my rudeness by telling her my opinion of the charlatans currently peddling their lunacies in Okotoks. Instead, I settled for neutrality. "I just don't find that kind of stuff very helpful."

145

"How do you know?" Sadie asked. "Have you ever consulted a psychic?"

"No," I admitted. "Unless you count one Saturday afternoon when I was in junior high school and a bunch of us went downtown to see Madame Gisella, the Hungarian Gypsy princess. There was a little restaurant on First Street East where she used to read tea leaves every weekend. We saved up our allowances and away we went. We thought we were very daring and sophisticated."

Madame Gisella was terrific. She wore all sorts of bangles and scarves and enormous gold hoop earrings. We were a pack of pimply thirteen-year-olds from the suburbs out on a Saturday spree but she had treated the four of us like women of the world, discussing our love lives as if they actually existed. We were thrilled. The only trouble was that Madame Gisella's Hungarian accent was so thick we could hardly understand a thing she said. It didn't matter much. We still thought she was wonderful.

"Ah yes, dear old Madame G.," Sadie laughed. "I remember her Hungarian highness very well. Her real name is Gail Jordan and she was born in Red Deer. It's too bad you met Gail when she was in her Hungarian princess phase because she really does have something of the gift."

"You mean she's still around reading tea leaves?"

"Madame Gisella retired a number of years ago, but Gail's still around. I think she uses a crystal ball now. She may even have a booth at Maud's fair. I heard that she was doing the fair circuit these days."

"Maud says that you're the best card reader she knows but that you disapprove of doing it for money."

"I think 'disapprove' is maybe a little too strong. I don't

mind what other people do but I wouldn't feel comfortable charging money for readings myself."

"Where did you learn?" I asked.

"It's not something you learn," Sadie answered. "It's something you are. It's a gift."

"But don't you have to know what each card means and be able to arrange them in special patterns? You aren't born knowing things like that."

"That's true. There are certain skills you have to develop," she conceded. "But unless you have the gift all the skill in the world would be useless. It's a little like music. You could practise all your life, but unless you have the gift of music inside you, you'll never be a real musician."

I thought of the Goldbergs and my plodding efforts and felt a little chastened.

"Would you like me to read your cards?"

"Wouldn't it be a waste of your time?" I asked. "You already know I'm not a believer."

"It doesn't matter whether you believe or not," Sadie said.

"Won't I upset your vibrations or something?"

"Oh Phoebe, you are funny," she laughed heartily. "Having you here has done me a world of good." She put away the last of the cups and closed the cupboard door. "Thank you for staying on to talk. I know you're not the kind of person who feels comfortable talking like this with strangers and I'm grateful to you."

"But I don't feel like you are a stranger," I said truthfully. "For some reason I feel like I've known you a long time."

"Who knows? Maybe Maud's right and you have." Sadie's grin made her look twenty years younger. "Now come on. I'll get the cards and we'll go out to the garden and do a reading."

She went into the dining room, opened a deep drawer in the oak buffet, and took out a large biscuit tin with a photo of Buckingham Palace on its lid. The tin was filled with decks of cards, each in its own box except for one which was wrapped in a silk paisley scarf. Sadie removed this deck, collected a floppy straw garden hat from a hook in the kitchen, and led the way back out to the patio.

I pulled a couple of chairs up to the table while she adjusted the umbrella to block the rays of the late-afternoon sun from shining directly in our eyes. Then she unwrapped the cards and spread the scarf on the table. The scarf was very old, its brown and gold silk threadbare in places and cracked along one of the folds. She put the deck of cards down on it carefully.

"You don't use tarot cards?"

The deck on the cloth was a much-used fifty-two-card stack of everyday playing cards backed with a picture of purple pansies, all scratched and worn with age.

"My grandmother taught me how to read the cards and she always used an ordinary playing deck. I'd be surprised if she'd even heard of the tarot," Sadie said. "These cards belonged to her. So did the scarf. I sometimes use them on special occasions."

"They're beautiful," I said, pleased that Sadie regarded me as a special occasion. The old cards and their scarf had developed the kind of beauty that comes to objects that have been handled often and with love. I suppose it's more of a feeling than anything else – the same kind of feeling you get from an old, worn toy. At least that's where I've felt it most often.

"That wouldn't be everyone's first reaction but I suppose they are beautiful in an odd sort of way," Sadie agreed. "They're beautiful to me because they remind me of my grandmother. Sometimes I think I can still smell her perfume on the scarf. I've had them so long they're like a part of me." She began to shuffle the cards. "You know, Phoebe, I don't think I'm a person who cares very much about things. Or, at least I'm not a person who cares about having a lot of possessions. But if I were running from a fire I know I'd try to save Grandmother's cards. Tracy teases me about being buried with them, and on my crazier days I don't think that's such a bad idea at all. Maybe I'll just do that – I'll take them with me when I go." Sadie laughed but I didn't think she was joking. She handed the deck to me. "Now, you shuffle these and, when you feel you've shuffled them enough, cut the deck into three stacks from right to left. Then gather up the cards again in the same direction and give them back to me."

The old cards felt much heavier than modern plastic ones. I wondered how many hands had shuffled and cut them before mine. I carried out Sadie's instructions and passed the cards back to her. She dealt them face up onto the scarf in a triangular pattern. I hadn't seen any arrangements like it at the psychic fair and told Sadie so.

"My grandmother taught me this way," she said. "I think she invented it herself."

"How does it work?"

"Each side of the triangle represents a different aspect of your life. This one is for your head – it stands for practical things like money and work and how you think and how you make your way in the world. This next one is for your heart – how you feel about things, your relations with other people. The last one deals with your physical health. But you can see that they're all part of a bigger pattern and a card at one point can influence all the other cards."

"Head, heart, health," I repeated. "One more H and your grandmother could have been a charter member of the 4-H Club."

"Well, she was a farmer's wife so it wouldn't surprise me."

"You left a joker in the pack." I pointed to the man in cap and bells at the top of the triangle.

"Well of course I did," Sadie smiled. "Life is full of surprises and so are the cards."

"Is the joker good or bad?"

"He can be good, he can be bad – it all depends on what surrounds him. He can also mean that things are not what they seem, that what looks obvious may not be so obvious after all. He's a trickster."

"Is he good or bad in my cards?"

"Let's have a look and see." Sadie bent over the table, studying each side of the triangle separately. Then she leaned back in her chair and looked at me. "Is there anything you'd like to ask?"

"Not really," I said.

"Then I'll tell you some of what I can see here. Stop me if you want to ask a question. First, I know that you're a very intelligent and talented young woman but the cards didn't have to tell me that because I've talked with you and seen your films. I also know that you live alone and that you've been married once but it didn't work out. Cyrrie told me that. What he didn't tell me, and what I see here, is that you're going through a very lonely period in your life just now. So lonely you sometimes even miss your ex-husband."

"I never thought that could happen, but you're right. I have missed him lately. I guess I must be a little lonely. Either that or totally crazy. Our marriage was a disaster area."

"A little lonely?" Sadie looked at me sceptically.

"Well, maybe more than a little," I admitted. "But everyone gets lonely from time to time. It's part of being human, isn't it? Besides, you didn't need the cards to guess that I might be lonely."

"Didn't I?"

"I live alone in an isolated place in the country. I mostly work alone – nature photography is a very solitary kind of job. I think all of that makes me a pretty obvious candidate for loneliness. But I've felt this way before. It'll pass."

"That's what you're worried about, isn't it? You've been lonely before, but this time it's different. This time the loneliness has gone so deep and lasted so long you're beginning to think it will never go away. You're beginning to wonder if you'll feel like this for the rest of your life."

"Sadie, I don't mean to be rude but I don't think I want to do this right now. Please, could we stop?"

"Certainly, Phoebe. Any time you like. I'm sorry if the cards made you feel uncomfortable." She began to gather them up from the scarf.

"No, it's my fault. I guess I'm not very good at this kind of stuff."

"You're just a very private person."

"And you're not?"

"Me?" Sadie laughed. "What's to know about me? I'm an old lady who likes to garden, that's all. I was left a widow when I was forty-two. I worked as a bookkeeper at the Co-op for twenty-some years. I raised a daughter and a granddaughter. Children and gardening. That's it."

"How long have you worked on this garden?"

"Bill and I moved here when he came back from the war.

We designed the basic shape together. We spent a lot of time out in the hills looking for the perfect tree and shrub for every spot. Each of them has a story."

"Would you tell me some of them?"

"I'd love to but you'd better be sure you really mean what you say. Tracy says I'm a terrible bore about my garden. Get me started and you'll probably be here all night."

"I'm not going anywhere. At least not until you drive me. So bore away."

"Come on." Sadie pushed back her chair and stood. "I'll put the cards away and then I'll take you on a tour of my favourite plants while we still have enough light."

Sadie's large garden included the yard behind Tracy's house as well. The space was divided into three sections arranged like the leaves on a three-leaf clover. Each section featured plants found in one of the main geographical areas of southern Alberta. Even the shrubs and trees were appropriate – wolf willow and snowberry for the prairies, mountain ash and juniper for the foothills, alpine larch and Rocky Mountain rhododendron for the mountains. Scattered through each of the sections and tying them together, the domestic cultivars provided the civilizing touch that said this is a garden, a work of art as well as nature. Right now, honeysuckle and Saskatoon bushes bloomed side by side and under them a profusion of bleeding heart, late tulips, and lady's slipper.

The shadows in the garden grew long as I followed Sadie and her plants from the prairies to the foothills. By the time we reached the mountains the shadows had given way to dusk and a muted pink sunset glowed behind the pines.

"It sure chills off once the sun goes down, doesn't it?" Sadie said. "Maybe we'd better save the mountain orchids for next time. You will come again, won't you Phoebe? I've enjoyed this evening very much."

It was dark by the time Sadie drove her little red Chevy through my gate. The dog came bounding out to greet us, his earlier sulks forgotten.

"Thanks for the ride." I closed the door and held Bertie's collar while she backed out of the drive.

"Sadie!" I called after her. "Wait a minute." The Chevy stopped abruptly. "What about my joker? What did he mean?"

"That's a surprise, Phoebe." Again the youthful grin. "You'll just have to be patient and wait."

"But how will I know when it happens?"

Sadie didn't answer. Instead, she waved a jaunty goodbye and drove off into the night.

9

Despite the fact that I'd been up since before five, it took me ages to get to sleep that night. It was after one by the time I finally put down my book and turned off the light. An hour later, the telephone rang.

"Phoebe, wake up!" Candi's voice came at me through layers of dreams. "You've got to go to David Cavendish's bookstore in Okotoks right now."

"What's happened?" I sat up, swung my legs over the edge of the bed, and looked at the clock. "For God's sake, Candi, it's the middle of the night."

"I know. But Tracy needs help. I'll meet you in Okotoks as soon as I can."

"What's the matter? Has she had an accident or something?"

"No. She's okay. I just got a call from her. It's David Cavendish. Somebody beat him up. Apparently it's pretty bad. Tracy's with him at the bookstore. She wants me to come but I'm at home and it'll take me an hour to drive out there. Can you go stay with her until I get there? She really needs some help."

"Sure. But what can I do? I've never even met the guy. Besides, it sounds to me like he needs a doctor. Why doesn't she call an ambulance and get him to a hospital?"

"Because David refuses. He won't go to a hospital. Tracy says he won't even let her phone a doctor."

"What do you mean he refuses? Who gave him a choice? For all they know he's behaving irrationally because he's in shock or something. Why doesn't Tracy just go ahead and call an ambulance?"

"Come on, Phoebe, are you going to help her or not?"

"Yeah, okay. I'm on my way."

I pulled on jeans and a sweatshirt and ran a comb through my hair. The dog opened one eye, rested his chin on the side of his basket, and watched me put on my runners. As I grabbed my jacket and opened the door to leave, he sighed a little, tucked his nose under his tail, and promptly fell back to sleep. I envied him. I didn't want to be awake. I especially didn't want to be awake and dealing with Tracy and her troubles. Why she couldn't simply ignore David's protests and phone an ambulance was beyond me. Then again, she'd let Jonathan use her as his personal punching bag and that was beyond me too.

There were no other cars on the road between my house and Okotoks. I slowed to a stop for a badger dazzled by my headlights and waited while it escaped the beams and scuttled to safety across the ditch. I sat a moment longer, gazing up at drifts of stars so clear and bright against the fathomless black that they seemed close enough to dust the treetops. Me and a badger and a trillion stars. It felt like the two of us were the only living creatures out under the foothills sky that night. A few minutes later I drove into the sleeping town with its empty streets and darkened houses. The occasional insomniac's solitary light only sharpened the lonesome feeling.

I pulled up in front of David Cavendish's bookstore. I knocked on the plate-glass door and a few seconds later a dishevelled Tracy turned the bolt and let me in. She did not turn on the lights.

"Where's Candi?" She shot the bolt behind us.

"She's on her way," I said. "She'll be here as soon as she can. What happened?" A slice of light shone from the crack of an almost-closed door at the back of the store.

"They beat David up. They kicked him, Phoebe. They kicked him in the face."

"Where is he?"

"In his office." Tracy led the way past rows of books towards the light. Near the door, a large wire bookrack lay on its side, its contents scattered over the floor. The fallen paperbacks looked like someone had spattered them with red paint. The red blotches continued through the door and into a small office where David Cavendish sat huddled in a desk chair bleeding into a towel. He lifted his bruised and bloody face from the towel and looked up at me. At first I thought he was squinting against the glare of the harsh overhead neon but what I took for a squint turned out to be swelling. His left eye was completely shut. The rest of his face wasn't much better. A wide cut ran through his hair down his left temple to an inflamed and distended ear. His upper lip was split in two places and, worst of all, his nose seemed to have moved at least an inch to the left. It sat squashed onto his cheek, oozing a steady trickle of blood. He muttered something to Tracy through the gap of a missing front tooth. She knelt beside him and explained who I was.

"Good to meet you, Phoebe." David offered me his right hand with painful slowness. I couldn't believe it. Here was a guy with a nose like a mashed plum and his front teeth in his pocket and he was still busy minding his manners. As he lifted his hand I saw him notice that it was covered in blood from the towel. He wiped it on the equally bloody front of his striped pyjama top with great care, examined it again and decided that the pyjama treatment had only made things worse. After some thought, he gave the hand a slow swipe along the leg of his jeans and held it out to me again. I clasped it gingerly.

"David, we've got to get you to the hospital," I said. My palm felt sticky but I managed to resist the urge to follow his example and wipe it on my jeans.

"No, it's okay. I just need to rest a little," he mumbled, slurring his words like a drunk. "No hospital."

"David, you're not okay," I tried to reason with him. "For starters, you've got a broken nose. Unless you want it pointing at your left ear for the rest of your life you've got to get to a doctor."

"I go to a hospital and they call the police. I'm sick of police. I don't want to talk to them anymore. No more police."

"Look, for all we know you could be bleeding inside. You have to go to a hospital."

"David, Phoebe's right." Tracy's hand trembled as she brushed back a straggling lock of uncombed hair and looked up at him. "You could be hurt real bad inside. You need help."

David was about to protest again but began to retch before he could speak. For a few seconds he abandoned himself to the pain of the spasms. Then he vomited blood down his pyjamas and over the desk. He slumped back in misery while Tracy dabbed at his chest with the bloody towel in a futile effort to clean him up.

Right then, the contents of my stomach came pretty close to joining David's. I swallowed hard a couple of times and did my best to ignore the stinking puddle on the desk as I reached across it to pick up the telephone which he had mercifully managed to miss. I started to dial the emergency number.

"No ambulance." He dropped a gory paw over the phone cradle and cut off the line. "We'll go in the car. You're right, I do need to go to a hospital but I don't need an ambulance. Just the car." Vomiting blood seemed to have had a positive influence on David's attitude towards hospitals.

"Tracy, go find some blankets," I said. "We have to keep him warm on the way." I remembered all those first-aid instructions about how you were never to move an accident victim and felt vaguely guilty. However, if David had managed to make it from the store to the office and into his chair all by himself, he could probably manage a fifteen-minute car ride with a little help from me and Tracy. Besides, anything was better than standing around watching him bleed into that towel.

While Tracy went upstairs to David's apartment above the store to fetch a blanket, I ran out, started my car, and turned the heater on full blast. I returned to find her wrapping a big Hudson's Bay blanket around his shoulders. She spread a fresh towel over his lap and placed a large mixing bowl on top of it.

"I brought a bowl in case he has to be sick again before we get there." Tracy was an old hand at dealing with the aftermath of beatings.

Fortunately, David's office chair was on wheels so we pushed him in it through the store, out the front door, and over to the car. Tracy and I supported him on either side while he eased his way out of the chair and into the front seat. It was a messy process for us and a painful one for him. I was pretty sure

David had some broken ribs to add to his miseries. Tracy tucked the corner of the blanket under his legs and put the mixing bowl back on his lap.

We drove to the Oilfields Hospital along the same route Candi and Ella and I had taken last Friday in the path of Jonathan's ambulance. David reeked of vomit and blood. The car was stifling hot, which made the smell even worse. I longed to roll down my window but, despite the car heater and his thick wool blanket, David had begun to shiver. He also seemed to be falling into a doze. Or maybe he was losing consciousness. Either way, I figured we'd better keep him awake until we got him to the hospital.

"Don't fall asleep, David," I shouted at him. "David! You mustn't sleep."

"Sorry." With a mighty effort, he pulled himself back to consciousness.

"Talk to me," I said. "It'll keep you awake. Tell me what happened. Who did this to you?"

"I caught some kids robbing the store."

"David lives above the store," Tracy added unnecessarily.

"I heard noises downstairs so I pulled on a pair of jeans and my shoes and went to have a look. I think they must have got in through a basement window." David's broken nose made him sound like a man with the world's worst head cold but, on the positive side, he had at least regained a measure of control over his mouth and no longer slurred his words.

"How many of them?"

"Two. When they heard me they ran out of the office and knocked me down. Then they kicked me around."

"Did you recognize them?"

"No. Everything happened too fast." David paused, lifted the mixing bowl to his chin, and contemplated his reflection in its stainless-steel depths. I offered up a silent but heartfelt thank you when he at last lowered the bowl, still empty, and continued with his story. "They looked like every other teenage boy in town."

"What were they wearing?"

"Nothing unusual. Jeans, baseball caps, dirty runners. You know, what all the kids wear."

"Do you keep a lot of money in the store?"

"Only the cash float – sixty dollars."

"It's enough," I said. "But I can't figure out why they'd stick around to beat you up. Most kids looking for cash want to get in and out as quick as they can. It doesn't make sense for them to hang around just to kick you. What happened?"

"I don't remember much," David said. "The whole thing is pretty hazy. I don't even remember them leaving. All I know is that after a while I was lying on the floor and I was alone. Then I managed to get to the office and phone Tracy. She came right over, didn't you Tracy? You came right over after I called."

"That's right," Tracy said. "David called and I came over to his place. Then I called Candi. Right after I saw what had happened to him, I called Candi. Didn't I?"

"Yeah. You did," David agreed.

You didn't need to be one of Maud's clairvoyants to know that the pair of them were lying. Even I could tell that this account of David's beating was pure fiction. However, he and Tracy weren't making up the story for my benefit. This was a practice session, an opportunity for them to coordinate their lies and get their stories straight. They knew they'd have to come up with an official version of the night's events when we got to the hospital and this was the dress rehearsal. They were going to have to work on a few of the details. Like the shoes, for instance. No running shoe I'd ever seen could have opened a cut like the one on David's head. Something bigger and heavier in the footwear department had done that, something like work boots with metal toes.

"Why didn't you call the police?" I asked, curious as to how they were going to explain away this glaring omission.

"I must have fainted," David said. "I don't remember anything until Tracy got there." Not a bad story considering the shape he was in, but it did leave Tracy holding the bag.

"When I got there and saw all the blood and David almost unconscious and everything, I guess I must have panicked," she said. "I mean I really didn't know what to do or anything when I saw him sitting there all bloody, and in all the confusion I forgot about the police. I got confused and forgot." Well, that bit obviously needed some extra polish but, from what I'd seen of her, I knew she'd pull something together in time for the big performance. "Besides, David's right," she continued. "We've had too many police asking us questions. What good would it have done to call them? They'll never catch those kids."

"You were too confused to call the police but you weren't too confused to call Candi," I said.

"Oh no, Candi! I forgot to leave a note on the door of the bookstore," Tracy wailed. "Candi will get there and she won't know where we've gone." Tracy was also a pretty good evader. Lying and evasion. Two skills she'd probably had to develop into an art form just to survive life with Jonathan Webster.

"Don't worry about Candi." I could see the lights of the hospital ahead. "She'll figure it out." I slowed down for the turn into the driveway. "Why can't you tell me what really happened?" I asked David. "No police, no hospital – what's the real reason?" We pulled up in front of the emergency door.

"I'll go get someone to bring a stretcher." Tracy was out of the car and into the hospital the second the car stopped.

David didn't answer my question. Instead, he held out his hand to me again. "Thanks Phoebe. You've been a good friend and I don't even know you. I hope we can talk sometime." He tried to smile and made the cut on his lip start to bleed again.

"David, why won't you tell the truth? A couple of teenagers out for a little easy B&E cash didn't do this to you. What really happened?

He looked at me. "Phoebe, I wish . . ." He hesitated and then with a painful shrug turned away and buried his head in the mixing bowl.

A few seconds later a nurse and an orderly lifted him onto a gurney and wheeled him into the hospital. Tracy held his hand all the way to the desk but they made her stay behind when they carted him off to the ward to assess the damage. That put the two of us back in the waiting room with the old *Reader's Digest*s. I considered asking Tracy some more questions about what had happened but she was a far better liar than I was a questioner so the whole exercise would have been pointless. Instead, for the next twenty minutes while she sat and stared at the linoleum, I read through the "Life's Like That" column in a stack of the *Digest*s. The linoleum was probably more interesting.

Finally, a very young doctor came to talk to us. It makes me nervous when doctors are younger than I am, but Cyrrie says I'd better get used to it because the older you get, the younger they get. Despite her obvious weariness, this one was relentlessly upbeat and chipper, a cheerleader with a stethoscope for a pompom. Maybe it was her way of coping with too much work and not enough sleep – just switch to auto-cheerful and let it fly.

"Your friend is going to be A-okay. He might be a little sore for a while but it doesn't look like there's any internal damage. He got off pretty lightly – a broken nose, couple of cracked ribs, mild concussion, a few cuts and bruises – nothing much to worry about."

"But what about all the blood?" Tracy said.

"They bleed buckets those scalp cuts," the doctor continued blithely. "They look pretty gruesome but mostly they look way worse than they are. He really hasn't lost all that much blood. That cut on the left side of his head was a mess but it's all stitched up now. His nose might need a little more work but basically, he's going to be just fine."

"But he was vomiting blood," Tracy protested.

"That's nothing to worry about," the doctor airily dismissed her concerns. "He'd swallowed a lot of blood from his broken nose and woofed it up, that's all. Like I said, he might be a little uncomfortable for a few days but he's going to be fine." Uncomfortable or in agony – I guess it all depends from which end of the stethoscope you experience the pain.

"When can he go home?" Tracy asked anxiously. "Can we take him now?"

"I'd like to keep him in overnight, just to keep an eye on him. You don't want to take chances with even a mild concussion."

"Can I see him?"

"For a few minutes. The police are going to want to talk to him tonight too. Mr. Cavendish said you hadn't called them before you came so we took care of it for you. They said they'd send an officer along to ask you some questions." The doctor turned abruptly and set off for the ward at a brisk pace trailing Tracy behind her.

I opened another *Digest* and started in on the disaster of the month. The cafeteria was long closed, but one of the nurses kindly brought me a cup of coffee from the staff lounge. I hoped it would help keep me awake but it seemed to have the opposite effect. I could hardly keep my eyes focused on the page. I must have nodded off because next thing I knew Candi was shaking me gently by the shoulder. She'd already removed the cup from my hand.

"Where's Tracy?"

"In with David." I put the magazine down and rubbed a nasty little kink in my neck. So much for falling asleep sitting up. "The doctor says he's going to be okay. No serious damage done."

"Who beat him up?"

"Apparently he interrupted a couple of teenage boys burgling the bookstore. At least that's the story he and Tracy are handing out for public consumption."

"What do you mean, public consumption? What's going on?"

I told her exactly what had happened from the time of my arrival at David's bookstore. "I don't know why," I concluded my story, "but neither of them is telling the truth." I stood and stretched and looked out the window at the first rosy greys of dawn. A police car turned into the hospital drive and pulled up at the front doors.

"Maybe they were afraid," Candi said. "Maybe someone is threatening them. I'll bet this is connected with Jonathan's death somehow."

Tracy arrived back in the waiting room just as the Mountie from the car walked through the emergency admitting doors. He spoke to the nurse at the desk who pointed in our direction.

"Are you the women who brought David Cavendish to the hospital tonight?" His boots were burnished to such a lustre that I could see the ceiling lights reflected in their toes. The rest of the man's broad-shouldered six-foot-four was a credit to his footwear. He looked gorgeous in his uniform and knew it. I wondered how he managed to cope with the sheer splendour of himself when he wore the red dress uniform.

"We brought him," Tracy pointed to me. "Phoebe and me. I'm David's friend, Tracy McMurtry."

"Miss McMurtry, I'd like to ask you a few questions about what happened tonight." The voice matched the looks.

"It's pretty late," Tracy said. "Couldn't it wait until morning? David's going to be okay. That's what really matters."

"This will only take a minute or two. It's important that we talk while things are still fresh in your mind. Your friends can stay with you." He pulled out a notebook and we all sat down together in the waiting room.

The constable was polite but perfunctory. His questions were totally routine and he didn't seem surprised by or much interested in any of the answers. I was pretty sure he hadn't recognized Tracy's name and so hadn't made the connection between her and Jonathan Webster. The first questions he asked were for me and Candi – our names and addresses, our relation to Tracy. He recorded all this carefully in his book. Then he moved on to Tracy. She stuck pretty much to the story she and David had concocted earlier although she did come up with a more elaborate reason for not calling the police first thing.

"You see, I thought it would be quicker if we drove David to the hospital ourselves. Waiting for the police and then waiting for an ambulance could have taken a lot of time. In all the shock and confusion, I'm afraid I probably wasn't thinking too clearly. All I could think about was getting David to a doctor as fast as possible."

She didn't mention why she had the presence of mind to call Candi, nor why, if she and David were in such a hurry to get to the hospital, they had waited until I came and drove them. Tracy didn't have to explain because the constable didn't bother to ask. This surprised me. Neither Inspector Debarets nor Constable Lindt, the only other police officers I had experienced in action, would have been this sloppy. This guy might score a full six for artistic impression but he was zip for technical merit.

"Right." He closed his notebook and stood. "Thanks Miss McMurtry. That's all for now. An officer will come around tomorrow morning to have a look at the store. Will someone be there?"

"I guess I will be," Tracy said. "Someone's got to clean the place up."

"Don't do any cleaning or tidying before the officer gets there. Just leave everything as it is. I'll try to arrange for someone to be there around eight."

He went back to the admitting desk, spoke with the nurse again, and then followed her into the ward. If his questions to David were as routine and by the book as the ones he'd asked Tracy, then David didn't have much to worry about.

"What time is it?" Candi asked.

"Almost five," I yawned. My mouth was fuzzy with sleep and bad coffee and the rest of me felt rumpled and grumpy.

"Let's go have some coffee." Candi, on the other hand, looked like she always does, fresh and crisp and immaculately groomed. I swear they could ring a fire alarm in the middle of the night and she'd be awake and out two seconds later looking perfect. It isn't fair.

"I've had too much coffee," I said. "I want to go home to bed."

"What's the point?" Candi countered. "You'd only have to get up in an hour anyway. Remember? You promised you'd help me edit this week's 'Lifestyle' and we're booked for nine this morning."

"I'd forgotten," I admitted. Now that Ella was on maternity leave, editing duties for the season's last episode of "A Day in the Lifestyle" had fallen to Candi. In a moment of weakness, I'd volunteered to help.

"Maybe you could drop me off on your way to Phoebe's place," Tracy said.

"Come with us," Candi insisted. "Have some coffee while Phoebe gets ready for work. We'll take you home on our way into Calgary. It's more convenient that way." It wasn't, but Tracy didn't feel like arguing with Candi any more than I did.

The world was dew-fresh and new under the five o'clock sky and every bird in the foothills sang its song to the morning sun. There seemed to be a meadowlark for every fence post and telephone pole on the road between the hospital and my house. Tracy and I drove in silence, windows down, listening to their concert. Candi followed in her car. I wasn't surprised that Tracy had chosen to drive with me. I suspected that she was avoiding Candi and her inevitable questions.

I put Tracy to work making coffee and toast while I tidied the bed away and opened the patio doors to the deck. Candi took the dog for a short walk. Bertie had been so overwhelmed with delight to find her at his door when he woke up that he needed a calming run in the pasture to help him recover from the thrill. The morning was still too chilly to sit out on the deck so when Candi returned we ate our toast at my dining-room table.

"What really happened last night?" Candi put down her mug and looked at Tracy.

"You heard what I told the policeman," Tracy answered.

"Yeah, I heard," Candi agreed. "But I still don't know what really happened. Tracy, why won't you tell us the truth? What are you afraid of?"

Tracy didn't answer. She sat looking miserable, her coffee mug clasped in both hands.

"All this is connected to Jonathan somehow, isn't it? Is someone threatening you?"

Tracy started to cry.

"Come on Tracy, you can't keep on lying and then crying about it. You've got to trust someone," Candi said gently. "It might as well be me and Phoebe. Tell us what happened. Maybe we can help."

Tracy stared into her coffee mug. None of us spoke. Finally she broke the silence. "You have to promise that you won't tell anyone what I'm going to tell you."

"You know we can't promise you that," Candi said.

"Then I can't tell you anything."

"Look Tracy, Jonathan was murdered and someone beat up David. Those are facts. They're not going to go away, no matter how many lies you tell," Candi said. "Please, tell us what's going on. We can't help you if you don't tell us the truth."

Another silence, this time a longer one. Finally Tracy made her decision. She wiped her eyes on the back of her hand, took a gulp of cold coffee, and started to talk.

"Two guys came and beat him up. They didn't come to rob the store. They came to beat up David."

"Start at the beginning."

"It started pretty much like David said. We'd just gone to bed when we heard a noise in the store. He went down to see what it was. I put on some clothes and went after him and there were these two guys waiting for us in the office."

"Did you recognize them?"

"No, not exactly. Well, sort of, I guess."

"Either you did or you didn't," Candi said. "You can't sort of recognize someone."

"I mean that I'd never seen them before but I did recognize one of their voices. The fat one. He phoned me yesterday morning. He said that Jonathan had owed his boss a lot of money and that he was coming around to collect."

"How much did Jonathan owe?"

"Forty-three thousand. I said I couldn't pay. I told him I didn't have any money. He never even answered me. He just hung up."

"What did they look like?" I asked

"Like I said, one was real fat. He had a big tattoo on his arm. A woman and a snake. It was disgusting. The other was sort of skinny and he had bad acne. His hair was in a pony-tail."

"Sounds like the pair that came to your house last Thursday night," I said. "The ones that the Three Graces described."

"Did these guys say anything?" Candi asked.

"Plenty," Tracy said. "They said they'd come to collect their boss's money. I said I'd already told them I didn't have that kind of money, and that's when they started beating David. They knocked him down and started kicking him. I tried to stop them but what could I do? They just kept on kicking him. Then they said they'd be back later this week for the money and if I didn't have it then they'd beat me up too."

"So why didn't you call the police?"

"Because they said if I told the police, they'd hurt my grandma."

"And you believed them?"

"Of course I believed them," Tracy replied with feeling. "I'd just watched them beating David. Why wouldn't I believe them?"

"Did they say who sent them? Did you get a name?"

Tracy shook her head. "They just called him the boss. They never said his name. They said that Jonathan owed their boss money. That's all."

"But you knew all along Jonathan was in debt," Candi said. "And that puts us right back where we left off yesterday afternoon."

"Candi, I swear I didn't know anything about any debts," Tracy protested vehemently. "Not until I got that phone call yesterday. Jonathan owed me money but that's the only debt I knew about. Honest. I only knew about the times he borrowed from me."

"How much did he owe you?"

"Some." Tracy shifted her gaze to the coffee mug again.

"How much is some?"

"Well," again the hesitation. "Quite a lot I guess but I'm not sure exactly how much. They were kind of unofficial loans. I mean I don't have any IOUs on paper or anything like that so I guess I couldn't actually prove that I loaned anything to him. Jonathan said that we didn't have to make the loans official because we were like husband and wife and what was his was mine and what was mine was his."

"Except he didn't have anything," Candi said.

"He did at first," Tracy protested. "I know you guys didn't like him but he wasn't always like he was when you met him. When I first knew him he was wonderful. Before the gambling started. That's when he changed."

"When was that?"

"A few months after we started living together. He and Eddy had been in business for about six months and I'd worked for them all that time. That's when they sold me my five per cent of Foxy Locks and when I moved in with Jonathan. He'd bought a big house by the Elbow River. The backyard ran right down to the water. We even had a canoe. It was beautiful."

"Business must have been pretty good if he could afford a house on the river," Candi said. "How did you pay for your five per cent?"

"A few years ago, I inherited a trust fund from my father's estate. My dad died when I was three and left a little bit of insurance money for me that started the fund. I guess the trust company that looked after it did a pretty good job because there was really quite a bit of money. I mean it wasn't a fortune or anything but I thought it was a lot. I used some of it to pay for my share."

"So you had a house, a business, and a trust fund. Sounds to me like you were sitting pretty. What happened?"

"Jonathan's gambling happened. It's hard to say when it got so out of control. I mean it started out okay. It was even sort of fun. Sometimes when the weather got too depressing in the winter, we'd hop a plane for Vegas for a few days. We'd play some golf, take in a couple of shows, play a little blackjack in the casinos. I enjoyed it. The only thing was that sometimes it was hard to get Jonathan to leave the casino, especially if he was down, but we always had to go catch the flight home."

"Did you take these trips often?"

"We only went about once every few months at first. Then we started to go a little more often. Sometimes I couldn't get away so Jonathan would go without me. Then pretty soon he started going without me all the time. By then, all he wanted to do was gamble so I was just in the way. Sometimes he'd miss the plane home. He always had a good excuse but I knew it was because of the gambling."

"He only gambled in Las Vegas?"

"No, he used to go to casinos here in Calgary too. You know, those charity things. He didn't like it as much here because the house skim in Alberta is so high. The odds aren't nearly as good here as they are in Vegas but he still went."

"He gambled at the track too, didn't he?"

"Jonathan spent a lot of time at the track. He read the racing form every day. Not that it helped him much. I think he lost pretty badly last season." Tracy's story matched Sandra's. "I'm pretty sure he did some sports gambling too, you know football point-spread stuff. But I don't know where he did that. I don't think it's legal here."

"Did he always lose?"

"Not always. Especially not at first. Actually he won quite a lot sometimes. The trouble was he never knew when to quit. I guess he couldn't quit. He'd go right back and lose whatever he'd won."

"And he always played for high stakes?"

"No, that came later too. When we first went to Las Vegas he'd take five hundred dollars for both of us to gamble with. He'd say, 'If we lose this babe, then we're done.' And I think he meant it. Sometimes we'd come home a little down, sometimes we'd be a little up. Except for once. I guess it was the third or fourth time we went to Vegas that he won pretty big. He hit on one of those crazy giant jackpot slots and won twenty thousand dollars. He gambled with that for the rest of our stay and we still went home with a couple of thousand."

"And that changed things?"

"Yeah, I think it did. After that it wasn't good enough to take our five hundred. We had to take the twenty thousand. He called it his lucky stake."

"But I thought you said he only had two thousand of it left."

"Tell that to a compulsive gambler. I don't know how many times he lost that twenty thousand. I know our house by the river went pretty quick. That's why we moved out to Okotoks. The house there belongs to my grandma and she let us have it for nothing."

"Is that what happened to the business? Did it become a part of the lucky twenty thousand, too?"

"I don't know for sure but I think so. I never did get to know all the details about how Foxy Locks went down. You'd have to ask Eddy Sedge about that."

"Is that when you started lending Jonathan money? When the business went broke?"

Tracy shook her head. "No. I'd started before that. My money was supposed to keep the business afloat. He told me we were having some temporary cash-flow problems and that my money would make all the difference."

"How much of a difference?"

"Twenty thousand the first time. Ten the next. Thirty the last time."

"Tracy, that's sixty thousand dollars!"

"Plus the original twenty I'd put up to buy in."

"Eighty thousand dollars! Didn't his partner say anything?"

"Jonathan told me not to tell Eddy about the money. He said he knew that Eddy was ripping him off somehow, that Eddy was the reason Foxy Locks was in trouble in the first place and he didn't want him ripping me off too."

"But his partner must have known. How could he not know about sixty thousand dollars cash on his books?"

"I don't know," Tracy said. "I'm only telling you what Jonathan told me because that's all I know. Anyway, the money didn't do any good because the business still went bust."

"Do you think Edward Sedge was ripping him off?"

"If he was he didn't do a very good job. Eddy's back working at La Maison and from what I hear he's as broke as I am."

"That was all your money? The eighty thousand."

"No. I still had a bit left. It's what we lived on until Jonathan lost the last of it. That was some time near the end of February."

"What have you been living on since?"

"My mom and stepfather send me money for my birthday and Christmas. Plus I did some card-reading. And I had a real job at a little beauty shop in High River for a while. It was strictly blue rinse but I didn't care. I liked it there."

"Why did you leave?"

"They said I wasn't regular enough. They needed someone they could count on. I wasn't feeling too well a lot of the time back then."

"Is that because Jonathan was beating you?"

Tracy nodded, dumb with misery and shame. "He'd only done it a few times before that. Sometimes when he'd lost real bad. But he was always sorry after. He always said he was sorry and I know he meant it."

"But he'd started to beat you more often."

Again the nod. "I didn't have any more money left to help him. I couldn't do anything."

"Why didn't you leave him?"

"I know that must be hard to understand," Tracy said. "I don't honestly know why myself. I guess I was so afraid of him I couldn't leave."

"Couldn't you have gone to the police and had him charged with assault?"

"You think that would have stopped him? Look Candi, Jonathan was crazy. The guy was totally nuts. You couldn't

174

tell what he was going to do next. He could have killed me. You know the police can't do a damn thing about men like Jonathan."

"What about the ozone machine business? How did he get started in that?" I asked.

"Inspector Debarets wanted to know about that too," Tracy said. "Jonathan had always been a health nut. When I first met him he was into eating all this special stuff and exercising every day. That never changed. Except the exercise maybe. Sometimes when he was gambling a lot he didn't have time to work out. Anyway, this guy who used to sell us some of our supplies at Foxy Locks had a line on these machines and he sold one to Jonathan, gave him a real deal on it. A little later he asked Jonathan if he'd like a franchise to sell SuperOs through the salon. Jonathan wanted to do it but Eddy wouldn't let him. Then after the business went bust, Jonathan called the guy and asked if the franchise was still available."

"How much did that cost you?"

"Only a couple of thousand. Jonathan already had his own machine that he could use to do his sales pitch."

"I still can't figure out how those things are legal," I said. "Where's the Department of Health and Welfare when you need them?"

"There's not really much they can do. SuperOs aren't sold as medical equipment and they don't come with any kind of guarantee," Tracy explained. "If you buy one you have to sign a contract that says you're voluntarily taking part in an experiment and that if you get hurt it's your own fault. It's all pretty complicated."

"Couldn't people sue the manufacturers or something?" Candi asked.

"Good luck finding them. A European company markets them but the machines are actually made somewhere in Southeast Asia. It'd be nearly impossible to track down the manufacturer. Besides, even if it doesn't do any good, the SuperO probably doesn't do much harm either."

"But Tracy, the SuperO killed Jonathan," Candi said with more patience than I could have mustered. "I'd call that harmful."

Tracy started to cry again. "You guys, what am I going to do? How am I going to get that money? I can't let those men hurt Grandma."

"Maybe you could make a deal with their boss," Candi suggested. "He doesn't care about your grandmother. All he wants is his money. Maybe you could arrange to make regular payments or something. Sort of take over Jonathan's account."

"How can I arrange anything with him when I don't even know who he is?" Tracy wailed.

Candi thought for a moment. "Phoebe," she turned to me, "do you know any loan sharks?"

10

"Putting this stuff together is harder than it looks, isn't it?" Candi placed the finished tape of this week's "A Day in the Lifestyle" in its case. "I thought I'd planned it out so carefully that it would only take us a couple of hours, but it's almost one. It never takes Ella this long."

"Ella's a really good editor." I pushed my chair back from the editing console. "And she's had a lot of practice. You'll get a lot quicker when you've done as much of it as she has."

"Ella's such a fuss-budget you sometimes forget how good she is at her job," Candi admitted. "I miss her."

"Me too." I stood up and stretched.

"I guess I'd better stick this in Ella's filing cabinet." Candi gathered the pages of her script.

"What about the tape?"

"I've got to get it duped. I promised Ella I'd bring her a copy before the program airs this week." We started down the hall to Ella's office. "Then what about bookies?" Candi asked. It took me a minute to realize that this was a direct continuation of our early-morning conversation. "You don't know any loan sharks but do you know any bookies? Maybe Jonathan owed a bookie." She spoke as if there had been no six-hour interruption.

"Why on earth would I know a bookie?"

"Well, you've worked for News." Another piece of Candi logic zoomed past me.

"So that means I'm a gambler?"

"No. But it means that you might have photographed a bookie when you were on a story. You know, covering the criminal element and all that."

"Sorry. Not one single illegal bookmaker ever crossed my lens. Actually I never photographed that many criminals of any kind when I was with News. Unless you count politicians."

"Look, we've got to be able to find a way to contact whoever employs those two goons that beat up David. There's a connection between that beating and Jonathan's murder. I know it. After all, they were out at Jonathan's house that night. Their boss could have sent them to kill Jonathan."

"Why would they kill Jonathan when he owed them money? That doesn't make sense. He was worth more to their boss alive than dead. Besides, the Graces said they didn't go into the house."

"Yeah, I guess you've got a point," she conceded. "But I still think there's a connection and we've got to find out what it is. Only how are we going to talk to this boss guy if we don't know anybody who can help us find him? I mean, other loan sharks and bookies would know who he is but we don't know any of them so where does that leave us?" We went into Ella's office. Candi dropped the script into the top drawer of the filing cabinet. "Unless . . ." she paused, "unless we know somebody who does know. Somebody like Cyrrie." The drawer closed with an emphatic little thump.

"Cyrrie? That's ridiculous. Unless the garden club has taken to making book on petunia of the year Cyrrie's even less likely to know a bookie than we are."

"Come on, Phoebe," Candi insisted. "Cyrrie has spent a lot of time at the track, he knows all kinds of people there. Maybe he's heard a name or something. Or maybe someone he knows will know. It can't hurt to ask him, can it? I'm on my lunch break. We can go right now."

We found Cyrrie in his garden pruning a dogwood bush. Edith was busy in the house finishing the lunch dishes.

"My dears, what a pleasant surprise." Cyrrie put down the secateurs and took off his gardening gloves. "May I offer you something? A cup of tea, a glass of lemonade?"

"No thanks Cyrrie," Candi declined. "I don't have much time. I have to be back at work before two. We came to ask you if you know any bookies."

"You certainly don't believe in beating about the bush, do you Candida?" Cyrrie said when he stopped laughing. "And may I ask why you need the services of a bookmaker? Are you ladies planning an important wager?"

"Well," Candi hesitated, "it's kind of complicated."

She was right. We could hardly come right out and tell Cyrrie we were looking for a pair of under goons who had beaten up David so we could track down the boss goon. He'd think, with some justification, that we'd taken leave of our senses.

"Tracy thinks that the bookie Jonathan dealt with still has some of his money," I plunged in. "You know, some bets that he actually won. Candi thinks if we can find out who it is then maybe Tracy can get some of the money." Usually I'm a rotten liar but I felt this wasn't a bad effort for an amateur. It had a certain improvisational freshness. Maybe I'd been around

Tracy enough lately that some of her natural talent was rubbing off.

"To help her pay for his funeral." Candi added what I thought was an unnecessary flourish. Even I know that the first principle of the successful lie is keep it simple.

"I had no idea that illegal bookmakers were in the habit of returning money to their deceased clients' estates." Clearly, Cyrrie had not bought our story. "How refreshingly altruistic of them."

"We don't know for sure whether they do or not," Candi admitted, "but it couldn't hurt to ask, could it?"

"Hunting down criminals to ask them for money seems to me to have a distinct potential for hurt," Cyrrie said. "Do you think what you're doing is wise? Shouldn't the police or Tracy's lawyer be looking after this?"

"We're not hunting anyone down," Candi protested. "We just want to talk to Jonathan's bookie, that's all. We need to talk to someone who could help us find him and we thought that you might have heard a name when you were at the track. You know, someone who could at least give us a lead. Another bookie maybe."

"Sorry but I don't know the kind of people at the track who know bookies. I'm not even certain that there are such people as illegal bookmakers anymore. There are so many places to gamble legally nowadays, there can't be much call for their services."

"So we've reached a dead end." I tried not to sound too relieved.

"And you've never ever even heard the name of a bookie in Calgary?" Candi was not willing to admit defeat so readily.

"Well, I wouldn't quite say that," Cyrrie admitted. "I have

met Two Bob Roberts. He was a patient of Andrew's for many years." My uncle had been a dentist. "I believe he's living in the Hillside Home now. If he's living anywhere, that is. The man must be ninety if he's a day."

"And he's a bookie?" Candi asked. "This Two Bob person?"

"Robert Roberts the Second. He's been retired for years. And bookmaking wasn't actually his full-time business, it was more of a sideline. Two Bob was a plumbing contractor who did a little bookmaking. Mostly for people he knew – friends or friends of friends, that sort of thing. Nothing that would upset the law very much. Andrew told me that Two Bob had learned bookmaking from his father, the first Robert Roberts. The father had been a bookmaker in England before he immigrated to Calgary sometime around the turn of the century. I guess bookmaking was in the Roberts' blood."

"And you know this old guy?" I asked. "Two Bob the Second."

"Yes. I met him long after he had retired. He still liked to come to the track on an occasional Saturday afternoon. Andrew introduced me to him. He's a charming old chap."

"Is the Two Bob family still in the bookmaking business?" I asked.

"I have no idea," Cyrrie said. "I know Two Bob had a son but I believe he was killed in a car accident a few years ago. There was a grandson too. I remember he used to bring the little fellow to the track now and then. The grandson was about your age Phoebe, so that would make him old enough to run a business by now."

"Could you arrange for us to talk to him?" Candi asked. "Two Bob the second, I mean. Not his grandson."

"I suppose I could but there wouldn't be much point, would

there? After all, the man retired years ago. He isn't likely to know much about the current state of illegal gambling in Calgary."

"Do it for us anyway, won't you Cyrrie?" Candi coaxed. "It's all we've got."

"Come inside and I'll phone the Hillside Home and see what I can arrange for you. At least you can't get yourselves into any trouble talking to old Two Bob." Cyrrie gave in to Candi's persuasion, but it was obvious that he did not believe his elderly acquaintance would be any help to us whatsoever. We followed him into the house and left him in the kitchen looking up the Hillside Home's number in the phone book while we went to say hello to Edith.

Edith had finished the dishes and was in the living room with her feet up reading the *Herald*.

"Are we still on for tomorrow?" I asked her.

"The bread for the picnic sandwiches is doing its first rise right now." Edith folded the paper and put it on the floor beside her chair.

"I'll pick you up at nine," I said.

"It makes me so angry that you have to drive all the way into town to get me, Phoebe. If only I could hire a car while I'm here. God spare me from bureaucrats and their stupid rules and regulations. One little accident in January and they won't let me drive. So unfair. Everyone has the occasional fender-bender, as you Canadians call them." For Edith, bashing the car was at least a bimonthly event. Her Rover spent more time in the body shop than it did in her garage. Edith had landed herself in the hospital a couple of times too, one of them for a serious concussion. Her driving was a constant worry to Cyrrie. "And if all the people who've had insignificant little accidents were not allowed to drive, the roads would be empty. Surely one or two tiny scrapes are not sufficient reason to take away my licence. I know they wouldn't do that to a young person."

In her last "tiny scrape," Edith had sideswiped a fish van. The Rover and Edith survived with minor damage but the van was a write-off. Fortunately, its driver only suffered a broken arm and a mild concussion. The accident was deemed to be entirely Edith's fault and her driver's licence was suspended. Her reign of terror on the Essex country lanes had come to an end.

"Not to worry, old girl. I'll drive you out to Phoebe's." Cyrrie joined us in the living room.

"But it's blatant ageism, Cyril. Isn't that what they call prejudice against old people now? Ageism?" Edith wasn't about to be mollified so easily.

"I've set up an appointment for the two of you to see Robert Roberts the Second at eleven o'clock on Wednesday morning," Cyrrie said. "The nurse I spoke to says he's looking forward to it. Here's his room number at the home." He handed Candi a slip of paper.

"You spoke to a nurse, not to Mr. Roberts himself?" I said. "Is there something wrong with him?"

"If you mean has the old boy gone gaga then no, there's nothing wrong with him that way. He's just hard of hearing, that's all. He finds talking on the phone very difficult so the staff at the home pass on his messages. That's why you'll have to go there and talk to him in person."

"So there's nothing wrong with his memory," Candi said.

"He's 'bright as a button,' and that's a direct quote from the nurse I spoke to," Cyrrie said. "She sounded kind so I forgave her the expression. Even if he isn't much help to you, I expect the old boy will enjoy your visit. As I remember, Two Bob has quite an eye for the ladies. Fine-looking fillies – that was his term for good-looking young women. And fine-looking fillies you are, the pair of you. Exceptionally fine-looking fillies."

"Cyrrie, you just made that up," Candi said.

"Did I?" he teased.

"Do stop yawning, Phoebe." Edith smothered a yawn of her own. "It's so contagious."

"Sorry." I did my best to suppress the next one but only succeeded in making my eyes water. My missed night of sleep was catching up with me.

Candi looked at her watch. "I have to run or I'm going to be late for work. Come on, Phoebe, I'll drop you off at the station so you can pick up your car." Candi, on the other hand, was still going strong.

By the time I did a little grocery shopping and picked up my dry cleaning, it was nearly four when I got home. I phoned Ella to tell her we had finished editing the program and to make a date to see her and Margaret Phoebe Candida on Wednesday afternoon. Sitting down while we talked was a mistake. By the time I hung up, I could hardly keep my eyes open. The only thing that kept me from diving between the sheets was the realization that if I went to bed at four I'd be wide awake and ready to go by eleven and that would screw up my sleep schedule for another day. Instead, I took the dog for a walk along the creek that marks the west boundary of my land and separates it from the forest reserve. When we returned I decided I would probably do more harm than good if I tried to work on anything that demanded concentration, so instead, I did a major house-clean. For me, a major clean means that you actually move the furniture when you vacuum.

"Why aren't you bald?" I asked the dog as he followed me and the vacuum cleaner round the room. "I've picked up enough of your hair in this machine to knit a pair of corgis. And what about those disgusting nose prints on the patio door? How many times have I told you about that nose? God, you're a slob Bertie." He wagged his tail.

By the time I'd finished cleaning it was eight-thirty and the house looked great. I showered and then heated a can of chicken-noodle soup for dinner. I managed a half a bowl before I finally gave in, crawled into bed, and slept straight through until seven the next morning.

Cyrrie dropped Edith and the picnic basket off at my house a little before ten. The cloudless sky was a deep, intense blue, the kind of blue that promises a hot day to come.

"Did you bring something cooler to put on later?" I asked. Edith was wearing a tweed skirt and jacket, a wool pullover, a well-polished pair of brogues, and a Tilley hat that Cyrrie had given to her. It was an outfit made for the cool damp of the English countryside. "It's supposed to get pretty hot later on."

"It's hot now." Edith fanned herself with her hat. She has a distinctly British attitude towards heat. She regards twenty-five degrees Celsius as uncomfortably hot and anything over that as a tropical heat wave. Even up in the foothills, Edith and those heavy tweeds were not going to find happiness together on a sunny June afternoon in Alberta. "But I didn't bring anything cooler because I thought the tweeds would be good protection against mosquitoes."

"I don't think there'll be many mosquitoes where we're going. Besides, I've got some insect repellant in my workbag so we'll be okay. Let me lend you some lighter clothes."

With some misgivings, Edith exchanged her wool sweater for a T-shirt but she refused to swap her tweeds for a cotton skirt.

Finally, with Edith in the front seat, the dog in the back, and the picnic lunch and my camera equipment stowed in the trunk, we set off for Okotoks and Sadie Nightingale's house. Sadie was waiting for us on her front steps looking very comfortable and sporty in white slacks, a red cotton T-shirt, and runners. She had a red and white sweatshirt draped over her shoulders and a Blue Jays baseball cap perched on her short grey curls. I could see Edith eyeing her outfit enviously. Sadie climbed into the backseat with the dog, I aimed the car west, and our expedition to the Sheep River officially began.

I love the drive up the Sheep. Just west of Turner Valley the road begins its climb into the hills. Soon the view opens out onto the river valley itself, wide and sprawling against the backdrop of the Highwood Range. This morning, the mountains' snowy peaks reflected the morning sun in a dazzle of white on blue.

We crossed Macabee Creek. The late snow and spring rains had caused the usually small stream to overflow its banks and fill the marshy area on either side with its muddy brown water. A couple of hundred yards from the road, a moose grazed in the grassy shallows. I couldn't resist stopping to take a shot of him although, strictly speaking, I already had more than enough of this kind of footage in stock.

I pulled the car off the road and got the camera and tripod from the trunk. I put the zoom lens to maximum and the moose's massive head filled the viewfinder. If I hadn't had Edith and Sadie with me, I'd probably have gone down into the marsh to get a closer shot. However, it was just as well they were along because I had so much work to do for *Right in Your Own Backyard* on this excursion that I had no time to waste chasing a moose who wasn't in the script. Today was Mountain Torrent Day.

The moose raised his head to sniff the wind. His nose dripped water, and strands of soggy grass trailed from his mouth. I called to Edith and Sadie to come have a look at him through the viewfinder. They had followed me out of the car but were so busy talking to each other that they could barely spare a minute for a quick squint. The pair of them had no time for wildlife that morning. They were too involved in the odd and totally absorbing process of becoming friends. They seemed to be telling each other the story of their lives and, since they'd both lived long and full ones, condensing the narratives into a few hours' talk demanded their full attention. By the time we climbed back into the car and continued on our way they'd got through their childhoods (Sadie's happy on a farm near Drumheller and Edith's so-so in a London townhouse) and made it to the point where they met their husbands (Sadie at a church dance and Edith at a country house weekend). At times, I'm sure they forgot I was there. In a way, listening to them felt like eavesdropping. But it was fascinating. I found out all sorts of things about Edith that I'd never known before.

It's only about thirty-five kilometres from Turner Valley to the picnic area where I planned to park Edith and Sadie while I worked. Today, thanks to my frequent stops, the trip took us well over an hour. The road itself is pretty good, although there are steep drops off the shoulder and in a couple of places the curves are very sharp. The last eighteen kilometres, from the government information centre on, are only open to traffic from mid-May to late autumn. This year, due to the late winter, the big gates hadn't swung open for the season until the end of May. In spite of the hard winter and heavy spring rains we'd had, the pavement was in surprisingly good shape. A road crew had already been at work repairing the frost heaves and filling the worst of the pot-holes with tar and gravel.

They should fill in the Texas gates too, I thought to myself as we hit one and bounced across. I'd been so caught up in the story of Edith's courtship that the gate had snuck up on me and we'd taken it too fast.

"What on earth was that?" a started Edith exclaimed just as she was about to accept a proposal of marriage.

"A Texas gate," Sadie answered. "The road to the Sheep is full of them. So the cattle won't stray."

"Oh, you mean a cattle grid," Edith said. "We have them all over England. Texas gate," she sniffed. "Trust the Yanks to think they invented them."

"You find them all through the foothills too," Sadie said. "Darned things can be pretty hard on your car."

"Not if you drive reasonably." Edith, who has never driven a half-sane mile in her entire life, let alone a reasonable one, cast a severely pointed look in my direction.

The higher the road climbs into the hills, the more frequent the Texas gates become. I drove over them very sedately but Edith and Sadie were too busy talking to notice either the gates or the cattle grazing at the side of the road. They didn't even pause for breath when I pulled off the road into the parking lot at a viewpoint high above the river. I got out of the car and stood at the barrier looking down at a Sheep River I didn't recognize. It thundered through the steep rock walls of the narrowing gorge with a volume and violence I'd never seen before. I got the camera and took some shots. These ones I would use in the film but the sight was so unusual that I wanted my own record too.

We arrived at the picnic area at the end of the road shortly before twelve. Edith and Sadie had made it up to the birth of their children. This time they actually noticed that we'd stopped.

"Would you like to go have a look at the river?" I asked. I could hear the rush of fast-flowing water even before I opened the car door. "It's just over there." I pointed in the direction of the sound.

"We could do with a little walk to stretch our legs," Edith said, climbing out of the car.

"And we can watch you do some filming," Sadie added.

"I don't think I'll start shooting until after lunch," I said. "The light on the water won't be quite right yet."

"Well, let's go scout things out then. Come along, Bertie," Edith whistled to the dog.

We set out past the picnic tables along the trail under the tall spruce trees. Half a dozen cows and their calves had settled down on a small patch of open grass near the last table. The babies lay sleeping in the sun while their mothers grazed around them. They looked up as we passed, curious, following us with their large liquid-brown eyes. The sound of the water grew louder with every step. I stopped to look at some wild violets nestled in the grass beside the trail, rather wishing I had brought the camera. The dog and the two old women strolled on ahead. I caught up to them at the river. We stood together at the edge of the cliff, looking down the sheer rock face to the churning muddy-white water fifty feet below. Even in years when its water level is low, here, near the Blue Rock campground, the Sheep River is always a raging mountain stream. But today, its rage had turned to fury. The dog planted himself well behind us, a prudent distance back from the edge. Bertie is not one to indulge in what he considers pointless machismo.

I turned to speak to Edith but my shout was lost in the roar of the water and in the shock of fear that clutched my throat. A deathly pale Edith swayed dizzily, caught in the grip of vertigo. The next few seconds passed in a slow-motion eternity as her knees began to buckle and she teetered forward towards the abyss. I reached out for her, my arm heavy as in a nightmare. I grasped a fistful of T-shirt and pulled her back from the edge. She stumbled into my arms.

Sadie saw what had happened and stepped back from the edge herself. She put her hand gently on my shoulder and the world returned to normal speed. I let go of Edith's shirt. My knees felt watery with relief. Edith sat on the ground breathing deeply, her eyes closed. The dog nudged her with his nose and licked her face. At last, she looked up. A little colour had returned to her cheeks. Sadie and I helped her back to the picnic area and sat her down at one of the tables. Now we could at least hear ourselves talk. I got the picnic basket and Sadie poured us all a cup of coffee from the thermos. She made Edith put three lumps of sugar in hers.

"I'm so sorry," Edith said. "I've never had much of a head for heights and when I looked down that cliff and saw the water rushing . . ." She shook her head and looked at me. "Phoebe, you saved my life." Her eyes filled with tears. "I feel like a foolish old woman. Such an old woman."

"Vertigo has nothing to do with age," I said. "Lots of people suffer from it."

"Heights bother me too," Sadie said. "I don't get vertigo but I do have a horrible fear that one day I won't be able to control myself. I'll jump off. It's odd because I'm not a suicidal person at all. But I really have that fear of jumping very strongly. It's a horrible feeling."

So much for our quiet picnic in the hills. Maybe Ella is right. She claims I'm a magnet for trouble. And now I'd just marched two old women with height phobias up a mountain gorge where I'd nearly lost one over the edge and had the other one leap in after her. Makes you wonder.

"Phoebe, dear, you're wool-gathering. Do come back to us." Edith startled me out of a horrible daydream in which I was explaining to Cyrrie why his sister wasn't coming home. Ever. "Come on, drink your coffee while it's hot. I'm sorry I frightened you so badly but we're all safe now." She was back to her usual brisk British self and very much in control. "Is it too early for lunch?"

"Not for me," said Sadie. "Being out in the hills always makes me hungry."

"It seems to have the same effect on the mosquitoes," Edith said. "I think we could use some of that bug spray you brought, Phoebe." I fetched the insect repellant from the car while Edith and Sadie opened the picnic basket and organized lunch.

Edith's sandwiches were very good, even the bread. It didn't seem to have quite the heft of her usual loaves.

"Sorry about the bread," Edith apologized. "I think it's the flour or maybe it's the altitude, but my Calgary bread always turns out a little on the airy side. I simply can't bake a proper loaf when I'm away from home."

"I know what you mean," Sadie agreed. "I used to try baking bread when I went to visit my daughter in Brazil but it was a disaster every time. Not one proper loaf in all those visits."

"How long has your daughter lived in Brazil?" I asked.

"A long time," Sadie said. "She's lived in São Paulo for at least fifteen years and they were in Brasilia for five years before that."

"You must miss her dreadfully," Edith said. "Do you visit her often?"

"I used to try to see her once a year. I thought it was very important for Tracy to keep in contact with her mother so either Amy would come to us or Tracy and I would go down to Brazil. Amy and Cliff have always been very generous about tickets. But in the last few years we haven't seen each other as often. Now that Tracy is a grownup working woman she sometimes finds it hard to get away, and the truth is it isn't quite so important now as when she was little."

"Don't you ever go to visit by yourself?" Edith asked.

"I did a few times but I found it very difficult. They lead such a different kind of life from me. Not that Amy and Cliff aren't kindness itself. They're very good to me. It's just that there's too much of the old-fashioned prairie socialist in me to feel comfortable with all that luxury."

"So Amy and Cliff are well off?" Edith said. Once again, the two women seemed to have forgotten my presence. I ate my sandwich and kept quiet.

"Well off? No," Sadie laughed and shook her head. "Amy and Cliff are not well off – Amy and Cliff are stinking rich. He's a mining engineer and he's made a fortune at it."

"Now Sadie, there's nothing wrong with having money, is there?" Edith said a little defensively. While she's not exactly stinking rich, Edith does have a certain aroma of affluence about her. Her late husband, Tom, left her what she'd call comfortable and I'd call loaded.

"I don't know," Sadie said. "I guess it depends on what you do with it. I only know it makes me feel very uncomfortable to live in the lap of luxury in a place where lots of people don't even have a proper roof over their heads. Once, when I was visiting São Paulo, Estella took me to visit a friend of hers who lives in the favelas, the slums. I'll never forget it. I was afraid every minute I was there, but I was ashamed too. I could go home whenever I wanted, home to Amy's mansion full of servants or home to my own safe little house in Canada. But they were stuck in those hovels forever. That was home." Sadie paused for a moment and drank some coffee. "It's the children that break your heart. Estella took some clothes and money for her friend but she's not a rich woman herself. She can't afford to do very much."

"Who's Estella?" Edith asked.

"My daughter's housekeeper. She's a good friend of mine. During one of my visits, Amy and Cliff had to go off for a few days on a business trip. I was all alone in that great big house except for the servants and none of them but Estella spoke any English. I was feeling lonely and probably a little sorry for myself. Anyway, I was very down in the mouth when Estella took pity on me and invited me back to her place for a few days. She and her husband live in a small house about a mile away from my daughter's. It's the only place in Brazil that I've ever really felt comfortable." Sadie smiled as she remembered.

"One Sunday all Estella's children and grandchildren came to the house to meet me. I helped her and her daughters cook a huge feast for everyone. We all had a wonderful time even though their English was almost as shaky as my Portuguese. Besides, Estella was there to translate for us when things got too confusing. Edith, I wish you could meet her. I know you two would really get along. Estella and I write to each other all the time. Her written English is a little odd, but it's a whole lot better than my written Portuguese."

"You can speak Portuguese?" Edith sounded impressed.

"Only a little and very badly – I can get around the stores, ask directions to the washroom and that kind of thing. But I could never have a real conversation like we're having now. I guess I speak what you'd call tourist Portuguese."

"Well, it can't be any worse than my finishing school

French," Edith said. "I once spent the most terrible year in a Swiss hellhole that passed itself off to desperate British fathers as a school for young ladies. I've never been so miserable in my life as I was at that place. I've not been back to Switzerland since. To this day, the sound of a cuckoo clock puts my teeth on edge."

"Oh dear," Sadie laughed. "You'll have to remind me to stop mine when you come to visit. Tracy gave it to me when she was little and I love the silly old thing. It's very elaborate. It even has a music box that plays after the bird is finished cuckooing. It took me a while to get used to hearing 'The Blue Danube' every hour on the hour night and day but now I think I'd miss it. Funny how you can come to love the most awful gifts, simply because you love the giver."

"I wonder why it is that children have such a passion for frightful clocks?" Edith said. "My son once presented me with a mantle clock that has a dreadful little porcelain ballerina who stands in front of the works and twirls her tutu every time the pendulum swings past her behind. Roddy thought it was madly elegant when he was nine years old. Well, the man's over fifty now and I still have that wretched ballerina in my sitting room. I couldn't bear to part with her."

"Where does your son live?" Sadie asked. "Does he have children?"

The sun was now directly overhead and work called. Edith and Sadie barely paused for breath when I got up from the table and went to the car where I collected the camera and tripod. I got out my lightproof black bag and reloaded the film magazine. I put an extra magazine in my workbag and set out for the river with twenty minutes worth of 16mm film and an afternoon of perfect light ahead of me. I looked back at the picnic table in the shade of the pines where the two women were still absorbed in their conversation. The dog sat beside them, his eyes riveted on the remaining ham sandwiches, a study in canine optimism. None of them noticed me wave as I turned the corner on the path and walked out of sight past the dozing cattle and on to the river.

I set the camera on its tripod not far from the place where Edith had nearly fallen over the edge. I had planned to take a shot of a tiny strip of pebble beach nestled in the curve of the opposite bank. But that was on paper. Today, the little beach was completely submerged. So too were the small caverns that, over the ages, the water has carved out of the rock all along the gorge. Right now they were underwater caves. However, I did get some pretty spectacular footage of a log that chose that moment to sweep downstream. The log's speed as it crashed past the rocks was a dramatic measure of the force of the water. Sometimes you get lucky.

I continued up the stream, stopping to film as I went. To me the whole afternoon passed in what seemed like a few minutes but, by the time I noticed a change in the light, it was well after four o'clock. When I got back to the picnic table, Edith and Sadie weren't there. I had just stowed the last of the camera gear back in the car when the two of them appeared strolling along the road with the dog. Poor Edith looked very hot.

"We've had a lovely afternoon, Phoebe," Edith said. "First we cleaned up the lunch things and then each of us commandeered a picnic table and had a little snooze and then Sadie read my cards. Now we've just been for a little stroll up the road." Her brogues were dusty and the afternoon sun had turned her nose a bright pink. "Sadie took me to see the campground. Do you know they have facilities for horses here? What a wonderful place Alberta is. You can even take your pony on a tenting holiday. Perhaps that's what Cyril's horse needs."

The drive home took much less time than the drive out. Shortly after five we were back in Turner Valley.

"May I keep you company on the drive to Calgary, Phoebe?" Sadie asked. "You could drop me off after you take Edith home. That way you wouldn't have so far to go by yourself."

"What a very good idea," Edith agreed. "Cyril would be delighted if you'd stop and have a look at his garden. I say," she paused, "perhaps it would be just as well if we didn't mention anything about that little spell of mine on the cliff to him. He's such a worrier."

Cyrrie had dinner waiting when we arrived back in Calgary. He insisted that Sadie and I stay and share the curried chicken and rice. Bertie drooled his way into the kitchen following the wonderful smells. I poured him a bowl of dry dog food from the bag I keep at Cyrrie's. Cyrrie mixed in a couple of spoons of the curry. No wonder Bertie loves him.

After dinner, I helped Cyrrie clear the table and do the dishes. Bertie lay in the middle of the kitchen floor just so he'd be on hand in case Cyrrie tripped while carrying the curry bowl and found himself in need of a faithful friend to lend a paw to help clean up the mess. When it comes to food, the dog leads a vivid and ever-optimistic fantasy life. Sadie and Edith continued their marathon conversation over coffee in the living room.

"Those two have certainly hit it off," Cyrrie said.

"They've been at it all day. I don't think they've stopped talking since we left Okotoks."

Before we left for home, Edith and Sadie made a date to get together the next afternoon for a shopping trip. Edith was determined to buy herself some sportier clothes.

Sadie and I drove most of the way home in silence. Maybe she'd talked herself out for the day or maybe we were both too occupied enjoying the long, shadowy evening. The sun had settled to a glow behind mountains that were now visible only as dark shapes in the mauve twilight. The evening star shone above them.

"I remember teaching Tracy to make wishes by the evening star." Sadie broke the silence. "She was too little to know what a wish was but she loved the words of the rhyme. She's loved poetry all her life. She writes poetry, you know. At least she did before she met Jonathan. Some of it's very good too. They published two of her poems in the high school yearbook."

By the time we pulled up in front of Sadie's house the sky was black and full of stars. She opened the car door but made no move to get out. She looked at me. "Phoebe, do you think murder is ever justifiable?"

"If it is, then I guess we don't call it murder," I said. "It's self-defence or defending your country or whatever. You're thinking about Jonathan, aren't you?"

"It's hard not to. It preys on my mind. Sometimes it feels like I've hardly thought of anything else since Friday. Except for today with you and Edith. I managed to forget about it for a while and I'm very grateful to you both for that."

"Sadie, I know things must seem pretty grim to you right now but you mustn't worry. Inspector Debarets is going to catch whoever did this. Tracy and David will be okay. You can bet on it."

"Can I?" She looked at me quizzically. "I wonder what odds Jonathan would give me on that?"

11

Candi phoned me early the next morning to remind me that
we had an appointment with Robert Roberts the Second at
eleven. We arranged to meet in front of the Hillside Home at
five to the hour. Personally, I agreed with Cyrrie that we
weren't going to find out much from Two Bob. But at least
talking to him would provide an outlet for Candi's sleuthing
instincts, which seemed to have gone into overdrive in the last
few days. She also passed on the latest news about Jonathan.
His death was now officially a murder, which was no surprise.
The police had released his body for burial. The funeral was
set for Saturday.

I loaded a reel of work print onto the editing bench and
managed to get in a couple of hours worth of shot-sorting
before I had to leave for Calgary. Traffic was light and I
reached the city a little early. Even the crosstown traffic wasn't
too bad so I indulged and took the scenic route by the river,
west on Memorial Drive, under the Centre Street Bridge, and
along to Fourteenth Street.

The Hillside Home is located exactly as its name implies,

halfway up the North Hill a few blocks west of Fourteenth. I decided to approach it from the top of the hill mainly so I could catch a glimpse of the bronze statue of Robert the Bruce as I drove past the Jubilee Auditorium. Mounted on his warhorse, the Scottish hero occupies a place of honour in front of the theatre, gazing out to the mountains over a city he could not have imagined in a land that for him did not exist. As a child, I thought it was the most wonderful statue in the world and even now, for all its kitschy overtones, I still love it. Then again, I love the Boer War memorial in Central Park too – the slightly larger than life bronze of a soldier on his horse. Nick claims I'm a case of arrested aesthetic development. I think I just like statues of horses.

By some miracle, I found a parking spot on the car-jammed street in front of the home. Candi was not so lucky. She trotted up the hill to the main entrance at five past the hour carrying a big bunch of daffodils and a plastic vase.

"Sorry to be late. I had to park at the bottom of the hill." We hurried up the walk to the front door. "I sure hope Cyrrie's right and the old guy's still with it."

"You ever met a bookie before?" I asked as we entered the building and walked through the lobby to the elevators.

"Never," Candi said. "At least not the gambling and horse-racing kind." She pushed the up button.

"What other kinds are there?"

"Phoebe, there are lots of other kinds of bookies," she stated, very matter-of-fact. "There are bookies all over the place."

By now, experience should have taught me never to play the straight man for Candi but, no matter how hard I try, curiosity always wins out. "Such as?"

"Such as insurance men, for instance."

"Insurance salesmen?" I laughed. "My uncle is an insurance broker. He's the biggest stuffed shirt in Calgary. He'd have a heart attack if he heard you calling him a bookie."

"Maybe he prefers to call it something else," Candi said. "But your uncle's still a bookie. Or at least he works for bookies. I mean, look at it this way. Insurance guys decide what the chances are that your house will burn down or that you'll die before you're fifty or you'll total your car. That's their odds line."

"I think they call them actuarial tables."

"They can call them what they like, they're still an odds line. And when you pay your premium you're making a bet. So if the insurance guys have made their book right, if they've done a good job of setting the odds, then the premiums they collect from people whose houses don't burn down pay for the houses that do and always with a nice big chunk of money left over for the insurance company. That's book-making. It's just that it's bookmaking on respectable stuff. Geez this thing is slow." She poked the elevator button a few more times.

"When did you get to be such an expert?" I asked, filing away her dissertation on insurance bookies for use at the next family gathering that included Uncle Stuart.

"Yesterday at the public library. When I knew we were coming here to talk to Mr. Roberts I went to the library after work and read up on bookmaking. Nick went with me. He wanted to look up some stuff on horses."

The elevator finally came. We waited while a load of Hillside residents, along with their walkers and wheelchairs, disembarked on their way to a very early lunch in the dining room. At last, the doors sighed shut behind us and the elevator began its stately progress to Mr. Roberts' floor. That elevator had a truly geological sense of time. Entire species could have evolved while we travelled up through the strata of the second and third floors. Some of them may even have passed to extinction before its doors opened languidly in front of the fourth-floor nursing station.

Old folks homes depress me. Even the good ones bother me and the Hillside Home is one of the best. Maybe they're too much like hospitals – the wide doors, the wheelchairs, the metal and Formica furniture, the pervasive smell of antiseptic and institutional cleansers. Or perhaps it's the ever-present reminder that age and decay come to us all that gets me down. On the positive side, I'm always amazed at how cheerful and kind most of the people who work in them are. I think they deserve medals. One of them pointed Candi and me in the direction of Robert Roberts' room.

His door was half open. He sat in a wheelchair facing the window with his back to us. All we could see of him was the back of his wispy-haired white head. I knocked on the door. The head didn't move. I knocked again, this time longer and louder. Still nothing.

"You have to make more noise than that if you want him to hear you." A young woman stopped her laundry cart beside us. "Mr. Roberts," she shouted as she went into his room and touched him lightly on the shoulder. "Mr. Roberts, you have some visitors." She turned his chair to face us and a slightly startled Robert Roberts blinked his very blue eyes and smiled. The thick lenses of his big horn-rimmed glasses magnified his eyes slightly and seemed, by some optical trick, to intensify the blue as well. "You have to talk real loud and right to him." The young woman went back to her laundry cart and continued down the corridor.

"Ladies, ladies, do come in." Robert Roberts spoke in a

strong and steady tenor, a voice still free of the treble trembles of age. "You must be the two girls that young Cyril Vaughn phoned about on Monday. Said you wanted to ask me some questions about bookmaking."

I suppose Cyrrie would seem young to someone as old as Robert Roberts. However, for a man of ninety he looked to be in pretty good shape, perhaps a touch thin and frail but still very tall and straight in his chair. He wore a blue-grey tweed jacket over a light blue shirt, a canary-yellow waistcoat, grey trousers, and suede loafers with rubber soles, the kind of shoes my Great Aunt Phoebe always referred to as brothel creepers. The ascot tucked into his shirt collar had just a touch of the vest's yellow woven into its mostly blue paisley. In his day, Robert Roberts must have been an extraordinarily handsome man because, white hair, wheelchair, and all, he still cut a pretty dashing figure.

"Hello Mr. Roberts. My name is Phoebe Fairfax," I announced loudly as I walked through the door. His room was bright, airy, and institutional. The only decoration of a personal nature was a small oil painting of a grey horse that hung on the wall opposite the bed.

"How do you do, Fanny." He shook my hand.

"Not Fanny, Mr. Roberts." I raised the volume another notch and, following the laundry woman's advice, spoke directly to him. "My name is Phoebe. Phoebe Fairfax."

"Sorry Phoebe," he pointed to his ears, each of which had a tiny hearing aid embedded in its folds. "Don't hear very well these days, I'm afraid. Got these things turned up as high as they'll go but they don't work worth a spit. Ears are just too blessed old, I guess." He let go of my hand and then turned to Candi. "There's no need for you to tell me your name, young lady. You're Candi Sinclair and you're a real favourite around here. Everybody in the place watches your program. I can tell you, it sure beats bingo."

"Thanks for seeing us, Mr. Roberts." Candi shifted the bouquet of daffodils to her other arm and shook his hand.

"Please, none of that Mr. Roberts stuff. Just Bob or Two Bob. I answer to either." Candi gave him the flowers. He inhaled the bouquet's spring smells. "'And then my heart with pleasure fills, And dances with the daffodils.' Had to learn the whole of that off by heart when I was a boy in school. Funny thing, memory, isn't it? Have trouble telling you what I ate for dinner last night but I could recite that poem for you like I'd learned it yesterday. Wasn't much of a kid for poetry either."

Candi filled the vase with water at Two Bob's bathroom sink. She placed it on the table next to the bed, reclaimed the flowers from him, and began to arrange them in it.

"Daffodils always remind me of my mother." Two Bob watched Candi and the flowers. "That was her name, you see. Daffodil. Had four sisters – Jonquil, Iris, Poppy, and Mabel. Don't know why poor Mabel didn't get a flower name too. Maybe the old man put his foot down.

"Of course, Mother got called Daffy but there wasn't anything daffy about her at all. Very practical woman. Had to be. Had a lot of courage too. Women did in those days. Arrived in Calgary with me in her arms and my sister May just walking. Spent her first summer here in a tent by the Bow River while my father built their house. That was 1906. Twenty years old she was, fresh from England and living in a tent by a river in the real wild west. Must have been something for a Newmarket greengrocer's daughter, eh?"

Candi put the last flower in place. She perched on the edge of the bed. I sat in the easy chair at its foot.

"Newmarket. Isn't that the horse-racing place in England?" She began to direct the conversation.

"That's right," Two Bob said. "Big racing place, Newmarket."

"Was your father from Newmarket too?" Candi continued at top volume.

"He was. A Newmarket man, born and bred."

"Cyril Vaughn told us that your father was a professional bookmaker."

"A bookmaker's assistant and a good one. Had a fantastic head for numbers, Dad did. Make your head spin how fast he could add a column of figures. Sort out a line on a dozen horses quicker than you could say their names. But that was back in England. Gave it up when he came to Canada. Promised my mother before they got on the boat. Very straight-laced in her own way, Mother. Sometimes wonder how she and Dad ever got together. She didn't want anything to do with gambling. Dad promised her a new start in a new country and a good thing he did as it turned out. Got here and found out book-making was illegal. Poor Dad." Two Bob smiled and shook his head. "Couldn't imagine a place where it was against the law for an honest man to place an honest wager with an honest bookmaker. Was a real shock to him that."

"If he'd given up bookmaking then how did he support his family?" I asked.

"Sorry, Phoebe." Two Bob shook his head and pointed at his ears again. "Didn't quite catch that."

"Money," Candi said. "How did he earn a living?" For some reason, he seemed to find her voice much clearer than mine. He understood the question with no difficulty.

"Learned bricklaying. Very good at it too. Never had any trouble finding work. Raised me and four others and none of us ever hungry." As long as Two Bob could hear, he had no trouble at all keeping up with the conversation.

"But no more bookmaking?" Candi asked.

"Well, not officially," he grinned. "But every now and again Dad would take bets on the Grand National or the Kentucky Derby or sometimes the occasional local race, although there weren't all that many back in those days. Only did it in a small way. Just for friends. Nothing the law and Mother couldn't look the other way for."

"Then bookmaking was never a full-time job for him here?" This time I tried lowering the pitch of my voice as well as raising the volume. It seemed to work.

"Oh no. Calgary was far too small a place back then even if it had been legal. Couldn't possibly have made a living making book in those days. Not unless you were willing to take on dog fights and the like and Dad wouldn't have any part of that. Disgusting things dog fights and so are the men who go to them. The dregs. Makes you sick to think about it." Two Bob shuddered a little in revulsion. "No, Dad never made book on anything but horse races and neither did I. Sport of kings, girls." He leaned back in his wheelchair and thumped its arms for emphasis. "The sport of kings."

"Did you learn how to make book from your father?" I asked.

"I was never a patch on Dad with figures but he did teach me to set up a pretty good line. For a plumber, I wasn't a bad bookmaker at all." He laughed heartily at his own joke. "Always went by Dad's golden rule – bookmakers never gamble."

"Bookmakers never gamble?" Candi said. "I thought gambling was their business."

"But that's just it, Candi," Two Bob said. "For a bookmaker, gambling is a business and, if you make your book properly, no matter what horse wins, you make money. See that fellow up there?" He pointed to the horse in the painting. "Jackie Sparkles. Best horse ever bred in Western Canada in the humble opinion of yours truly. Made me a lot of money Jackie did, but I never gambled a nickel on him."

"But other people did," I said.

"Did they ever. The betting boys couldn't put enough down on his races. Jackie was a very big star around here back in the old days. Even people who never bet in their lives wanted a couple of dollars on his races. Some of them bet against him, some of them bet for him, but I made money on all of them." Two Bob looked up at the painting. "Took me and the missus to Hawaii that fella did. Back in the days when you took the boat. Caught the train to San Francisco then the Lurline to Honolulu. What a trip that was, Jackie." He smiled and gave the grey horse a nod and a small salute.

"Do you ever go to the races now?" Candi asked.

"My grandson takes me to the track every once in a while. But it's awkward with this damned hip of mine, if you'll pardon my French. Can't even walk to the paddock to check out the horses. Kind of takes the edge off it. Besides, everything's changed – the grandstand, the betting windows. Everything. Did you know you can put a bet down now and never have to talk to another living soul while you do it? Tim showed me how. You just touch numbers on a thing that looks like a tele-vision screen and out pops your ticket. No, nothing's the same. Course, nothing's the same anywhere when you're my age and you'd have to be a fool to think it could be."

"The horses are the same," I said. "They don't change."

"You're right about that, Phoebe," Two Bob smiled up at the painting. "Lovely creatures and always will be."

"So you don't do any bookmaking at all these days," Candi steered us back on track.

"Haven't made book for years. Only ever did a little of it on the side anyway. Just like Dad," Two Bob said. "But I think I could still work out a pretty fair line even now. It's something you don't forget."

"Do you know anyone who does?" she asked.

"Anyone who makes book? No," he shook his head. "I'd guess that bookmakers like me are as dead as the dodo. There are so many places where they'll take your money now that an honest bookmaker wouldn't have a hope. Casinos and lotteries and what have you. And all of it legal. Amazing, isn't it? Who'd have guessed that someday the government would be the biggest bookie of them all."

"What about sports gambling?" Candi said. "You know, football point spreads and stuff like that. Somebody must take those bets."

"If they do, I don't know them. Never did. I've been out of the game for twenty years but like I said, I was strictly horses even then. I don't know anything about what goes on now. Besides," he raised his bushy white eyebrows and looked at us shrewdly, "why do you want to know?"

"We're not asking for us," Candi said. "It's for our friend."

"Oh yes, it always is, isn't it?" Two Bob nodded sagely. "And you can tell your friend from me that girls like you shouldn't be gambling. It's strictly a sucker's game unless you know what you're doing. Even the ponies. I made book for nearly fifty years and I can only name you two men who made money off me over the long haul. Now, I can see that you're both very nice girls and, believe me, you've got far better things to be doing with your money than throwing it away . . ."

A loud knock interrupted Two Bob's lecture on the evils of gambling.

"Hey Grandpa, are you ready for lunch?" A tall, smiling man breezed through the door, his tie loose, the top button of his shirt undone, and the jacket of his grey summer-weight suit slung over his shoulder. Despite the business suit, he brought the vitality and energy of outdoors with him into the little room. Even the air seemed to smell fresher for his presence. "Sorry, Grandpa. Shouldn't have barged in. I didn't know you had company." He leaned over the wheelchair and gave the old man a hug.

"That's all right, Tim. You're in for a treat. I'm glad you got here in time to meet these ladies. Candi Sinclair and Phoebe Fairfax, this is my grandson, Robert Timothy Roberts." The old man's smile said everything there was to say about his feelings for his grandson.

Tim was about my age. I could see the family resemblance between him and his grandfather but his eyes were even bluer than Two Bob's and his close-cropped hair was jet-black. It curled tight against his skull like wool on a black lamb. I found myself wanting to touch it. I shook his hand instead.

"So, are you going to be on 'A Day in the Lifestyle,' Grandpa?" Tim asked. Everyone recognizes Candi.

"The ladies are here to talk to me about bookmaking."

"You're doing a program on gambling?" he asked with genuine interest.

"Well, not exactly," Candi hedged. "It's more of a background thing."

"Oh, you mean like a history of gambling in Calgary?"

"Your grandfather has just been telling us how he learned

bookmaking from his father," I said. "Do you know the business too?" If you don't want to answer questions, ask some of your own.

"Me? I'd go broke in a day." Tim laughed and I found myself smiling along with him. With a small shock, I realized I would be content to spend the rest of my afternoon smiling as long as he was around. God, but I wanted to touch that hair. "Grandpa tried to teach me but he gave up. He's some sort of mathematical genius but I have trouble adding two and two without my calculator."

"I'm afraid there was nothing left for the lad but to go respectable. Tim's a lawyer," Two Bob beamed.

"Since when did lawyers get more respectable than bookies, Grandpa? Most people would say it's the other way round."

"Will you ladies come out to lunch with us?" Two Bob asked.

"I'm afraid I already have plans for lunch," Candi said. "But I'm sure Phoebe would love to go. Wouldn't you Phoebe?" She nudged me surreptitiously.

"Oh. Lunch. Yes," I said, too startled to protest. "Thank you. Lunch would be very nice."

"Then why don't you go on ahead while I find my hat," Two Bob said. "Tim and I will catch up to you at the main entrance."

Candi said her goodbyes and the two of us headed for the front door, leaving Two Bob to use his bathroom or whatever the euphemistic finding his hat implied. This time we took the stairs and less than a minute later we were standing outside in the noon sun.

"Well, that wasn't much help, was it?" Candi put on her sunglasses.

"Not much," I agreed.

"So what are we going to do now?"

"About finding Tracy's loan shark? I don't know. Give up maybe?"

"Too bad Two Bob couldn't give us a name." Candi ignored my suggestion just as I knew she would. "It would've been a place to start."

"I'm glad we came to see him anyway. He's a really interesting man."

"And his grandson ain't half bad either," Candi said with her best dirty-old-lady leer.

"He seems very pleasant."

"Pleasant? Pleasant? The man is gorgeous and all you can say is he seems very pleasant. What's the matter with you, Phoebe? Are your hormones on holiday or something?"

"I've stopped listening to my hormones. Every time they point me at a man he turns out to be a jerk. I married on the advice of my endocrine system and look where it got me."

"So no one's asking you to marry the guy. You're going out for lunch with Tim and his grandpa and that's it. Look," she took off her sunglasses and stabbed the air with them for emphasis, "just because your ex-husband is a truly major-type dork does not mean that every man you find attractive is automatically a dork too."

"Please Candi, no more of this beating round the bush. Go ahead – be blunt. Don't feel you have to spare my feelings."

"And you can laugh all you like but you know that what I'm saying is true. So you married a jerk. That doesn't make every guy who likes you a jerk. I mean, if I hadn't seen you panting after Tim's curls back there, I'd figure you were practising to join a convent or something."

"It sure is easy to tell when people are in love," I countered.

"They keep trying to sell the idea of romance to everyone else."

"Whose talking romance? I thought we were discussing lust."

"How's Nick?" I asked pointedly.

"Nick is wonderful. I'm crazy about him and I'm going to be late meeting him for lunch if I don't get going." She started down the walk and then turned back. "Hey, I almost forgot to tell you. Cyrrie phoned Nick about his horse. Nick's going to channel him on Friday night. Want to come?"

"You mean Nick is going to have a little heart-to-heart with Prairie Fire? That I wouldn't miss for anything."

"I'll call and let you know what time." Candi headed off to her car again, this time at a run. "Hope you and your hormones have a fun lunch," she called back over her shoulder.

I sat on one of the park benches that dotted the lawn in the little park across the street from the home and basked in the sun while I waited for Two Bob and Tim. Its rays beat down on the back of my head and shoulders. I closed my eyes. A feeling of lazy well-being slowly seeped through my body. The dog is a devoted basker and, at moments like this, I begin to understand his dedication. I felt someone sit down on the bench beside me and opened my eyes.

"Did I wake you?" He smiled. My hormones smiled back.

"No, I wasn't asleep." I shook my head and stretched. "Not quite anyway. Where's your grandfather?"

"Grandpa sends his apologies. He's decided that he's too tired to go out for lunch today."

"Candi and I shouldn't have stayed so long. We probably wore him out. I'm sorry." And also disappointed. No Two Bob, no lunch with Tim.

"Don't apologize. There's absolutely nothing wrong with him. He's not tired, he's matchmaking."

"Matchmaking?"

"Grandpa told me that he thinks you are one very fine filly. He gave me ten bucks and told me to take you out for lunch." Tim tried to suppress a grin but couldn't. "I'm supposed to ply you with wine at the Palliser."

"Do you get to keep the change?"

"I guess Grandpa's imagination hasn't kept pace with inflation. But hey, it's the thought that counts. Maybe I could ply you with a sandwich in Riley Park instead."

On our way to the park we stopped at a deli on Fourteenth and bought coffee and sandwiches. The park was crowded with other lunchers. We found a free bench in the shade of a huge poplar tree near the paddling pool. Children splashed and laughed and sailed small boats under the watchful eyes of their minders. Over in the direction of the cricket pitch, a gangly black dog with a red bandanna round his neck played Frisbee with his shirtless owner.

"Do you work for 'A Day in the Lifestyle' too?" he asked. We unwrapped our sandwiches and started to eat.

"I'm a photographer. I work for 'Lifestyle' two or three days a week. I spend the rest of my time making natural history films, mostly in the foothills."

"Sounds like a good life," Tim said. "And a pretty busy one. It was nice of you to take the time to come and see Grandpa. It does him a lot of good to meet new people. He really enjoyed your visit."

"It was mutual," I said. "I enjoyed talking to him."

"He's worried about you, you know. He thinks you and Candi are involved in some sort of gambling scheme."

"I know he didn't believe us when Candi told him we had

come to see him to get some help for a friend. But it's true. We know a woman who's having trouble paying off her boyfriend's gambling debts. We want to talk to the guy who loaned him the money but we don't know who he is. We were hoping Two Bob could give us the name of a bookmaker, somebody who could help us find him." I felt I owed Tim at least this much explanation for worrying his grandfather.

"Why doesn't the boyfriend look after his own gambling debts?"

"He's dead."

"Good reason. But then his estate should pay them."

"The debts are his estate."

"Big estate?"

"Forty-three thousand due by the end of this week."

"Big enough." He peeled the plastic lid off his coffee and poured in the contents of a packet of sugar. "So why are you and Candi looking for the lender? It seems to me that for forty-three thousand dollars he's going to be kind of anxious to get in touch with your friend."

"He already has. That's the problem."

"What did he do? Send his loan officers out with a reminder notice? They're usually big guys who carry baseball bats instead of briefcases." Tim was uncomfortably swift on the uptake. "Is your friend okay?"

"She's scared and there's no way she can pay the money on time and that's why we have to talk to this guy. Candi and I are hoping we can at least negotiate a little time for her."

"You could also negotiate yourself into one hell of a lot of trouble with these people, Phoebe. You and Candi shouldn't be doing this."

"Last time I bothered to look I seemed to be an adult. I can take care of myself. I've been doing it for a long time."

"Please," he said. "Don't be offended. I'm sorry if I came off sounding sexist or patronizing or whatever but I know what I'm talking about here. I work in the Crown Prosecutor's Office and I've seen enough creeps like this to last me a lifetime. I've seen what happens when the muscle goes into action and it ain't pretty. This is not like defaulting on your mortgage at the bank. These guys would just as soon repossess your kneecaps as look at you. Believe me, I wouldn't mess with them. If I were your lawyer, I'd advise you to tell your friend that she isn't responsible for her dead boyfriend's debts and, if this guy he owed money to is threatening her, she should go to the police."

"That's what we did tell her," I said. "But it's not that simple." Tim waited for me to elaborate.

"So, are you going to tell me about it or not?" he said. "Maybe I can help."

"There's nothing more to tell." I would have liked to tell him the whole story right from our first meeting with Jonathan but discussing Tracy's troubles with a lawyer from the Crown Prosecutor's Office was out of the question. Still, I hated lying to him. Somehow, everything to do with Tracy lead to lies.

"You must really like this friend of yours."

"Actually, I don't." The words were out before I was aware of what I'd said and they were honest words. I did not like Tracy at all. She was manipulative and an habitual liar and her manipulations were now making a liar out of me with a man who deserved better. "I just met her a few days ago, but she's an old friend of Candi's and we promised to help her out. I know you're right. We shouldn't mess around with this. To be honest, I'm not feeling too great about going to see this guy – if we ever find him that is. But I know Candi won't give up and I can't let her do it alone."

"Last time I looked, Candi seemed to be an adult. I'll bet she can take care of herself too."

"Touché and a point for your side." I laughed, mostly at myself. "But it still doesn't change anything."

"You're not going to give up on this, are you?"

"Nope."

"How are you planning to find this guy now that you know Grandpa can't help?"

"I'm not sure, but Candi will figure something out. Maybe we'll start hanging out in gambling dens looking desperate. Orphans of the bingo storm or something."

This time it was his turn to laugh. He scrunched his napkin and sandwich wrapper into a ball and tossed it over his shoulder in a fancy hook aimed at the garbage container ten feet to the left of our bench. It bounced off the rim. I did a straight shot with mine and centred a perfect basket.

"No fair," he said, collecting his paper and putting it in the container. "Mine was a way trickier shot."

"They don't give points for tricky. Mine went in."

We sat in silence for a while, sipping our coffee and watching the Frisbee dog leap and run. He seemed as energetic as ever although his owner was looking very red in the face and a lot slower than he had when we first sat down.

"Phoebe, I wish you'd let me help you with this. And before you tell me to mind my own business, please just listen to what I have to say." He raised a hand to cut off my protest. "I'm pretty good friends with a couple of the police officers I deal with at work. Maybe they can tell me something about this guy you're looking for – he may even have a record. Chances are pretty good that at least they'll know who he is. So if you know anything at all about him, tell me and I'll ask around. No names, no strings, just information. Might save you and Candi a lot of hours hanging around all those bingo dens."

It was a reasonable offer and one I probably didn't deserve considering all the things I hadn't told him.

"I have a description of a couple of men who work for him. I think they're his loan officers. One's fat and has a tattoo of a naked woman on his arm. The other is younger and very thin. He has bad acne and a greasy ponytail. And that's it. I don't know any more."

"If the police have anything on them, that should be more than enough. Where can I get hold of you?"

"I work at home a lot. You can call me there." I wrote down my phone number on a slip of paper. "If I'm not in, I have a machine."

"I'll call you tonight and let you know how I'm doing. Is this a Calgary number?" He looked at the paper and slipped it in his pocket.

"I live in the country, in the foothills. Not far from Millarville."

"Lucky you."

The black dog loped over to our bench, his Frisbee in his mouth. His owner lay collapsed on the lawn, guzzling orange juice from a big container. The dog dropped the Frisbee at Tim's feet and looked up at him expectantly. In one graceful, fluid movement, Tim picked up the disc and tossed it in an arc high over the exhausted owner's head. The dog followed its flight in a straight line, leaping over his prostrate master, and catching the Frisbee just before it buried itself in a carefully tended flower bed. He dashed back with his toy.

"Sorry fella," Tim stroked the silky black ears. "I've got to get back to work. It's time for me to go fight crime and keep Canada safe for democracy. Maybe this nice lady can stay and play with you."

"Sorry. It's time for the nice lady to go make a major contribution to nature cinematography and thus help preserve the Canadian wilderness for future generations."

"Hey, we're really something, aren't we?" he said and, for half a moment, I half believed him.

12

I stopped off on the way home to visit Ella and deliver a welcome-to-the-world present to Margaret Phoebe Candida. Ella and Marty live in a tiny house in Bridgeland, on one of those streets that make an abrupt drop down the North Hill to the Bow River. Their street is so steep that the sidewalk in front of the house has steps and a handrail. I parked the car, turned its wheels into the curb, and pulled hard on the parking brake. I found Ella in the screened back porch sitting with Maggie in her arms in a big easy chair that Marty had moved out from the living room for them. The porch faces north and its screens are covered with Virginia creeper so, even on hot summer days, the interior is shady and cool.

"Hi. Am I disturbing you?" I whispered.

"Not at all. It's good to see you. That door isn't locked. Come in."

"I've brought Maggie a present." I navigated my way round the cedar lawn chair which, along with Ella's chair, a footstool, and a basket of Maggie's clean laundry, pretty well filled the tiny space.

"You don't have to whisper. She isn't asleep."

"It's a hobby-horse."

"Yes, I can see that, Phoebe," Ella said with what was for her a surprising display of patience.

"Try pulling the reins."

I held the horse while Ella gave the reins an obedient tug. The hobby-horse emitted a loud, long, and very spirited whinny. Ella laughed and I swear that Maggie smiled too.

"It's wonderful," Ella said. "And trust you to find it. What's his name?"

"That's up to Maggie," I said. "See, the batteries go in this slot under the mane. They're supposed to last for ages."

"Not with Marty around they won't. He's already building houses with the Duplo his aunt sent. At the rate he's going Maggie's toys are going to be worn out before she's old enough to play with them. Please, Phoebe, do sit down. This porch is too small for people to pace in." I sat. "Candi says this week's program looks pretty good. Does it?"

"It's not bad," I said. "Even the interview with Maud came off all right. I thought you'd have seen it by now. Didn't Candi have a copy made for you?"

"She dropped it off yesterday after work but I haven't had time to watch." Truly, Ella was a changed woman. "But I did see some of the footage you shot – the part with that man who got murdered – it was lead item on the news this morning."

"Jonathan Webster," I said.

"Yeah, that's his name. Why did you shoot so much tape of him? I can understand the stretcher and ambulance shots, but why all that stuff in his booth? It looked like you knew something was going to happen."

"We got stuck taping him because Candi knows his girlfriend," I said. "Turns out they were good friends in high school."

"I can't believe it," Ella shook her head in what I'm pretty sure was genuine dismay. "Magnets for trouble. I leave you and Candi alone for half an hour at that fair and look what happens."

"It's hardly our fault," I said indignantly. "We didn't murder Jonathan."

"You know I noticed Webster when I was walking around the fair making up the shot list," she said. "I thought he looked terrible then. Did you see how green he was? It's hard to believe a person could actually be that colour. Was the girl in the booth with him Candi's friend?"

"Long black hair?" I asked. Ella nodded. "That was Tracy."

"She kept looking at him," Ella continued. "She was messing around with some stuff at the back of the booth and she kept glancing up at him and then down again. Almost like she didn't want Webster to catch her watching him. It was odd."

Margaret Phoebe Candida made a snuffly baby sound. Ella gazed fondly at her daughter. I shifted around on the chair and put my feet up on the footstool.

"Phoebe, what on earth is the matter with you today? First you pace all over the porch and now you can't sit still. You've been squirming around on that chair ever since you sat down. What's up?"

"Nothing's up. I probably just need some exercise."

"Well, that's not what you look like. You look like you're
. . ." Ella paused for a moment, slightly taken aback, as if she'd just noticed something odd. "Phoebe, you look happy."

"So I'll go for a run when I get home."

"No, really. I'm not kidding. You do. You look happy." She sat back in her chair and looked at me, rather puzzled.

Maybe motherhood had addled her wits. Ella never talks like this. She's the one woman you can depend on not to discuss feelings – her own or other people's.

"Can I hold Maggie?" It was time for a change of subject.

"Only if you promise to sit still. Twitchy people make babies feel insecure."

I cuddled Maggie while Ella folded the laundry and played with the hobby-horse. She was still moving a little more slowly than usual. Then Maggie decided she was hungry so I gave her back to her mother. I left them in the porch, bathed in the cool, green, dappled light, Maggie at Ella's breast nursing contentedly.

I did go for a run when I got home. The dog watched glumly as I changed into shorts and a T-shirt, put on my running shoes, and did some warmup stretches. When I opened the door to leave, he sighed ostentatiously and flopped down in his basket. Bertie loves to go for walks but he flatly refuses to accompany me on runs. As far as he's concerned, unless you're allowed the leisure to sniff every tree along the way, follow phantom scents through the underbrush at whim, and chase the occasional rabbit, then what's the point? Truth be told, I tend to agree with him. Running purely for exercise is a bore but a run for fun is different. I don't go at it in a very organized way – I simply alternate running and walking until the running parts get shorter and the walking parts get longer and I reach the point where my body knows it's had enough.

Unlike the dog, the horses love to come running with me. At least Pete does. As a former racehorse, Elvira has far too professional an attitude to running to make her a comfortable companion. She has a nasty tendency to leave me choking in her dust. Pete, on the other hand, is willing to indulge my puny human legs and lack of equine stamina. He gallops on ahead, but he comes tearing back every few minutes to check up on me. Best of all, if we go too far and I get too tired, he lets me ride home on his back.

He and Elvira and the foal came running when I whistled at the pasture fence. Pete stomped around and pawed the ground in excitement. He recognized my running clothes. I fed Elvira a few carrots, led her and the foal into the corral, and closed the gate behind them. Then I opened the pasture gate and Pete and I took off for the stream that marks the west boundary of my land. For a roly-poly pinto of advancing years, Pete can make pretty good time. He had run to the stream and back to me three times before I reached the water's edge. Pete raced ahead through the water, into the trees and up the long stretch of hill that marks the beginning of the provincial forest reserve. This time he didn't return but I knew I'd find him grazing government grass in the meadow at the top of the hill. I crossed the stream and followed him into the cool damp of the woods. My lungs heaved huge breaths of piny air as I pounded my way up the steep trail, its litter of fallen needles and poplar leaves soft and springy under my shoes. I ran all the way to the top of the hill, out of the trees, and into the sunlit meadow where I sprawled gasping like a fish.

My breathing had almost returned to normal when Pete ambled over to where I lay and nudged me with his long nose. I got up and we strolled together across the lush carpet of new grass with its scattering of wild flax and fleabane daisies, down the shallow slope to the bottom of the valley. There we alternately ran and walked south for another half-hour before we turned around and mostly walked back to the meadow. By this stage even its gentle rise made my legs wobble. Back at the top of the hill, I climbed gratefully onto Pete's sturdy back and he took us home at a sedate pace, down the trail through the woods, over the stream, and up to his corral.

Elvira whinnied and trotted over with the foal to welcome Pete home from his adventure. While the returning hero had a drink from the water trough, I fetched his curry comb and brush. As soon as I finished grooming him, he lay down in the middle of the corral and had a dust bath. I gave Elvira and the baby a brush too. Because my working hours are irregular and I'm often away from home, my next-door neighbour's teenage son usually looks to the care and feeding of the horses. He'd be over later to give them their evening oats. I doled out the last of the carrots I'd brought and then went back to the house.

I showered and changed into a clean pair of shorts and a white broadcloth shirt that's been washed and ironed so many times it's softer than silk. I worked at the editing bench for a few hours before I took a break and made myself a sandwich which I ate out on the deck. I sat outside and read for a while before the lengthening shadows and gathering mosquitoes told me it was time to go in, clean up the kitchen, and get back to work. I managed the first two, but got waylaid by the piano before I made it back to the editing bench.

It felt like a Cole Porter sort of evening. As a propitiatory offering to the mosquitoes, I began with "I've Got You Under My Skin." I was just about to delight them with my delicious rendition of "Delovely" when the dog barked the single, discreet woof that tells me we have company. I heard a car pull into the driveway. Bertie and I went to investigate.

"I was in the neighbourhood so thought I'd drop in and tell you what I managed to dig up on your loan shark." Tim unfolded his six-foot-two from a very businesslike four-wheel drive, the kind of vehicle that looked like it could take some pretty tough offroad work in its substantial stride. I'd longed for one just like it for years. Ah well, maybe after a few more contracts that actually paid.

He stood beside the 4x4 and held his hand out to the dog who sniffed at it cautiously. "I'm on my way to Medicine Hat. I have a conference there for the next couple of days and since your place is on the way it made more sense to stop by than phone." My place is on the way to Medicine Hat the same way Los Angeles is on the way to Dallas. They're both south of Calgary.

"I'm surprised you found your way." I flapped my hands in an effort to disperse the squadrons of mosquitoes whining around my head. "My house isn't all that easy to find."

"I cheated. I phoned the television station and Candi gave me directions so I didn't have any trouble. I haven't been out this way for a long time. I'd forgotten how beautiful it is." He slapped at the back of his neck. His hand came away bloody. "Except for the mosquitoes."

"They're pretty bad tonight." I whacked a pair that were biting me through my shirt and succeeded in smearing blood all over the white cloth. "We'd better go inside." Before we went into the house, I dusted Bertie's fur with my hands in an effort to dislodge the mosquitoes that I knew were hitching a ride on him.

"Were you working?" Tim noticed the editing bench still loaded with the work print.

"Pretending to." I closed the screen door behind us. "I was goofing off when I heard you pull into the drive. Would you like some coffee?"

"Thanks." He followed me over to the kitchen corner while I filled the coffee-maker and flipped the switch. "This is one very impressive kitchen," he said. "You must really like to cook."

"My ex-husband did. I'm just your average, everyday, put it on your plate and eat it up sort of cook. The kitchen was Gavin's brain child. He loves cooking."

"So does my wife," Tim said. In the space of a breath, anger chased disappointment and a dozen other outraged emotions through my body. The sonofabitch was married. "When we split up she got the kitchen. The rest of the house went with it."

"What did you get?" I did my best not to sound as relieved as I felt. Overt expressions of delight at the news of someone else's defunct marriage are not in the best of taste.

"An apartment in Sunnyside and visiting rights. I get my daughter every other weekend and half the school holidays."

We went out to the living room and sat on the couch with our feet up on the old poplar-plank coffee table while we waited for the coffee to brew. The table is made from trees that Uncle Andrew cleared off the land to make space for the house. The dog settled down in front of the door to the deck directly in the path of the cool, mosquito-free breeze that blew through the screen. He kept a watchful eye on Tim.

"So what's with our loan shark?" I asked.

"Sharkette actually," Tim said. "Her name is Shelley Watson. She owns a small trucking company out in Highfield."

"A woman?" I was very surprised. Crime is one field of human endeavour still dominated almost totally by men. Just consider the number of men in jail as compared to women. It's hard to believe, but that ratio is even more lopsided than the ratio of men to women with tenured positions on university faculties.

"A woman and a very attractive one. According to my

sources, Shelley Watson is nineteen years old, beautiful, and smart. Well, actually more than smart," Tim amended. "Apparently she's a bona fide genius of some kind. Her IQ is off the charts."

"How did you find her?"

"I talked to a couple of friends on the police force. One's a detective and the other's a beat cop. They both recognized Shelley's loan officers from your description. Seems they're a pretty well-known pair. They've been with Shelley since their juvenile court days. All three of them were habitual runaways, forever being picked up for shoplifting, break and enters, prostitution – the kinds of crimes that mean survival for street kids. They looked out for each other and they survived better than a lot of kids do, mostly thanks to Shelley. Intelligence like hers gives you an edge even in an environment like that."

"How old was she when she ran away from home?"

"It's hard to say. The detective I talked to remembered picking her up for prostitution when she was thirteen. He says that she was a very astute businesswoman even then. She'd found her own special market niche. None of this tight clothes and a ton of makeup stuff like every other hooker on the block. Shelley used to cruise in a Girl Guide uniform."

"So how does a thirteen-year-old Girl Guide grow up to be a nineteen-year-old loan shark?"

"She married Red Watson. He owned a trucking company. He had a lot of other small but crooked irons in the fire too – the loan-sharking operation was only one of them. He was getting on for sixty when he married Shelley. She was fifteen. He'd been one of her best customers."

"Where were her parents? That young she would have needed their consent, wouldn't she?"

"Prove to the court you're pregnant and you can get married

when you're twelve," Tim said. "Anyway, no matter how she wangled it Shelley was Mrs. Red Watson all legal and official."

"He must have had a real thing for Girl Guides."

"This little Girl Guide was probably a lot more than Red bargained for. He may have been four times older than her, but Shelley was four times smarter."

Tim followed me to the kitchen while I poured the coffee. The dog came too. He sat and stared at the cupboard from which an occasional cookie has been known to emerge when guests are around. This time his optimism was misplaced. I'd forgotten to buy digestives last time I went to the supermarket.

"You know Phoebe," Tim took a sip of his coffee, "one of the oddest things about this whole business is that from all reports Shelley and Red had a very happy marriage. I know it sounds sick – the dirty old man marries his child prostitute – but apparently he doted on her and she loved learning about the business and they got along just fine. As a matter of fact, soon she knew more about Watson's Trucking than he did. Turned out the kid had a real flair for all kinds of business – trucks, loans, what have you – didn't take long before she was the family expert, not him."

"Are she and Red still together?"

"He died. Had a stroke the night of Shelley's nineteenth birthday and died a week later. Left everything to his wife."

"When was that?"

"Around this time last year."

"So she's been loan-sharking for a year," I said. "That fits with what Candi's friend told us."

"Not entirely," Tim said. "Shelley's not taking on any new customers. Apparently she's gradually steering the business out of the loans and the other questionable stuff and going legit. She's ambitious. She's got her sights set on the business big-time and with her kind of brains and some working capital from Red's estate, she'll probably make it. My guess is that she's realized small-time loan-sharking isn't worth the hassle or the bad reputation if it goes wrong."

"Then why is she still lending money and why does she send those two creeps out to do her dirty work?"

"The loan accounts that are still active likely date from Red's time and she's not willing to write them off. Probably there's too much money involved. As for the loan officers, it's like I said, those guys and Shelley go back a long time together and they still look out for each other. The two of them work for her now and whenever they get into trouble she's there to bail them out. Just like old times. The one with the tattoo did a few months for his part in a drunken brawl but that's the only adult jail time either of them has logged, which must rate as some kind of miracle."

"So, you're telling me that Candi's friend is in hock to a widowed, teenage, genius ex-hooker turned business tycoon?"

"Yeah. That about sums it up," he said. "It's a weird one, isn't it?"

Before I could agree with him, the phone rang. It was Candi wanting to know if Tim had showed up on my doorstep.

"Tim's here now," I told her pointedly. "And he's tracked down the loan shark." I got away with the condensed version of what Tim had told me by promising to phone her later. Even so, she wouldn't let me hang up until I'd recapped the Saga of Shelley, which took a few minutes. The story sounded even more bizarre in the retelling. While I was on the phone Tim took his coffee and wandered over to the piano. He sat on the bench and leafed through the music on the rack next to it. I finally said goodbye to Candi after promising that we'd set up a time to talk to Shelley Watson.

"You play?" Tim nodded at the piano.

"Strictly for my own enjoyment," I said.

"I see you've got some violin music as well as piano." He held up a book of Bach sonatas for violin and piano. "You play the fiddle too?"

"No. The violin scores belong to my brother. He's the family fiddler. We used to have to play together in the music festival every year when we were kids. Our parents thought it would do good things for us, give us poise and all that. It didn't and we hated it."

"What's this?" He held up a folder full of tattered old sheet music tied together with a piece of string.

"A collection of tangos. They belonged to my Uncle Andrew. He was a dentist and one of his patients was from Argentina. She gave them to him. They're quite old. Most of them were published in Argentina in the thirties and they're all by Gardel. That was his heyday I think, late twenties, early thirties."

"By who?"

"Carlos Gardel. He was as big a star in South America as Fred Astaire was in North America. They even declared a national day of mourning in Argentina when he was killed in a plane crash. At least that's what Uncle Andrew told me. My uncle was a big tango fan."

"Do you ever play them?" he asked.

"Occasionally. I haven't for a while." I hadn't looked at the folder since Andrew died.

"Just a minute." He bolted off the stool. "Wait right here." He handed me his coffee mug and ran out the door. The dog bounded after him. They reappeared a minute later. Tim carried a battered violin case. He put it on the coffee table and took out the violin. "I take it with me whenever I have to go out of town. I play it at night before I go to sleep. It helps me relax."

"That must really enchant the people in the room next door."

"You're just jealous because your piano is too big to fit in your car. Now, come on, let's do some of these tangos before I have to leave for Medicine Hat. Give me an A so I can tune this thing." I sat at the piano and hit the A above middle C. "I think we should start with one you know really well so I can hitch a ride on the piano."

"How about this one in honour of your family roots? It's about horse racing." I opened the yellowing sheets of "*Por Una Cabeza*," "By a Head" in English, and put it on the music stand. Uncle Andrew had pencilled in an English translation of the lyrics. Typical tango stuff, they compared love to a lost horse race in which a man has no control, a game of chance where fate rules. Tango lyrics are usually about love and loss and the cruelty of fate. The music, however, is exclusively about sex. At least that's how it felt that night in my house when Tim and I started to play.

We were a little shaky at first but pretty soon we were sailing. Far from needing to hitch a ride, Tim's violin soared and sang above the piano, its voice clear and strong. There are subtle rhythms within the tango's insistent forward beat and he found them all. He stood close behind me so he could read the music over my shoulder. I could feel the heat of his body on my back. We followed each other instinctively, building to each crescendo and pulling back through each diminuendo until we reached the tango's climax and our last chords pulsed through the foothills night. Playing tangos with Tim was not like playing Bach with my brother. Not at all.

The next day, Candi took an early lunch hour. I picked her up at the station and we drove to Watson's Trucking in Highfield, an industrial district just off the Blackfoot Trail. Highfield is not a neighbourhood that goes overboard on greenery unless you count the weeds growing out of the cracks in the parking lots. We drove past an assortment of strip malls and warehouses until we pulled up in front of the cinderblock building that housed Watson's Trucking and two other businesses. Watson's was the last in the row of three identical glass doors that led to the business offices inside. A couple of Watson rigs were backed into the two loading bays that occupied the rest of the building. I pushed open the door to the front office. A sleigh bell tied to its inner handle with a grubby piece of string announced our arrival.

Inside was a no-frills, strictly business kind of office, the sort of place that looks like there's never quite enough time to get anything done but the essentials. A receptionist's desk made of metal and Formica faked to look like wood grain faced three chrome and vinyl armchairs lined up along the opposite wall. On the desk, a sea of business forms and invoices threatened to drown the computer. Behind the receptionist's chair, a closed door with Shelley Watson's name stencilled across its frosted-glass window led to an inner office. A large colour photo of an old-fashioned step van painted with the Watson's Trucking logo hung above the chairs. It was the room's only decoration aside from a framed eight-by-ten of two children on the receptionist's desk. Suspended from the ceiling, directly over the front door, a small television camera surveyed the scene below.

The receptionist's desk was empty. The chrome chairs were not. A fat man with a large tattoo of a naked woman on his hairy arm lounged in one. I suspected that the fat covered a mound of muscle. A somewhat younger and much thinner man with acne and a greasy ponytail occupied another. Tattoo and

Ponytail. No question that we'd found the source of Jonathan's loans and David's broken nose.

"Sweet Jesus." Tattoo shook his head in mock wonder. "I think I just died and went to heaven. Will you look at the tits on that blonde one?"

"They're nice tits," Ponytail nodded his carefully considered agreement. "They're very nice." He stopped worrying his pimples for a moment and cast a seriously appraising look in my direction. "But this one has a better ass," he concluded gravely. "You have a very pretty ass, ma'am." He smiled sweetly at me. Clearly, Ponytail's truck was a tire or two short of a set.

"That's just cause she's wearing pants and you can see it better, dickhead. I'll bet the blonde one's ass is even better than her tits if you could get a look under that skirt."

"Excuse me. We're looking for Shelley Watson." Candi reacted with the Canadian female's first line of defence. She pretended she hadn't heard.

"Shelley's real busy," Ponytail said earnestly. "And Rhonda's busy too. That's Rhonda's desk." He pointed to the receptionist's desk. "We're looking after things out here for her."

"And you can sit down right here and wait until they're done being busy." Tattoo ran his stubby, none-too-clean fingers in a slow circle round the seat of the empty chair between him and Ponytail then rested his hand palm-up on the vinyl.

"They can't both sit there." Ponytail gave the problem serious consideration. "There's only one chair."

"My friend," Tattoo smirked, "as long as I've got a face, these women got a place to sit."

"Look, if you're trying to make me sick, you've done it," Candi said icily. "Just tell your boss we're here."

"Hey, what's wrong with you lady? Can't you take a joke?" Tattoo turned to his companion. "You know what? I think we got ourselves a couple of lesbians here. They can't take a joke. They don't like men. Yeah, that's what we got ourselves – a pair of goddamn dykes." He turned back to Candi and me. "Hey, you girls really dig doing it to each other?"

"If you're the alternative," Candi said.

It took a while, but the meaning of her remark finally sunk in. Tattoo's face flushed with anger.

"You fucking dykes." The venom in his voice was frightening. He raised his fist and started up out of his chair but seemed to think the better of it. He glanced up at the security camera and subsided back onto the vinyl. The camera must have been attached to a recorder and, angry as he was, Tattoo had enough sense not to punch Candi for taped posterity. "You goddamn fucking dykes."

"Yeah," Ponytail nodded sagely. "Fucking dykes."

"You know," I said, in my best conciliatory tone, "I think we got off to a very bad start here. Maybe we could try again. Right from the beginning."

"You're right," Candi agreed. "Hi. I'm Candi Sinclair and this is my associate, Phoebe Fairfax. I'm sorry but I didn't quite catch your names."

"Fuck off," Tattoo said.

"Well, Mr. Off, would you please tell Ms. Watson that we're here to see her." Candi gave him her best smile.

"Fuck off," Tattoo repeated. Now he was frustrated as well as angry. He was smart enough to suspect that Candi might be laughing at him but, if she was, he didn't get the joke.

"Candi," I said, "I have a feeling that Mr. Off isn't comfortable with this last-name formality. I think he's probably accustomed to more casual forms of address."

"You're right, Phoebe," Candi agreed seriously. She turned back to Tattoo. "Look Fuck, tell your boss we're here."

Tattoo leapt to his feet just as the door to the inner office opened. Two women stood on the threshold. One was very young and pretty in a fresh-faced high school cheerleader sort of way. She wore a business suit, so expensively cut and beautifully tailored it was worthy of Ella. Actually, the suit was too sophisticated. It made her look like she was dressed up in her mother's clothes. The other woman, looking pleasantly middle-aged in her flowered print dress, sat down at the receptionist's desk.

The business suit looked at us and then at Tattoo and Ponytail. She took the situation in at once. Tattoo subsided back down onto the vinyl.

"What are you two doing here?" she snapped. Despite her youth she was very much the boss. "You can't have finished cleaning that rig already."

"We're on our lunch hour, Shel," Ponytail explained thoughtfully.

"Not any more you're not," she said. "And not in here. Now get lost." They did.

"Are you Shelley Watson?" Candi interrupted.

"What can I do for you?" the young woman answered.

"We'd like to talk to you," Candi said.

"Sorry but I have an appointment. If you need a truck, Rhonda can help you." She started back into her office.

"It's important," Candi said. "It's about Jonathan Webster."

Shelley turned abruptly and looked at us. "Then I guess you'd better come in." She motioned us into her office. "You've got ten minutes."

Shelley's office, while hardly opulent, was at least a little less spartan than the outer room. Here the chairs were covered in cloth, not vinyl, and a conservative beige broadloom hid the industrial grey lino. However, her desk was simply a larger version of Rhonda's and the filing cabinets behind it were surplus-store green. Art seemed to be Shelley's one indulgence. A couple of Jack Snow lithographs kept company with a Gissing oil on the wall behind Candi and me, and a truly wonderful small bronze of a horse chasing a wolf occupied a place of honour on a specially lit shelf beside the desk. The bronze was an original Charlie Russell. I'd only seen one like it before and that was in the Buffalo Bill Museum in Cody, Wyoming. That kind of art doesn't come cheap. I wondered how much of the gallery was the work of the trucks and how much was thanks to Jonathan Webster and idiots like him.

"What can I do for you?" Shelley sat behind her desk and motioned us to two chairs in front of it. The harsh noon sun shone in through two narrow windows behind her. The back lighting emphasized the severe lines of her suit while it outlined her hair in a halo of gold. She looked like an underage angel on her way to a businessman's funeral.

"My name is Candi Sinclair. This is Phoebe Fairfax. We've come about Jonathan Webster," Candi repeated.

"What about him? I read in the paper that he was dead." There was nothing in the least angelic or even youthful about Shelley's hard, flat voice. It was the voice of a woman who had heard it all and said a lot of it too.

"He owed you money, didn't he?" Candi continued. Shelley did not reply.

"We know he did. We also know that you sent those two charmers we met out front to get the money off him and when you found out he was dead you sent them back to get it out of his girlfriend." Shelley maintained her silence.

"So then they beat up her boyfriend and threatened to hurt her grandmother. Now what's the point of that? How is threatening old ladies going to get your money back? Tracy can't pay you. She's broke. Besides, she doesn't owe you any money. Jonathan did."

"Supposing any of this is true," Shelley said, "what's it to you?"

"We're her friends," Candi said. I didn't disagree. It wasn't the time to discuss the finer points of my relationship with Tracy.

Shelley relapsed into silence. I could see that she was sizing us up, deciding if we were official trouble come to plague her or exactly what we claimed to be, a couple of bumbling amateurs out to help a friend.

"Did you know Jonathan?" she asked at last.

"We only met him once," Candi replied. "Just before he died."

"What did you think of him?"

"What can you tell in ten minutes?" Candi shrugged. "Besides, he was really sick when I talked to him."

"What about you?" She turned to me.

"I thought he was a four-star piece of shit."

Shelley smiled. It wasn't what you'd call a warm smile but it was better than the lizard looks she'd been giving us up to now.

"Hey, let's be fair," she said. "Maybe if you'd known him a little longer – say twenty minutes, half an hour – you might have only given him three stars. I mean the guy was a pretty good hairstylist."

"You could be charged with assault for what those two guys did to David Cavendish," Candi pointed out indignantly.

"I don't think that's very likely, do you?" Shelley said. She had evidently decided Candi and I were as harmless as we looked. "Tracy isn't going to tell the police anything more than she has to. The way I figure it, she's in enough trouble already with Jonathan murdered and her the main suspect. Why would she add another motive to the list? And you've got to admit that having a guy rip off your money to pay his gambling debts might make you feel like murdering him. Especially if he beat you up too." Shelley made her point. "No. I don't think Tracy is going to tell the police anything about this. Not the Tracy I know."

"So you know Tracy," I said.

"Of course I know Tracy. I used to go to Jonathan and Eddy Sedge's hair salon. Jonathan cut my hair until they went out of business. I got to know him and Tracy pretty well. She even read my cards once."

"Did the cards tell her that you're a loan shark?" Candi asked.

"I'm no loan shark," Shelley bristled. "I'm not in the money-lending business. I'm the president of a trucking company."

"You lend people money and, when they can't pay, you send those two goons out front to beat them up. That doesn't sound like the trucking business to me," Candi said.

"I occasionally do a friend a favour. That's all," Shelley said. "Jonathan was a friend. I did him a favour."

"Some favour," Candi said. "David's nose is never going to be the same."

"I'm sorry this David guy got hurt," Shelley said. "That should never have happened. They were only supposed to talk to Tracy. They got a little carried away. But Tracy can take some of the blame herself. If she'd returned my calls, nobody would have got hurt. I got sick of leaving messages on her machine."

"Then Tracy knew you'd loaned Jonathan money," I said.

"Of course she knew," Shelley said. "Last time he came to me she sat where you are now and watched him sign the note."

"And now you're claiming she owes you forty-three thousand dollars," Candi said.

"Forty-five," Shelley corrected.

"It was forty-three thousand last week," Candi said. "Where did the other two thousand come from?"

"Interest."

"That's not interest, that's extortion."

"No," Shelley said matter-of-factly. "It's five per cent a week and I think you'll find that, compared to what you call loan-sharking, five per cent is pretty reasonable."

"But that would be over two hundred and fifty per cent a year!"

"No, it wouldn't," she disagreed again. "It's five per cent, per week, compounded weekly."

"But that's usury. It's illegal. Nobody can charge that kind of interest."

"I can."

Even Candi had no reply to this.

"Look, I'm not in the money-lending business and I'm not a bank." Shelley leaned back in her chair. "Like I said, I occasionally do a favour for a friend, that's all. Jonathan came to me and said he needed some help so I helped him. He'd come to my husband for help before and he was always good for the money. He knew exactly what he was doing and the terms he was doing it on. People make their own choices. I never pulled any tricky stuff on Jonathan. He made a free choice."

"Don't you think you might be out of luck this time," I said. "After all, the guy is dead."

"I don't believe in luck. I've seen what happens to people who believe in luck – they die broke. I believe in compound interest."

"But how can Jonathan pay you?" Candi said. "He's dead."

"Tracy isn't."

"But Tracy doesn't have any money. You know she's broke. Where's she going to get forty-five thousand by the end of the week?"

"That's really not my problem, is it?" Shelley looked at her watch. "Look. I don't want to be unreasonable here. Tell Tracy to return my calls and we'll talk. Tell her I'm willing to give her to the end of the month. She should be able to come up with something before then. Anyway she's got until June thirtieth."

"That's not enough time. You could at least give her until September."

"No way," Shelley shook her head. "She'll probably be in jail by then."

"In jail?"

"For murdering Jonathan," Shelley said. "Not that anyone would blame her. Your friend is right. He was a shit."

"You can't be serious," Candi said.

"June thirtieth. That's it." Shelley got up, collected her briefcase from the floor beside her desk, and walked to the door.

"June thirtieth but with no more interest added," Candi bargained.

Shelley hesitated for a moment. "Ah, what the hell. I must be getting soft. Okay, no more interest compounded until July first. But no money by then and nothing changes." She opened the office door. "And now that we've got that straight I have to leave or I'll be late for class."

"You're a student?" Candi asked.

"I'm in commerce at U. of C. Part time." Shelley said this with genuine pride and an uncharacteristic shyness. "In another two years I'll have my degree. Then maybe I'll go to grad school." For the first time, she sounded as young as she looked. "Anyway I've got to get going. This is a special summer seminar series and it's my turn to give the paper."

"What's your topic?" I asked, curious.

"Business ethics."

13

"Tracy lied to us," Candi said.

"Yet again," I agreed.

We were back in her office at the station. On the small monitor perched on top of the filing cabinet, an announcer silently mouthed the news. Then my footage of Jonathan at the psychic fair came on the screen. I reached over and turned up the volume. Since Jonathan's death had officially become a murder, my tape was hot stuff. This time the News boys had added some of their own footage of Tracy walking from her house to her car. They'd also found out about the beatings and the gambling and were having a field day safe in the knowledge that the dead can't sue for libel.

"But why? Why would she lie to us?" Candi was genuinely puzzled. It was a rare moment.

"Probably because she thought we didn't have a hope in hell of tracing Shelley and if we hadn't got lucky with Two Bob and Tim she'd have been right." The item on Jonathan ended and I turned down the volume on the monitor.

"But that still doesn't tell us why."

"Maybe it's how she survived life with Jonathan. It's a way of protecting herself."

"But why does she need protection from us? We want to help her, not hurt her. All we're doing is trying to get at the truth. Why can't she see that? Unless maybe she's protecting somebody. Maybe David killed Jonathan and Tracy's protecting him. God knows the man had a good enough reason to want Jonathan out of the way. So did Sadie Nightingale for that matter. It must have been hell for her watching what Jonathan was doing to Tracy, beating her up and all. And Phoebe I know you think Tracy is sort of a drip . . ." This was an understatement. In my view, Tracy gave the term drip whole new dimensions of dampness. "But she really would do anything to protect her grandma. All the same, this lying is crazy." Candi leaned back in her chair and put her feet up on the desk. "I mean look at all the people who had a motive for killing Jonathan and the opportunity too. What about all those people the Graces saw that night at the house? Which reminds me, Edward Sedge is the only one we haven't talked to yet. We'll have to take care of that soon. We've got a lot to ask him."

"Candi, we are not the police. We don't have any right to go barging around asking a lot of questions. Why would Edward Sedge talk to us? What makes you think he'd want to discuss his relationship to Jonathan with a couple of strangers."

"We'd never met Shelley Watson before today and she talked to us."

"Shelley talked to us because she wants her money back. Edward doesn't have any reason at all."

"Oh yes he does. Or at least he will. He'll have to talk to us because he's going to cut your hair. I'll make an appointment right now." Feet back on the floor, she reached across her desk for the phone book and started to look up the number for La Maison.

"Wait just a minute here," I protested. "Why me? If you're so keen to talk to Edward Sedge then get him to do your hair."

"Phoebe, you know that Ralph would have a fit if I let anyone but him touch my hair." Ralph is Candi's regular stylist. He specializes in the calculatedly unkempt look, the kind of artful mess that takes constant applications of both skill and money to maintain. Ralph's salon overlooks the money in Candi's case, rightly figuring that they recoup their investment in the "Miss Sinclair's hair by My Mane Man" credit that rolls by at the end of every edition of "A Day in the Lifestyle." "It's taken him over a year to get my hair in shape. Besides, he'd be really, really hurt."

"Well, how do you think Vera's going to feel?" I said.

"Who's Vera?"

"My stylist. The Vera of Vera's House of Beauty in Turner Valley."

"I don't mean to be rude," Candi cast a critical eye over my hair, "but how long has it been since your hair and Vera saw each other?"

"I guess it's been a while," I admitted grudgingly. I hadn't been to the House of Beauty – one chair, one sink, two dryers, and coffee from the restaurant next door – since last winter. Unlike Candi's, my hair manages to look messy without the aid of regular salon visits. "Do you know how much they charge at La Maison?" I decided it was time to open a new front. "I couldn't afford to walk in the door, even if they'd let me."

"So I'm paying for half," Candi said. "Come on, Phoebe, give yourself a treat. What've you got to lose besides a few split ends and a little money?"

"A little money?" I was fighting a losing battle. "You call that little?"

"Look, if I make the appointment in my name I'm pretty sure they'll give me a discount. Places like that always do if they figure they can get some advertising mileage out of it."

"Somehow I think they're going to notice that I'm not Candi Sinclair when I show up for the appointment."

"But I'm coming with you so what can they say?" She dialled the number, made an appointment for Saturday morning at eleven-thirty, and negotiated a fifty per cent discount on the regular price.

"Jonathan's funeral is this Saturday, isn't it?" I asked.

"Two o'clock Saturday afternoon at a funeral home somewhere off Elbow Drive. Jonathan wasn't religious and neither is Tracy so it's more of a memorial service than a real funeral. There's not even going to be a burial. His body has already been cremated and right after the service Tracy wants to scatter his ashes. . . . Oh no."

"What's wrong?"

"I promised Tracy I'd get hold of a rowboat and I forgot all about it until now. Dammit Phoebe, where can you rent a rowboat?" From funerals to rowboats – this time even I couldn't follow. I must have looked very puzzled because Candi actually backtracked and did a little explaining. "Tracy wants to scatter Jonathan's ashes on the Elbow River behind the house they used to live in. She says it's the only place where they were really happy. So we need a boat – a rowboat or a raft or something like that."

"Why can't Tracy walk down to the river and scatter him from the bank?"

"Because she wants to do it right behind their old house and you have to go through people's yards to get to the water there," Candi explained. I didn't look convinced. "I mean Tracy can hardly march up to some stranger's front door and say, 'Excuse me, but would you mind if I cut through your yard because I want to toss my murdered boyfriend's ashes in the river at the bottom of your garden.'"

"Are you sure it's legal to scatter ashes on the river in the city? I think the law is pretty particular about what you do with human remains."

"So who's going to know?" She reached for the phone book again. "I guess we're going to need a trailer or a car roof-rack or something to put the boat on to haul it to the river, aren't we? What should I look under? Maybe I'd better start with B for boats. Why didn't I remember to do this earlier?"

"Would a canoe do?" I asked. "If a canoe would be okay then you can use Alex's. It's sitting in my parents' garage. There's a roof-rack there that you can put on your car too." My brother Alex lives with his wife and two children in Vancouver but his beautiful red canvas and cedar canoe still lives at home. I occasionally use it but mostly it just sits on the garage rafters collecting dust.

"That would be great except for one thing," Candi paused. "I've never been in a canoe. Would you mind coming with us and driving the thing?" This time I didn't bother to argue.

After Candi went back to work, I stopped in at Cyrrie's to return the wool sweater that Edith had left at my place the day of our Sheep River excursion. He was sitting in the garden preparing for the Monday board meeting of his arts foundation. A tall stack of grant applications sat on the table beside his garden chair. Edith wasn't home.

"She and Sadie Nightingale have gone off shopping together. Edith wants some clothes. I think she's determined to look as sporty and up-to-date as Sadie." He put the application he was reading down on the pile and took off his reading glasses. "It's wonderful that those two have hit it off – good for both of them. I'm so busy getting ready for this meeting in Edmonton I've been neglecting Edith, but she's having such a good time with Sadie that I don't think she's even noticed. And maybe having Edith around is helping poor Sadie through this dreadful business of Jonathan Webster's murder. Have you seen the television coverage? They're really making a meal of it."

"I know," I said. "I shot some of the footage they're using. I bet they'll be out in full force for the funeral. It's on Saturday."

"Sadie told me that this morning. I promised I'd take Edith. Are you going?"

I told him about my part in Tracy's plans for scattering Jonathan's ashes. "So," I concluded, "I promised Candi I'd get Alex's canoe. Do you have a key to Mom and Dad's garage? I have a house key but not one to the garage."

"I have a key," Cyrrie said, "but it's not going to do you much good. Don't you remember? Tony and Carolyn borrowed the canoe to take on their holiday to Prince Albert National Park." Tony is my other brother, the violin playing one. Carolyn is his significant other, at least that's how she refers to herself. "Carolyn is going to write an article about following in Grey Owl's footsteps or paddle strokes or whatever for some German magazine. In any case, you're out of luck, my dear, because the canoe is in Saskatchewan."

I drove home feeling very put out. I was annoyed with myself for having forgotten about Tony's canoeing holiday but I was even more irritated with Tracy. For someone I'd known less than a week she was proving a major nuisance. Now, thanks to her, I'd get to spend Friday rounding up a canoe and Saturday afternoon sprinkling Jonathan in the river. Personally, I'd have said good riddance and dumped him in the ashtrays at the Elbow Lodge Casino.

When I got home, Bertie and I went for a walk along the stream. Then I settled down at the editing bench to finish the work I'd neglected while playing tangos with Tim. It was almost eight before hunger pangs reminded me it was time to stop and make myself a bite to eat. I was halfway to the kitchen when the phone rang. It was the tango man himself.

"Where are you?" I asked.

"In my hotel room in Medicine Hat."

"Playing your violin?"

"I'm thinking about it but I miss your piano."

"The folks next door won't."

"Did you talk to Shelley Watson yet?" he asked.

"Candi and I went to see her today and you can tell your police friends they were right. She's really something." I gave him a carefully edited version of our visit to Watson's Trucking.

"So you managed to negotiate some extra time for Candi's friend," he said. "Good going."

"Not all that good. Only until the end of the month."

"That's way better than I thought you'd do."

"It should give her a little room to manoeuvre."

"And now can I persuade you to forget about loan sharks and Candi's friend and her troubles and spend some time with me?" he asked. "It would make my grandfather very happy if you did."

"Are you telling me that Two Bob's happiness is at stake here?"

"Absolutely."

"Then my time is yours."

"What would you say to spending Saturday hiking in the Kananaskis, then back to town and dinner? You like Szechuan food?"

"Szechuan is great and so is the Kananaskis and I'd like to very much but I have to go to a funeral on Saturday."

"Don't tell me," Tim said. "The boyfriend."

"None other."

"Funerals don't take all afternoon. Why don't you meet me after? We can do something then."

"Because I'm going to be cruising down the Elbow River scattering boyfriend ashes. If I can drum up a canoe, that is." I found myself telling him the story of the funeral, the ashes, and the part my brother's missing canoe was to have played in the whole dreary drama. All the irritation I'd felt earlier in the day came flooding back.

"Phoebe, there's no need to get in a twist about this. I've got a canoe which I will be more than happy to put at your disposal Saturday afternoon."

"Really? You have a canoe?"

"And a couple of paddles to go with it."

"You're sure you wouldn't mind?"

"I'd get to be with you so why should I mind? Look, after the funeral I'll meet you at Stanley Park. We can put the canoe in the water there. You paddle down the river and toss the boyfriend and then you float downstream to where I'll be waiting to pick you up."

"You could meet us by the footbridge," I agreed. "You know, the one beside the racetrack. You can drive really close to the water there."

"So there's your boat problem solved. And then we'll have the rest of the day to ourselves."

We talked for a while longer. Neither of us wanted to hang

up. I hoped Candi was right and my hormones weren't playing another obnoxious joke. They were certainly playing at something. That night I dreamed of black-haired men with curls like lambs and canoes that never tipped.

Next morning, I went back to work at the editing bench. Aside from a leg-stretching walk with Bertie at lunchtime, I managed an uninterrupted day. By mid-afternoon, my shoulders felt cramped and my eyes were tired from looking at flickering images on the tiny screen so I decided to call it quits and go for a run with Pete. When I got back, there was a message from Candi on my answering machine inviting me to join her and Nick for an early dinner at her place before Nick's channelling session with Cyrrie's horse.

Calgary's Friday rush-hour traffic was heavy but it was all headed away from the city centre so it didn't slow me down much. I arrived at Candi's apartment a little before six. She lives on the top floor of a big old red-brick house in lower Mount Royal. When I arrived, she was busy tossing the salad and Nick was slicing a baguette. He was very quiet for Nick. He gave me my usual big hug and a kiss and then went back to his bread board. He remained subdued and abstracted all through dinner, eating very little and refusing a glass of wine. It reminded me of the way he behaves before the opening performance of one of his plays. Candi drove us to the track in her car. Nick hardly said a word all the way there.

"It's packed in here." Candi surveyed the backstretch parking lot in some dismay. "I forgot this was a race night. Cyrrie's supposed to meet us at the gate at seven-thirty and it's almost that now. Maybe I'll drop you guys off and go find a parking spot."

Nick and I got out of the car and strolled over to the race

office. We stood outside by the gate in the warm June evening, listening to the call of the fourth race over the backstretch loudspeaker. "And they're off to a good even start." The track announcer's voice floated on the still, dusty air. By now, Nick looked not simply abstracted, but a little queasy as well.

"Are you feeling okay, Nick?"

He shook his head in mute misery and swallowed a couple of times. "Jesus Phoebe, how did I get myself into this? I'm scared shitless of horses."

"Then why did you say you'd do it, you idiot? It might be different if you actually believed any of this guff but really Nick it's . . ."

"Phoebe, don't start that again," he interrupted. "Look, I need a friend here. I'm a dying man. I'm about to be trampled by a racehorse right in front of the woman I love."

I couldn't help laughing even though the poor man truly did look miserable.

"The horse is not going to trample you." I tried to be reassuring. "Prairie Fire is a very well-behaved animal and Sandra and Cyrrie will be right there with you. Besides, who says you have to go into Prairie's stall to channel him? Why can't you just stand at the door and hold his halter? Look, you're the one who's supposed to be the expert here so you can make up the rules to suit yourself. You're the actor – improvise."

"You don't think it would look phony if I didn't actually go into the stall with him?" He brightened a little.

"Pet channelling? Phony? Nick, how could you even think such a thing?"

"See, there you go again." He shook his head sadly. "You poor woman. Totally out of touch with higher forms of communication." For the first time that evening, he almost sounded like the real Nick.

The fourth race had been over for five minutes before Cyrrie and Sandra Doyle walked up to the gate from the backstretch and Candi hurried over from the parking lot. After Cyrrie registered us with track security we headed for the barn. Candi and Nick walked ahead with Sandra who talked non-stop, delivering a highly technical explanation of Prairie Fire's symptoms. Nick was too busy keeping a nervous eye peeled for passing horses to listen but, even if he had, he wouldn't have understood a word. Cyrrie and I followed behind them.

"Cyrrie, why are you doing this?" I asked. "You don't really believe that Nick can communicate with animals, do you? I'll bet Edith put you up to it, didn't she? Are you doing it for her?"

"You ask far too many questions, my dear. You always have. Now why don't you simply relax and enjoy the evening? If it would make you feel better, think of it as a form of entertainment."

"But Cyrrie," I protested, "you're far too rational to believe any of this stuff. I know you are. I can't understand why you're doing it. It doesn't make any sense."

"And what does?" He shrugged and smiled serenely. We entered the barn and walked down the row to Prairie's stall. "Now Phoebe," Cyrrie cautioned as we approached the others, "I don't want you giving Nicholas a hard time tonight. Let the man do what he's here for."

Edith was waiting for us in her new runners and a denim jacket with matching slacks. She even had a baseball cap with the Flames logo on it. The tweeds were history.

"Nicholas, are you certain that having all of us around won't disturb you?" she asked.

"Yes," Cyrrie agreed, "maybe you'd sooner be alone with the horse?"

"No, no. Please stay," Nick answered rather too quickly. "Having people around doesn't bother me at all. As long as it won't upset Prairie Fire, that is," he added as an afterthought.

"Why don't you ask him?" I said. Cyrrie shot me a warning look.

Before Nick could protest, Sandra opened the stall door and led Prairie out. The horse stood quietly, looking at us with amiable interest. He'd lost a little weight since I'd last seen him.

"Here," Sandra thrust the halter shank into Nick's trembling hand. "See what you can do with him." She joined the rest of us, leaving Nick alone in the middle of the barn holding the horse. For a moment, I half expected him to drop the rope and run, but he stood his ground. He even managed to put a tentative hand on Prairie Fire's neck. Then, for a few minutes, horse and man simply stood together quietly. The rest of us were silent too, but all the while I kept waiting for some drama from Nick, at the least a few flamboyantly theatrical gestures. But he remained still, his attention focused on Prairie. At last, he turned to us.

"It's something to do with his mouth," he said with quiet assurance. "I think his teeth are bothering him."

"But the vet checked his mouth last week," Sandra said. "He couldn't find a thing." She took Prairie's halter shank from Nick.

"Did he take X-rays?" Cyrrie asked.

"No," Sandra said. "He thought since he couldn't see anything and Prairie was eating and seemed to be managing a bit okay that his mouth was probably fine."

"It's his mouth," Nick repeated with a confidence that surprised me. "And whatever it is, it's somewhere on the left side. Probably the lower left."

I had to admit that he was improvising brilliantly. He had chosen restraint over dazzle and it was very convincing. For a moment, even I believed him.

"Then I suppose we'd better have Dr. Musgrove and his X-ray machine out," Cyrrie said.

"I'll call him and make an appointment," Sandra said. "But it's going to be expensive."

"So is keeping a racehorse who can't race," Cyrrie pointed out. "Thank you Nicholas." He shook Nick's hand. "It was good of you to come tonight."

"Let me know how he does," Nick said. "And remember that I guarantee results." He looked pointedly at me. "If it's not Prairie's mouth that's causing the trouble, then you don't owe me any money. Not a cent."

Except for Sandra, who had a horse running in the eighth, we all went back to Cyrrie's for coffee. Away from the barns, his ordeal by racehorse over, Nick's colour and spirits returned to normal. A good belt or two or three of Cyrrie's cognac and they were better than normal. In fact they were so good that he sang Sondheim songs in the car all the way home to Candi's place. He and Candi walked me to where I'd parked the car. They stood together under a streetlight, his arm around her shoulders, her's around his waist, and watched me drive off. As I turned the corner, a chorus of "A Weekend in the Country" boomed through the darkened neighbourhood.

14

The morning of Jonathan's funeral the sun shone, the birds sang, and the new grass in the pasture was drenched with dew. The dog came home sopping from his morning patrol. I dried his fur and wiped his feet on an old towel before we set off together on the drive to Calgary. Bertie is good about staying by himself but he gets lonely if I leave him for too long. Often, when I have lots to do in town, he comes with me and spends the day with Cyrrie. Both of them regard this as a great treat. When we arrived, he made his usual big fuss over Cyrrie and trotted happily up the walk with him. At least one of us was going to enjoy the day.

I got to La Maison a little early for my appointment. The salon occupies a recently renovated old two-storey frame house just off Seventeenth Avenue, not far from Candi's place. I sat in my car in the parking lot at the back of the building and waited for her. She came striding into the lot on the dot of eleven-thirty and hurried me around the house and up the steps to the front door. I turned the big brass handle in the centre of the imposing slab of oak and pushed. The door didn't budge.

"That's funny," I said. "It's locked. But they have to be open. They have customers." I rattled the handle.

"Maybe we should try the doorbell." Candi reached in front of me to a little brass plate with Please Ring engraved on it and pushed the button directly below. Seconds later, a tall, slender woman in her mid-thirties answered the door. She wore tailored cream slacks and a raw silk shirt. Her hair and makeup were as flawless and beautifully understated as her clothes. She ushered us into a small reception room off the entrance hall. There wasn't a sink or barber chair to be seen.

"Mr. Edward will be with you presently to discuss your styling needs. In the meantime, may I bring you some coffee?" She stood at the door with a dancer's poise.

"Thanks," Candi said. "That would be great."

The house had been renovated by a lavish and loving hand. The reception room was beautiful – oak woodwork and plenty of it, new hardwood flooring partly covered by a Persian rug, heavy brass door hardware, William Morris-style paper on the walls. Morning light streamed through the mullioned panes of the big east window. Even the French provincial furniture – usually not a style to my taste – was perfect. On the coffee table copies of *Vogue* and *Architectural Digest* lay casually scattered among the coffee-table books, some of which actually looked interesting. I had just opened one on the history of *haute couture* when the receptionist returned carrying a tray with bone-china cups and saucers and a thermos carafe of coffee. She set the tray on the table and then left the room. French doors on silent runners slid shut behind her.

"I don't believe this." I sat down on the chesterfield.

Telemann trickled from hidden stereo speakers and the faint scent of roses hinted at sachets of potpourri. "Where are the sinks and dryers? Why doesn't it smell like someone's getting a perm?"

Candi sat at the other end of the chesterfield and poured us each some French roast. Edward Sedge arrived before we'd finished our first cup. He was extraordinarily tall, six-foot-six at least, and broad-shouldered to match. His voice, however, was oddly high-pitched for such a large man. It verged on the falsetto.

"Hello, I'm Edward. Welcome to La Maison," he fluted, first engulfing Candi's hand in both of his enormous ones, then mine. He wore a pink and white striped shirt open at the neck, grey slacks, and the biggest pair of cowboy boots I'd ever seen. "More coffee?" Introductions complete, he refilled both our cups, poured one for himself, and sat down in the armchair opposite. He stirred a lump of sugar into his coffee and took a tentative sip. I was beginning to wonder if we were ever going to see a pair of scissors.

"Not to worry. We'll start cutting soon enough," Edward said as if he'd read my mind. "You see at La Maison we like to take a little time to get to know our new clients. That way we can design a hairstyle that suits your lifestyle or maybe I should say your 'Day in the Lifestyle.'" He chuckled at his own witticism as he put down his cup and looked closely at Candi. "But you know – and I'm going to be brutally honest here – if I were you Candi, I wouldn't change a hair. Not one single hair. Your look is totally perfect just as it is."

"Thanks Edward," Candi said. "But we're not here for me. You're going to be working on Phoebe today."

If this news dismayed Edward Sedge he certainly didn't show it. He reclaimed his coffee and continued to sip while he asked me a little about my work and what I liked to do on my time off, about what kind of clothes I wore most often, and, finally, about what he called my present hair-care program.

"Well, I wash it every morning in the shower and then I brush it." It didn't sound like much of a program, even to me. "I use a blow-dryer quite often too. Especially in the winter." I struggled for embellishments. "And I have a curling iron." With which, I neglected to add, I singe my ears from time to time.

"So, I guess we could put you down as a casual kind of gal," Edward said. "Sportif yet elegant."

"Pretty much," I agreed. I avoided Candi's eye by looking down at the sportif runners poking out from my elegant blue jeans.

"You know, you really do have wonderful hair, Phoebe." Edward stood up and walked around the table. His movements were quick and graceful. "It's thick and heavy and it's going to be a dream to work with." He ruffled my hair with his fingertips until it stood up in spikes. "Now shake your head." He stood, towering over me, watching the spikes fall back into a tangled mess. "Will you look at that natural wave," he said optimistically. "It just won't quit. And now we'd better get you shampooed. See you in ten." He left the room with a little wave and a smile.

"I thought we were here to ask this guy about Jonathan," I said when we were alone.

"We will," Candi assured me. "We need a little time to build up his confidence in us, that's all. Talking about Jonathan is probably going to upset Edward a whole lot so it's important for him to feel that he can trust us. I thought we'd wait until he actually starts on your hair before we bring up Jonathan."

"Oh yeah," I said. "I like that idea a lot. Get Edward really upset right when he's in the middle of cutting my hair."

"Phoebe, the man is a pro."

"Who will be holding sharp pointy things right next to my head."

"So no matter what else we accomplish here today," she continued blithely, "I guarantee that you are going to get one truly incredible haircut. Besides, just being here is kind of fun. I mean, don't you think this place is neat?" She drank the last of her coffee. "I could get to really like it here."

Unfortunately, as the morning progressed, I started to like La Maison more and more too. What I saw of the rest of the house was as beautifully done as the reception room and the service more than measured up to the surroundings. Everything about the place, from the pinky-peach smock that I traded for my T-shirt to the big, warm towel that the assistant who washed my hair wrapped around my head, made me feel cosseted and comfortable. I found myself calculating what I'd have to give up in order to finance regular visits. Eating perhaps, or maybe heat and light. By the time the receptionist ushered me into what she called Mr. Edward's studio, I had been totally seduced, the last feeble cries of my inner puritan smothered by sybaritic self-indulgence and rose-tinted lights. I was shameless.

I sat in Edward's barber chair and stared at my reflection in the huge mirror. Candi perched on a small chair with Queen Anne legs right next to his workstand. Nobody seemed to think it odd that she had trailed along with me. Who knows, maybe the world is full of women who take a friend along for moral support every time they get their hair cut.

Edward arrived and after a little more preliminary chat about length and bangs he at last got down to work. He pressed a switch with his foot, a servo motor hummed, and the chair rose into the air. With my head now at a comfortable working level, he gathered the top layers of my hair, pinned them up, and began to snip around the nape of my neck, his huge hands dwarfing the scissors. He had progressed as far as my ear when Candi spoke.

"Are you going to Jonathan Webster's funeral this afternoon?"

Edward stopped in mid-snip, perilously close to my left lobe. Even for Candi, this opening didn't earn big marks for subtlety.

"You're friends of Jonathan's?" he asked sharply.

"No, we're Tracy's friends," Candi said. "She told us that you guys were all partners in your own salon. That's why we're here. She recommended you." It was news to me.

"Tell Tracy thanks." Edward started back in on my hair.

"Tracy likes you," Candi continued. "I know she thought it was really good of you to let her have some shares in your business." Edward shrugged. I flinched. "It must have been a big shock when you heard about Jonathan's death. I mean, your former partner murdered and all."

Edward stopped work and stared over my shoulder into the mirror, his eyes fixed on Candi's reflection. "Jonathan Webster was the worst thing that ever happened to me," he stated flatly. "I lost everything because of him. The man was a psychopathic bastard and I hope he rots in hell. End of story."

"You mean you don't care who murdered him?" Candi asked.

"No one could murder Jonathan. Murder is something that happens to human beings. Vermin like my ex-partner get exterminated."

"Murdered, exterminated, whatever. The police are still going to arrest someone for killing him."

"Well, it ain't gonna be this cowboy if my lawyer has anything to say about it. And I wish they would arrest somebody – anybody. The sooner the better as long as it isn't me. Then maybe they'd leave me alone."

"It's been pretty bad with the police, has it?" Candi asked sympathetically.

"Bad isn't the word," Edward said. "They've been around every day, sometimes twice. They've talked to my boss and all my friends. They've even questioned some of my customers. My lawyer says it's one step this side of harassment. You're looking at suspect numero uno, top of the list."

"I thought Tracy was their prime suspect."

"Tracy?" Edward snorted. The scissors flashed back into action. "Jon had Tracy so beaten down she didn't have the guts to leave him, never mind murder him. Even when things were going good she was totally under his thumb and when they started to go sour . . ." He shook his head.

"Why did you sell her shares in Foxy Locks?" Candi asked.

"That was Jon's idea. Tracy had been with us almost from the start and she'd worked as hard as we had to build up the business. We were doing so well I said to myself, why not? She deserved a cut. It was the stupidest thing I ever did. It made the two of them majority shareholders. Trace always did what Jon told her, so selling her those shares was like giving them to him. From that day on, he could do what he liked without even telling me. That's when I really lost my salon. Not the day the receiver locked us out. That was just a little formality."

"But what about all the money Tracy loaned you guys to keep the business going? That must have been some help," Candi said.

"What money? Trace might have given Jon money, but I

guarantee you that the business didn't see a penny of it. Most likely some pony ran away with it or he threw it away on a roulette table somewhere."

"Tracy told us about his gambling addiction."

"Ah yes. One of Jon's many charming little quirks." Edward loosened the pins and the back layers of hair fell down my neck and around my ears. "Did she tell you about the beatings? That was another."

"She told us he owed a lot of money," Candi said. "You ever hear of a woman called Shelley Watson?"

"Yeah, I remember Shelley," Edward said. "Jon used to cut her hair. A weird kid. Married some old guy and got rich."

"That's her," Candi said. "And I assume you've met her business associates?"

Edward shook his head. "I don't think so. Shelley always came to the salon alone."

"Maybe you met them when you were out at Jonathan's place in Okotoks the night before he died?" Candi continued. "A fat guy with a tattoo of a naked woman on his arm and his skinny friend with bad acne?"

Edward dropped the scissors. They clattered over the parquet floor. He picked them up, put them on a tray, and fished a clean pair out of a drawer in his workstand. Then he caught a lock of hair in his comb and began to cut.

"Look, if you're here because you think I murdered Jonathan, you can forget it." The scissors continued their way around my head. "Yes, I'm glad he's dead." Snip. "And yes, I was at his house the night before he died." Snip, snip. "But no, I didn't kill him." Snip, snip, snip. My hair fell to the floor with increasing speed.

"Shelley's a loan shark," Candi said. "Those guys are her muscle. They came after Tracy. Did they come after you too?"

"That bastard." Edward spun the barber chair around with such force I felt myself slide forward. I clutched the arms to stop myself pitching onto the floor. "I lost a business, I lost a house, and I lost a lover before he was finished with me. Just when I thought I was finally rid of him, those two things showed up on my doorstep." I pushed myself back in the chair while he loosened the clip on the last hank of hair. It flopped down over my eyes.

"Jon was up to his super-oxygenated ass in debt. When he couldn't make his payments, the muscle paid him a visit. He told them to come see me. Said that I was his partner and that we'd used the money for a joint business venture. He told them that I'd make sure they got it back." The scissors sliced into my bangs. "They came to my house the day before he died. I explained to them that Jon and I weren't partners anymore, that I hadn't seen him for months, that I didn't know anything about any money. That's when they started threatening me. They said they might have to come visit me again. Did I like baseball because maybe they'd bring along their bats."

"What about the Thursday night in Okotoks?" Candi prompted. "Did you see them then?"

"I went to Jon's place that night to have it out with him but there was nobody there. I sat in the garden and waited for him. He never showed, but Fatso and Fungus Face did. I moved back into the bushes so they wouldn't see me. I left right after they did." He whirled me around to face the mirror again. "Have they been making trouble for Tracy?"

"They beat up her boyfriend and threatened her grand-mother."

"Doesn't surprise me," Edward said. "I sure hope for Tracy's sake that they're the only ones holding Jon's paper."

"You mean you think Jonathan was in debt to other loan sharks?" Candi said.

"Loan sharks, hustlers – you name it. Jon knew a lot of people who could get very nasty if they figured they'd been stiffed. I'd be surprised if Shelley Watson is the only one Trace hears from."

"So Tracy could be in danger."

"She was probably in just as much danger when Jon was alive and beating her. Maybe more. He really beat the crap out of her a couple of times and I heard it got worse after the business folded. Compared to that, this other stuff is only little gift from beyond the grave – a *memento mori* or whatever you call it. He left them for both of us. A little something to remind us of why we hated him."

"What was your gift?" Candi asked.

"You mean what do I hate Jon for most?" Edward contemplated both my head and the question for a moment. The scissors flicked past my eyes as he absentmindedly snipped a few stray strands from my bangs. "I hate Jon for still being able to make me feel like shit even now that he's dead. I have a good job, I'm living with a guy I love, I'm getting my life together again. But I can still feel his poison."

"Well," said Candi at her cheery philosophical best, "you're alive and Jonathan's a box of ashes. Right now, I'd say he's the one who should be feeling shitty."

The roar of the blow-dryer put an end to further conversation. Edward seemed to have regained his professional composure by the time he put down the dryer and dusted my neck with a soft brush. He held a mirror so I could see the new me from all angles. "You like?"

"Very much," I said and I did. My hair was a little shorter

than I was accustomed to but it seemed thicker and softer too. Once again he ruffled it with his fingertips.

"Now shake your head," he said. I did and this time my hair fell back into place following the path of its own wave. It was as if Edward's scissors had restored it to some sort of natural order.

He pressed the foot switch and the chair dropped to ground level. I stood up. My knees felt a little shaky. All in all, it had been quite a ride. Still, I had to admit that Candi was right. I'd had the haircut of my life.

15

By half past twelve we were strolling down Seventeenth Avenue ostensibly in search of pantihose but mostly enjoying the sun. We walked in silence for a while, carried along by the crowds of shoppers going happily about their business on a perfect June afternoon. Even here in the middle of the city I could feel the day pulling me. I tried not to think of the hike in the Kananaskis with Tim that I was missing but it rankled.

"Not a cloud in the sky and we're going to Jonathan Webster's funeral," I said. "What a waste of a gorgeous Saturday."

"But this morning was okay, wasn't it?" Candi asked. "I mean Edward did tell us some pretty interesting stuff."

I shrugged noncommittally. As far as I could see, all we'd found out from Edward was that, besides his business, he'd lost a house and a lover thanks to Jonathan. But maybe Candi had listened harder than I had. I was willing to admit that my concentration wasn't at its best with those scissors whizzing around my ears.

"You think Edward could have done it?" she asked. "He sure had the motive."

"But maybe not the opportunity. Remember, the Graces said they didn't actually see him go into the house."

"But they weren't totally certain that he didn't. Besides, he could have come back after they'd gone to bed."

"I don't think so. I think that Edward told us the truth. He saw Shelley's pals, he hid, then he left."

"You're probably right," Candi agreed reluctantly. "And that means we're back where we started." For the first time, she seemed discouraged. "But I was right about one thing, wasn't I?" she continued on a slightly more optimistic note. "You got a great haircut. It looks fabulous." I tossed my head and flipped my hair in what I thought was a pretty good imitation of the women in shampoo ads on TV. "Wow, Phoebe!" Candi applauded. "You do that better than Miss Piggy."

"What are you going to wear this afternoon?" I asked.

"I was thinking of my navy suit. You know, my Ella looka-like outfit. That thing was made for funerals. I still can't figure out why I bought it. Maybe I thought the people I interview would take me more seriously or something. Dumb. How about you?"

"My dusty-rose dress and a cream blazer – the silk one my mom brought me from China last year. It's about the most conservative thing I've got. I don't own any real funeral clothes."

"Thanks a lot for getting us a canoe," Candi said.

"Thank Tim. He phoned last night. He says he'll be waiting for us in the park right after the funeral."

"You want to leave your car at my place?" she offered. "Nick has volunteered to be our chauffeur as long as he doesn't actually have to go the funeral."

"Thanks but I think I'll change at Cyrrie's and catch a ride with him and Edith. I have to go back to Cyrrie's later anyway to pick up the dog so I might as well leave the car and my clothes there too."

Edith and Cyrrie were ready to go when I arrived. They are both great believers in arriving places in what they call "good time" and everyone else calls twenty minutes early. After remarking on my transformed hair they waited with growing impatience while I changed my clothes and put on my makeup. Despite what they obviously considered foot-dragging on my part, we still arrived at the funeral home fifteen minutes early.

A couple of television crews were there already along with some newspaper and radio reporters. The ladies and gentlemen of the press stood on the sidewalk in front of the funeral home looking very casual as they smoked and talked among themselves while they waited for something to happen. I understood their nonchalance. The funeral itself wasn't a hot news item so, unless they could wangle some words out of Tracy, anything they shot here would probably end up as cover for the latest piece on the murder investigation or, at best, a human interest sidebar. I waved to the guys from our station who waved back. This earned them a stern look from one of the two funeral chapel employees who marched up and down beside the sidewalk making sure that no one stuck an unauthorized toe onto their property.

Tracy and David Cavendish pulled into the parking lot right behind us, followed by Sadie in her little red Chevy. The video tape started to roll. Tracy ignored both the cameras and the questions that the reporters called after her as she and Sadie walked over to join us. The two of them looked very elegant if not particularly funereal, Tracy in a navy and white dress with a white blazer, and Sadie in a straw-coloured linen suit. David didn't get out of the car. His nose was packed in bandages and neat stitches ran the length of the cut on his head.

A few seconds later Nick dropped Candi off. She had indeed worn her conservative Ella suit but she'd given the tailored look a whole new spin. Candi had added a hat and not just any hat. This one was a very rakish version of the cloche in navy felt with a tiny half veil of net and a peacock feather that swept past her left ear and curled up over her head like a big, swirling question mark. The iridescent eye of the feather dangled at least six inches above the top of the hat. It bobbed up and down every time she moved her head.

We stood talking in the parking lot for a few more minutes. Despite the cameras aimed at us from the street, nobody was eager to go into the chapel. It was almost two when the funeral director came and spoke to Sadie. She told him our names and he assured her that we were the only ones who would be admitted to the chapel. Jonathan's funeral was to be a strictly private affair, no reporters allowed. He summoned his two assistants from the border patrol. They went to stand guard on either side of the door while he led us into the chapel and down the centre aisle. We formed natural alliances for the occasion. Candi walked with Tracy, and Edith with Sadie, while Cyrrie and I brought up the rear. Someone began to play Bach very softly on the organ. There was a slight commotion behind us. A large man, whom I pegged for a plainclothes Mountie, flashed his ID to the two men at the door, then walked briskly into the chapel and took a seat near the back.

The six of us sat strung out along the front pew in a space built to hold two hundred. Aside from the Mountie and the funeral home staff we were it, the congregation. Not counting Jonathan, of course. A polished wooden box containing his ashes rested on the raised dais in front of us. It sat on a low table to one side of a lectern.

"Do you think anyone else is coming?" I whispered to Cyrrie. "He must have had relatives somewhere." At the least, I thought a few of Jonathan's former business associates might show if only to make sure that he was really dead. Whether they'd be allowed in was another matter.

"If they were coming then they'd be here by now," Cyrrie said. "I should think we're it."

One cop and the six of us. Even for Jonathan, it seemed pretty sad. However, neither Cyrrie nor I had reckoned with the Three Graces. I heard their voices protesting from the door that they were friends of Mrs. Nightingale. Then the funeral director glided down the aisle and whispered something in Sadie's ear. As soon as she nodded a yes, the Graces bustled to the pew behind us and sat down. At the same time, the minister appeared on the dais in his black robes. So now we were ten plus the minister. Most of us hadn't known Jonathan, and the ones who did had detested him. Maybe Tracy loved him once but he had killed that love long before someone had killed him. I wondered if there was anyone truly saddened by his death. Surely, even the most miserable of us deserves at least one genuine mourner.

"That's Sadie's minister from Okotoks," Cyrrie derailed my morbid train of thought. "Mr. Churchill."

"And those women behind us are Sadie's neighbours," I offered in return. "The Three Graces." Cyrrie's eyebrows shot up demanding an explanation but the service had begun.

Considering the unpromising material he had to work with, Mr. Churchill did a pretty good job of dispatching Jonathan. He stuck mostly to readings and prayers and kept the personal comments to a minimum. At least I think he did although I'm not entirely certain because my attention kept straying to Candi's feather. So did everyone else's. I glanced back. Even the Mountie had his eye on the peacock.

"It is very sad when a life is taken from us too soon," Mr. Churchill began. Candi nodded her agreement. The peacock feather nodded too. As an attention-getter it had the ash on Clarence Darrow's cigar beat all to hell.

The Lord's Prayer, the Twenty-Third Psalm, a couple of readings, and one hymn later we were all back standing in the parking lot. Nobody said much. All in all, it had been a pretty depressing twenty minutes. Even the Graces were subdued. The Mountie wandered off to have a smoke. He stood well away from the rest of us out on the public sidewalk with what was left of the reporters and TV crews. The media ranks had thinned considerably during the funeral. Most of them had already packed up and gone and the few stalwarts left seemed to be thinking about doing the same. For them, today's story was over. They didn't know about Jonathan's ashes and his house by the river.

Nick and David sat in their cars waiting to whisk us off to our rendezvous with Tim and the canoe. After what seemed like an hour but was probably no more than five minutes, the funeral director appeared carrying a sturdy cardboard box which he gave to Tracy – Jonathan minus the polished wood. She marched over to David's car, opened the trunk, plunked the box next to the spare tire, and slammed the trunk lid down. It was the best shot of the afternoon but there were no cameras left to take it. The slam seemed to mark the end of the occasion and break some of the tension we were all feeling. Everyone began to talk at once and we were sent off to Stanley Park with hugs and handshakes but no tears.

Tim already had the canoe in the water when Nick and

Candi and I got to the park. Its red fibreglass hull bobbed in the current, tugging at the painter in his hand. Tracy and David and the ashes arrived a few minutes later. We made an odd group as we stood beside the river in the soft light under the trees, the men in their casual shirts and jeans, we women in our funeral finery, Jonathan in his cardboard box.

Candi and Tracy and I removed our high-heeled shoes and exchanged our blazers and suit jackets for large, faintly fishy, orange life jackets. David stood with his arms full of our cast-off clothing while Tim held the canoe steady and we tried to figure out how to get in without wading through a foot of water. Nick came to the rescue. He kicked off his sandals and, with a gallant flourish, swept me up in his arms, strode into the water, and placed me gently in the stern. Then he lifted Candi into the bow. He handed us each a paddle before depositing Tracy midway between us. She faced forward, leaning against a thwart, clutching the box of ashes. Then Candi pointed her peacock feather downstream, Nick gave us a little push, and the canoe slid into the current. Jonathan's funeral barge had begun its voyage through the city.

The Elbow is the source of Calgary's drinking water and, in the few kilometres between the reservoir and where it joins the Bow River, its flow is controlled by the Glenmore Dam. Where we were, well downstream of the dam, it is a small river, narrowing in some places to not much more than a few canoe lengths from bank to bank.

I explained to Candi that her main job was to make sure we didn't bump into any rocks or submerged debris although the water was sufficiently deep that I wasn't very worried about hitting anything. Then I showed her how to do a simple bow stroke but it really didn't matter whether she paddled as the current pulled us along speedily enough. We floated downstream in silence except for the background rumble of the city and the patter of water drops trailing off our paddles as they arced forward to their next stroke.

On the north bank, a narrow strip of green with a public path running through it provided a small buffer between the river and the noise of the heavy traffic on Elbow Drive. The path itself was busy with joggers and dog walkers and cyclists. On the south bank, the manicured gardens of big expensive houses swept down to the water. I saw a solitary gardener busily transplanting red geraniums from nursery flats into his flower bed but otherwise the gardens were deserted. So was the river itself. Except for a few mallards and a lone blue-winged teal who bobbed along beside us for a few yards, we were the only traffic on the water.

"We're coming to the swinging bridge." Candi broke the silence as we approached a small suspension footbridge. "Your old house is somewhere near here, isn't it?"

"It's right over there." Tracy pointed ahead to an enormous pile of a place, all glass and cedar and stark angles. "The one with the little boathouse. That's where we kept our canoe."

We drifted under the footbridge. Candi waved to a group of children crossing on their bicycles. Tracy began to struggle unsuccessfully with the lid on Jonathan's box. Her fingers slipped over the smooth cardboard. In frustration she slammed the box down in the bottom of the boat. Then, breaking every commandment in the canoeist's bible, she stood up and turned around to face me. The canoe tipped ominously from side to side as she moved. A startled Candi looked back over her shoulder. The peacock feather quivered in alarm. By some miracle we didn't capsize and, much to my relief, Tracy knelt down again.

"Here," she leaned over the thwart and thrust the box at me. "Open this thing."

The lid was held down by tight metal tabs, the kind you find on sample boxes in labs. I straightened their tips.

"Hurry up," she snarled, her hands stretching out to grasp the box. "Get the goddamn lid off. We're nearly there."

I pulled and the lid slipped off. She reached forward and yanked the box from me so roughly that once again we came close to tipping.

"Hey Trace, take it easy," Candi exclaimed in a worried voice. "Watch it or you're gonna have us in the water."

But Candi was wasting her breath. Tracy was beyond caution. Tracy was beyond reason. Tracy was out of her mind. She stared down into the bits of ash and grit that had been Jonathan. Her eyes bulged, she sucked air through distended nostrils, and the sinews of her neck stood out like cords.

"Come on. Come on." She thumped the bottom of the box on the gunwale as I steered the canoe closer to the bank and her old house. "Come on, come on, come on, come on," she chanted under her breath through clenched teeth, banging the box in rhythm with the words. Her face was only a few feet from mine, so close that I could see the flecks of spittle at the corners of her mouth, but I don't think she even knew I was there. I wouldn't swear that Tracy knew she was there. She was only aware of Jonathan. She held the box over the side and began to spill its contents into the water. All the venom, all the loathing and revulsion that she felt for him spilled with it. Now I knew what hate looked like. And revenge. And triumph. At that moment I knew, as surely as if I had seen her pour the poison, that Tracy had murdered Jonathan.

Bits of him drifted down into the water, on their way to rest in the cracks and hollows of green-slimed rocks and abandoned tires. Tracy shook the box hard trying to dislodge every speck of dust from the corners. She raised her fist and pounded on its bottom.

"Ow!" I cried out as a burst of pain shot through my right eye.

"What's the matter?" Candi twisted around in the bow as far as she could. I sat rocking in misery, my hand clamped over my eye. Tracy kept right on pounding Jonathan's box. "Phoebe, are you okay?" Candi called back to me. "What's wrong?"

"Jonathan," I howled. "There's a piece of him in my eye." Tears poured down my cheek.

"Tracy, will you stop beating on that thing and help Phoebe," Candi ordered. Tracy continued to slam the box with her fist, drumming the last of Jonathan out of her life.

"Tracy!" This time Candi shouted but still Tracy didn't hear.

"Tracy!" Candi tried one last futile shout before she reached back and whacked her old friend over the head with her paddle. Where words had failed, the paddle seemed to do the trick. The box slipped from Tracy's hands into the water. She clutched the gunwales, hung her head over the side of the canoe, and vomited. When at last she raised her head, it was a sane Tracy who looked at me out of normal eyes.

"Guess I'm not a very good sailor, am I?" She scooped up some water and rinsed her mouth. "Phoebe, is there something wrong with your eye?" It was as if she had returned from another world.

"Grit," I said. "I've got a piece of grit in it." That grit felt as big as a boulder. I tried to open my eye. Big mistake. It didn't hurt all that much but I couldn't keep the lids apart.

"Hang in there, Phoebe. It's only a few more minutes to the Stampede Grounds." Candi did her best to sound positive but

I could hear the worry in her voice. "Look, you can see the office towers from here. That means it's not far now."

I couldn't look. Now I was having trouble keeping my good eye open. It seemed to want to close in sympathy with its injured friend.

"Mission Bridge ahead," Candi kept up her encouragement. "Actually, Phoebe, I think you'd better hang a left pretty quick or we're going to bonk into it."

I did as I was ordered and thanks to Candi's navigating, we avoided hitting not only the Mission Bridge but the Twenty-Fifth Avenue Bridge and both the MacLeod Trail bridges too. I have no idea if we missed them by inches or by yards. I couldn't see. Even when I did manage to open it, my good eye was so full of tears that the city passed by in a blur. Tracy produced a Kleenex from the pocket of her skirt. I drenched it in no time.

"There are the guys," Candi called as we floated under the last of our bridges, the one that brings traffic from Spiller Road into the Stampede Grounds. I heard Nick and Tim calling to us from the shore beside the racetrack. Under Candi's direction, I steered towards their voices. I felt a little bump and then a rush of relief as the bow hit the shallow bank. Our afternoon cruise down the Styx was at an end.

Two hours later only the gauze patch over my eye convinced me that the whole afternoon had really happened. I sat in Candi's living room, enveloped by a big easy chair, working my way steadily down a large medicinal Scotch. Candi occupied the other chair. She had accomplished far less with her dry vermouth. We were waiting for Tim and Nick to return from stashing the canoe back in its garage.

"How long do you have to wear the patch?" Candi asked. She and Nick and Tim had hurried me to an emergency clinic where a doctor put some anaesthetic drops in my eye, whisked out the offending bit of Jonathan, and told me I had a scratched cornea.

"The doctor said I could probably take it off later today as long I wasn't in bright light. My eye is going to be a little sensitive for awhile but he said that it should be okay in a day or so. Eyes heal fast." I swallowed a slug of Scotch and felt it warm my insides.

"Well I think Tracy could have been a little more concerned." It was the first time I had heard Candi truly irritated with her friend. "I mean she could at least have hung around long enough to make sure you were okay." Tracy and David had headed back to Okotoks right after we landed. "I guess she really lost it this afternoon, didn't she? What was going on back there, anyway?"

"Back where?"

"In the canoe, just before you got the grit in your eye. I thought for sure she was going to dump us all in the river. What was all that pounding and stuff about? I couldn't see."

But I had seen. I remembered the hate on Tracy's face and how, at that moment, I had been so certain of her guilt. Now, I wasn't certain at all. For starters, I know I'm not at my best when raw emotions are flying. Here in the calm of Candi's living room, the gut feeling that I had taken for truth on the river now seemed more like a gross overreaction to an emotionally charged situation. Of course Tracy had hated Jonathan. She had good cause. And at the end of a week of death and police and funerals, her emotional resources must have been pushed to their limit. Scattering Jonathan's ashes may have been the last nudge. Tracy had every reason to slide over the edge to hysteria. I had no right to follow her.

"I don't really know what happened." I tossed back the last of my Scotch. "I guess Tracy must have been a little hysterical."

"A little?"

"She had reasons. Some pretty good ones. And we really don't know what happened to her in that house, do we? Maybe that's where he started knocking her around. Remembering that would be enough to get anyone a little hysterical." I didn't like Tracy and here I was defending her. It had occurred to me that perhaps my growing dislike for her had been a factor in triggering my reaction in the canoe. I wondered, would someone you love trigger the same reaction or would you see their hysteria in a different and more forgiving light? "Anyway, after I got the grit in my eye, I couldn't see either."

"So what are we going to do now?" Candi asked.

"Tim and I are going out for dinner and then he's going to drive me home." The doctor had told me I wasn't to drive until the eye felt totally comfortable without the patch, probably not until Monday. "And somewhere in there, I've got to go to Cyrrie's to pick up Bertie."

"I didn't mean that," Candi said. "I meant what are we going to do about this mess that Tracy's in?"

"I don't know," I hesitated. "But I think we should talk to the police. Tell them what we've found out."

"That wouldn't be fair to Tracy," Candi said. "Besides, what can we tell the police except for some stuff about Shelley Watson and Edward that they probably know already?"

"We can tell them that Tracy is a compulsive liar," I said. "And that Jonathan was swindling Maud."

"And that David Cavendish and Sadie both hated him," Candi continued the list. "But can you honestly see any of this coming as news to Inspector Debarets?"

"Look, if Tracy is innocent," I reasoned, "then what harm can we do her by talking to the police?"

"I don't know. Probably none," Candi conceded. "But the whole idea still makes me uncomfortable."

"And holding back information from the police makes me uncomfortable," I said. "Candi, we're mixed up in a murder. It isn't right not to tell what we know."

"Jonathan was such a slime it isn't right that someone's going to be punished for killing him. Maybe there are some murders you should be allowed to get away with." Candi echoed the Three Graces' sentiments. However, this is not a point of view shared by the RCMP. The law doesn't say it's wrong to murder good people but okay to hold open season on creeps. The police machinery would grind along as relentlessly on behalf of the egregious Jonathan as it would for an honourable man.

"Maybe we should go talk to Inspector Debarets," Candi agreed, much to my amazement. "But only with him. I don't want to talk to anyone else. I mean, what if we got stuck with an idiot like that Dudley Do-Right at the hospital. Talking to somebody like him would only make things worse. It's Inspector Debarets or no one." She was adamant.

"Let's phone him now and make an appointment," I said in a bid to forestall second thoughts.

"But it's Saturday."

"So, Mounties work on weekends. He'll probably be there." But I was wrong. Inspector Debarets was not in his office. "He won't be back until Tuesday morning," I announced as I hung up the phone.

"How can he not be there when we need him?" Candi said indignantly.

"Give the man a break," I said. "Maybe he's working on one

of his other cases. Or maybe he has a day off. Even inspectors take a day off now and then."

"Well he picked a very inconvenient time to do it."

"I'll call him again first thing Tuesday morning."

Tim and Nick returned shortly before six. Tim and I refused the offer of another drink and left to go get Bertie. I didn't think Nick and Candi would miss us much.

We found Cyrrie home alone working on his stack of grant applications. Cyrrie is a great worrier so it took me some time to convince him that my scratched cornea was not all that serious. I didn't tell him the source of the grit that had done the scratching.

"The doctor promised it would be all healed by Monday," I assured him. "But I can't drive until then so would it be okay if I left my car in your garage? I'll pick it up Monday morning but I don't want it sitting out on the street all weekend." The side of Cyrrie's double garage that used to hold Uncle Andrew's car is now empty.

"Give me your keys and I'll move it later," he said. "And remember that I'm off to Edmonton on Monday so I'll leave the keys on top of the fridge for you."

"Your grant committee meeting?" I asked.

"The whole day. The plane leaves at seven and I won't be back until late evening. I expect Edith will be very happy to see you. I'll tell her you're coming. Maybe the pair of you could go out for lunch together. I do wish this confounded meeting hadn't come right in the middle of her visit. Bad timing, I'm afraid."

"Where is Edith?" I asked.

"Out to an early dinner and a movie with Sadie. They're off to swoon over Anthony Hopkins."

"Would you like to have dinner with us?" Tim offered.

Cyrrie beamed at him. I could tell he was delighted to see me with Tim. It had been a long time since I had brought a man with me to his house.

"We're going to Hong Kong Hattie's," I added, knowing that it's one of Cyrrie's favourite restaurants.

"Such a kind offer but I really can't tonight," he said. "I simply must finish reading these wretched applications. We can't risk the world losing a potential Picasso simply because I neglected his application for a plate of ginger beef. So off with the pair of you and enjoy your dinner." For all his excuses I could tell that Cyrrie was as busy matchmaking as Two Bob.

Bertie wagged his tail in anticipation as we drove across town, convinced that we were headed somewhere good. He was crestfallen when Tim and I left him in the car and went into the restaurant. Hong Kong Hattie's dishes up its consistently excellent food in a very modest strip mall near the Marda Loop. It's a straightforward kind of restaurant with a linoleum floor, Formica tables, and paper napkins – a place where you pay for the food and not the decor. As usual, it was packed. We sat at a table next to the window, right in front of where we'd parked. I waved to Bertie. He sat on the front seat of Tim's 4x4 and glared back resentfully.

"Couldn't we at least save him a fortune cookie?" Tim asked as the waiter brought our food. "It doesn't seem fair us feasting away in here while the poor guy looks in the window." Bertie dropped his ears and hung his head a little lower.

"Don't let him guilt-trip you," I said. "He's brilliant at it. Bertie could get a job in the movies. I know for a fact he can do at least three variations on that martyred look he's using on you now. Nick should be that good an actor."

"You know, you're not such a bad actress yourself," Tim said. "Right now I'd say you're doing a pretty good imitation of a cheerful dinner companion. What's wrong? Is your eye still hurting?"

"No, it's fine," I said. "I guess maybe I'm still in a bit of a daze. It was quite an afternoon."

"Phoebe, I know who the boyfriend was."

"I thought you would by now."

"Those ashes were Jonathan Webster's, weren't they? And Tracy's a suspect in his murder."

"I guess she is," I said. "She lived with him so she's bound to be on the list." I placed my chopsticks over my rice bowl. My appetite had gone.

"Do you want to talk about it?" he asked.

"No, I don't. At least not right now. I'm going to talk about it with the police. Candi and I are both going."

"I think you should," he said. "Word around the office is the police are getting pretty close to an arrest."

"Who?"

"Even if I knew I couldn't tell you and I don't know. Nobody knows except the people working directly on the case. The officer in charge of this one plays his cards pretty close to the vest. Leaks that big just don't happen when Inspector Debarets is in charge."

"I wish we had never gone to that damned psychic fair."

I was fed up with Tracy and her lies, and fed up with me for allowing myself to get involved. I even had a little free-floating peevishness left over for Candi and what's more my eye did hurt. Not very much. Just enough to make me feel sorry for myself. My spirits plunged at the thought of having to recite the tale of my doubtful part in the whole mess to Inspector Debarets.

"Hey," Tim reached across the table and took my hand in his. "You look like a lady who could do with some music to cheer her up." He smiled and in spite of my sulks I felt myself smile with him. "I've got my violin with me." He nodded in the direction of the 4x4. The rays of the evening sun slanted in the window, catching his black curls in their light. "Want to go to your place and tango?"

We drove home through the sunset and into the dusk, leaving the noise and smell of the city behind. I rolled down my window and let the wind sweep the staleness out of my lungs and my mind. I did the same at the house. It had the airless feel of a place that has been shut all day. I pulled back the big patio door and opened all the windows to the breeze blowing down off the Rockies.

The coyotes howled their eerie music while Tim and I stood together on the deck and watched the last of the light fade behind the first range of mountains. Finally, the cool of evening gave way to the chill of night and we went inside to make our own music. This time the violin stayed in its case and the piano remained unopened.

16

Monday morning poured rain and the tops of the hills were lost in cloud. We were back to our wet spring weather with a vengeance. It was cold too, not much above freezing. Edith could haul out her tweeds again. In typical foothills fashion, the temperature had dropped thirty degrees Celsius overnight. Sunday had been sweltering. Today I wouldn't have been surprised to see snow. On the cheery side, the doctor had been right about my eye. This morning it felt as if nothing had ever happened to it.

Tim had stayed for the rest of the weekend. Our time together made murder and funerals seem like part of some other world. We talked and made love and went for walks and made love. We laughed a lot too. Falling in lust has much to recommend it. The happiness of gratified sexual desire may be a fleeting thing but, on a sunny day in spring, hormonal euphoria can feel like the answer to the questions of the universe. Even today's rain couldn't wash the feeling away entirely.

Tim left very early for Calgary and his job. He'd be back around eight for dinner, which he volunteered to bring with him from town. We said goodbye. It took awhile. I watched the 4x4 drive off into the mist and then went back to bed, pulled up the comforter, and listened to the rain beat down on the roof and lash against the windows.

It was still raining when I woke up again at nine and so gloomy that I had to switch on the lights. They flickered a little when the furnace fan kicked on. I phoned my next-door neighbour and made arrangements for Bertie and me to get a ride to town with her. Every Monday morning Barbara goes to Calgary to do her grocery shopping and visit her mother. She has two dogs of her own so she never minds a little Bertie hair on the car upholstery. She'd pick us up at ten. The dog did not seem all that keen on our expedition. It was the kind of morning that sensible animals spend curled up asleep and he hadn't budged from his basket.

"Come on," I ruffled his ears. "You're a companion animal so do your job and keep me company." He yawned, crawled out of the basket, and stretched luxuriously, first extending one back leg and then the other. He managed to stay awake long enough to crawl into the back of Barbara's car where he slept soundly all the way to Cyrrie's house.

I rang the front doorbell but there was no answer. Sometimes Edith's hearing isn't all that great. My guess was that she was at the back of the house where it's harder to hear the bell. I pulled the collar of my raincoat a little tighter and ran around to the kitchen door. Bertie bounded ahead of me. I knocked but there was still no answer. There were no lights either. It was almost as dark in Calgary as it was in the hills and lights shone from windows all along the block, but not at Cyrrie's. I knocked once more and then gave up, used my key, and stepped gratefully into the warmth of the kitchen.

"Edith, it's me, Phoebe." My voice rang through the house

but there was no reply. I took off my coat. The dog shook the raindrops off his fur. "Edith," I called again into the silence. "Come on, Bertie, let's find Edith." He followed me from room to room as I looked through the house. "She's probably just walked over to the store," I said, beginning to feel vaguely uneasy. "She'll be back in a minute or two. We'll wait." He wagged his tail at the sound of my voice.

I pulled up a stool and sat down at the island that serves as Cyrrie's kitchen table. Bertie went back to sleep at my feet. A copy of that morning's *Herald* lay on the counter in front of me. I read my way through the first section and then turned to the comics. There was still no sign of Edith. My unease ballooned into full-blown worry.

Maybe she'd taken the bus downtown to shop for more clothes. If so, it was odd that she hadn't left me a note. Maybe Cyrrie had forgotten to tell her I was coming. Or maybe she'd . . . I pulled myself up short. Here I was fretting about a woman who was perfectly capable of taking care of herself. Edith was old but she was neither feeble of body nor weak of intellect. Seventy-eight is not synonymous with senility and if Edith wanted to spend a wet Monday going about her own business then who was I to worry as if she were a child and a rather simple one to boot.

I roused Bertie and reached for my car keys on top of the fridge where Cyrrie had promised to leave them. They were wrapped in a note from Edith.

"Darling Phoebe,
Too dreary a day to stay at home. Am off to the shops. May even stay downtown for lunch and take in a matinee. Sorry I couldn't wait.
Edith"

I felt like an idiot.

I locked the back door behind me and walked through the dripping garden to the garage. My car occupied Andrew's half. Cyrrie's side was empty. He must have driven himself to the airport, which struck me as a little odd since he hates the hassle of parking there and usually takes a taxi. However, this morning's weather had probably put early cabs at a premium. I didn't envy Cyrrie his flight. Even on the best of days, air currents off the Rockies can turn the Calgary–Edmonton run into a roller-coaster ride.

Bertie sprawled across the backseat and was asleep before I'd backed out of the garage. I drove out of the alley feeling restless and at loose ends. I guess I was still a little high from my weekend with Tim. I'd hoped to shoot some film in Cyrrie's yard after lunch but the weather had put an end to that plan. I didn't really feel like going home to work at the editing bench. I decided to swing by the station and see if Candi was free for lunch. After that, I'd go home and work. Really, I would. Procrastination is the freelance worker's road to hell. I'd work all afternoon.

Candi wasn't in her office but Nick was.

"How's the animal-channelling business?"

"It's finished." He sat slumped behind the desk in Candi's chair. "I'm not doing it anymore."

"You got an acting job! That's great! What's the part?"

"No, I didn't get an acting job," he said. "I've just quit channelling, that's all."

"But why? Come on Nick, what's happened?"

"Have you talked to Cyrrie lately?" he asked.

"Not since Saturday afternoon."

"He phoned me yesterday. They had Prairie Fire X-rayed

and I was right. It was his teeth. The vet said he has a condition called persistent root."

"What's that?" I asked.

"Cyrrie said it's something that occasionally happens to horses when they get their adult teeth. A sliver of an old baby tooth's root stays in the jaw. Sometimes it doesn't bother them, other times it can hurt like hell."

"Then how come Sandra and the vet didn't notice?"

"Apparently it's pretty hard to detect until it really starts to swell and hurt and the horse quits eating. When it first starts, they just seem kind of off like Prairie did, so it's hard to know what's wrong." He paused and looked up at me. "But Phoebe, I knew what was wrong. You were there. You heard me tell them."

"Congratulations," I said. "I can't believe it but congratulations. You're brilliant. How did you do it?"

"That's the point. I don't know how I did it," he admitted. "I can't explain it. I took one look at that horse and somehow I knew his jaw hurt. Prairie had exactly the same look on his face that my sister had right after the dentist pulled her wisdom teeth."

"You must remember to tell her that," I said. "She'll be so pleased." Nick's sister is a very successful fashion model.

"And now I've got half the owners and trainers at the track calling me to channel their horses. My phone has been ringing all morning. That's why I'm hiding out here. I had to get out of the house." He stood up and walked over to the window.

"So why quit when you're such a success?"

"Because it scares me, that's why," he said. "I know zip about horses but, sure as I'm standing here, I knew that Prairie's teeth were hurting him. So you tell me – how did I know that?"

"I have no idea," I said. "Ask Maud. Maybe you were a vet in a previous life."

"Phoebe, please don't make fun of this. I'm serious." He looked out the window at the rain beating down on the cars in the parking lot. "This feeling that you know something, it comes over you just like that." He snapped his fingers. "But you don't know how you know or why you know or where the feeling comes from and it's frightening. It's probably hard to understand if you've never felt anything like it yourself but believe me when it hits you, it hits like a ton of bricks. It's totally overwhelming. And then when Cyrrie told me that my feeling was right, the whole thing gave me the creeps. Really, it did. So no laughing, okay?"

"I'm sorry, Nick. I didn't realize you were so upset. No more laughing." I went to stand beside him. "And I think I do understand how you felt when you looked at Prairie. I've felt something like it myself. But you can't trust those kinds of feelings. That's all they are – feelings."

"Mine was dead on," he said.

"So you were right this once. That doesn't mean it was anything more than a coincidence."

"Yeah? Well, I'm still not going to channel any more animals. Or anything else for that matter. I'm finished for good."

"Hi Phoebe," Candi breezed into her office. "You coming for lunch with us?"

"Where are we going?" I asked.

"I'm into cheap and lots of it today," Nick announced. Apparently, his psychic jitters had not affected his appetite. "How about liver and onions at Howie's?"

"Sounds good to me," Candi agreed, which made me think she must be in love for real.

We were about to leave the office when the phone rang. It was Tracy. We stood and waited while Candi talked, or rather while she listened and made an occasional monosyllabic reply. Finally Nick got bored and went to drive his car around to the front door so Candi and I wouldn't have to walk through the rain. The man has an incurably gallant streak. It must be all those costume dramas. I wandered over to the window and watched him hopping over the puddles in the parking lot just as Candi concluded her conversation with the ominous words, "I'll ask Phoebe and call you back."

"Ask Phoebe what?" I said.

"Tracy is worried about her grandmother. Sadie's not at home and Tracy doesn't know where she is."

"So? I'm not at home, you're not at home, lots of people aren't at home. What's the panic?"

"Apparently Tracy and Sadie had a late breakfast together and then Tracy went to look after the bookstore for David. Sadie said she was going to finish some letters she'd started on the weekend. She was already working on them when Tracy left. Tracy forgot her purse at Sadie's place so she phoned to make sure it was there but there was no answer. She kept trying. Finally she closed the store and went back to the house to check. Sadie was gone."

"Maybe she went to the store or over to a neighbour's for coffee. It's not like she's too old and feeble to know what she's doing. Sadie is a perfectly competent adult. She doesn't have to sign out every time she goes to buy a loaf of bread." I remembered my own reaction to Edith's absence and felt a little guilty.

"Tracy thinks Tattoo and Ponytail have taken her somewhere."

"That is absolutely ridiculous. Why on earth would they do

anything to Sadie now that Tracy has until the end of the month to come up with the money? Shelley Watson promised that nothing would happen before July."

"Don't be so sure. Remember what Edward told us," Candi said. "Maybe Shelley isn't the only shark in the water. What if Edward is right and there are some others out for blood?"

"Candi, that is paranoid nonsense."

"Maybe it is," she conceded. "But it wouldn't hurt to go out to Okotoks and check, would it? It's only a few miles out of your way."

"My way? What's this my way stuff?"

"I'd go myself but I can't get away from work this afternoon." At least this time she had the grace to sound a little guilty. "I have a production meeting at one thirty and it's after twelve now."

"Where's David?"

"He's in Calgary today to see some doctors about his face. That's why Tracy was looking after the store. She tried to phone him but he'd already left the plastic surgeon's office. He's supposed to go see his dentist this afternoon but right now he's somewhere between appointments and she can't reach him. That's why she called me. I told her I'd ask if you'd go. It would only take you a couple of minutes to stop by Sadie's place."

"To do what?" I asked.

"I don't know," Candi said with some exasperation. "Talk to Tracy. Reassure her. Keep her company until David gets back or Sadie comes home or something. Come on, Phoebe, the woman has been through hell. Give her a break."

"All right, I'll go," I agreed ungraciously. "But if Tracy's so damn worried about Sadie then why doesn't she phone the police."

"I think the police are probably the last people she wants to talk to right now," Candi said.

"Tim heard that they're going to make an arrest soon," I said.

"I guess he couldn't tell you who it is, could he?"

"No, he couldn't," I said. "Besides, he didn't know."

"Who do you think?" Candi asked. "I don't mean who do you think did it – I mean who do you think they're going to arrest? It's going to be Tracy, isn't it?" she added before I could answer.

"She's probably pretty high on the list," I agreed. "She sure had some good reasons to want him dead."

"Do you really think she did it?"

"I think she could have," I admitted, remembering the look on her face as she dumped Jonathan's ashes into the river. "Tracy's probably capable of murder, but so are lots of people if they're pushed far enough. What do you think? Did she kill him?"

"I honestly don't know," Candi said sadly. "But I do know that if Tracy goes to jail for murder it will be like the end of her life too. And David's."

"What about Sadie?" I said. "She loves Tracy as much as it's possible for one human being to love another. She must be feeling pretty desperate."

"All this misery for a lousy bastard like Jonathan Webster." Candi looked as downhearted as I've ever seen her. "There really is no justice in the world, is there?"

The raindrops began to look suspiciously thick as I drove south through the city along the MacLeod Trail. By the time I arrived in Okotoks and pulled up in front of Sadie's house they had become big, wet snowflakes that melted as soon as they hit the pavement. Bertie is fond of paying social calls so he gave me one of his best martyred looks when I made him stay in the car while I went up the path to the house. Tracy was waiting for me at the door.

"I know you probably think I'm getting hysterical over nothing Phoebe, but my grandma doesn't do stuff like this. She just doesn't." Tracy started to babble before I'd even got inside. She seemed very wound up and talked so fast that she could have given Maud a run for her money. We stood together in Sadie's crowded little entrance hall.

"Stuff like what?" I asked.

"Like leaving and not telling anyone where she's going."

"Was Sadie supposed to meet you here? Were you coming home to have lunch with her or something definite like that?"

"No," Tracy admitted. "Not really. Nothing definite. But Grandma told me she was going to stay home and finish up her gardening letters. All sorts of people write to her with questions about their gardens and she answers every single one of them. She spent most of yesterday writing letters. She said it helped to take her mind off Jonathan."

"Maybe she finished them and took them to the post office," I suggested.

"But she would have been back ages ago if she'd gone to the post office," Tracy said. "Oh Phoebe, I just keep thinking of what those two creeps did to David and how they could be hurting my grandma right now and it would all be my fault." She started to cry. So far, I didn't seem to be a raging success as a source of reassurance and comfort. Then again, the tears might simply be dramatic embellishment for another of Tracy's elaborate lies. I couldn't tell anymore and I didn't much care.

"Is Sadie's car in the garage?" I asked.

"I don't know. I never looked. Why?"

"Because if her car isn't there then I don't think you have

much to worry about. The people who beat up David would hardly make Sadie drive her own car to her own kidnapping, would they? If the car is gone then she's off somewhere on her own and she's perfectly safe."

"I never thought of that," Tracy said, drying her eyes on the sleeve of her sweater. "Come on, let's go check the garage."

She led the way through the living room towards the back of the house. I stopped short in the dining room. The big biscuit tin where Sadie kept her cards stood on the table.

"Hang on a minute." I looked in the box. There was no paisley scarf. I checked through the decks of cards. Sadie's favourite, the old pansy set, was missing too. Suddenly, Tracy wasn't the only one worried about her grandmother.

"You know," she tapped the lid of the box, "I'll bet Grandma went somewhere to do a reading." As my anxiety mounted hers seemed to diminish.

"Maud told me that Sadie doesn't do readings away from home."

"Mostly that's true but Grandma does make some exceptions." She put the lid back on the box. "Like for invalids and people in old folks homes. I'll bet you anything that's where she is now."

We hurried out to the garage. Tracy opened the door. The little red Chevy was not inside. I stood and stared at the empty space. My heart felt as cold and heavy as the snow falling on the garden. I'm not psychic but I knew exactly where Sadie and her car had gone.

"Gee, I feel like such a jerk," Tracy jabbered with relief. "I guess I really lost it this morning. I'm sorry I hauled you all the way out here. Come on, let's go inside. I'll fix us a bowl of soup."

"Thanks, but I've got to go."

"Are you okay, Phoebe? You look a little white. I'll bet you're cold. Are you sure I can't get you a cup of coffee or something?"

I know I must have answered her but I don't remember what I said. I ran around the side of the house and back to the car. I started the engine, turned on the headlights, and headed west to the cloud-shrouded hills. I drove as fast as I could through the snow. As the road climbed higher, the temperature dropped and the snow no longer melted when it hit the ground. The trees were turning white and the pavement was covered in slush.

I took the first Texas gate at full speed and the car rattled in protest. It woke the dog. He climbed into the passenger seat and sat next to me bringing with him the reek of damp dog. Bertie's supposed to stay in the back of the car but this time I didn't make him go back to his own place. I was glad to have the comfort of his warm furry presence beside me, pong and all.

I passed the information centre and began the climb to the lookout point. There wouldn't be much of a view today. The higher I climbed, the thicker the snow became and soon I could only see a couple of hundred feet ahead. I was glad to be driving in the inside lane, the one that hugged the rock wall where the road had been blasted out of the hill. A lane away, the cliff dropped to the river hundreds of feet below. I passed the sign for the turn-off to the viewpoint parking lot and slowed down a little as I neared the curve at the crest of the hill. That little decrease in speed probably saved my life. It gave me a split-second to react. Good luck gave me a place to go.

A grey car appeared around the corner racing directly towards me in the wrong lane. It caught me between a rock and nothing – sheer rock wall and a drop into nothing. I chose the nothing. It's softer. I swerved across the yellow line towards the edge of the cliff and hit the brakes. I felt the wheels leave the pavement but instead of hitting air, they skidded across the gravel of the parking lot. The left fender scraped along the barrier rails as the car slid to a stop, its front bumper resting against a support post. The beams of the headlights shone over the cliff into the swirling whiteness.

I turned my head to look at the car that had so nearly hit me. It had slowed but it hadn't stopped. I saw red taillights disappear down the hill and into the snow storm. A grey sedan. The kind of car that my parents and Cyrrie and hundreds of other Albertans drive. The kind of car so unremarkable as to be unnoticeable until it almost kills you.

I heard a horn blaring and suddenly realized it was mine. My elbow was resting on the steering wheel. I sat and waited for my heart rate to slow to something like normal. Even Bertie looked a little shaken. He leaned over and licked my face. I rolled down the window and took a few deep breaths of cold, damp air. I listened to the muffled thunder of the unseen river in the valley far below and shivered.

I left the window open as I drove the remaining fifteen kilometres to the Blue Rock recreation area. Somehow, I felt like I needed more air than the cramped space of the car could supply. I didn't meet any more cars which, considering the weather, was not surprising. Even the range cattle had vanished into the shelter of the trees. I hoped that the parking lot at the end of the road would be as deserted.

It wasn't. Sadie's red car sat parked in almost the same spot we had used last Tuesday. It was covered in an inch-thick layer of slushy snow, which meant it had been there for some time. I pulled in beside it and went over to investigate. Bertie walked beside me. I brushed the slush off the windshield and peered inside. Four white business envelopes lay neatly stacked on the dash. I tried the door. It wasn't locked. I reached inside for the envelopes. The first was addressed to Tracy, the second to Sadie's daughter in Brazil. The third had a man's name I didn't recognize over the address of an Okotoks law firm. The last one was for Inspector Debarets. I tossed the letters on the driver's seat and began to search for the missing cards and paisley scarf. I looked in the glove compartment and in the map pocket and even felt under the seats but they weren't there.

I gathered up the letters and put them back on the dash. I leaned against the car watching the snow fall and listening to the distant roar of the river. The dog nudged my hand with his nose, impatient with the delay. He thought we'd come to the Blue Rock to go for a walk and, in a way, I guess we had. I closed the car door and walked up the same path, now wet and slippery, that Sadie and Edith and I had taken to the river's edge. Patches of snow lay on the ground. I saw what might have been the edge of a footprint in one. Bertie dashed here and there through the underbrush, chasing smells along the ground and into the snow. Soon, he carried a little white drift on top of his nose. I reached the edge of the cliff and looked over. There was nothing to see but the swollen mountain stream. Its water looked leaden in the dull-grey light.

I didn't notice the shoes until I turned back to the parking lot. I wouldn't have seen them at all if Bertie hadn't run ahead and found them first. A pair of runners had been placed neatly, side by side, under a small spruce tree. Its sheltering branches almost obscured them from view. Sadie's aviator glasses were tucked tidily into the right shoe. I left them where they were and trudged back to the car.

I drove back down the road as far as the information centre.

As usual on a weekday, no one was there and the place was locked. I used the pay phone outside to call the police. Then I returned to the Blue Rock to wait for them. Once again, I pulled in beside Sadie's car.

The weather seemed to be warming up a little. I watched the snowflakes turn first to sleet and then to rain. The rain washed the slush off Sadie's car and melted the patches of snow on the ground.

I leaned back and rested my head against the seat. I felt cold and weary and sick at heart. Bertie edged over and leaned against my side. I could feel the warmth of his fur through the thick cloth of my raincoat. I put my arms around him, buried my face in his neck, and wept.

17

Forty-five minutes later, an RCMP cruiser pulled into the parking lot. The spit and polish constable emerged looking every bit as splendid as he had last week at the hospital. Even his rain slicker looked as if it had been starched and pressed. He got out his notebook and wrote down my name and address but I don't think he remembered me until I reminded him of our first meeting at the Oilfields Hospital the night of David's beating.

We walked over to Sadie's car and I showed him the stack of letters on the dash. I could tell he wasn't convinced they were suicide notes. I took him up the path to the spruce tree and Sadie's shoes but he still didn't believe me. It was only when I told him about Sadie's connection to Jonathan Webster that I felt I was beginning to get through. When he finally figured out that, in his words, Sadie Nightingale was like Webster's mother-in-law, sort of, it seemed to galvanize him.

We went back to the cruiser where he spent the next ten minutes on the radio. Then he asked me a lot of questions about how I knew where Sadie had gone. I tried to explain that it wasn't one single thing but a lot of little ones that had led me to the Sheep River. I told him about Sadie's love for her granddaughter and how Jonathan had abused Tracy, about Sadie's reaction to Edith's attack of vertigo and how she wanted to be buried with her old set of playing cards. Then I told him how Sadie had loved the hills, how she and her husband had gathered a garden there. He wrote down what I said but I know he didn't really understand what I was telling him. Maybe I didn't understand it all myself.

Then we waited. The constable saw that I was cold so he gave me a cup of coffee from his thermos and turned the car heater on high. He'd never be commissioner but the man was kind. It was five o'clock before the reinforcements arrived in three squad cars followed by a couple of vans. Suddenly the place was swarming with police. With the precision of long practice, they began to perform the set rituals of their inquiry into violent death. It was all there – the yards of yellow barrier tape, the cameras, even two men with wetsuits and scuba gear although what use they'd be in a river like the Sheep was beyond me. I saw Constable Lindt walking up the path to the river lugging a large aluminum case. I don't know whether she saw me.

A plainclothes officer came and asked me a lot of questions. Like the constable, he wanted to know how I knew where Sadie had gone. I told him. I don't think he really understood either. He asked me if I'd seen any other cars on my drive up to the Blue Rock and I told him about the grey sedan that had forced me off the road. I showed him the scrape along the driver's side fender of my car. He got one of the officers to take a sample of the paint and measure the height of the scrape from the ground. He asked me again and again to describe the other car – the colour, the year, the make, the licence plate.

Grey and not too old. It wasn't much but it was all I could say for certain. He wasn't pleased. We went back to the cruiser. I longed for Inspector Debarets.

Then the plainclothes officer left and I sat alone and waited. Constable Lindt and another officer walked back from the river. This time I waved to her. She smiled back but didn't come over to talk. She and the other officer got into their cruiser and drove off. Then the plainclothes officer came back and asked more questions. It was after seven before he let me leave with the promise of more questions the next day.

Bertie was sound asleep on the backseat when I got into my car and headed home. The rain had dwindled to a drizzle. I drove past the viewpoint and saw a Mountie bent over the barrier rail. I guessed that he was collecting samples of my scraped paint and measuring the height of the rail.

By the time I turned into my driveway, the rain had stopped completely but the evening was still overcast and dreary. I fed Bertie. He started to eat but then looked up from his bowl and barked his single someone's there woof. Then I heard the car. It was Tim. I had completely forgotten our plans for the evening.

"Here's dinner – dolmades and Greek salad." He held up a large paper bag in one arm, pulled me to his side with the other, and gave me a kiss. I wrapped my arms around him and held on tight. He tried to put the bag of food on the counter. I didn't let go. "Hey Phoebe, are you all right?"

I shook my head and told him what had happened. I was very grateful when he didn't ask a lot of questions. "And now I've got to phone Cyrrie and Edith and tell them," I said. "And Candi." The police would tell Tracy.

"You go do your phoning and I'll heat dinner. Come on." He extricated himself gently from my grasp and led me over to the couch. "You need some food. Your hands are like ice and you're white as a sheet."

I let him take care of me. He brought me the phone, poured me a glass of wine, and lit a fire in the big stone fireplace. Bertie polished off his dinner and came to doze by my feet. I sat and stared at the phone. I was on my second glass of wine before I could bring myself to dial Cyrrie's number. I had just begun to punch the numbers when I heard the car. Bertie was so sound asleep that Constable Lindt knocked on my door before he woke up enough to bark. She looked cold and tired.

"I was on my way home and thought I'd stop in and make sure you were okay. You had a pretty rotten afternoon." For a stuffed shirt, Jenny sometimes does some surprisingly nice things. "How are you doing?"

"I'm okay, Jenny. Thanks. Come on in and have a glass of wine and something to eat. You look bushed."

I introduced her to Tim, who repeated my offer of food and wine.

"Thanks but I'd fall asleep before I finished the glass," she said. "I wonder if I could talk to you alone for a couple of minutes, Phoebe?"

"If you'll excuse me, I was about to take the dog for his evening stroll, wasn't I, Bertie?" Tim grabbed his coat and prodded the sleeping dog with the toe of his shoe. Bertie blinked and yawned and plodded out after him.

Jenny sat down wearily on the couch beside me. "You were right," she said. "Those letters on the dash were suicide notes."

"Have they found her?" I asked.

"No, not yet. They'll start searching again in the morning but it's not an easy job. That river is so fast and deep right now that it's pretty near impossible."

"Then you think she jumped."

301

"In her letter to the inspector, Mrs. Nightingale was very explicit about what she intended to do."

"Why?" I asked, although I wasn't altogether certain I wanted to know. "Did she say why?"

"Because she didn't want to be arrested for Jonathan Webster's murder and spend the rest of her life in prison. The letter was a confession."

"No. Sadie didn't murder Jonathan. You can't think that. It's not true. Not Sadie."

"I'm sorry, but that's what she said in her letter."

"Sadie murdered Jonathan." I said the words again as if repetition could somehow make me believe them.

"I guess she couldn't stand by any longer while he abused her granddaughter so she killed him. She gave a very detailed description of how she did it. It fits exactly with our forensic evidence. It has details only the murderer could know for certain."

"Why are you telling me all this?" It was unheard of for Jenny to volunteer what I knew must be confidential police information.

"Because I've just come from telling Tracy McMurtry about her grandmother and I figure you have the right to know as much as she does."

"You had to tell Tracy?" No wonder the poor woman looked exhausted.

"They always make me do that kind of stuff. They say it's because I need the experience but I know it's because they don't want to do it themselves. Having to tell people that someone they love has died is the worst part of this job."

"Maybe they make you do it because you're a woman."

"That's probably part of it," she agreed. "We're supposed to be sensitive and understanding and all that crap, aren't we?"

"You won't get into trouble for telling me, will you?"

"By tomorrow or the next day everyone's going to know, so I don't suppose anybody's going to care much. The police can't keep it a secret when someone dies. Besides, you were the one who knew where she'd gone, not Tracy. I thought you deserved better than reading about it in the *Sun*."

"How did Tracy take it?" I asked.

"You don't want to know," Jenny said. "And now I've got to go home or I'm going to fall asleep sitting here." She got up and walked to the door.

"Jenny, can I ask you one more question?"

"You can ask, but I might not be able to answer. I've already told you more than I was authorized to tell Tracy."

"I heard that the police were very near to an arrest on this case."

"That's true," she acknowledged.

"Were you going to arrest Sadie?"

"No. We weren't."

After Jenny left, I phoned Cyrrie. I couldn't put off telling him and Edith any longer. Cyrrie answered on the first ring.

"Cyrrie, I'm glad you're back," I said.

"Only this minute, my dear. I just walked in the door. The wretched plane was late and when I finally did get back to Calgary the airport was so swamped it took me half an hour to get a taxi. I thought I'd never get home."

"Is Edith there?" I asked.

"Right here filling the kettle. Did you want to speak to her?"

"No, that's okay. I want to talk to you."

"Then talk away. It's always a pleasure to listen to you, my pet."

"Not this time, Cyrrie," I said. Then I told him what had happened.

"Are you all right, Phoebe?" he asked when I had finished. "I don't think you should be alone. Edith and I will come right now. Or would you sooner come here?"

"Don't worry about me, Cyrrie. I'll be fine. Tim is here." Tim and Bertie had just returned from their walk. "He made me a fire and brought some dinner and I'm fine."

It took a while to convince Cyrrie that I was okay but finally he said goodbye and went to tell Edith about her friend. I knew that Edith would need a brother tonight.

I made my last call of the night to Candi. She had already heard the news. David Cavendish had phoned her earlier.

"He said that Tracy totally flipped out when the police told her," Candi said. I thought of poor Jenny. "She was so hysterical that they had to call a doctor. He pumped her full of sleeping stuff and she's out for the count. How are you doing, Phoebe? Are you okay? I'm so sorry I didn't go out to Tracy's place with you. I should have been there too."

"That's okay," I said. "Nobody could have guessed this one. Did David tell you that Sadie left a letter confessing to Jonathan's murder?"

"Sadie murdered Jonathan?" Candi echoed my words. "That's impossible."

"That's what I thought but I guess it isn't. She left a letter. It tells how she did it and why."

"How do you know all this?"

"Constable Lindt told me. I don't think she was supposed to but she was really upset because they made her break the news to Tracy. I think she told me more than she should have."

"I still can't believe it," Candi said. "Oh God, Phoebe, how can everything be so horrible?"

The sky cleared overnight and Tuesday morning was hot and sunny. At least I think it was. I spent most of it indoors at

RCMP headquarters in Calgary answering questions. I did get to see Inspector Debarets – he was the one doing the asking. We sat in his office while he and another officer took me over the details of the previous day. Like their colleague out at the Blue Rock, they concentrated on how I knew where Sadie had gone and on what I remembered about the grey car. I had nothing new to say on either topic. Then they asked me about my relationship with Sadie – where we had met, how long I had known her. I told them everything from my first meeting with Tracy at the psychic fair to finding Sadie's shoes and phoning the police. The only thing I didn't mention was that Constable Lindt had told me about Sadie's suicide note and her confession of murder. Finally, the other officer left and Inspector Debarets and I were alone.

He turned off his tape recorder and came to sit in the other chair on my side of the desk. He stretched his long legs in their impeccably tailored blue pinstripes out in front of him, undid the button on his suit jacket, and leaned back in the chair. It was as informal as I'd ever seen the inspector. "You were quite right, you know. The letters you found in Mrs. Nightingale's car were suicide notes. In the one addressed to me, she confesses to Jonathan Webster's murder but I think you know that already."

I didn't bother to deny it. "I find it very difficult to believe that Sadie was a murderer."

"I've been a police officer for over twenty years, Ms. Fairfax, and I've met many murderers who I would never have believed capable of the crimes they committed. But they were and I gathered the evidence to prove it."

"Can you tell me what evidence you have against Sadie or is that confidential?"

"We have her confession."

"Is that enough?"

"In itself, probably not. But several of the things Mrs. Nightingale told me in her letter are things that only the person who murdered Jonathan Webster could have known. Our forensic evidence confirms that. And it, I'm afraid, is confidential so you will simply have to take my word on it."

"So your investigation is over," I said. Inspector Debarets did not contradict me. "A few days before she died Sadie asked me if I thought that murder was ever justifiable. I thought she was worrying about Tracy. I didn't know she was talking about herself."

The inspector reached over and removed two typewritten pages from a folder on his desk. "This is a transcript of Mrs. Nightingale's letter to me. I think you should hear a little of it." He put on his reading glasses. "'Dear Inspector Debarets: I am confessing to the murder of Jonathan Webster. I will not waste your time by telling you my reasons for committing this crime because you know them already. I will also spare you the ramblings of an old woman's troubled conscience and not attempt to justify either what I have done or what I am about to do. It is enough to say that I have lived a long and, until recently, a very happy life. That I choose to leave it rather than spend such time as remains to me in prison or put my family through the agony of a murder trial is my own business. Jonathan's murder, however, is another matter.'" The inspector looked up from the pages. "The rest is her very detailed description of exactly how she murdered him. I can't read it to you. Besides, I don't think it's something you would want to hear." I looked at him but no words came. There was nothing left to say. I had heard Sadie's sane and steady voice speaking through his telling me that the unthinkable was true. "I know she was your friend, Phoebe. I am very sorry."

That evening, Sadie's suicide was reported on the local news. By Thursday, after the police had released the news of her confession, it was lead item. It was pretty sensational stuff and page-one stories made the most of Guilty Grandma Confesses. The police declined further comment except to say that the case was now closed. By Saturday, the story was back in the city pages and on Monday it had disappeared. It made a couple of sporadic appearances over the next couple of weeks, but there was really nothing new to report.

I went back to work on *Right in Your Own Backyard*. The weather held and I managed to put in long afternoons filming in Cyrrie's garden. Tim and I spent most of our free time together. We didn't do a lot of talking. The worry that maybe we'd discover we didn't have all that much to say to each other niggled at the back of my mind, but our silences were still so golden that I did my best not to think about it. I bumped into Maud one afternoon at the supermarket. She was still suing the Queen. "A Day in the Lifestyle" aired its program on the psychic fair and pulled off the highest rating in its history. Nick did get an acting job. He was off to Saskatoon for six weeks to play Mercutio in a tent by the river. He didn't want to leave Candi. Prairie Fire had the rogue root removed from his mouth and was back training splendidly. Tracy and David announced their engagement. In other words, life was back to normal. Yet somehow, it wasn't.

The first day of summer, four days before Edith was due to fly back to England, she and Cyrrie and I attended a service for Sadie at her church in Okotoks. Candi went with us. It wasn't a really a funeral because they still hadn't found Sadie's body. Unless they found her, she could not be considered legally dead until seven years from her disappearance.

Funeral or not, the church was packed. Maud arrived a little late and squeezed in beside us in the pew behind Tracy and David and the Three Graces. Even Shelley Watson showed up. Later Candi told me that Shelley and Tracy had reached a compromise. Shelley agreed to forgive Jonathan's debt if Tracy would promise not to go to the police. Now that Tracy no longer had anything to fear from the police, Shelley had lost her leverage and, like any good businesswoman, she knew when to cut her losses.

After the service, the ladies of the church served tea in the church hall. Candi stayed to help Tracy who was still looking a little shaky. Cyrrie and Edith and I went home. Edith had hardly said a word about Sadie's death. Every time one of us mentioned her friend, she changed the subject. Cyrrie thought the whole thing must have hit her pretty hard but I couldn't tell what she was feeling behind that British stiff upper lip.

Exactly four weeks from the day that Jonathan died, I drove into Calgary to say goodbye to Edith, who was booked to leave that afternoon on a four o'clock flight. I arrived to find her and Cyrrie in a great flap. Edith had lost her passport.

"I don't know when I last saw it, Cyril. If I did then the damn thing wouldn't be lost, would it?"

"Have you had it out since you got here?" he asked.

"I took it downtown with me the day you went to Edmonton. I wanted to cash some travellers' cheques and it's always easier if you can show them your passport."

"Could you have left it on the counter at the bank?"

"Of course I could. I could have lost it anywhere downtown. It could have fallen out of my handbag for all I know."

"I don't know what the proper procedures are for travellers who've lost passports but maybe we should call the people at Air Canada and ask what to do," Cyrrie suggested.

"I'm not going anywhere." Edith was truly upset. "It's all

simply too distressing. I'll phone the British Embassy about the passport and get Air Canada to rebook my flight. Now let's have some lunch. I refuse to be buggered by bureaucrats." I don't quite know what she meant by that last remark but it did have a good ring to it.

The procedure for dealing with lost passports turned out to be fairly complicated. Nevertheless, three days later, Cyrrie had Edith adequately documented and rebooked for home. This time her flight left in the evening. We had dinner together at Cyrrie's before we drove her to the airport and waved goodbye at the security gate. Cyrrie was very quiet on the way home. I think he missed Edith already.

He made us some coffee while I stacked our dinner dishes in the dishwasher. We took our coffee out to the garden. The evening air was heavy with the scent of sweet rocket. A robin hunted for worms in the freshly watered lawn.

"You're very quiet, my dear," Cyrrie said. "Is something troubling you?"

"I was about to ask you the same thing. You're pretty quiet tonight yourself."

"I don't mean just tonight," he said. "You've not been right since Sadie died. What's wrong?"

"I'm okay." Sometimes I wish Cyrrie did not know me quite so well.

"You've got a funny way of showing it," he said. "Are you sure you don't want to talk about it? It sometimes helps."

"Sadie's not dead." I blurted it out. "They still haven't found her body and they never will. She's alive. I know she is."

For once Cyrrie was at a loss for words.

"Sadie didn't jump into that river. She faked it and Edith helped her. She's in Brazil."

"In Brazil?" Cyrrie found his voice.

"São Paulo."

"Phoebe, that is preposterous. Why on earth would Sadie do something so monstrous as fake her own death?"

"To protect Tracy. Sadie knew that Tracy had murdered Jonathan."

"How could she possibly know that?"

"Maybe Tracy told her. You know, get it off your chest by confessing to grandma. I'm not exactly sure, but somehow she knew, right down to the last detail. She also knew that the police were getting ready to make an arrest. Sadie isn't stupid. She knew what was going to happen. They were going to arrest Tracy."

"You think that Sadie faked her own suicide and confessed to murder to get Tracy off the hook and that Edith helped her." He put down his coffee cup and looked at me. "No, Phoebe, no. You're not making sense."

"But Cyrrie, it does make sense. Everything fits together. It does. I know it does."

"Calm down," he said. "Let's look at this logically. Come on, take it step by step."

"The morning you went to Edmonton I came to pick up my car." I began as calmly as I could. "You told Edith I was coming but when I arrived she was out. So was your car. I thought you'd taken it to the airport."

"I took a cab like always," he said. "You say my car wasn't in the garage?"

"Your car was on its way to the Sheep River. Edith drove it. She met Sadie up there. Sadie had come in her own car. She'd probably planted the shoes and the glasses by the time Edith arrived. She put the suicide notes on the dash and then the pair of them drove to the airport in your car. The weather was a bonus. It meant that the likelihood of anyone else being up at the Blue Rock was small. But even in nice weather it's usually pretty deserted on weekdays."

"How can you possibly know all this?"

"Because they nearly ran me over a cliff. That grey car was yours. I know it was."

"Did you see the licence plate?"

"No," I admitted. "It was snowing too hard to see the plate but I did get a look at the car. They slowed down for a few seconds. I saw the red of the brake lights. I guess they wanted to make sure I hadn't gone over the cliff. Then they took off again."

"Heading for the airport," Cyrrie said, clearly not believing a word I was saying.

"Right," I agreed, ignoring his scepticism. "They went to the airport. And when they got there Edith gave Sadie her passport and put her on a plane to Brazil. That's where Edith's passport is now, in Brazil with Sadie."

"Phoebe, that's nonsense," Cyrrie stated flatly. "How could Sadie possibly use Edith's passport? Her photograph is in it."

"Edith and Sadie are both old, they both have short grey hair and brown eyes, they're both tall – it's enough. Nobody looks at old women. They're boring and harmless and nobody pays any attention to them. Sadie looks enough like Edith that her passport photo would do just fine."

He thought about this for a moment. "It won't wash, my dear. It really won't," he shook his head. "Stop and think for a moment. It's really not that easy for someone to disappear unless they truly are dead. How could Sadie vanish without leaving some sort of paper trail? What would she do for money? Even if she left the country with nothing more than the clothes on her back how could she buy a plane ticket without taking funds from her bank account or using her credit cards? How would she live when she got to Brazil?"

"Edith," I said. "Edith has lots of money. Edith has paid for everything. Why do you think she and Sadie spent so much time shopping. They weren't simply bringing Edith's wardrobe up-to-date. They were shopping for Sadie."

"And why Brazil?" he continued. "If she's a fugitive from justice, Sadie can hardly go marching up to her daughter's house and knock on the door, can she?"

"She didn't go to her daughter's place. She went to her daughter's housekeeper. I heard her telling Edith about Estella. She's a good friend of Sadie's. Estella would help her," I said. "Cyrrie, I'm right. I know I'm right. I can feel it."

"For someone who speaks so disparagingly of psychic phenomena, you're certainly putting a great deal of faith in your feelings," he said. "But what real proof do you have? You say you think my car might have run you off the road. As far as I can see that's it. Your whole theory is based on a momentary glimpse of a very common make of car in the midst of a blinding snowstorm. I'm sorry. It's not enough. Not nearly."

"But the car was on the wrong side of the road," I protested. "It was driving on the English side."

"If the visibility was as bad as you say, then that isn't too surprising, is it?"

"Then where was your car because it wasn't in your garage?"

"I'd be willing to bet that it was out joyriding with my totally irresponsible sister. You know how frustrated Edith is by not being able to drive. She probably gave into temptation and went for a spin to a shopping mall."

"But Cyrrie, they haven't found Sadie's body."

"And perhaps they never will," he said softly. "There are a hundred places where Sadie's body could be caught in that river. Maybe it will be swept downstream later in the season when the water level recedes, but it's just as likely that it never will be found. You told me the caverns along the bank are mostly underwater now. Sadie's body could be stranded in one of them."

"What about Edith's passport?"

"Phoebe, much as I love my sister, you know as well as I do that Edith losing her passport is about as unusual as the sun rising in the east. Edith does things like that all the time. Remember what happened last time she was here?"

"She lost all her travellers' cheques," I admitted.

"You thought very highly of Sadie, didn't you?"

"We just seemed to hit if off right from the start. We were friends, good friends. I know she felt the same way about me."

"Yes, I think she did," he agreed. "So why don't you be a good friend to Sadie now and let her rest. Did you tell your theory to the police?"

"What do I have to tell them? They work on evidence not feelings. And you're right. All I really have is a feeling that Sadie is still alive. Maybe I only have that because I want it to be true."

"Are they still pursuing the case?" he asked.

"Constable Lindt told me that Sadie's confession gave details only the murderer could have known. Inspector Debarets said the same thing. My guess is that the police don't know for certain that Sadie murdered Jonathan, but they can't prove she didn't."

"And the Brazilian connection – I'll bet the police did some checking there."

"Constable Lindt told me that they checked Sadie's phone

bills and there was only one call to Brazil right before she died. It was to her daughter's house but her daughter hadn't been home, only the housekeeper. They got the São Paulo police to do some checking too. They didn't find anything."

"What about Sadie's bank accounts?" Cyrrie's questions continued.

"There was no money missing from her accounts."

"Her charge cards?"

"They were still in her wallet."

"Were any of her clothes missing?"

"No. Only the ones she was wearing. And her passport was in the drawer where she always kept it."

"No money, no charge cards, no clothes, no passport," Cyrrie listed them off. "And that's just for starters. There would be dozens of other problems to solve before you could pull off the kind of disappearing act you're suggesting."

"Then Sadie and Edith solved them."

"Phoebe," he said gently, "can you honestly believe that Sadie and Edith could outwit the police forces of two countries?"

"How can I know what to believe if they can't find her body?" I said.

"My dearest child," he took my hand in his. "Don't torment yourself like this. It could be that Sadie didn't kill Jonathan. Maybe you're right and Tracy did murder him. But if that's so then Sadie sacrificed her life for Tracy and there's nothing you can do about it. Sadie's dead. Nothing will bring her back. Let her go."

"But that means Tracy will get away with murder and Sadie will never be able to come home."

"Sadie is never coming home again," he said quietly. "You must accept that, Phoebe."

We sat together in the garden and watched the evening shadows blend into the long blue summer twilight. I heard children's voices calling their dog home. Then I heard their mother calling the children.

"I guess I should go now." I looked at my watch. "I was supposed to be at Tim's place half an hour ago." We carried the coffee things into the house.

"Before you go, there's something from Edith that she asked me to give you," Cyrrie said. "I almost forgot." He went to his desk and pulled out a large manila envelope. "Here. She left strict instructions that I was to give this to you after she left."

I took it from him and slit the top with my car keys. Inside I found another envelope, a white one, business size. My name was written on it in the same hand that had addressed the envelopes in Sadie's car. I ripped it open.

"Well?" Cyrrie said. "Come on. Don't keep secrets. What's in it?"

I held up the joker from Sadie's old deck of fortune-telling cards. The heavy cardboard felt familiar to my touch.

ACKNOWLEDGEMENTS

I would like to thank the people who helped me with this book. My thanks to Joanne Walker for sharing her love and knowledge of horses; to Dr. Owen Olfert and Dr. Bruno Schiefer for their expert knowledge of agricultural pesticides; to Linda Blasetti, Ginny Dowdle, and George Karaki for helping me to find my way around Okotoks and the Oilfields Hospital; to Debbie Massett and the Western Development Museum for their help with antique playing cards; to Gwen North, Judith Kent, Karen Scott, Judi Boe, Linda Bardutz, Pat Ward, and Gary and Laura Salisbury for dotting the i's in details too numerous to mention; to Dr. Lucinda Vandervort, who knows about things legal; to the eagle-eyed Heather Sangster, copy editor at McClelland & Stewart; and to my editor, Dinah Forbes, who helped and encouraged me as a writer long before I had the pleasure of working with her on *Seeing Is Deceiving*.